MY MASTER
MY KING

BOOK 2 OF 'THE ALPHA KING'S HATED SLAVE'.

(This should not be read as a standalone, as it is a direct continuation of the first book "My Slave, My Property")

By KISS LEILANI

AUTHOR'S NOTE

This is a dark romance that contains triggering situations such as forced-sex, graphic violence and gore, pedophilia(not depicted), abuse, slavery, trauma, rape and *very* sexual situations. This book is highly rated 18 and not intended for children. While it is ultimately about hate, revenge, processing and healing, if you're sensitive to these topics, this book may not be for you.

DEDICATION:

It'll be weird to dedicate this book to my family, so I'll dedicate to my beloved readers and fans. I love each and every one of you and I hope you enjoy this book as much as I did writing it.
If you know me or my family before, then for the love of all that is dark, smutty and unholy, avoid this book! You'd better not be the reason my granny/mama finds out about this book and starts giving me *the* eye in family gatherings.
Also to my lovely editor, Melanie Lopata, you're a lifesaver and you're the very best!

My Master My King

TABLE OF CONTENTS

PROLOGUE.

Once upon a time, a slave was a princess.

Once upon a time, another slave was a prince.

Once upon a time, the princess's father enslaved the prince and his people after killing his parents.

After ten years in slavery, the prince and his people escaped slavery and killed the king who enslaved them.

The prince took over the land again and became a king to his people. His name was King Lucien.

Ten years in slavery by the king who hated him so much, King Lucien had the worst life anybody could ever have. He was a scarred king; a king who could not father a child. A king with so much hate and pain in his cold heart. A king with demons. His past, his experience, his memories and his nightmares were his demons. Demons he had to fight every day. Demons who lurked at the back of his mind, waiting to devour him. Demons that were driving him to the blink of insanity. His demons were his worst enemy.

No. His worst enemy was the daughter of the man that enslaved him—the daughter of the man that gave him his demons. Her name is Princess Danika.

Like I said in the beginning,

Once upon a time, a slave was a princess.

King Lucien enslaved the princess, Danika. She was his slave. His property. His possession. To hurt and to kill. To do with whatever he wished. And he wished to do a lot. To hurt her so much.

But there was a problem.

Princess Danika was nothing like the daughter of a monster should be. She was everything opposite.

Her presence made his burdened shoulders light-weighted. Her soft caress cracked bits of ice around his cold heart. Her melodic voice brought him peace. Her soft touch kept the demons at bay.

She made him sleep. Him, a man who had not slept well in the past fifteen years.

King Lucien did not understand how that was possible. It had him confused.

Who is this woman? It was a question he asked himself in the privacy of his own mind.

Who is this woman? What is it about her.?

He did not like that he had to ask himself those questions. She was his slave—a woman he hated so deeply. She was the daughter of King Cone.

And yet...

Those questions and his demons were starting to battle for supremacy in his mind.

CHAPTER 1. DESPAIR.

Danika walked back to her bedroom after she left the king's quarters. She couldn't push the words he said to her away from her mind. *"Just for the evening, I will be your king and not your master."*

It made her heart light just thinking about it. But then, her heart didn't stay light for long.

How had she allowed herself to fall for him? She fell in love so deeply; it hurt just thinking about it.

She opened the door to her room to see Sally sitting on the bed, sewing a dress, and at the same time, she seemed to be in thought.

"My princess!" Sally smiled at Danika as she saw her standing at the door.

Danika tried to smile back, but it came out shaky. Her heart was hurting too much, squeezing the life out of her chest.

The smile disappeared from Sally's face, replaced by concern and panic. "What's wrong? Are you alright, my princess?"

Tears rolled down Danika's cheeks. She ran across the room and threw herself into Sally's arms. "Oh, Sally! What am I going to do!?" Danika sobbed, her body trembling.

Sally was shocked about her princess's reaction, and she became more worried. She hugged her princess's head to her chest and started patting it in reassurance, even though she was becoming more panicked.

"What is the matter, my princess? Please, talk to me. Is it the wicked mistress? Did she hurt you again? Drag you by the hair? Is it the king? Did he punish you for yesterday?" Sally asked the last one dreadfully.

"Oh, Sally! Right now, I think it's something worse," Danika whispered, trying to get ahold of herself.

Sally let out a deep sigh of relief. The king hadn't hurt her physically. That was a sure relief. But..."What could be the problem?" Sally whispered worriedly.

Danika pulled back and sniffled, wiping the tears from her eyes. "I'm in love with him," she blurted out.

Sally blinked in confusion. "In love?" She said the words like they were foreign terms.

Danika nodded, sniffling again. "I've fallen in love with King Lucien, Sally."

That was when it dawned on Sally. Her eyes widened In sheer horror. "Oh no!"

Danika nodded miserably. "I don't know how it happened. I don't know. But it's true; I can feel it!" She looked at Sally with eyes full of sorrow and pain. "How d-did this happen? How did I allow myself to fall for my master? Not just any master, but King Lucien?"

"Please, stop crying, my princess. It's not a death sentence." Sally tried to console Danika, even as her heart started to burn.

"It's worse than a death sentence, Sally. My father hurt him to hell, and he hates me so much. He has hurt me a lot, and his eyes are so cold when they stare at me. How could I have fallen for him so deeply?" she cried. "This will not end well at all for me, Sally. He might as well order my execution when he finds out."

Sally's hand went to her wet cheek, and she forced her princess's eyes to meet hers. "Listen to me, my princess. You're overthinking this. The king is the most unpredictable man I know. No one can predict or know what he will do next. So, instead of worrying yourself to death, why don't you try to put it away from your mind and live in the moment? In the best way you can?"

Danika found herself nodding to her words. "You're right; you're right." She started wiping her cheeks.

Sally nodded, helping her wipe it clean. "Yes. You're the one that always says that we shouldn't waste time on things we can't change. So, why don't you do so now? And I want you to know that love is

4

not an offense or a crime, too; you always say this to me." She placed her hand on Danika's chest. "It's in here. Love. It's yours. *Your* feeling. Your secret. You have fallen for the king. For your master. It's okay, my princess. You have a big heart. It's okay to love," she whispered to her like a mother would console a child. "You have a pure heart. It's okay to nurse these feelings for him. You cannot tell your heart whom to love. Everything is going to be alright. Everything."

As Sally crooned to her in consolation, Danika felt a burden lifted from her shoulders. Suddenly, she felt better.

It's okay to love him. It's okay to nurse these feelings for him. You cannot tell your heart whom to love. Everything will be fine.

"Oh, Sally. Thank you so much," she whispered in sincere gratitude. She leaned up and kissed Sally tentatively beside her lips.

Sally glowed under the heartfelt tenderness. "You're welcome, my princess."

"You were in thought when I got in here," Danika remembered. "Is everything alright? How is Chad?"

Sally startled a little bit. Her cheeks reddened, "You knew?"

"That you have feelings for the king's personal assistant and bodyguard? Yes, I do."

"Oh, my princess. It's so frightening, caring for such a man of status. Such a good and great man. I'm just a slave, and most of the maids in this palace find him attractive and always wants to get his attention."

"And does he give it? His attention?" Danika asked softly.

Sally shook her head, not having to think about it one bit. She had never seen Sire Chad give his attention to any female at all.

"I thought as much. He's such a gentleman, Sally. And I'll tell you the truth. I think he has feelings for you too."

Sally gasped in disbelief. "That is just ridiculous, my princess. He...speaks to me with respect, and he is always a gentleman to me. But I wouldn't mistake it for anything else." There was sadness in her eyes as she made that statement.

Danika wanted to reassure her the more, but she didn't. She wasn't sure of the big escort's intentions towards her best friend, and the last thing she wanted was for Sally to ever get hurt. Just the thought of something like that happening filled her chest with dread. She changed the topic.

"Remeta is still with her mother, right?" Danika asked.

"Yes. Madam Baski took her into the forest to gather herb leaves and seeds."

"Okay. The king invited me for an evening walk with him." She finally confided the source of her inner joy to Sally.

Sally's eyes widened. "Really!? He did!?"

Danika felt her cheeks heating up. "Yes."

"Oh, that is so great! I'm so happy, my princess! We must get you prepared. You need your slave's outing wear, and you--"

"Calm down, Sally. I've not gotten my outing wear yet. Baski said the tailor would be done in a few noondays," she reminded her excited best friend.

Sally waved her off, jumping up to her feet. "Not to worry about that. I have spare outing wear, and I also have some money with me." She clapped her hands excitedly.

"Money for what?" Danika asked curiously.

"To take the outfit to the tailor in town. We must get it designed with lace and a little silk."

"But...You can't do that, Sally. Only privileged people have laces and silks in their clothing."

"There is no law that forbids that, my princess. The only problem slaves have is that there is nowhere to make money, and they are very expensive. But you don't have to worry about that, my princess." Sally waved her off, walking to her wardrobe to go and search for her outing wear.

Danika watched her silently as Sally attacked her bag with sharp hands. She couldn't help the smile that touched her face. She also couldn't imagine being able to survive here without Sally. She would never be able to pay Sally back for everything she did to her, but she was not giving up.

"There. Found it." Sally raised the plain green dress from her back. "I'm going downtown now. We need the tailor to put some lace and a little silk. My princess must look so beautiful."

Danika knew she was in thought and was talking to herself, so she didn't say a word. Instead, she watched Sally adoringly.

"We need to get it really ironed too. Yes, ironed. Mended and ironed. Then a little bit of lace and silk!" Sally stared up at her princess, then, "Oh, my princess—you're going to be so beautiful!"

"Does it matter? If I am?" Danika sighed. She knew the king wouldn't care one bit if she was.

"Oh, but it matters a lot!" Sally grinned at her in reassurance.

"What brings you here, Mistress?" Karandy asked, curiosity overriding everything else. He was kneeling before her and couldn't stop wondering what the king's mistress was doing there—visiting him.

Karandy wasn't a privileged person; he was lowborn. The king's mistress shouldn't be near him, but there she was in his small living room.

She was looking around the house, but she looked deep in thought. Her big, beautiful corset covered the floor she stood on, sewed with so much lace, and glistening with diamonds. She smelled of money. Power. Privilege. Everything he had always wanted.

"Do you know the slave called Danika?" she asked him at last, her eyes resting on his face.

Just at the mention of her name, anger infused Karandy. Of course, he knew that bitch of a woman. That whore that almost got him killed!

"Yes, I know her, mistress." He tried to keep his violating, loathing reaction to himself, but Vetta saw right through him and smiled in satisfaction.

"Oh, you'll do."

"What do you want from me, mistress?" Karandy asked.

.

.

CHAPTER 2. BITTER VETTA.

Vetta turned away from him. "Danika is overstepping her boundaries in the palace. After everything we suffered from in the hands of her father, we don't need to suffer more in *her* filthy hands. The king hates her very much; he wants to keep her as his slave by his side. But I want her really messed up and trashed around. So many look at her and still see her former status around her," she hissed out calmly. "I don't know how that is possible when she's dressed in rags, but I want to put an end to that too."

She allowed him a moment to digest that, then she continued. "The king still sees her that way because he is the only male that has taken sexual pleasures from her body. He also deflowered her."

"But I heard that the kings have introduced her," he said, still reeling from the knowledge that it was the king that deflowered Danika, and that could have only been months ago when she became a slave.

Virgins in their world were as rare as snow in summer. It was impossible, except for young females under the age of twelve. Even privileged females have ordered their slaves to pleasure them from time to time. And she had been a pure, untouched female few months ago? Just the thought had his dick hardening for her after a few weeks of trying to put her away from his mind.

"Yes, the king introduced her...to kings. Men of privileged status. They are the only ones who have known her body," she resented. "She is a slave, and a slave should tumble with lowborns and the lowest of the low. She still carries herself like a princess. But when she truly tumbles with lowborns, then she will see herself as the trash she is. The king will see her as one because we will make it look like she was the slut that begged for it. He is an unpredictable man; he might even order her execution."

Karandy nodded his understanding, listening attentively.

Vetta looked away. "When I was a slave, I never forgot the way it felt when an unwashed man who has tumbled the mud forces his body on mine. No matter how you wash, you still feel dirty—even though I was born a slave. I want Danika to know that feeling. She was born a princess, so the feeling will be worse. The king's aversion for human touch was because of this," she revealed.

"The king hates human touch?" he asked.

"Everybody's." *Except for Danika,* she fumed in her mind, remembering what she saw last night.

Karandy wasn't offended about it being thrown in his face that he was a lowborn and had tumbled in the mud. Instead, he kept himself from feeling too excited about where this was leading. "So, what is the plan?" he asked.

"I will send the messenger bird to you when it's time. I will bring the slave out of the palace into the woods. You and any number of men you came with can attack us; throw me aside because I'm not late King Cone's daughter. After all, you all came specifically for her. You can have your way with her. Whatever you want to do, but don't kill her." Vetta looked at her manicured nails with a little smile on her face. "I need to see the results, so don't kill her. I want to watch the life drain out of her while she's still alive, and I want the king to watch it too."

Karandy always knew that this mistress had a wicked streak in her—he had always suspected it whenever he saw her in town—but now, he was faced fully by what she was capable of. He almost pitied Cone's daughter. Almost. He bet that she was still traumatized from whatever those kings did to her in that courtroom. The woman carried her body like it was made of gold. And it *was* gold.

She was a princess. Not just any princess, but the princess of the Mombana kingdom, the most powerful kingdom of all the twelve kingdoms. So, yes, her beautiful body was indeed gold, coupled with the fact that she was unsoiled months ago and had only known the beds of kings—men who have eaten power so much they didn't know what to do with a woman's body anymore.

"Your wish is my command, Mistress. I can't wait to hear from the messenger bird." He licked his lips; his dick fully lengthened at the plan. What he knew was to come. He couldn't wait to put his hands on Danika. The things he would do to her.

Revenge and lust crowded his visions.

"Good." Vetta threw a wrapped sack of coins at him. "That is half of your payment. I will give you the rest when it's done."

His eyes widened. It was a considerable amount of money he thought as he pressed his hand to the coins. "Thank you so much, Mistress."

She pulled her cloak over her head and walked past him to the door, swinging it open. "Wait for the messenger bird."

She walked through the door and slammed it shut.

"What do you think!? Oh, what do you think, my princess!?" Sally cried excitedly as she unwrapped the dress in front of her.

Danika was dumbfounded at the beauty of the dress. The plain slave wear Sally went out of the house with wasn't so plain anymore. Silk was sewn beneath it and lace outlined the upper part of the red wear. "It is so beautiful, Sally!"

"I know, right!?" As she looked at the dress, a huge smile was on Sally's face. Then the smile fell. "I know it's nothing compared to the dresses you are used to, though."

"Don't go there, Sally. That's the past, and this is the present." She took the dress from her. "This is the best dress I've had presently. I wouldn't trade it for anything."

The huge smile was back again on Sally's face. "Really? You really like it?"

Danika closed the distance between them and hugged her closely. "Yes, I love it. Thank you so much."

"You're welcome. Isn't the day looking so bright, my princess?" She beamed.

"It is. And the only person brightening up the day is you, my Sally."

Sally pulled back then and stared at Danika's hair in concentration. "Your hair is all messed up. I'll get it into a beautiful braid just like when we were in Mombana. We might not have the expensive pins and needles, but I can still get it looking so beautiful with what we have."

Danika smiled in gratitude and started towards the bathroom. Sally watched how she walked so gingerly and bit her lips in worry.

"What is it?" Danika asked when she caught the look.

"Your walk. Are you hurt, my princess? The king—did he hurt you?" she asked with concern, dreading the answer.

Her assessments reminded Danika about her sore muscles she never really forgot. A flush spread through her face and she shook her head at Sally. "No, he didn't. At least not in the way you think."

She let out a huge sigh of relief. "Thank heavens. I thought you must have knelt all night or whipped because your father is dead, and it's your fault that the poisoned arrow traps caught him."

Danika shuddered at that. She couldn't even begin to imagine what would have become of her if he had punished her for that. "No, he didn't."

"Have you seen Madam Baski?"

"Yes. I saw her and Remeta when you went into town with the dress. She has given me herbs, and I got to play with Remeta. She's doing so much better."

"Yes, she is. I'm so glad about that, my princess. The ghosted one? No one will call her that mean name again. I hope you've applied the herbs. You can't walk this way to the evening walk," she added with a purse of her lips.

Danika let out a soft laugh at the look of seriousness on Sally's face. She had taken it upon herself to ensure she had a good evening.

"Yes, I've applied the herbs, Sally." Her cheeks reddened the more when she remembered the way Baski took one look at her and her brows had shot up.

"But he is sick. How did this happen?" Baski asked with just one look at her.

"I...erm, we..." she'd swallowed tightly. "He ordered it," she'd said at last.

A smile had crossed Baski's face before she wiped it clean and began attending to her. "I'm happy to know that he's doing better. I will go in later in the day to see him," she'd said.

Now she reassured Sally that she'd be fine, but she did need a little sleep.

"You can sleep all you want, my princess. I have your back right here." Sally was determined to make sure that no one would wake her up too.

Danika smiled at her in gratitude. "What would I have ever done without you, Sally?"

She waved her off with a smile. "You could have done so much and more. But I'm not letting you go. I stick like glue."

The king was in the library in the inner room, reading a book in concentration, when Vetta announced her arrival.

"Where have you been all day?" he asked without raising his head from the book.

She was standing just outside the library and bowed her head. "I went into town to shop for new laces."

"You didn't take the carriage. No maids or servants," he added.

Her heart skipped. "I didn't, my king. I needed a moment alone, and I was going into town, so I didn't bother to take them with me."

He finally raised his head and stared at her. "Nowhere is safe, Vetta. You must be careful wherever you're going. Take a few guards with you and the carriage too."

Her heart fluttered at his obvious concern for her, even though his face didn't look it. "I will keep that in mind, my king."

"I have been looking for you."

That gave her mixed feelings. Why would he be looking for her? Is it because he wanted her company? Or because of something else?

"I am sorry, my king." She bowed her head.

"You can come in." He turned his attention back to his book.

She entered and walked towards him. "How is your health, my king? I was too worried last night; I couldn't sleep."

"I am fine. The wound is healing."

She sighed softly. "So, even in death, King Cone still torments us."

He stiffened at the mention of his name. He said nothing.

Vetta pushed on. "My king, don't you think your slave should be whipped for what happened? She should pay for the pain her father caused you."

"She is already paying for that; she is my slave." He didn't spare her a glance.

"But my king---"

"My battles, Vetta. I can fight my battles. I do not need help or assistance. I am not weak."

"I'm so sorry, my king. That wasn't my implication." She lowered her head to him even as anger filled her insides.

"She nursed me all night. Cried for me." He paused and raised his head as if in remembrance.

What!? That bitch! Vetta did her best to keep her voice calm. "I know she must have been pretending to care. She is trying to get on your good grace, my king. Don't let her; it is all pretense. She is the daughter of the most manipulative man ever born. Of course, she will be manipulative too."

Calmly, the king closed the book, and his eyes met hers.

.

.

CHAPTER 3. THE KING: His Reprimand. And his heart.

The king closed his book and turned his attention to his mistress. "My slave does not manipulate me, Vetta. She has not been manipulative; if she is, it is left for me to find out. I haven't found out, so it will only be an accusation you make without basics."

He didn't believe her!? "But my king---" she began again.

"Let the subject drop," he ordered calmly, never one to raise his voice. He never had to.

Vetta snapped her mouth shut, raging in her mind. He wouldn't even listen to the things she had to say! Was he shutting her out now? "Your wish is my command, Your Highness." She bowed her head, biting her lips hard to keep the words in.

He picked up his book again and opened it. The silence stretched as he began going through the book again.

Vetta hovered over him, wanting to share this moment with him. He writes, reads, and works with Danika—the one thing she couldn't do. She hated it! She tried to see the words, but they may have well been written in Chinese. She was just too illiterate to know a word there, so she focused her attention elsewhere.

Vetta placed her hand on his hair, and he stiffened automatically at the contact. But he didn't pull away or order her away. She took it as a plus it was. Running her hand through the soft mass of curls, she reveled in it. He had the best texture of hair, she noted in a pleasing way.

"The reason why I've been searching for you all morning is because of Danika," he stated firmly, his concentration back on his book.

She ran her hands down his neck to his shoulders and back to his head again. "What about her, Your Highness?"

"You do not drag her by the hair or beat her up again for nothing from today onwards." He flipped through another new page and blew away the dust before reading.

Vetta's hands faltered on him and she stiffened. She wasn't sure she heard him correctly. "M-my king?"

"In this world, every day, I write petitions and notes and practice proceedings because of the maltreatment of slaves all over the twelve kingdoms. I must put a stop to it." He continued with a flip of another page. "Slaves are humans and are already in the lowest of the food chain. They suffer every day, and they labour day and night." He paused. "They do not need to be maltreated and punished for crimes they haven't committed—especially from people who have no right to execute punishments to these slaves."

Vetta was downright dumbfounded. She could only stare at the king, dread filling her heart.

He raised his eyes, spared her a glance, and then said, "Danika is my slave. She is not just any slave but the king's slave. I am the only one with the right to treat her unkindly and abuse her recklessly as I please; she is my property. She belongs to me. I will not tolerate it if my mistress punishes my slave when she hasn't done anything to deserve it." His eyes found hers. "Walking around with a burning scalp."

Her cheeks flushed with guilt at the mention of that. She averted her eyes.

"....or going around with a hand imprint on her cheek," he finished. "That should stop."

"My king. A-are you saying that I should stop p-punishing her?" She couldn't help asking, feeling chastised.

He nodded firmly. "When she does nothing wrong to you."

She opened her mouth. Snapped it shut. Opened it again.

He watched her with a giant frown before she finally snapped her jaws locked. "Your wish is my command, My king."

Silence ensued so thick in the air.

Vetta was so angry and hurt; it was in her composure. In every part of her being, she was almost shaking with it. The worst of it was that the king seemed angry too. When his eyes flashed, Vetta couldn't help thinking that he had remembered something, and whatever it was, had his body frozen and drawn taut like a bow.

She didn't want him to be angry at her because it wouldn't go well for her. "I...I am sorry for mistreating y-your slave, my king. It wasn't my intention to be hard on her. I just can't forget who she is no matter how I try; I c-can't forget what her father put us through."

He said nothing. But his eyes were on her and not on the book.

She dropped herself to her knees in front of him between his legs and unbuckled his belt. She unclothed his soft flesh and took him into her hand.

"I am not in the mood for this, Vetta," he said calmly.

"I will put you in the mood, my king." She was relieved that he was not ordering her away.

When she took him into her mouth and began pleasuring him, he let her. Eyes like bottomless pit watched her with an expressionless face. She closed her eyes and pleasured him, licking and stroking him while he grew hard in her hands. She relaxed perfectly and took her time pleasuring him. She had been with him for five years; she knew how to pleasure him, how to make his body feel for her. Want her.

It took longer than usual before he began enjoying her ardor, she realised when his eyes finally slid close, and he groaned at the back of his throat in pleasure.

As she continued stroking and sucking him, he ordered her to touch herself.

It was a pleasure session she had missed. She snaked her hand beneath her dress and rubbed herself with each stroke of her hand on him. Her muffled moans filled the air. When she had him wired up, she stood and pulled up her wears. She straddled him, sheathing him deep inside her with a cry until she was seated fully on him. She rode him hard and deep until he came with a grunt. She followed right behind him until they were both satisfied, their breathing mixed and erratic in the air.

Finally, she rose from him with a satisfied smile on her face. Her body was tingling everywhere.

He dressed, and pulled her closer, and palmed her cheeks. "You please me."

She glowed under the praise. She wanted to be the only person that pleased him. She wanted him to belong to her alone and would do everything to ensure that happened.

She bowed her head. "Thank you, my king. You please me, too, and I will remember your words for long."

He nodded dismissively.

She arranged her underthings and started towards the door.

"Vetta?"

She paused at the door and turned back to him. "My king."

He looked her in the eyes. "I was distraught yesterday, and I know you were too. You were worried about me, so I will pretend that I didn't know that you slapped Chad. I will chalk it up to things you did because of how worried you were, but it should not happen again. Ever."

What. The. Hell? He knew?

"T-thank you, my king," she stammered out, flustered. She didn't know that he would be able to remember that with how drugged up and sick he was.

"If it happens again, I will punish you severally for it. Nobody should ever disrespect Chad. He does not deserve it. He is more than an assistant to me. I will not have it," he stated in a gentle but vehement tone.

Chad is close to your heart!? What about me!? She wanted to scream at him. Instead, she lowered her head. "Yes, Your Highness."

"You can go now."

Vetta's heart was beating to death in her chest as she walked out of his room.

She put it all out of her mind. Instead, she withdrew her wrapped fertility pill from her corset and swallowed it down her throat.

Danika walked towards the king's door in the evening at the same time the door opened and the king came out of his room. She was nervous, and she didn't know why. It was an ordinary walk, not an invitation to any gathering or party. And yet, she was nervous. She was dressed up, and with the help of Sally, she had her hair arranged.

Danika stood before him and lowered her head in greeting. "Mast--" she paused, swallowed, and added, "My king."

King Lucien looked at her with the same expressionless face that had become his usual look. But his eyes slid through her body, from her simple wear to her beautifully styled hair. He did not understand how one woman would carry the beauty of several women. She was not wearing the series of jewelry women from prestigious families design themselves with, and yet, as she walked closer to him in that usual steady, regal walk of hers, his mind took him back to the few times he saw her as a princess in Mombana.

He remembered, specifically, the day he collared her. He was so enraged, and he hated the very sight of her so much. But it was imprinted in his mind how beautiful and regal she was as she stood there and glared at him with eyes filled with fire.

His brows knitted into a frown; he forced his eyes away and walked past her, leaving her to follow. She followed closely behind him silently, her eyes taking in his elegant kingly wear and the way he placed his hands behind his back.

Unbiddenly, Danika remembered what those hands had done to her the night before. Hotness infused her cheeks.

As they walked out of the royal quarters, Danika didn't realise he had slowed his steps until she walked beside him, her body almost touching his. A lightness and peace infused her heart as she walked. The guards bowed their heads in greetings to him as they passed, and the maids moved out of the way.

The moment they stepped outside the big building, Danika's eyes zeroed in on Remeta. She was standing beneath the big orchid tree, gathering its leaves and building a house. She was playing.

When she saw Danika, a big smile hit Remeta's face. She sprang up and ran to hug Danika but stopped short halfway because the king was with her. She bit her lips in indecision, standing still and not knowing what to do.

The sight of the girl playing with leaves a moment ago had some harshness, and the frown disappeared from King Lucien's face. He never got tired of seeing Remeta getting better.

"Go to her." He found himself nudging Danika's shoulders softly when she saw Remeta stop halfway.

"Yes, my king." She walked past him and motioned for Remeta.

At her permission, the smile lit up Remeta's face again. "My queen!" She shrieked as she ran closer and hugged Danika.

Danika wrapped her arms around her and closed her eyes affectionately. "How are you doing this evening, Remeta?"

"I am doing fine, my queen. Mama gave me herbs and made me drink potions! Mama said it'd make Remeta look more beautiful!" she confided in an excited voice.

Danika smiled and pulled back. "Mama was right. You are indeed looking more beautiful."

"Thank you, my queen." She beamed radiantly.

Danika felt the king come up behind her. His heat surrounded her even without his body touching hers. He didn't say a word, but she didn't have to look at him to know that he was watching Remeta.

"G-good day, my king," Remeta whispered shyly. Gingerly, she walked closer to press herself like glue to Danika.

King Lucien didn't take offense at her protective move. Instead, another crack of ice fell away from his cold heart that the move. "How are you doing today, Remeta?" he asked in a gentle voice Danika had never heard before.

"I am fine. Remeta was just playing with leaves. She likes playing with them when she is bored," Remeta informed him softly, ducking her head shyly.

Danika stole a glance at the king to see him watching Remeta warmly. There was no coldness in his eyes. No pain. No blank face. He truly cared for the fifteen-year-old, Danika realised inwardly. He cared more than he was admitting to the world.

Remeta turned to her. "Are you going out, my queen? You look so beautiful!"

Danika blushed. "I am taking a walk...with the king."

Remeta beamed and clapped her hands. "Can I come too!? Can I play with!? Can I tag along!? Remeta will be good! Promise!" She raised her hand in a vow.

Danika bit her lips, knowing that it was not up to her to decide, and Remeta was looking at her with wide, hopeful eyes.

"You can come with, Remeta," the king said softly before she even began thinking about what to say.

Remeta clapped her hands excitedly and bowed her head in gratitude to the king. "Thank you, my king! Thank you! May you live long! Have kids too! Oh, of course, you will have kids! Remeta knows this! Remeta knows this! Remeta is happy! Remeta is excited!" She was rambling to herself, clapping her hands as she skidded her way ahead of them.

King Lucien stood rooted to the spot as he stared at the excited girl who was already several feet ahead, jumping up to take leaves from each tree she passed.

.

CHAPTER 4. THE ABYSS OF MISERY. THE ISLE OF EMOTIONS.

After Remeta ran away, Danika couldn't help stealing glances at the king. There was so much pain in his eyes it made her heart burn. Why would he hurt this way? Oh, what did Remeta say to trigger a look like that on his face?

She didn't know when her arm rose of its own accord to rub soothingly on his back. She didn't know where the courage came from, but she found herself patting him.

King Lucien was deep into his head before he felt the soothing caresses on his back. Remeta had spoken about babies, and it had triggered painful memories—memories of when the healers and medicine men of the kingdom told him one after another that he couldn't father a child. Memories of the first year after slavery when he had desperately tried to prove them wrong, bedding so many women of the kingdom who had been all too happy to graze his bed. He had bedded so many he lost count, but none of those females had carried his fruit. He was so desperate then; it didn't matter who would carry his child. It didn't matter if it was a slave or an outcast; he just wanted to father a child.

But when none of them were able to carry his child, he knew then that, indeed, he could not father a child. In his cold heart, the knowledge hurt. It had been hurting from the beginning because he was a sterile king. Scarred and sterile. Broken.

Cone really did kill him completely. Repeatedly. In the deepest way a man could kill another without making him stop breathing.

And now, little Remeta innocently grinned up at him to speak of a child. It caused internal pain. For another person, he would have ordered her execution for saying such to him. But from Remeta, he could only remain deep in his head, being devoured by painful memories.

The soothing hand on his back dragged him back from the miserable abyss. It was as if all the demons of the past had vanished, and his head was clear again. He swiveled his head and stared at Danika. She had concern written all over her face, her eyes filled with warmth. But she quickly snatched her hand back to keep from getting punished.

It was at the tip of the king's tongue to ask Danika to put her hand back on him again—anything to keep those monsters at bay. But he didn't. Instead, he moved forward. Danika walked beside his stiff body. Tension radiated from him in waves.

They walked away from the vicinity of the palace. It was a long walk. With each step they took, the evening wind caressed them. The beautiful sight of the sun disappearing completely from the sky had Danika captivated.

It was refreshing, this walk away from the palace. Away from slavery and suffering—even for a moment.

It must be refreshing for the king, too, because the tension slowly left his body. They entered the woods, and the only sound in the air was the chirpings of birds and the howl of the wind.

They saw Remeta far ahead of them, laughing and chasing crickets. "See! My queen, see!" She screamed as she chased them around, her face radiating joy.

Danika looked at the king for permission, and he nodded his head, so she hurried ahead towards Remeta and joined her in chasing crickets around. It was funny how the crickets slipped from their fingers and led them in circles of a goose chase, and Danika found herself smiling alongside a laughing Remeta.

King Lucien stood quite far from them, using one arm to support the other. He pursed his lips in thought. It was a beautiful sight, seeing Danika and Remeta like that. He was captivated by the beautiful smile on Danika's face as she chased after Remeta, who was chasing after an evening cricket. His worries dissolved at the sight. A different kind of peace fell upon him. Away from the palace building, he allowed himself to lose himself in the evening walk's peace and serenity.

Closing his eyes, he breathed deeply. This was what he wanted. He can have this—even if it was just for this evening.

He felt a presence beside him and opened his eyes to see Danika standing before him. Remeta was nowhere in sight.

"Where is Remeta?" he asked.

"She chased a cricket down the river," she replied with a beautiful smile, pointing in the direction Remeta went.

He allowed his eyes to truly look at her again. Earlier in the afternoon, some oddities happened when he was with his mistress that left him baffled. It had been difficult for him to get hard for his mistress. He wasn't in the mood. He didn't want her. And when he was eventually in the mood, it was Danika that filled his thoughts. He'd always endured the touch of his mistress for the past five years; he was used to it. But today, he found it hard to endure it. While she moaned her pleasure, his head took him back to the night before when he had Danika in his arms. Her innocence and eagerness to please. The sweetness that was uniquely hers. The enjoyment from her touch alone. Her moans. The tightness of her body wrapped around his organ.

It took him a moment, but he forced himself to shut his mind away from the memories of it.

In the past, when he thought of memories, it meant horrors because he could only remember his time in slavery. For the first time, a memory for him wasn't dipped in horror.

He did not understand it. He could not comprehend it, but it was what it was. Who was this woman?

When he'd told her she pleased him, he was seeing Danika. He forgot for a few seconds that it was his mistress in his arms.

Now, he gave her words he'd always wanted to say to her but hadn't been able to let himself utter it before.

"You are beautiful," he whispered.

Danika's cheeks flushed red at the compliment, and she ducked her head. "Thank you, master."

He turned and started walking with his hands behind his back. "I am your king for this evening. Not your master."

The reminder made her glow. She decided to take a leap at fate. "Then can I ask you a question, my king?"

When he gave no reply, she bit her lips. She walked beside him in silence, inwardly cautioning herself not to overstep her boundaries again.

He stretched out his hand towards her and waited. She stared at this hand in bewilderment, wondering what the silent request was. She raised her eyes to his expressionless face—which was staring ahead—and there was no clue about it.

Surely, it wasn't what she was thinking.

"Put your hand on mine, Danika," he said, still not looking at her.

The words that sounded like an order and a request at the same time made her belly flutter. She placed her hand into his strong outstretched hand and watched as his fingers wrapped around her slender white ones. It was the first time he openly requested her touch—her hand in his. She forced herself not to think it special—not to let this gesture feed the feelings she already had for him. But it did. With each step they took together in the coolness of the evening, his hand in hers, Danika felt her heart reach out to him.

"You can ask," his deep voice came through.

"Huh?"

"You said you have something to ask. You can ask."

"My mother. I want to know about my mother," she whispered. His steps faltered, and he stared at her. She swallowed and rushed out. "She died when I was young. I don't know much about her."

King Lucien hesitated, then continued walking. "I don't know much about her either, but it was well known around the twelve kingdoms that she was a very good queen. Rumors have it that she never supported your father in anything he did, but it never stopped Cone. A queen can only do a little when it comes to her king," he provided softly as they came out of the woods to the riverbank.

They watched Remeta, who was on the other side of it, quite oblivious of the adults close by. They continued walking. The evening started blending into early night.

"The things Cone could never do, Queen Auroria tried to do. Going into the village regularly, sharing foods for lowborns. She treated everyone equally." He paused. "She was a good woman."

Danika's heart felt happy and relaxed as the king continued talking about her mother. She had never really known her mother except for the little her nanny told her, but hearing King Lucien talk about her was like a soothing balm on its own. The same mouth that snarls her father's name in sheer hatred spoke so gently and analytically about her mother.

They came to a wooden bench beside the riverbank, and Danika was happy when his hands were on her. Then he led them to that chair. She sat beside him, and he talked steadily. She listened attentively, her eyes soaking up this moment as they watched his face and the river before them. Such a beautiful sight. She stored this moment in her heart, knowing deeply that she was the first person to share such an intimate moment with him—the first person he had talked to for such a lengthened period of time.

Finally, he turned and pinned blue eyes on hers. "Always, I ask myself who you are. How a monster like Cone could birth a woman like you." He paused. "For the first time in my life, I let myself wonder...what if you take after Queen Auroria and not King Cone?" he confessed, his eyes holding hers intensely.

Danika seized breathing. Out of the corner of her eyes, she saw Remeta disappear to the other side of the woods. They were alone again. The world around them fell away because she was lost in the ocean that was his eyes. She didn't know how to answer his question, and she wasn't trying to.

She could only glance at him. Her hand in his. Her body surrounded by his.

"You will never betray me, will you, Danika?" he asked suddenly, his eyes searching hers.

She shook her head. "I don't know how to betray you, my king. I will never," she whispered.

"I do not like to be betrayed, Danika. I do not give trust easily, and when I give, I do not like it being thrown away. I am giving you a little. Do not ever throw it away," he stated firmly.

Danika didn't know why he was saying those words to her, but she was determined to let him see that she could never do anything that would hurt him. This man who had hurt her so much. This man who had hurt more than any other human being she had ever known. She would never do anything that would hurt him. She did not have the heart for it.

Danika pressed closer to the king, so nothing separated their body from touching. The scent that was uniquely his enveloped her. She let her feelings for him show blatantly in her eyes—for him to see her sincerity. "I will never betray you, my king," she vowed because she knew full well that she did not have the heart to hurt him. She did not know the betrayal he was talking about, nor did she know what aspect he was talking about. But it didn't matter. She knew she would never be able to do it.

Tears filled Danika's eyes suddenly, and she looked at him through glassy eyes. This must be her curse, to love a man who would never love her back. A love that was forbidden. An abomination. When the embarrassing tear dropped from her eyes, she tried to avert her gaze, but his hand went to her chin and stopped the movement. He forced her gaze right back at his. How he looked at her, she didn't know what was going through his mind. And when his gaze lowered to her lips, a frown crossed his features.

She swallowed tightly, wondering what was going through his mind.

Suddenly, his head lowered, and his lips found hers.

CHAPTER 5. SILENT WORDS.

When Baski came out of the palace to search for Remeta, Uyah told her that she saw Remeta going for a walk with the king and the slave princess. Baski was surprised that the king would let Remeta tag along, which also brought a smile. Recently, she had so much to smile about. Her baby, her Remeta, was getting better as days went by. Healing didn't happen all at once. As a gradual process, Remeta was getting well.

It was the early hours of the night, and Remeta had to take her potions. Baski went in search of her, taking the river straight instead of going through the woods. She heard a feminine footstep laughing and chasing the chirps of crickets and smiled again, knowing she had found Remeta even before she saw her.

"Remeta, it's time to go," Baski called as she came out in the clearing and saw her daughter holding a cricket.

"It is?" Remeta pouted at her mother. "But the king and my queen are still at the riverbank."

At the riverbank? Baski still couldn't comprehend how the evening walk between the king and his slave would be. An evening walk was the best pastime for relaxation, letting out steams, letting go of worries, of calm and serenity. The king always liked going alone the few time he went.

It made her wonder how it was going between them, and Baski didn't know if it was curiosity or worry that the king might be punishing her that drove her to the few steps forward and strain her neck to oversee the riverbank.

The king was kissing Danika.

Umm... No.

Baski blinked hard to clear whatever it was that entered her eyes, causing the hallucination. She looked again with clearer eyes. The image hadn't changed. She gasped.

"What is it, Mama!? Can Remeta see!?" Remeta was already walking towards her as she asked.

Baski quickly held her daughter and started taking her away from the premises. "No, Remeta cannot see. It's the waters of the river swallowing its bank. It's n-nothing."

"The river is being mean. Does it want to kill its bank?"

"That's the way rivers do. They have to flow around. They don't stay in a place. Their banks understand." She led Remeta into the woods as she said distractingly.

"Oh. So, it's a river thing?" Remeta asked.

"Yes, it's a river thing."

"Are you sure my queen will not be angry at Remeta because she left without telling her?"

"No, I'm sure your queen will not be angry."

"Is she not your queen too? She is everybody's queen," she said to her mother as they walked.

"Whoever is Remeta's queen is also Baski's queen," Baski deadpanned.

"Because Baski is Remeta's mother?"

"Because Baski is Remeta's mother," she confirmed with an affirmative nod.

"Can Remeta tell her mama that she loves her?"

Baski stopped suddenly and stared at her daughter. In the past few days, she had added weight and looked brighter than ever. Tears burned the back of her eyes. Baski had begun to lose hope that she would see her daughter this way. "She can," she said hoarsely.

Remeta grinned and hugged her. "I love you, Mama."

Emotions crowded Baski's throat. She hugged her back. "I love you too, my daughter. I love you so, so much."

She could never thank Danika enough. She could never thank the creator enough for bringing Danika into their lives. The things she did for her Remeta—for the king.

That woman was sent by the creator to their people, Baski thought as she continued leading Remeta back to the palace.

King Lucien was kissing her.

The thought was just running around in Danika's head without actual penetration. She was too shocked—too dumbfounded.

The brush of his lips were tentative at first, an unhurried sweep of his mouth against hers. Every muscle in her body locked up; he made a low sound deep in her throat that sent shivers down her spine.

The king was kissing her.

His lips caressed hers again, nibbling and clinging to them until they parted with a gasp. He deepened the kiss with a thrust of his tongue.

The knowledge finally hit home. The king was kissing her!

Danika's eyes were wide open. Her senses went into overload, firing in every direction. The kiss was everything she could've imagined a kiss to be and then some. Sublime. Explosive.

Danika's heart fluttered wildly from a yearning so deep that darts of pleasure shot through her veins as his tongue plunged deep into her mouth. His tongue licked hers, and his lips sucked hers. She moaned into his mouth, her hand tightening in his. His tongue parted her lips and swooped inside again, tasting her, seeking her warmth. She felt his hand at the back of her neck, holding her to his ardor, and she felt her heart racing against her chest. Her eyes slid closed, and she gave herself over to the kiss.

His lips were soft, and he tasted male. She held onto him for dear life while he plummeted her lips for so long, she didn't know how long had passed.

The sound of the flowing river, the chirping of birds, their erratic breathing, and her soft moans filled the air and surrounded them.

When he pulled his lips away, Danika was dazed and drunk from his kisses, her lips red and swollen.

King Lucien didn't know where the urge to kiss her lips came from, but when she sat down on the wooden bench, he couldn't stop noticing the plumpness. He'd given in to impulse.

Now, he wished he hadn't because he wanted her more. He wanted to do a lot of things to her—*with* her. It did not make sense.

He glanced into the dazed blue eyes staring up at him, his hands holding her soft body to him. His eyes lowered to her lips before he used his eyes back to hers. He had already started this evening; he would allow himself to enjoy it as it lasted.

Tomorrow, he would keep on his responsibilities as a king to his people. Tomorrow, he would remind himself about his duties. He would remind himself that she was his slave and the daughter of Cone. But for this evening, he would let himself enjoy this peacefulness. This serenity. This calmness that comes from her presence and a walk away from duties and obligations.

"Are you alright?" he asked with a crease of his brow.

"I'm fine," she whispered. She licked her lips, and she could still taste his tongue.

When he pulled away, Danika moaned about the loss of his body on hers. The kiss had overwhelmed her, and her body was all hot for him.

They stared at the river in front of them while her thoughts were only in the slight distance separating them. She hadn't recovered from the long night she spent in his arms last night, but her aching body still longed for his. She would be there if he demanded her in his bed again tonight. She would let him have her anyhow he wanted her— even if it hurt or felt way too good. That's how much she loved him.

Night had fallen, but Danika didn't want to go back. She wanted this moment with him to last forever. And so, when the king lowered his head to her shoulder and closed his eyes, Danika felt a warmness settle over her.

"My king?" she whispered.

"Mm." He didn't open his eyes.

She hesitated. "Can I pat your hair?"

A pause. "You can."

Her left hand was still circled in the protectiveness of his, so she curled her other hand to his hair and began patting softly and rhythmically. The early night slowly began falling into a night. The darkness was welcomed, too—a world of theirs.

They hadn't said anything for a long while, but they never had to—two people who communicated better in silence than in words.

Finally, the king raised his head. "We have to go back."

"Yes, my king."

He finally let go of her hand and got up. With his hands behind his back, he began walking back to the palace. She followed him, only a step behind him. They took the shorter route back to the palace.

They arrived, and a messenger was waiting for the king in front of the palace. He bowed his head as he saw the king. "I bring a message, my king."

"A long one?"

"Too long. It's a matter of the court, Your Highness. I was sent from the kingdom of Navia," he answered with his head bowed.

"By King Valendy?" he asked with a frown.

"Yes, Your Highness."

"It must have been a long journey. Guards?" he spoke in that usual calm manner of his.

Two guards came out of the palace and knelt. "Yes, Your Majesty."

"Escort the messenger to the royal court. I will be with him shortly," he ordered.

"Yes, Your Majesty." They turned and started doing the king's bidding.

King Lucien walked past them into the palace while Danika followed closely behind. They walked through the long hallway of the royal quarters before they cut through the hidden wing of the king's bedroom.

The three guards at the door bowed their heads to him. One of them quickly opened the door.

He strode past them, and Danika followed. The guard locked the door behind them.

Inside his chambers, she stood waiting as he walked towards his desk and held up the big bundle of scrolls. He extracted more than five new scrolls and spread them on the desk. He left the desk, strode to the inner room, disappeared inside the library, and came out minutes later with some written parchment.

"I want you to read and translate these words into those scrolls on my desk. Can you work alone while I'm not here?" His expressionless eyes were trained on her face.

Danika found herself nodding her head, even as it dawned on her that he wasn't dismissing her. He wanted her to stay in his chambers, to work alone while he went to listen to the messenger.

At her nod, the king walked to the desk and kept the parchments beside the scrolls. "Wait for me right here in my chambers."

"Yes, Your Highness." Another night with him? She swallowed tightly. It filled her with fear and excitement. Every moment with him was welcomed. Every moment with him was precious—especially after his kiss.But her body was still aching so much she had barely recovered from the previous night, and so, the thought of spending another night in his arms had her filled with trepidation.

The king ordered the guards to bring a smaller desk and chair for Danika. Within minutes, they brought it in and put it beside his desk. The guards left and they were alone again.

The king took a step to leave and stopped. He turned back to her and kissed her again. This time, the kiss was long and hard. He took her lips like a man would take what belonged to him. He devoured and ravished her mouth to the extent they shared the same air.

Danika tore her lips away from his and let in deep gasp of air when all the oxygen in her body depleted.

He pressed his forehead to hers while she gasped loudly. "You will be spending the night in my bed again tonight, Danika. Do not leave."

"I'll be here, Your Majesty," she whispered breathily.

Then he turned and walked out of the door.

.

CHAPTER 6. THE HEAVY WEIGHT OF DUTY.

C had entered his bedroom and was most surprised when he saw Sally sitting down on the chair by the side of the bed. His eyes mirrored his surprise. "Sally?"

Nervousness had Sally's fingers picking on the seams of her clothes. "It's me," she whispered.

When Baski told her that her princess would be spending the night in the king's quarters, and Remeta would be sleeping in her own bedroom, Sally decided to use the opportunity to see Chad. He had been avoiding her, and when they come across each other, he'd always keep his eyes averted, not looking her in the eyes. After the things Baski told her about his behaviour the other night, Sally knew that she had to make the move or he'd keep blaming himself and avoiding her.

"What are you doing here?" he asked, forcing himself to look away from her. She looked so small and beautiful sitting in that chair. Seeing her in his bedroom had a fierce primitive urge run through him. He'd always wondered what it would feel like to have her in his personal space.

That was before he did the horrendous thing he did to her the other night.

"I came t-to see you," she said, forcing her tone to be brave.

He averted his eyes. "You shouldn't be here. A man's abode was no place for a lady. It will only cause scandal and bad reputation."

"I'm no lady, sire. I'm a slave. I have no reputation to protect. And b-besides…" She swallowed tightly. "You know more than the others that I'm very soiled."

Chad flinched and glanced fierce eyes at her. "Do not ever say words like that again. The things you went through did *not* make you soiled. You're the purest person I know. Your heart above others makes you pure."

Sally didn't understand why he'd say or think something like that about her. She watched his face hesitantly to know if he meant it. She had never seen a more sincere face before. "T-truly? You mean it?" She ducked her head in shame. "The kings, they…hurt me b-badly."

Chad didn't like the pain and shame in Sally's eyes. He forgot all else, walked closer and held her shoulders. "They are the monsters with impurities. Not you, Sally. You were the victim. They are the monsters. It was not your fault."

Tears filled her eyes. "Don't you think it's time to tell yourself that, Chad?"It was the first time she had ever called his name alone without any horror to it. His name on her lips had his body reacting, and he cursed himself for it.

"What?" he forced himself to ask, not understanding what she meant.

She looked him in the eyes. "Don't you think it's time you tell that to yourself? What happened wasn't your fault. You aren't the monster."

His jaw locked and he tried to pull away from her, but she held him tight. Her wide innocent eyes implored him.

"You don't understand, Sally," he groaned at last.

"I do. If it's not my fault, then it's not your fault either. Please, s-stop avoiding me. It hurts me." She lowered her head on his chest and laid herself bare to him in a few words.

"I don't ever want to hurt you, Sally. I just---"

"Shhh." She placed a finger to his mouth. "If you don't ever want to hurt me, then please, stop pushing me away."

Chad looked down at her helplessly. She deserved so much better than him.

But he didn't think he could keep pushing her away. May the creator helped him with how much he wanted to make that girl his.

34

Danika was in the king's chambers translating and writing when she heard the angry voice of the mistress outside.

"I said let me in right now!" she barked at the guards.

"The king said we shouldn't let anybody in, Mistress," one of them said apologetically.

"But the king is not in there," the mistress hissed.

"He's in the royal court. But his slave is inside, and the king gave orders not to let anybody in."

Silence. Only silence met the guard's words. Danika heard nothing else.

Vetta, on the other hand, was stunned that the king was not inside his bedroom but Danika was. And he'd ordered no one else in? Why? Could it be that she was under some kind of punishment? Had he finally decided to punish her for all the wrongs she had been doing? Excitement had Vetta's heart swelling. She needed to know what was happening.

She kept her voice fierce as she yelled to the guard, "Let me in this instance!"

"But Mistress---"

"Now!" she yelled.

The guard quickly worked the locks and opened the door for her. She strode past him into the king's chambers and stopped short at the sight in front of her.

Danika was seated at a desk beside the king's desk with the king's scrolls and parchments spread out in front of her.

She wasn't getting punished. She was working. She was working alone in the king's chambers.

Vetta's blood ran cold. Anger replaced excitement. "What do you think you're doing!?" she hissed.

Danika bowed her head slightly in acknowledgment. "The king ordered me to work for him while he attends to matters of the court."

"He-he left you all alone here in his chambers? Why?"

"I don't know, Mistress. I'm not entitled to know why the king does the things he does. He only said that I shouldn't leave because I'll be spending the night in his bed," she explained calmly.

35

Vetta bit her lips hard to keep from spewing the curses that filled her mouth. She had been spending the night all the time in this bedroom lately. The same bed that had been there for quite some time, and she, Vetta, never slept on it before. Not until he had Danika on it.

He'd warned her to stop punishing Danika unnecessarily, or she would have slapped the devil out of Cone's daughter just for sitting on a desk beside the king's. She fisted her hands. She longed to put her hands on Danika, see her hurt and hear her scream.

Calm down, Vetta. Stay Calm. It's only a matter of time.

She calmed herself inwardly with those words. Indeed, it would only last for a little while, and then she'd set her plans in motion. Slow and steady always wins the race. Also, a little bit of patience.

"Alright then. Tell the king I'll see him in the morning." Vetta turned and marched out of the bedroom.

Danika watched her in puzzlement. She'd expected the mistress to behave badly again—to beat her up or draw her hair like she always did. She wondered why the mistress didn't do anything like that. Did the king grant her reward?

She didn't know. She wished that would be the case as she picked up the inked feather and continued writing.

Away from the king's chambers, Vetta walked far away from the palace. She might not know much about reading and writing, but she knew how to send signals and how to interpret them. She tore out a piece of her clothing and wrapped it up as she entered the woods, then whistled to a messenger bird.

The bird came and perched on Vetta's arm. She tied the piece of clothing to the leg of the bird and sent it in the direction of the former slave trainer's house.

She smiled as she watched the bird fly away.

It was well past midnight when the king walked into his chambers. Heavy burdens stood on his shoulders, his face hard as a rock. The lightness that surrounded him as he left his chambers had long

36

departed from him—especially after he heard the news of why the messenger came.

The king always knew that this day would come. He'd always done his best not to think about it. But finally, it was here. A day when he'd have to do the greatest duty required of him.

He had to take a wife. He had to have an heir. He had to form an allegiance with another great kingdom.

King Valendy had always been a good king, and he'd always supported well. When it came to support, King Lucien knew that he had the support of that king.

King Valendy had sent his messenger to give him the message that would be of help to him. The day before, Lucien had taken an arrow in the chest and was sick, so he hadn't been able to attend the court meeting with other kings in the kingdom of Ijipt. Valendy had suspicions that King Moreh might be after his throne, thinking to attack Salem and take over everything. It was just suspicions, but it wasn't without basis.

A kingdom without a queen, an heir, or allegiance was bound to be a center eye for many greedy kings.

And if anything happened to the king, the kingdom would be taken over.

He'd been sick yesterday, and his kingdom had been vulnerable to attacks. If anything had happened to him, Lucien's people would suffer again. His people have suffered enough. They would never have to suffer again; that would not happen. Not even over his dead body. He would always put his people above himself. That was the duty of every great king. That was the duty he would perform over and over again without any regret.

King Valendy had offered his daughter, Princess Kamara. In other words, he had offered his allegiance to his kingdom. If he married Princess Kamara, Lucien would be accepting the allegiance of a powerful kingdom that'd back him up against all the fights he knew would come in the future. The fight for more freedom for lowborns and more laws against the scurrilousness of slaves. The fight for the greater cause.

He'd sent the messenger back with a message of his own. Yes, he agrees to marry Princess Kamara. And yes, he was accepting his offer for the allegiance of the two kingdoms.

Now, the king leaned against the wall and stared at the woman who had fallen asleep with her head resting on the desk. He watched the smooth rise and fall of her chest in sleep. His shoulders were heavy with the burden of duty. His heart was heavier with the knowledge that he was about to take a queen when there was no hope for an heir coming from him.

His demons had resurfaced over the course of the evening. And now they haunted him.

.

CHAPTER 7. THE CALM BEFORE THE STORM.

D anika felt someone watching her. That was how she woke. She stirred, and her eyes opened to see the king standing a few feet away. He was leaning against the wall, and his eyes were on her.

At first glance, he looked deep in thought. He looked so troubled; she wondered what the matter could be. What was the message that the messenger came with? Seconds later, the troubled expression cleared his face when he saw her wake and was replaced by his usual blank face.

"My king," she whispered. Then she bit her lips. Was it time for her to call him master yet? She peeked a glance at him, but thankfully, he didn't call her out on it or reprimand her.

"Were you able to write two scrolls?" he asked, still leaning against the wall.

"I wrote four," she whispered.

"You did well."

She basked under the praise. Then the silence descended, and she found her nervousness enfolding her—nervous about what would come next. If she made any movement, she could still feel the soreness from the demands he made on her last night. Her thighs still ached where she gripped and rode him. Her cheeks heated up, and she lowered her head, picking nervously at the seam of her corset.

"Did you sleep well?" his deep voice came again.

"Yes, my king."

"Good." He finally pulled away from the wall. "Because you'll be needing it for tonight."

His shoulders were heavily burdened by his duties, but in these chambers, he could at least drop them aside. He didn't have to think of getting married. He didn't have to think of his inability to produce an heir to his throne. He didn't have to think at all. At least for the night. With the woman whose very touch could make him lose himself. Whose touch brought him peace and calm. He could forget everything and lose himself in the warmth of her body, of her arms. He could let himself have her and sleep so well.

Even if it was just for the moment. Even if it was just for tonight.

"Get up and undress for me, Danika," he ordered at last.

Danika's heart skipped three beats and then ran away from her chest. He wasn't ordering her to strip like he usually did. Instead, he was requesting her to undress for him. "Yes, Your Majesty." She stood on shaky legs and began pulling off clothes while he watched her like a hawk, his face not revealing anything.

Danika wished a day would come when he'd undress her himself. But then again, if wishes were horses, beggars would have been riding by now.

The room's silence was only disturbed by the ruffle of clothing as she undressed. Finally, she stood naked before him. He'd never seen a body so beautiful. So smooth, soft, and flawless, like the princess's. Being a slave hadn't been able to do anything to erase that.

Danika didn't want to risk being ordered to the table. She didn't want to risk being shoved into with her hips pressing achingly on the cold hard table—not after the memorable evening they had.

Not after his sweet unforgettable kiss.

So, without being ordered, she let her shaky legs carry her to the bed. She climbed onto the softness and silk covering it and laid down on her back. Her shy but loving eyes found his. Her legs pressed together.

Finally, the king pulled away from the wall he'd been leaning on and walked closer to the bed but stopped short suddenly. Indecision crossed his eyes. Danika didn't know what was going through his head as he stopped suddenly, his eyes staring blankly at her neck. She saw the moment when he made a decision and his face took on its usual blank look. Then his eyes held hers as he began undressing.

She gasped softly. Just like last night, he was going to take her naked. He wasn't going to blindfold her, and he wasn't going to take her fully clothed. Only this time, he was undressing fully for her. She'd only seen bits and pieces of his skin, but now, she would see him fully unclothed. Danika felt humbled that he was trusting her that way, and at the same time, her nervousness only skyrocketed.

He stood naked in front of her, the moonlight glow of the night feeling the bedroom. He looked like an avenging angel. He was all big, bulky and hard everywhere. The moonlight gave his scars a glow of some kind; they looked mighty beautiful to her, like a second skin.

Was it the moonlight or her love for him shining through her eyes?

"Don't you have anything to say?" he asked challengingly.

"You're beautiful," she blurted out. Red marred her cheeks with the admission.

He frowned, his eyes searching her face. He must have seen what he was looking for when all tension left his body and his face relaxed. "A man's body is not beautiful, Danika. A woman's is."

"Yours is to me," she whispered bravely. She allowed her eyes to stray past his waist. Her eyes flashed embarrassingly and jumped back to his face.

"What am I going to do with you?" he seemed to be asking himself.

She felt too naked and exposed lying down there, so she raised her hand and beckoned him to her. "Please."

The bed dipped as he climbed onto it, and his body covered hers. His hands went to her thighs, and he parted them in the silence of the night to sit fully in between her legs. King Lucien didn't want to have thoughts tonight, but he still wanted to keep a little bit of himself. He wanted to lose himself *in* her but didn't want to lose himself *to* her. He wanted to hold onto control.

But when he came down on her, she paled instantly. All the blood drained from her face when it looked like he would take her without preambles. Without preparing her body. Without touching her. No, that cold man wasn't the one she wanted. She wanted the man that drew pleasures from her body last night. The man she went on a walk with. The man that kissed her senseless.

So, she leaned forward and placed her lips on his. He stiffened momentarily. But only for a moment. "Oh, hell!" The words sounded like a surrender. And then, he was kissing her back.

Hot. Hard. Rough.

He didn't pull his strokes. Instead, his lips devoured hers. Danika didn't mind; he was finally kissing her again, and that's all that mattered. She closed her eyes and held on to him as he ravished her mouth with wet, deep kisses, with a ferocious hunger that weakened her knees. It was as if he finally unleashed the hungry demons in him on her—as if he finally let go of the control he'd been trying to hold onto.

His lips devoured hers. In one quick shove, he had her hands pinned in the hard confinement of his above her head. Her body was trapped beneath his hard body and his unleashed demands on her. She moaned as his tongue plunged into her mouth, sweeping inside and plundering, owning. And she was kissing him back just as much, heedless of the sharp pang of pain that came from her thighs where his leg shoved her leg wider for him.

The flames that started burning in her blood from the first time he kissed her by the side of the river erupted into a sudden inferno, and she was lost, only distantly aware that she was gasping and grinding helplessly against his hip, her hand holding his shoulder and her mind blissfully empty beyond a formless depth of want, and desire, and carnal need. So much need.

Then he tore his lips away from her mouth, his breathing as erratic as hers. "What are you doing to me?" The question was rhetorical, so Danika hadn't bothered to crack her tuned-out brain for what to say to him. His big body surrounded hers, blanketing her.

She felt safe. Sheltered.

Danika hadn't allowed herself to see the red flags of how she'd feel safe in the most unsafe place, how she'd feel sheltered in the most dangerous place.

He kissed her ear. "I... I..." He wanted to talk to her, but he couldn't say the words. He only rained kisses down her neck and back to her ear. "God, Danika. I want you so much," he finally admitted.

Knowing the admission didn't come easy for a man like King Lucien, and hearing him say that meant everything to her. "I want you too. So much." She clung to him.

She heard him swallow. "I need...."

"Whatever you need, you can have. Take whatever you need," she whispered, caressing his shoulder with a shaky hand.

"I do not understand the things you do to me..." he trailed off, sounding confused and angry at the same time. Then he slid down a bit, angled his head and took her rosy nipple into his mouth. At the same moment, his hand spread her thighs wide apart and he shoved into her in one deep plunge all the way to the hilt.

Chad lay with Sally on the bed. She rested her head on his chest while he patted her head rhythmically. They were fully clothed. He was running his hand through her long auburn hair while she kept her eyes closed, listening to the soft thuds of his heartbeat.

Sally didn't know how much time had passed since they'd been conversing. He'd promised her that he would no longer avoid her. He'd ordered his food and hers, and the guards had brought it in. They talked as they ate. She'd found out a lot about him that she never knew before. It was the most cherished time of their lives, the moment they were spending together. Especially now.

Chad finally admitted to himself that he had feelings for Sally. Deep-rooted feelings. And so help him, Creator, but he didn't think he could keep denying them.

He must be very selfish for wanting to keep something so precious to himself. Something so beautiful. He must be selfish, but he wasn't letting her go again. He couldn't. "I care about you," he blurted out, breaking the silence around them.

Sally looked up at him shyly. "I care about you too, Sire. I..." She swallowed. "I love you."

He shuddered at the admission and pulled her close. "God, Sally. How can you say words like that?"

"I say them because I m-mean them. I love you, Chad. Or I wouldn't be here. I wouldn't be lying in your arms."

"I love having you here in my arms. God help me, but I love it too much." He tilted her cheeks and kissed her passionately.

Her fears deserted her, and she kissed him back just as passionately. She pressed closer to him as his mouth took hers tentatively. Her body warmed all over. Chad wanted her so much; his phallus had gone so hard and thick it was almost painful. But he forced himself to stop kissing her.

"Please." She clung to him, not wanting it to end.

"No. No, Sally," he groaned, trying to get his breath under control. He pulled himself away from her. He wouldn't dishonor her or disrespect her by knowing her body carnally outside the bounds of marriage. She was sacred and precious to him; he wanted to perform all the sacred rites of marriage before taking her to his bed.

Tears stung Sally's eyes at his rejection. He didn't want her. He didn't even want to put his hands on her. Was she too dirty for him?

"Am I?" She swallowed tightly and forced herself to ask, "Am I too dirty for you?"

"What!?" he asked in bewilderment, not understanding why she would ask a question like that. Then he saw the tears falling from her eyes, and it was like a sucker punch to his jaw.

"Sally..." He reached for her.

But she pulled away from him in sheer embarrassment and pain. She got up and ran out of his bedroom, her heart breaking in two at his blatant rejection.

.

CHAPTER 8. THE NIGHT THAT WILL LIVE ON.

When Chad saw the pain in Sally's eyes before she ran away, he knew that he couldn't let her go for the night just like that. He didn't know what he had done to hurt her, but he was determined to find out and make amends.

"Sally. Wait," he called as he chased after her. He reached her down the hall, took hold of her hand, and halted her. "Please, wait."

She turned with tear-filled eyes. "What is it, Chad? Oh, please leave me alone."

She was already so ashamed that she offered herself to him and was rejected. Now, she wondered where she'd found the courage to make such an offer. She had never been a friend of sex because it hurt. She had her few experiences all the while she did her best to feed the slaves of Salem—to make sure they ate. Coupled with the things the kings did to her, she had become more afraid of it, and frankly, she wasn't sure that she could carry through any sexual intimacy—not even with Chad.

So, where had Sally gotten the courage to offer herself to him like that?

"Please, hear me out, Sally. I don't know what I did to hurt you. It's not my intention to hurt you," he groaned.

She swiped her hand across her cheeks to wipe the tears. "You don't want me," she accused. "You don't want me. Maybe because I'm dirty to you!"

45

"Whatever gave you such an idea!? How can you think of something so absurd!?" he asked in blatant confusion.

"In your bed. We were k-kissing, and then I repulsed you and you pulled away from me!" she accused sorrowfully.

He began to understand where she was coming from and shook his head adamantly. "No, Sally. You will never repulse me! Ever! I didn't pull away because I didn't want you. I pulled away because I wanted you *too* much. But I didn't want to disrespect you by taking you to my bed without going through the legal processes."

"The legal processes?" She sniffled, not understanding what he meant.

"Yes. I..." he paused and swallowed. He was suddenly nervous and dreadful. What if it wasn't what she wanted? What if she rejected him?

He wasn't exactly a hot shot. He wasn't really that big of a catch, and he was no longer a normal man because of the things he went through in slavery. What if she didn't want to spend her life with him?

She saw the looks and her curiosity was piqued. She searched her eyes, waiting.

"I... I want to marry you, Sally. I want us to get married. I want you to be my wife...if you'll have me," he finally rushed out.

Sally was dumbfounded. The look in her eyes showed her speechlessness.

"I do not understand the things you do to me..." He trailed off, sounding confused and angry at the same time. Then he slid down a bit, angled his head and took her rosy nipple into his mouth. The same moment, his hand spread her thighs wide apart and he shoved into her in one deep plunge all the way to the hilt.

Danika screamed at the unexpected move and tears burned the back of her eyes. All of a sudden, she felt full. Too full. And it burned. It burned so badly that she began pushing at his shoulders, pained whimpers tearing from her throat. Wet eyes pleaded with his.

He pulled back, pulling out of her completely when he saw how much he'd hurt her. It took so much from him to be able to pull away completely because of the incredible feeling of her tight body clamping hard on him.

She breathed a sigh of relief and gratitude when he pulled out, but at the same time, she felt bereft from the separation of their bodies.

His mouth on her breast began moving, and she felt each tug of his lips on her lower belly. He didn't try to penetrate her again. Instead, he focused his ardor on her plump rosy, tipped breasts. Slowly, the burning sensations disappeared, replaced by a throbbing of longing. Wetness coated her womanhood; her moans interrupted the silence of the night. Her moans and the suctions of lips.

His eyes were closed, his cheeks moving as he alternated between both globes. Her hand held his head to her body, her head thrashing on the pillow.

"Oh, please! Please!" Her body felt too hot. She was mindless for him now; she pushed her lower body towards his in silent pleas.

He finally let go of her red puckered nipple and buried his face in her neck. His hot breaths fanned her neck, and his breathing hitched as she felt his phallus nudging her again.

She couldn't help stiffening.

"Relax. Relax for me, Danika." His voice was hoarse.

"I'm trying! I'm trying," she whispered to him when the request/command penetrated her haze.

His lips buried at her throat as he began to work his hardness inside her. Short, fierce thrusts that opened her and stretched her. She gasped at the invasion, her hand clutching his broad back. Her inner muscles protested, fisting his hardness so much he groaned. He kept his thrusts short but hard and fierce until he was able to slide the last inches inside, seating himself fully inside her.

"Oh..." she breathed, feeling him so thick and hard, wedged deep inside her until there was no boundary between pain and pleasure.

"I want to lose myself in you, Danika. Can you take me?" he breathed into her ear.

Danika wasn't sure if she could, but she nodded anyway, her love for him driving her deeply under. Even if it was momentarily, she wanted him to lose himself to her.

It didn't matter how painful it might be.

Something in his words—in his expression—told her that this night wouldn't be happening again anytime soon.

"Yes," she whispered in affirmation.

A shudder worked through his body. Then he leaned up and took her lips into a fierce kiss as he began moving. Slow at first. Then he picked up the pace.

Within moments, he lost all control. He rocked his hips into her quickly, pulling out to the tip before slamming back home. Her body jerked each time he hit her center, which tightened her up and squeezed her phallus. He was only slightly aware of her tongue in his mouth because his hardness felt too glorious. He thrust into her harder, and she threw her head back and broke their kiss. She groaned loudly, and he took the opportunity to lean back a bit and grab both her hips in his hands.

"Hold onto me," he growled.

She made a little noise in her throat that almost sounded like a squeak, but she obeyed, gripping his forearms with her hands and wrapping her ankles around his calves. The headboard slammed the wall soundlessly as he moved rhythmically, and his manhood claimed her femininity. Each push was fast and deep—almost violent—as he grunted and bottomed out in her, burying himself balls-deep with every thrust. She went from crying out to wailing as he pounded her and pounded her until there was sweat running down his back and into his eyes from his hairline.

She feared that he'd break her in half. *This time around, he might truly break her in half.*

Danika wondered how it was possible that a man who rarely talked and was always so emotionless could be such a wild lion in bed?

He hit her dead-center and she sobbed incoherent words, her head thrashing on the bed. Her hands gripped him tighter with each pound of his hips. King Lucien ran his hands up her sides and focused on her breasts. He loved the way they felt in his hands—perfectly round globes of soft skin and pebbled nipples. He pulled at them and wanted to suck on them more, but he liked the pace inside her way too much to temper it.

Pleasure was zinging through his body—more than he'd ever had in as long as he could remember.

And he only wanted to pound her harder. The urge rode him hard.

Suddenly, he needed to take her from behind. It was a need that was already driving him mad. So, he pulled out, and she whimpered under him as he got up on his knees and wrenched her hands from his arms.

"Get on your hands and knees," he snarled. "Spread those legs for me."

His voice was quiet, but his tone still made the words an order. His tone was deceptive—a complete contrast to the fierce urge riding him.

She complied immediately, whimpering a little as she moved up on her knees and her hands gripped the sheets. Her body was shaking.

He grabbed her hips and slammed his thick organ back inside of her. Her ass was fabulous, and he dug his fingers into the soft flesh as he moved. She was fucking tight this way, and every time he slammed up into her, she cried out and her womanhood tightened up.

He closed his eyes for a moment, tilted his head back, and focused on the feeling of her wrapped around him as he plunged deep into her. When his eyes opened again, he looked down to where his organ was sliding in and out of her for a minute, but the sight was too disturbing; he had to close his eyes or he'd release. Instead, he leaned over her back and slid his hands up her sides and around to grip her breasts.

He pulled at her nipples—not hard at all, but enough to make her body jerk with a little more stimulation. She moaned, clawing on the sheets. He placed a hand on the back of her neck. With just a little pressure, he guided her head to the pillow and waited for her to turn her face to one side before he leaned in with a little more weight, holding her there.

He was slamming into her so much, her back bowed as a scream tore from her throat. His phallus was an iron-hard length of agony and ecstasy plunging inside her now. His hands gripped her hips, almost bruising in their strength as he pounded her so hard and fast she swore he would batter his way into her womb.

And he was already there.

Each stroke he hit at the mouth of her womb until the small opening caused a different sensation at the broad head of his shaft.

"King Lucien!" she yelped as shards of painful pleasure overwhelmed her. She shrieked with each plunge of his hips and push of his hands on her hips for her to meet his strokes, driving him harder, deeper, feeling her release begin tightening in her womb with each thrust.

"Damn you," he groaned, pushing her flat on her back, his legs inside hers.

Most of his weight held her down as he continued slamming into her body. She was crying out, sweating, and practically shaking. The thrusts inside her were rough, primitive. He pulled her to her hands and knees and took her just as hard. So hard they shook the bed, shafting inside her as she began to fly, as though he pierced her spirit and set it free with the exquisite pleasurable pain ripping through every nerve ending in her body. Even the air around them seemed to obey his will. He caressed her exposed flesh and licked at her nipples as she fought to hold herself in place, breathed over her sweat-dampened skin until the pleasurable pain became overly much to bear.

"King Lucien." Her wailing cry was desperate, shocked, as rapture began to flame around her.

"Heavens, Danika." His voice was guttural, so rough, so deep it was animalistic.

The familiar unbearable pressure began in her womb this time. It was too overwhelming and unbearable, and she began wailing and thrashing beneath him.

But he didn't pull his punches, slamming into her harder as he felt his release barreling its way towards him.

And then, it happened.

Suddenly, she felt every muscle, every bone in her body lock in place as something began to swell inside her womb.

It wasn't pleasure. It went beyond ecstasy.

Her vision turned dark, and she began to shudder, deep hard tremors shaking her body as she felt her release begin to pulse through her. The muscles of her inner flesh tightened and swelled, trapping him inside her. She heard his agonized, shocked groan, then felt her womanhood ripple as her release reached its height, milking his flesh, stroking him until she felt the hard, heated pulse of his semen inside her. He was growling behind her, whispering something as his body jerked and shuddered against her own.

Danika lost all the energy in her body and collapsed beneath him, unable to maintain the strength in her arms or any part of her. Her cheek pressed into the sheets as she fought the agonizing tightness in her inner body. Something was happening inside her, and the pressure of it was hurting her. She didn't know what it was, and it scared her. Her muscles spasmed with each furious spurt of seed King Lucien released, and each shattered male groan at her ear.

"Danika." He lay against her back, his voice tortured. "Sweet God. Danika . . ."

She jerked with the hard spasm that tore through her at his voice, then his own dark groan at her ear. King Lucien didn't know what was happening to her. He'd never seen anything like it. She'd released violently before, but never like this.

For a moment, it prickled him that his demands from her had truly harmed her badly. But he dismissed the absurd thought as soon as it came.

"Easy." He found his hand caressing her back gently, soothingly. "It's okay."

"My king. My king. My king." She was crying, whispering his name, her eyes closed.

She wouldn't stop jerking with each claw to her womb.

"It's okay." One hand smoothed her damp hair back as the other slid down her hip, her thigh. "You're okay."

One last shuddering tremor racked her body before she felt exhaustion swamp her. True exhaustion.

Her breath shuddered from her chest, and softly, gently, darkness closed around her. Her breath evened out, and consciousness began to be lost to her.

Remeta was sleeping in her mother's bed in the servant's quarters, where she'd brought her after she'd fallen asleep in Danika's bedroom.

A smile crossed her sleeping features. "Prince is here," she whispered in her sleep, then, followed by a slight sad frown, she added, "But will Prince stay?"

CHAPTER 9. COURTING WEEK.

Four weeks later, Sally came out to the backyard to see her princess washing her clothes. Sally would have rushed to take the clothes from her before, but today she didn't.

Her princess needed the distraction. She needed the activity to get her mind off painful things.

Her princess turned then and saw her. She smiled at her. "Sally..."

Sally forced herself to beam at her. "My princess. Do you need my help?" she offered anyway.

Danika shook her head. "No. I'm fine."

Sally bit her lips. It hurt just having to come to say this to her princess.

Danika saw the pain and indecision in Sally's eyes. She dropped the piece of clothing back into the small river and turned to Sally. "What is it?"

"Princess Kamara w-will be arriving today," she finally spoke helplessly. "We have to be ready to welcome her chariot."

"It's courting week already?"

Before royalties were married, sometimes there was courting week. Courting week could last for more than one week, but it didn't exceed one month. Princess Kamara had requested for courting week, and her request was granted.

"Yes, it's courting week," Sally replied sadly.

Danika swallowed tightly and she forced a smile. "It's okay, Sally. I'll be ready. You tell Baski that I'll be."

Sally's relief was apparent. She wanted so much to go closer and hug her princess tight, but she didn't. The protective rise of her shoulders and the pain she was working so hard to hide was written all over her face. Sally knew that her princess was doing her very best to be strong. If Sally hugged her, her princess might burst into tears. It wouldn't be the first time.

"How are the linens you went to buy?" Danika forced a smile, trying to brighten Sally up because she knew that Sally was worried about her.

It worked. Her former personal maid grinned excitedly. "I bought them! Oh, my princess, it's so beautiful!"

"I knew they'd be. You've always had such a good taste in wears." Sally was getting married to Chad, and it made Danika happy. Sally's happiness had always brightened Danika's day, and for the past three weeks, she had Sally's happiness to live on.

"Oh, I just forgot. The seamstress is waiting for me in our bedroom. I'll be back, my princess!" she gasped, and Danika nodded, watching her as she left.

Once she was gone, Danika's face fell. It had been four weeks since she came out of the king's bedroom after the night they'd spent together. Four excruciating weeks.

That was the last night she'd slept in the king's arms.

The last time she and the king had sexual intimacies.

Since then, the king barely summoned her. And when he did, she would sit beside him to help him write and translate. To help him work. And even that had stopped. The king hadn't summoned her in more than a week. He was back to being her master, and she was back to being his slave. It shouldn't hurt; after all, that's what they were.

But it did hurt. It hurt so bad.

Sometimes, Danika found herself wondering if that walk in the woods ever happened. Whether the night that followed it happened or it was just her imagination. But then again, she knew for sure that it happened because it had taken her days to be able to walk without a wince—days for the aches in her body to leave completely.

"I want to lose myself in you. Can you take me?"

The remembered words spoken quietly into the night made her shiver. He'd almost killed her.

Baski had made her herbs and potions, but she still felt the results of his demands from her for days to come.

Another shiver worked down her body. Whenever she remembered that night, it never stopped making her body feel warm. He'd really unleashed himself on her; he'd almost killed her. For a moment, she thought she'd died too.

But she'd woken the next afternoon feeling better than she'd felt in a long time. Except the aches in her body and the soreness, her insides felt great. So, she'd dismissed the feeling. She'd ridden in euphoria for days, until Madam Baski gave her the news about the king's impending marriage.

Danika picked up the washed clothes and squeezed water out of them then walked to the horizontal pole and began spreading each clothes out to the sun. Till today, she still couldn't forget how much the news had hurt. Her heart had torn from her chest, breaking into pieces. She had walked to her bedroom and cried the rest of the day away.

She had always known that her love for him stood no chance at all. He was a king, and she was a slave. He was king Lucien, and she was Danika, the daughter of King Cone. It was a love that was forbidden from all angles, and she knew that there was no hope. But it didn't make it hurt less at all.

Finally, Danika had wiped her tears. As much as the knowledge hurt, she couldn't even blame the king for making that decision. She was once royalty, and she understood.

Her father had been making plans to marry her off to another kingdom before he died. He had wanted to form an allegiance with the kingdom of Yana, and the prince of that kingdom was fifty years old. At least Princess Kamara was a lucky one for being marched with King Lucien, Danika reasoned to herself with a hurting heart.

But another thing that made her heart ache was that it wasn't a love match. If any man deserved to be happy, it was King Lucien. He deserved a woman who could make him smile and be happy.

But sadly, love and duty do not always go the same angle.

It hurt her severely, and even after three weeks, it hadn't hurt less. But if Princess Kamara would make the king happy, then, it would be bearable for Danika. She just have to bear it; she had no choice. She wished the king all the happiness life had to offer. Maybe then, the guilt of what her father did to him would finally leave her.

She paused and leaned her head on the cold hanging rail. *If the guilt might leave her, would her love for him ever leave her?*

When Baski gave her the news one week after the night she'd spent with the king, it made her wonder if that was the reason the king had stopped summoning her to his bed, stopped summoning her to write. Why he just stopped...everything.

She opened her eyes, shutting the pain out and continued the work she was doing. Exhaustion racked her body, turning her body to liquid, but she ignored that too.

She had been sick lately. She was always tired; nausea had become her companion. The cravings too. It felt like her body was no longer hers, and it had been feeling that way for a while.

Danika ignored it. She was sick, and she knew that it was because of everything that had happened lately, the emotional blows to her heart and the king's renewed aloofness. The king's impending marriage.

Princess Kamara. Danika knew her. The few gathering of princesses her father had allowed her to attend made it possible for Danika to know most of the princesses in the twelve kingdoms. She had been their leader, too, because she was the princess of Mombana, the strongest kingdom.

Danika walked to the small pavement afterwards and lowered herself on it to rest her tired bones. Tears prickled her eyes.

That saying about how the mighty have fallen.

That saying about going from grace to grass.

All because of her father's greed and evil heart.

He destroyed everything her grandfather and ancestors had worked for and ruined Mombana in just fifteen years of being king.

"I hate you, Father," she whispered tearfully. She hated him so much for putting her through everything.

Princess Kamara and the other princesses always respected her in their gatherings, while only few rebelled behind her back because they didn't have the guts it takes to speak about it to her face. Others solidly respected her. They bowed to her. They didn't speak when she was speaking. It was in the rule of things—in the teachings of old which princesses spent most of their lives learning. And today, Danika would stand and wait on Princess Kamara. Today, she would bow to her and do work and duties for her.

She didn't know Princess Kamara personally, but she could distinctly remember a tall and beautiful woman who was her age.

Does she rebel?

Would she make life more hell for her than it already was?

Would she hate her more than the mistress did?

Would she hurt her?

The mistress's mood had become blacker lately; she was always so angry and raging—more than usual. Danika didn't know why, but she did her best to keep out of her way. She didn't want to be an outlet for the wicked mistress.

The tears fell from her eyes and Danika wiped them clean. But wouldn't it be better to be an outlet for the mistress? At least when the mistress whipped her, Danika wasn't sure it hurt more than the pain she was feeling now. The only pain that competes with what she had been feeling lately was the pain of what the kings did to Sally.

She wiped her tears again. She needed to be strong. She had to.

"No matter what happens. Do not forget that you're royalty."

The king's words whispered in her mind. Those words had always been her strength in weakness. Her comfort in sorrow.

More tears fell.

Creator, she feels so sick and very dizzy.

"You can't fall asleep, Danika. You must be awake and get ready to welcome the princess's chariot," she whispered to herself.

Sally went in search of her princess after fitting into her dress. She came out of the backyard and stopped short when she saw Danika sitting on the pavement, her head leaning on the wall.

She was sleeping.

It hadn't been the first time Sally had found herself sleeping in a corner lately, but she knew her princess had a lot going for her too. Tears prickled Sally's eyes. She wished it would go away and her princess would be happy again. It wasn't the moment for her princess to sleep because they had a duty to see about the coming princess. But Sally didn't want to wake her princess. In fact, she didn't want her princess to join the crew that would welcome Princess Kamara, even though that was how it should be.

She resolved her heart to that. She would do everything possible to spare her princess that special degradation and humiliation.

Sally saw a guard passing and rushed to him. "Please, can you help me, sire?"

The guard stopped and bowed to her in respect. "What can I do for you, my lady?"

Sally flushed. The palace workers had been more than respectful to her since they learned about her upcoming marriage to their leader. They were always eager to do things for her, to help her. They even addressed her like she was a lady of privilege.

She hadn't been able to get used to it, but they wouldn't stop.

"It's my prin---" she paused, reminding herself that she couldn't address her as her princess in public.

Remeta could get away with openly calling her "my queen," but another person would have her head separated from her body and nailed in a spike for such insolence.

"Please, can you help me bring her?" She pointed at her princess, not having whatever it took to call her by her name yet. "To our bedroom? I don't want her to wake, or I would have woken her up," she requested softly.

"I will do that, my lady." The guard bowed again and proceeded to walk past her towards Danika. He lifted her as gently as possible and began carrying her inside the palace. Sally followed closely behind them. She really wished it would go away and her princess would be happy again.

.

CHAPTER 10. PRINCESS KAMARA.

Henna stared at her princess in the carriage. Princess Kamara had her professional 'princess look' on her face: haughty lift of her chin, a blank unsmiling face, eyes straight ahead, mouth snapped together. A typical princess look.

But one thing about a personal maid's relationship with her princess was that the personal maid already knew her princess really well, having been with her for so many years.

"Everything will be alright, my princess," Henna tried to say in consolation.

"Stay away from me, Henna," Princess Kamara snapped.

Henna watched the way her princess's hands tightened on the beautiful silk and lace corset she was wearing. Her hands had been balled into fists since their carriage entered the kingdom of Salem. It had only remained tightened as the journey progressed, and she wasn't making any move to loosen her fisted fingers anytime soon.

It will hurt by the time she finally loosened it, Henna thought sadly. Already, her hands are as white as a sheet. Henna took a deep breath in resignation and faced forward, keeping away from her like she was instructed.

It just hurt her that her princess was unhappy. She hated seeing her unhappy.

Princess Kamara could only stare ahead. She reminded herself to blink occasionally, so that the traitorous tears that had been burning the back of her eyes wouldn't blur her vision.

She didn't want to be away from her kingdom.

She didn't want to be making this journey.

She didn't want to marry King Lucien.

She didn't want to marry any king.

She didn't want to rule over any kingdom.

She did not want to be here at all. She didn't want any of this.

She'd cried and pleaded with her father, but her father could be a very stubborn man. All kings were.

She always knew that when he discovered her secret he'd have her married off immediately. She'd always known, and that was why she had kept it a secret. But he'd found out anyway. After six months, he found out about her love for a peasant.

Princess Kamara blinked hard. This tears better not make it down her cheek, or she'd be very mad.

No princess should ever have anything to do with a peasant. A princess should never fall in love with a peasant, a man with no royal blood in him. It was almost a sacrilege. It should never be done.

She kept telling it to herself all the while she visited her peasant in secret and watched as Henna and her friend—who was an herbal woman—treated his injuries and nurse him back to health. She'd kept telling that to herself all the while Callan stared at her with deep blue eyes while he laid on the bed. She told herself for six months whenever she visited to check on his health.

She just didn't know when her heart stopped listening to her head—when her heart stopped listening to her and decided to betray her. She didn't know how she became obvious with her love for Callan—when she became so obvious that her father noticed.

It must have something to do with when she became too happy. She was never very happy before. Not until she met Callan.

He'd sent the guards after her one day and found her out. She closed her eyes tight to ward off more traitorous tears.

Keep strong, Kamara. You're a princess. A strong princess does not cry in public. As she chided herself, her hate for one of her father's mistresses surfaced.

Mistress Donna. She was the one that advised her father to marry her off after her secret was out. Her father had listened to the advice of his favourite mistress.

Oh, how she hated that mistress.

She had pleaded with her father, but he had already made up his mind. A memory plagued her.

"Please, father, please!" she cried and pleaded with him, kneeling on his bed chambers.

"Stop pleading like a coward, Kamara. I didn't raise you to be one," he'd said to her with an angry scowl.

"I'll stop loving him, I promise you. But p-please don't marry me off. Don't send me away, please. I'll stop," she'd cried, unable to help herself.

"I know you'll stop loving him, Kamara. This is just a momentary madness, but I know it will stop when you marry a man and channel your love elsewhere." King Valendy had turned away then. "You can stop loving him by loving your husband."

"But Father!"

"Leave, Kamara. I will not change my mind," he'd snapped at her.

Kamara accepted this courting week because she knew that would only delay the wedding.

"We're here, my princess." Henna's voice dragged her back to the present.

Princess Kamara found out that the carriage had stopped moving. She looked through the small peephole of the window to see a huge, beautiful palace.

Indeed, they arrived.

Princess Kamara finally unclenched her numb hands. She took a deep breath and reminded herself never to let a tear fall.

Her mother always told her that a strong princess did not cry in public.

Vetta glared at the old healer sitting in an old wooden chair of an old, rutted house. She was in the blackest of moods and so angry she could start a fire with the way she boils.

"These fertility pills work none! I have been taking them for the past four weeks, and nothing works! Nothing!" she hissed angrily.

The blind healer dropped her walking stick with shaky hands beside the way. "They were supposed to work on the first few days. Even before you get to the third pill."

Vetta snorted. For a shaky old woman dressed in rags, she sure had a strong voice that was in contrast with her small old physiques.

"Before I get to the third pill!?" She threw the small empty can of pills to the floor. "I've finished all eight pills in four weeks, and I'm not pregnant."

The healer cocked her head to the side in thought. *Oh, that's weird.*

"Of course, that's weird. Considering that you were supposed to be the best healer in all the twelve kingdoms!" she hissed.

"Are you sure you have a womb and your man can father a child?"

The blunt question took her aback. She glared daggers at the woman. "Yes, I have a womb, you moron. I've carried a child before. And my man can father a child." Of course, the king could father a child. She did not doubt that because a king couldn't be unable to father a child. So, it's definitely because of the damned pills. Vetta glared at the healer harder.

The old healer couldn't see, but Vetta would've sworn that the woman knew how bad her expression was because she sighed in resignation.

The healer got up and walked to one of the beat-up shelves in the back. She came out later with a bottle of liquid. "Here. That's a potion for fertility. It was strong and only recommended when one of the couples has a problem that makes a child impossible."

Vetta grumbled incoherently and took the potions from the old woman. She slipped it into her pocket, still not feeling better.

It was courting week.

The only rule of courting week was that the king would dedicate all his personal time to his future queen. That meant no having sexual intimacies with the mistresses or the slaves.

Only the princess would graze the king's bed during this period. Not her. And definitely not that bitch Danika.

A happy and sad development, Vetta thought. She wouldn't be in the king's bed, but Danika would not be either. But she didn't know how long the princess planned to stay, and she didn't know how long the courting week would last.

"Argh!" she huffed in anger. Then Vetta dropped the money bag on the table and marched out of the rutted house in the woods. "Princess, my foot! Marriage, my feet!" she hissed as she marched. To that day, it was still hard for her to believe it. Hard for her to take it in. Marriage!?

Vetta had been so focused on that bitch, Danika, she forgot that there was something called 'forming an allegiance between kings.'

Now, a new bitch would dare step foot into the palace and into the life of her Lucien to rip where she did not sow!?

Over her dead body.

Both Danika and the spoilt princess would have her to deal with! She would not spare anyone of them at all! That was all the more reason Vetta needed those pills to work. It had become a chore to get the king to have sexual intercourse with her lately. Vetta didn't know why, but she knew that things were changing. Was it because of his numerous duties lately? Or because he was taking a new wife? Or because of Danika?

Vetta didn't know anything anymore. She'd be damned before she sat back and watched it happen!

As for the new princess, she'd bet she was as spoilt and stupid as they come. She'd be just like the wind.

It would be so easy to blow that particular wind back to her father's kingdom.

Danika woke up twice. The first time was to quickly relieve her bladder that disturbed her. The second time was also to relieve her bladder. When she woke the third time, it was late evening. She cursed herself inaudibly as she pushed herself to her feet.

"Oh, heavens! Oh, heavens! Oh, heavens!" she gasped as she sprang up with so much force the wall closed in on her. She froze, staggered to maintain her balance, and waited for the room to stop spinning. When it did, she hurried out of the room. She couldn't find

Sally or Remeta. Being late evening, she was sure that Princess Kamara must have arrived hours ago, and she hadn't been there to welcome her.

"Oh, Danika. Why did you have to sleep for so long?" she questioned as she hurried away from the royal quarters.

Vetta had just stepped into the palace when she saw Danika walking in a hurry, her eyes flying around as if she was looking for someone.

But she wasn't looking in the direction she was walking.

Vetta took the opportunity and walked into Danika, causing the both of them to collide.

"Oh, I'm sorry---" Danika began saying when she collided with someone, only to look forward and see that it was the mistress she collided with.

"How dare you!" Vetta slapped her hard across the cheek.

The force of the blow whipped Danika's head to the side, a burning pain spreading through her body. She curled her hands into a fist to keep from caressing her stinging cheek and giving that horrible mistress the satisfaction of seeing how hurting the blow was.

Vetta smiled inwardly. She had always wanted to do this. Always. It had been so long since she touched Danika because of the king's warning that she should never touch his slave if she did nothing to deserve it. Well, now she had eventually done something to deserve it by almost running her down in the hallway. She kept smiling inwardly.

Outwardly, Vetta glared daggers at Danika. "Did you want me to fall!? What? So, now you attack me in the hallway!?"

"I'm sorry for running into you, Mistress. I did not attack you," she spoke through gritted teeth.

Vetta had always longed to take out her anger on someone. She took a step forward and shoved Danika away with all her strength. "You dirty bitch!"

Danika fell. She tried to break her fall but could not, and her butt hit the ground so hard she cried out. The world tilted around her for the second time that evening. She was winded and almost felt like she would faint. Danika tried to get up, but she was so tired, and the world around her was still moving.

Then she saw a beautiful woman in golden silk and big designed laces walking closer to them. The elegance of her movements, the high rise of her shoulders as she walked in a sophistication that mirrored hers once upon a time.

The woman walked closer to them and straight to the mistress. She slapped the mistress very hard across the face.

"What the----" the mistress began.

But the woman slapped her again—this time, harder than the first time.

.

CHAPTER 11. THE PRINCESS. THE MISTRESS. AND THE KING'S SLAVE.

P rincess Kamara hadn't seen the king since she arrived. She heard that he had been in court all day, but she would be able to see him in the night. In the meantime, she was shown to her room which was decorated and well-equipped specifically for her.

She'd spent her afternoon and evening walking around the palace, just looking around and getting some fresh air with Henna. Kamara was still hurting, and anger was in still in her heart. She wanted to be in her father's kingdom, not here. She missed seeing the face of Callan. She hadn't able to see him for some weeks because her father had forbidden her from doing so.

The consequence of disobeying his orders was that Callan would be whipped.

She wondered how he was doing now.

All these were in her thoughts as she walked through another hallway of the palace, only to see a woman slapping a slave hard across the face.

Princess Kamara look at the oppressor who was dressed in expensive silk and a well-designed corset that embraced her upper body like a lover's arm with high-quality lace that covered the rest of her body and the ground she walked on. A mistress, she'd realized immediately. She'd heard that the king had one mistress, which was very hard to believe because other kings and men of privileged status had more than fifteen. The lowest she'd heard about was five. Her father had eight mistresses.

This must be the only mistress of King Lucien. Kamara cocked her head to the side and wondered what was special about the woman that she had to be the only one. Or was it because of the king himself? She'd heard stories about the king—about his time in slavery and his freedom. Everyone had.

Why was this mistress slapping this slave?

Not her business, she told herself solidly as she started walking away from the aggravating scene. She hated mistresses so much because of Mistress Donna, but that wouldn't make her take it out on other mistresses.

"My princess?" Henna's voice came from behind her.

"Yes, Henna?" She swiveled her head to the side to see her personal maid staring at the mistress and the slave.

"Isn't that Princess Danika?" Henna asked.

She whipped her head towards the scene and watched it again— really watched the scene.

It *was* Princess Danika. She saw the moment when the mistress shoved her away and she fell.

Kamara found her legs carrying her to the scene even before she could give it a second thought. She walked straight to the mistress and slapped her really hard across the face.

"What the---" the mistress began.

She slapped the mistress again, this time harder than the first time. Her body was almost vibrating with the force of her anger.

"How dare you put your hands on her!? How *dare* you!? Do you know who she is!? Even if you come from the noblest of families here in Salem, I'm sure your whole family would bow their heads and lick the ground Princess Danika walked on. How dare you put your hands on her just because her status was reduced!? How dare you!?" Princess Kamara raged. Needing more outlet for her anger, she slapped the stunned mistress the third time, and then, she grabbed hold of her hair and yanked on it really hard.

"Ouch! Let go! Now!" Vetta snarled angrily, her scalp burning and her cheeks stinging. She never expected this from the new princess. Ever. It was just so unexpected, it left her stunned.

"The next time you put your hands on her like that again, I'll have you whipped! The only person that can alter that judgment is the king, and if he didn't or wasn't available at that moment, I'd whip you mercilessly! Am I making myself clear!?"

Vetta could only nod vigorously—anything to make the princess let go of her hair. Her hands itched to slap the princess back. It itched so damn much. But then again, there was still sense in her head. A future queen was the highest status, next to the king himself. The last thing she needed was the wrath of King Lucien. Or worse, King Valendy.

Princess Kamara finally let go of her hair and stepped back. "Henna."

"Yes, my princess!" The maid rushed forward.

"Get me water to wash my hands. I just got it dirty," she snapped.

"Yes, my princess!" Henna was already running out, knowing her princess and the way she was when she was in rage.

Apart from anger, Vetta felt a special kind of humiliation. *How dare this princess? How dare she!?* She glared at Danika who was still seated on the ground looking stunned. Even the bitch didn't expect that.

"I will tell the king about this!" Vetta vowed, her eyes filled with fire as she watched the princess in front of her. She knew exactly how to twist this event. She turned and stormed away. She needed to regroup! And then she would tell the king!

How dare she!?

Danika could only watch what was happening. She was too stunned. Too shocked.

After Vetta stormed off, Kamara turned her attention to her. She stretched out her hand. Danika placed her hand into hers, and she helped her up from the ground.

"Thank you so much for your help, Princess Kamara. I appreciate it," Danika said sincerely. She never expected that at all.

Kamara waved her off. "Oh, stop with the 'Princess Kamara.' Not from your mouth too. I get sick and tired of hearing it sometimes."

"Oh." She didn't know what to say to that.

"You can call me Kamara, and I will call you Danika."

"But that's not proper. I'm n-no longer a princess. I'm now a slave." Her cheeks flushed in embarrassment.

"The clothes don't matter. What matters is the blood running through your veins," Princess Kamara quoted. "My mother always says that to me."

"Your mother must be a good woman," Danika said hesitantly. This princess was not what she expected, but she felt relief filling her spine like a new breath of fresh air. She'd spend weeks worrying about the arrival of the new princess. How she'd behave towards her? If she'd make life more of a hell for her? Danika's relief was so apparent that she had to blink back tears. Princess Kamara was not a bad person.

Even if she was, at least she wasn't being bad now.

"Thank you so much for helping me with the mistress," Danika repeated, dusting off her dress. "She has always hated me."

"She's bound to. You're a king's slave. You should see the way the mistresses in our kingdom treat the king's slaves. It's all because of jealousy and greed."

"Really?"

"Yes. I don't know why they bother to do that. A mistress can never be a queen," Kamara stated.

And a slave could never be a queen either, Danika thought inwardly. Waves of sadness crushed through her.

Kamara began walking and she fell into step with her. The maids and servants that bypassed them couldn't help noticing that two princesses were walking together. One might be dressed in an expensive gown and the other in a simple gown devoid of lace, yet both emitted the aura of royalty. The steady footsteps. The high rise of their shoulders. The lifted chins. The graceful way their hands were buried together in their midriff.

Instead of a princess and a slave, palace workers saw two princesses on an evening walk. They bowed to both as they passed.

"I'm sorry about what happened with your father. We heard all about it," Princess Kamara said to Danika.

"I'm not. My father deserved what he got," she told the princess truthfully.

Princess Kamara shrugged. "He might have, but you sure don't. You know, I've always admired you. As Princess Danika, you were everything every princess wanted to be: regal, elegant, sophisticated and fierce. You spoke and wrote so well. Not to mention, reading so fluently. You were such a good princess and leader," Princess Kamara confessed, sparing Danika a sideways glance.

"I'm sure the princess rebels would have disagreed with you." Danika smiled at the reminder of a beautiful life that was once hers.

"The rebels are stupid."

"Thank you so much, Princ--- Kamara," she corrected herself softly.

"You're welcome. It must be hell being a slave. I can't imagine it." Kamara shuddered just at the thought of it.

"It takes some getting used to," Danika admitted.

Footsteps sounded and Henna came running back to them, carrying a bowl of water in which Princess Kamara washed her hands in, then Henna carried it away.

"You shouldn't let her beat you around, you know," Kamara said, wiping her hands. "The mistress, I mean. You were always so fierce; you shouldn't let that change because your status changed. People will walk all over you."

"Oh, but it has to change, Kamara. The things we do to survive. It's not easy surviving as a slave," she confided softly, staring into space.

"Yeah, I can't imagine. It must be tiring."

Danika found her condition so many things before, but she had never found it tiring. But the truth was that these days, she have become so tired of it. Would death really be such a bad idea? She asked that for the first time in a long time.

"You're right. Being a slave...It's tiring." A small sad smile crossed her lips. "But I think it's for the best—being in this position."

"Why?" Kamara asked curiously.

She looked her in the eyes. "Because I got to understand the heart of slaves."

"Oh…" Kamara cocked her head to the side as she thought about it.

"But I'm worried. I don't want you to get in trouble because you defended me," Danika said in concern, looking away.

Kamara was worried about that too, but she'd cross that bridge later. The only person she had no authority over was the king, and he might even punish her for it. "It doesn't matter, though. I got to release some of my anger on that mistress, and that's all that matters to me. I've been so angry…" She paused. "It's a long story."

Danika saw the pain that flickered in her eyes before she said the last words. She was going to ask her what the matter was when Baski came out of the palace building. "Danika? You're needed in the backyard."

"Alright, I'm coming," she called back.

Baski bowed her head to the new princess before she walked back to the building.

Kamara turned to her. "Till we meet again."

"Thank you so much for earlier."

"You've thanked me for it before." Kamara smiled a little before she straightened and began walking away.

Danika watched her with a hurting heart. Her thoughts went back to the king. Very soon, Princess Kamara would marry the king. She would grace his bed and she would bear his children. She would be the future queen of Salem.

The knowledge was hurting so badly, more than the pain Danika was feeling in her butt from her fall. But amidst that hurt, she was grateful that Kamara was a good princess. After everything the king had been through, he did not need a wicked woman—a woman like his mistress. And, if she would make the king happy, then it would be okay for Danika.

As she began walking towards the palace building, Danika's heart hurt and tears filled her eyes. She missed the king so much. Just the very sight of him. It didn't matter if she had to gaze upon him when he was wearing his usual scowl on his face.

She wondered how he was doing now.

Was he working well? Was he resting well? Was he sleeping well?

Did he ever think of her? Even for a little bit, did he ever think of her?

.

CHAPTER 12. A TROUBLED SOUL AND A SOOTHING SOUL.

Can a person live and breathe pain?
That was the question Lucien asked himself as he lay in the cold hard cage, his body hurting badly. His ribs felt like they'd been roasted in a hot blazing fire.

He could always deal with his pain on his own in private, in silence. But now Declan needs him. Declan needs him now.

He bit back a growl as he got up from the ground and walked to the bars that adjoined his present cage with Declan's cage.

"Hey," he growled out.

Declan opened his eyes and stirred. Lucien could see that he wasn't really sleeping. He was just forcing himself. At twenty-one, Declan had developed a very bad case of insomnia.

Just like every other slave. Some worse than others.

"Prince Lucien," he groaned, crawling closer. He placed his bruised hand into the outstretched hand of his cousin's brother.

"I'm so sorry. I'm so sorry, Deck. I wasn't able to protect you." Lucien's heart was so heavy in his chest.

Declan shook his head vigorously. Eyes red from crying beseeched his. "Don't, please. It's not your fault. I was only whipped. That's child's play compared to what you have been through."

"I was supposed to protect you." Lucien squeezed the cold hands of his little brother, tears of rage burning furiously at the back of his eyes.

"You have been protecting me for the past eight years. I've only gotten a little part of the things you've been through, and I will forever be grateful to you."

Lucien pressed his head at the cold bar, his eyes closed. Rage and pain had become a living, breathing thing inside him.

He didn't want this for Declan. He should never know a life like this.

"I'll get us out of here, Deck. I'll get every one of us out of here. You... My people... None of you deserve this. I'll get you out of here. One day, you'll wake up and be happy because you're free again. I'll make sure that happens," he vowed.

The silence of the night got interrupted by Declan's hitched breathing. "You don't deserve this either, my brother. And I know you'll get us out of this. I strongly believe it."

And it was there in his eyes, that strong belief. In Declan's face was that great trust he had.

Lucien made the vow every day, and his people never stopped believing in him. Not after eight years. Not after nine years too.

He kept holding Declan's hand until Deck fell asleep, his bruised hand holding tightly onto him as if he was afraid to let go.

As if he was scared that if he let go, the guards would come for him again. That Coza would brutalize him if he let go.

King Lucien sprang awake from the bed, his chest heaving.

He closed his eyes tight; the burning in his cold heart was so much he feared it'll burn him alive.

Can't breathe. Can't breathe.

Declan.

He was suffocating. The worst kind of nightmares. The most painful memories are always that of Declan's.

They always leave him in a rage. In pain. Disorganized. And dangerously close to tears.

He lived with the guilt that he had failed his people for the past ten years. He failed them by not getting them out of that hellhole earlier than he did.

But the guilt was nothing compared to what he felt about his cousin. He'd failed him in every way. He hadn't been able to keep the promise he had made to Declan. Instead of getting him free, he'd gotten Declan killed. Instead of making Declan see the sun again as a free person, he made him see the grave.

The pain was excruciating, and that was how the memories of it had lived in his head and replayed itself every night for the past few weeks that he hadn't been able to get some sleep.

He rose completely and got out of bed. He needed some fresh air—time outside to breathe. His own private haven was suffocating him.

He put on his long robe and walked out of his bedroom in the middle of the night. He hadn't been able to see his future bride today because of how busy and tight his schedule had been.

He'd spent all day in court and returned with a bad headache and so tired in his wary bones he'd thought that maybe—for the first time—he'd be able to go to a peaceful sleep.

He hadn't been more wrong. His demons haunted him. His shoulders tensed; restlessness was the very air he breathed.

Some nights were worse than others.

This was one of those nights.

Danika's bladder woke her up in the middle of the night. Afterwards, she wasn't able to go back to sleep again no matter how she tried. She shifted restlessly on the bed, turning to the other side and facing away from the sleeping Remeta. Then she closed her eyes tight and tried to go back to sleep. There was no sound in the night, just the usual silence and blackness.

Danika waited and waited and waited. Sleep eluded her. It was quite strange, because for the past few weeks, she had become very good friends with sleep.

And now, for the first time, it was deserting her.

Danika rose from the bed, ignoring the way her belly growled in hunger. She hadn't been able to eat dinner because she didn't have an appetite for the food that was cooked—another strange occurrence because she always had appetite for tomato bisque soup and roasted chicken.

She sighed, knowing that the sickness would soon leave her body. It had too. It was making her too tired lately, and she didn't want Baski to know. She did her best to hide it from her—from everyone. Her sickness. Her pain. Her emotional wreckage. She just had to keep being strong both for herself and the two females she had come to care for.

Danika stared at Remeta and Sally, who were sleeping beside her, quite oblivious of the world. She watched their laboured breathing. Finally, she got up from the bed when she was sure that sleep had really eluded her. She might as well go outside and get some fresh air.

She put on her sleeping robe and walked out of the bedroom. Out in the hallway, it took time before her eyes were able to adjust to the darkness.

She walked through the empty hallway, her harms wrapping around herself. It was cold outside. She kept her footsteps soundless so she didn't wake the guards that were sleeping around the corner. Those on duty just ignored her as she walked.

Finally, she came out of the palace building and froze suddenly.

The king? Every bone in Danika's body locked tight and she blinked her eyes several times to see clearly. She would know that back anywhere. Even without the expensive clothes, she'd know him anywhere.

It was truly the king.

He had his back to her, facing the wall, and was leaning against it. From afar, Danika could see his shoulders so tense. He held himself so stiff like a drawn arrow waiting to snap.

She drank in the very sight of him. Creator, how she has missed that sight. Warmth filled her inside, and for a moment, she forgot the coldness of the night because cool air wrapped around her like a lover's arms as she watched him.

It didn't matter that the night was so dark, she could still see him through the moonless night. She drank in the very sight of him.

But his restlessness was getting to her. She couldn't see his face, but she knew that he was so troubled.

How she could feel his pain from several miles away, she didn't know, but she could practically feel it so bad it was almost bringing tears to her eyes.

That was his weak moment and he wouldn't be having it outside if he ever thought anybody would see him. Danika knew that she was supposed to pretend that she didn't witness this moment and go back to her bedroom.

But she found her legs carrying her towards him even before she could try to talk her brain out of him. Not that she'd succeed, even if she had such conversation with her head.

He was in pain. And there was a supreme urge in her to soothe him.

She reached towards him and wrapped her arms around him from behind.

Danika.

When the feminine arms wrapped around him, he knew instantly who it was. He didn't know how he knew that the woman who was holding him in a slightly tight embrace, but he knew that it was Danika. Not Vetta and definitely not his future bride.

How had he known that? What exactly gave her away—made her touch so unique? Was it because a rare calmness settled over him the instant her arms made contact with his midriff or because all the voices of the past—demons of the past—in his head suddenly stopped talking and went silent?

Or perhaps it was because a certain kind of peacefulness suddenly settled over him, lifting his soul and soothing over the pain in his cold heart?

All those thoughts only made him stiffen his shoulders even more in rejection, but her arms tightened around him. He felt her head on his back, and then she swiveled her head to the side so that her cheek was left pressing into him.

"Danika." His voice was hoarse.

"My king," she whispered.

Her voice wrapped around him like a cloak, stronger than the soft arms around his middle. He had not realized how much he had missed that voice until he heard it whispering to him now.

"Let me go." It was supposed to be a command, but it came out like a call upon supplication.

"No. Please, let me hold you. You're hurting."

At the back of his head, it registered that it was the first time she was ever saying 'no' to him. The first time she was blatantly disobeying him. For him.

"Danika." This second time was a hoarse warning.

She shuddered against him, shaking her head wordlessly on his back. He felt wetness in his back and knew that it was her tears. *It is no longer as cold out here,* Lucien thought. His heart no longer felt so hurt and bereft. And it was all because of her.

Who was this woman?

How did she have such power over him? How could she manage to do the things she does so effortlessly with just a single touch?

Danika knew the moment all tension drained from the king's big body. He made a move and she loosened her arms around him. He pulled back from her and turned towards to face her. Blue eyes and a face devoid of emotions stared down at her.

Danika couldn't even begin to imagine the way she looked. She had tears running down her face, and her hair must be messy from tossing around in bed. She'd bet she'd lost some weight, too, because of how little she had been able to keep down. Lately, most of her food made it out of her mouth after eating. All that wasn't what was supposed to bother her. She'd blatantly disobeyed him a few moments ago, and he could easily have her head for that.

Surprisingly, it wasn't her main concern.

Her eyes raked over his body to make sure it wasn't physical discomfort that had him strapped against the wall. She was making sure he wasn't physically hurt. Tears of relief joined the tears that were already making their way down her cheeks as she saw that he was physically fine. He might be an emotional wreck, but physically, he was not hurt.

"You're fine." Love, concern and relief filled her voice as the whisper pushed out of her mouth and her eyes finally found his face.

His eyes flashed.

The silence of the night stretched as she looked him in the eyes, getting drunk from the very gaze of him. One could easily get lost in his eyes—eyes devoid of warmth and filled with pain.

Suddenly, he grabbed hold of her arm and tugged her closer to him.

One moment, the night air was caressing her front, and the next, her face was buried in his wide chest, and his strong arms were going around her in a tight embrace.

.

.
.

EPISODE 13. A STOLEN MOMENT.

When King Lucien pulled Danika into a hug, blanketing her in his strong arms, everything suddenly felt right in the world when she got over her shock from the gesture. She allowed her wet eyes to slide closed and she wrapped her arms around him.

It had been four weeks since she'd been in his arms. Four excruciating weeks of pain and misery.

Danika closed her eyes and tightened her arms around the king. It didn't matter if that moment was fleeting. If he regained his senses and pushed her away. What mattered was the moment—this stolen moment between them.

Since her status reduced and she became a slave, Danika learned to always live in the moment, because good moments are hard to come by when you're a slave.

Finally, he pulled back. She looked up at his deep blue eyes that weren't looking so troubled anymore.

"You weren't sleeping?" King Lucien's voice was deep, his eyes searching.

"I slept, my king." She'd keep calling him that for the night until he demanded otherwise. "I just woke up earlier and couldn't go back to sleep."

He walked past her then, slow, steady steps and with his hands behind his back.

Danika was torn. She didn't know if she should follow him or not. She wondered what had made him so stiff and restless that he had to leave his bedroom and cold out to the cold night.

"Are you coming?" He swiveled his head towards her without turning.

She nodded once and began walking towards him. She walked unhurriedly, her steps matching his. She fell only a step behind him.

It was a beautiful moonlit, cold night. She followed his stride. "Couldn't you sleep, my king?"

He kept silent for a full minute. "I haven't been able to sleep in a while." He glared at her like it was her fault.

"I'm sorry, my king."

His throat worked. He faced forward again. "It's not your fault," he sighed at last. "Tonight I had a nightmare."

She guessed as much. The king was a man with a horrible past, so it was only fitting to think that it was nightmares of the past that kept him awake. Nightmares her father created.

"I'm sorry." The whispered words came easily again, slipping from her mouth just as water slips through hands.

"I have a cousin from my mother's side named Declan. A fire accident took his parents when he was five and I was twelve. He was living with Queen Meetia, who was my mother's only surviving sister back then." As he spoke, he walked. Danika listened attentively, walking a step behind him.

This Declan he always dreamed of—the Declan she'd heard him call out in sleep a time or two. She felt good that he wanted to confide in her a subject that was so delicate.

"Queen Meetia died few months before we were enslaved. That was how Declan came to live with us. He was enslaved with us. I did everything I could to keep him from harm's way. It's not easy when you've got no powers and you're a target for a powerful man." He threw her a side glance.

Danika hadn't known what to say to that, so she kept mute but her chest felt tight.

He turned away again. "That life should have never known Deck. He'd been too sheltered. Queen Meetia made sure of that, especially when his parents died when he was a boy. Then, all of a sudden, he was exposed to the worst. The harshest part of life. I did all I could. They'd whip him and wouldn't feed him. I'd made sure to give him my own food—even when I'd not eaten for several days. I'd either give him or Remeta or Vetta. Baski and Chad never took it, no matter how much I command them to. The best days were those days we suddenly get a feast to eat. We didn't know where they were smuggled from, but occasionally, there was so much to eat it made those who had been so starved sick." He paused, his throat working. "Now, we finally know it came from Sally."

Danika did her best not to give any reaction at all. She'd fed them too, most of the times when Sally was unable to. However, she couldn't say that to him. It wouldn't change a thing. It wasn't enough to change the wrongs her father did.

"Sally is an angel," he continued. "And I'm glad Chad is getting married to a soul so beautiful. If any man deserves such great happiness that comes from a love match, it will be Chad," he said softly, his eyes flashing a bit.

And what about you? Danika wanted to ask so badly. *Don't you deserve it like he does?* She bit the words off, swallowing them down.

"A day came when I was brutally tortured. It was one of those torture sessions that brings a slave at the very blink of death. I was right there at death's door." His shoulders had gone tense, his eyes darkened and coldness was his expression. "The guards still came to whip me again, but Declan was there and he refused to leave. They whipped him badly and raped him brutally. He died right in front of me, and they took his body away," he said flatly.

Danika closed her eyes against the wave of pain. No one deserved a death like that. Definitely not his cousin.

Silence descended again. This time around it stretched longer. They'd long walked out of the premises of the palace, and now they're walking through the shortcut that led to the river. Danika wanted badly to apologize again, but she couldn't bring herself to say the words. Maybe because she knew that it would be the last straw for him if she did. It might turn him back to the master she knew her first few weeks in the palace.

"My nightmares were filled with Declan. That was why I couldn't sleep."

She did say it then. "I'm sorry, my king."

They reached the bench they'd once sat on four weeks ago. To Danika, it felt like ages since the king brought her there.

When he lowered himself to the wooden bench, she sat beside him, putting some distance between them.

They stared out of the river. In the middle of the night, the water was almost still. There were no waves, no tumbling. Just the beautiful sight of water beneath the dark clouds of the night.

Then he wrapped a strong arm around her and pulled her closer to him. He lowered his head on her shoulder and closed his eyes. "Let us be like this. Just for tonight," he murmured.

The tension left Danika's body and she melted into him. The memories of the past had not made him cold towards her because she was her father's daughter.

Thank you, Creator, she whispered in her mind. That was truly a stolen moment—a moment where there was no duty. No Cone's daughter. No master. No slave. Just a woman who loved a man so much. And a man who was about to be married to another.

Danika closed her eyes against the slash of pain in her heart. "My king?"

"Mm." His eyes remained closed.

"Can I pat your hair?"

"You can."

She curled her fingers into his jet black curls and began patting it rhythmically. He seemed to relax more against her, and his breathing came out in a sigh. She was acutely aware of his body beside hers— so acutely aware. The unique scent of his expensive cologne—which she missed those past few weeks—was all she breathed.

King Lucien felt whole again sitting there with his head to Danika's small shoulder and his eyes closed. The past few weeks hadn't been easy. Duty was never easy. He'd done his best not to think of her and to put all memories of her aside to be able to perform his duties as a king. He never expected it to be as hard as it was. But it turned out to be one of the hardest things he'd done, keeping her out of his chambers and his bed.

For the first time in so long, he could breathe easily again. The voices in his head had died down; his demons had disappeared; and now, only peace and serenity remained.

It was her; he had come to realize it a long time ago.

He'd referred to Sally as an angel, but in his mind, whenever he thought of the white garment dwellers in the home of the creator, Danika's image was the first that came to his mind. He was done questioning why it was so. Why it was her. Questions did not provide him with the answer. He hoped that one day he would have the answer to why the daughter of the biggest monster in the universe happened to be the bringer of peace, bearer of light, and the cloak of calmness.

"My king?" Her melodic voice filled the night.

"Mm."

"We have to go back to the palace. It's not safe out here for you at night without any bodyguards around."

You will protect me. King Lucien frowned. He did not know where such a thought came from, but it was there, and it dawned on him that he believed it to be true. She would try to protect him if anything happened. Not that he couldn't protect himself—he could, really well. But he knew that she would want to. He did not know how he knew that, but his instincts were saying it was true anyway. He had come to trust her that much, he deducted.

He only frowned harder and pulled away from her. "You're right. Let us go back in."

Danika rose first from the wooden bench, and a wave of dizziness slammed her with so much force she swayed on her feet and almost fell. Strong arms shot out and wrapped around her midriff, saving her from losing her balance.

"Are you alright?" he asked, his face scowling.

She nodded repeatedly as the waves of dizziness passed. "Yes. Thank you, my king."

But he didn't let go of her.

She stared down at his arms on her body. Instead of pulling away, he wrapped them more securely around her middle, pulling her closer to him. Then he lowered his head to her belly and kept it there. Butterflies spread out inside her; warmth sizzled in her. Memories of the first day he did something like that filled her mind. She practically wore her love for him in her eyes as she began patting his hair again.

King Lucien closed his eyes again. For a man that hated physical contact of any kind from people, he had been touchy-feely with her tonight.

But it was a stolen moment where duty did not have to matter. And he was feeling a different kind of pain that filled him.

The pain of his inability to father a child.

A king who could not produce an heir.

What would the world say about that? What would his people think about that?

Swiveling his head so that his cheek rested on her belly, and he allowed that pain to wash over him.

.

CHAPTER 14. ON A BEAUTIFUL MORNING.

Danika woke the following day with dual feelings. She felt sick and so much better at the same time. The sick part of it was the normal part. She understood it because she had been that way for a good while. But the better part?

She smiled wide as she remembered that last night. Or had it been early this morning?

That hug.

She closed her eyes and could almost feel his arms around her. The king had held her tight like he hadn't wanted to let go of her.

Then they'd walked. He'd sat with her and let her put her hands on him. He'd told her about his late cousin. He'd put his head on her belly.

Her hands rose and pressed to her stomach, her face glowing. She could still remember the way they'd stood there, and she was patting his head. They'd stayed for a long time too.

Such a sweet, sweet moment.

Later, they'd walked back to his chambers, and he'd let her lie down on his bed. He hadn't touched her intimately; frankly, she hadn't expected him to. It was courting week. The only rule was that the future queen had all the undivided attention of the king throughout that period. She was the only one who could grace his bed during that time.

That was why Danika had been surprised when the king asked her to lie on the bed. She'd laid, but he only laid beside her and watched her with eyes that saw too much.

She should have known that the king was too much of a moral man; he would honour that rule with respect to his future bride.

He'd surprised her again when he resumed talking to her, telling her about some time during his slavery. In return, she'd told him some stories of herself when she was a child, how she and Sally used to sneak to the village to watch festivals, how she had attended some of the princess meetings.

She deliberately excluded the name of her father from everything she told him. Any event that'll lead to saying her father's name—reminding him of her father—she made sure to scrap that event.

That was how they'd spent long minutes.

She was in the middle of telling him the story of one particular horror event that happened in Mombana when she was a teen—about a man that killed his own child—when he fell asleep. She'd stayed a few more minutes openly gazing at him as he slept, unabashed. She didn't have to hide her love for him or her feelings for him because he wouldn't see her.

Such a sweet, sweet fleeting moment.

Danika couldn't remember how long passed before she allowed herself to get up from the bed, wrapped the duvet around him, and walked out of his chambers back to her own room.

"Someone's looking so happy this morning, standing in the middle of the bedroom, her cheeks flaming as she gets lost in thought."

The sound of Sally's voice pulled Danika out of her own head. She smiled at her former personal maid. "Sally."

"Good morning, my princess. I can see the day looking so bright, my princess!" Sally whirled around two times; her cheeks stretched in a beautiful smile.

"The only person brightening up the day is you, Sally. I didn't get to see your dress yesterday. I'm so sorry. I was sleeping like a goon." She bit her lips guiltily.

"Oh, stop it, my princess. I made sure you slept for a long time too. Then I came back to look for you and couldn't find you. You don't know how shocked I was when I saw you with Princess Kamara." She made a face. "I hope she didn't hurt you."

Danika shook her head. "No, she didn't. Actually, she saw when the mistress was beating me around, and she came to my rescue."

"Your rescue?" Sally asked wide-eyed.

"She slapped the mistress three times and scolded her."

Sally's jaws went slack. "What!?" Her eyes were wide like saucers, filled with disbelief.

"Yeah, I was that surprised too. Creator, I never expected it."

"Oh... My... Creator. She slapped the witch of the west?"

Sally's disbelief was so comical Danika laughed. "Yes, she did. Then she took water from her personal maid and washed her hands clean for touching dirt."

Sally cringed. Then she was grinning. "I almost feel sorry for that wicked witch. She finally met her match."

"I'm worried, though. Vetta threatened to tell the king all about it. The king might punish Kamara."

"Or he might not. With the king, you never know. Let's just hope for the best, and in the meantime, let's go to the village and buy some clothing. You know we only have a few moments to spend together before I get married," she finished sadly.

"Don't be so dramatic, Sally. Of course we'll still be spending time together even after you're married," she told Sally with a smile, but her chest tightened. She was so happy that Sally was getting married to a man she loved, she really was. She just felt a burning in her chest whenever it reminded her that Sally would no longer be so close to her afterwards. She'd have to live with her husband. Take care of her husband and make him her priority.

"I'll really like to go into the village with you, Sally, but I have some chores——"

"Don't worry about chores. I already pleaded with two maids to do it as a favour to me. I'll pay them back." She grinned and clapped. "I want us to go into the village; it's been so long since you stepped out of the palace gates."

Danika smiled, staring at her. "Alright. Let me dress up, and we'll go."

Vetta watched the king, who was seated behind his desk, his brows furrowed together as he scribbled on the scroll in front of him.

"My king," she drawled as she looked towards his desk, getting behind it and behind him.

"What is it, Vetta?" he asked without breaking his concentration from the book in front of him.

"Let me give you a massage. You must be tense. You need to relax those muscles from time to time." She raised her hands towards his shoulders.

"Do not put your hands on me, Vetta. Not now. I do not need the distraction."

Vetta swallowed at the hardness of his voice. Sometimes it was really hard to deal with the king. "Alright, my king." She stepped back and forced a breezy smile. "Did you sleep well last night?"

His hand paused mid-scribble; his eyes flashed. "Yes. I slept well," he replied in a surprisingly gentle voice.

Did anything special happen the night before? Vetta found herself wondering.

"Why are you here? Is anything the matter?" He pulled out fresh scrolls and opened them.

"You gave me instructions few weeks ago that I should never put my hands on the slave again in punishment unless she commits an offense to deserve it, right?"

His hand pushed mid-scribble again, and his eyes found hers for a few seconds. Then the blue orbs went back to scrutinizing the papers in front of him. "Yes, I did."

"I have obeyed your wishes and your command, my king. But yesterday, the slave ran into me in the hallway. She pushed me down until I fell so gracelessly." Her voice was filled with fake pity and horror. "My heels were hurting—that particular part where King Cone burned me with a hot iron."

Just as she knew it would, the last statement got to him more than the others. He could still remember that event; Vetta knew this surely. That particular day after she'd had her miscarriage, the king had singled her out and branded her feet with hot iron.

"How are your feet?" His eyes were filled with concern as he looked at her.

Vetta had him exactly where she wanted him. "It hurt so bad the rest of the day.. Today I can only feel it throb from time to time," she lied smoothly. "When she did that to me, I felt so angry and punished her by giving her a mild slap on the face, but the princess—" she hissed the name out with so much hatred. "—came upon me and slapped me three times! She beat me up badly!"

The king's brows knitted together and he scowled. "The princess?"

"Yes. Princess Kamara—your future bride!" she said through gritted teeth. It would be over her dead body that the king would get married to that witch!

Silence met her outburst.

The muscle in his jaw ticked. He reached for a new feather and inked it in the bottle of ink in front of him. The silence only lengthened as he withdrew the inked feather and began drawing his letters again.

"My king!" she said impatiently.

"You know, Vetta, a king who wants to live long does not get involved with the problems, commotions, and malice between his women: the queen, his mistresses and his slaves," he lectured in a calm voice.

"But you got involved for the slave. And you warned me off her," she reasoned, trying to keep her anger in check.

"The slaves are the lowest in the rank and the most mistreated unjustly. You were once a slave; you know this."

Vetta did *not* like the reminder at all. "Yes, my lord."

He nodded without sparing her a glance. "I work hard to make sure some laws will be abolished and slaves will stop being seen as animals but instead like humans. That includes my own slaves."

"But my king, that princess slapped me three times! My feet and cheeks hurt all day," she allowed her voice to waver, sounding dangerously close to tears.

"I will speak to her about it," he let out finally.

"Thank you so much, my lord." It made her feel a little better—even though she expected more from him. "And w-what about the slave? Will you punish her too?" she added.

"You just told me that you've already punished her. I see no reason why I should do that too." He folded the well-written scroll and kept it aside.

"Y-yes, Your Highness." She balled her hands to fists.

"You may go now."

She bowed to him and started out of the door.

"Vetta?"

She turned. "Yes, my king?"

"Do not bring such matters to me again unless it's a critical case. You do well to settle it amongst yourselves while I see to more important matters and affairs of the state."

"Your wish is my command, Your Highness."

"You may go."

She walked out of the door feeling angry, hurt and chastised and kicked the wall in front of her with rage.

He would 'speak' to the princess and what about Danika!? She fumed.

Then an idea formed in her head that caused a smile to flash in her features.

He said to settle the matter between them and take laws to their hands, right?

She would be dealing with Danika today in a very, very bad way. She wouldn't be there when it happened so that no one would suspect anything.

.

CHAPTER 15. THE HOVERING DARK CLOUD.

"Guards," King Lucien called calmly, never one to raise his voice.

The door opened and Zariel entered. Chad had been scarce lately because he was preparing for his marriage. He had made a mental note to have some private time with his friend and helper since childhood soon.

"Your Highness." Zariel bowed his head.

"Tell Princess Kamara I summon her."

"Your wish is my command, Your Highness." He turned and hurried out of the door.

The king parked up his well-written scrolls and got up from his chair. He walked into his library towards the left end of the shelf where he had his last written scrolls lined up. He took his time arranging it according to date of when they were written for easy access and identification.

He was filling in the second to last scroll when the door opened, and a feminine voice called, "I'm in here, Your Highness."

King Lucien dropped the last of the tied price of paper on the shelf and closed the spread then strode out of his library, stopping at the door.

The first thing he noticed about the princess was her unusually wavy blonde hair that spread down her back and curled to a stop at her lower back just before her waist. Hair like Danika's. Danika had the exact shiny blonde hair with length so long it was beautiful.

He scowled. Why would he pick up such detail? When did he pick it up? He shut down such confusing thoughts and focused on the woman in front of him. He took it her facials and physiques. She was very young and a beautiful princess too.

He pulled away from the door of the library and strode deeper into his bedroom. "I apologize for my inability to meet with you up until this moment, Princess."

Princess Kamara held her lower gown and curtsied like she was taught all her life to do in front of a king. "You do not need to apologize, my king. I understand how busy it is for you."

"How was your first night in the palace?"

"I slept like a baby, My Lord."

Kamara wondered if he could see the trembles of her body. King Lucien looked nothing like she imagined. She'd heard words and stories about him and the things he went through in the hands of the former King Cone, so she'd warily prepared her mental health for seeing a King Kong or a scary Chimpanzee dressed in expensive wears.

The king was a handsome but terrifying man. There was a scar that ran across one cheek and disappeared into his neckline, giving him a savage look. And he was huge, like a fighter in royal wears.

Kamara swallowed, finding herself tongue-tied. Her only relief was that her big corset and veil must be hiding the shivers running down her spine.

"I hope your journey went well?" His deep voice filled the air as he walked closer and hesitated.

It was just three seconds hesitation before he stretched out his hand, palms out. A man that's wary of touch, Kamara observed as she placed her hand into his. He kissed the back of her hand in a gesture of respect and greeting as old as time.

"The journey was lovely," she lied smoothly.

"I'm glad. I hope your stay has been great."

"It has been good, my king. I've been exploring. It's so beautiful here." That part was sincere.

She took a step back from him. King Lucien didn't miss the move or the slight fear his future bride was trying to hide. He would have smiled if he knew how to. Instead, he pulled away from her to give her a little bit of space. "How is your father?"

"He's fine, My Lord. He sends his regards."

"And your mother?"

"The queen is fine, thank you." She curtsied again.

He scrutinized her again and decided that he made a good choice where she was concerned. She seemed rightly trained and beautiful. He could have done worse.

The same exact thoughts were running through Kamara's mind. He was everything she never expected, and that was...good, she guessed. She could have done worse. If it worked out between them, she would settle down with him.

Better him than a mustached-jaw, potbellied, fat and ugly sixty-year-old king, who most princesses have been unfortunately matched with.

On her way here, she'd wished he'd reject her because of everything she'd heard about him. She'd thought that if he rejected her, her father would match her with a better king.

But now, she looked at him and hoped he wouldn't reject her. It wouldn't save her from her father's decision, and it won't make it possible for her to be with Callan either, but if he rejected her, her father would only match her with another king, because that's the 'duty of a princess.'

A shudder sizzled down her body and she looked up at the king again. His blue eyes never failed to startle her; it was his most captivating feature.

Eyes just like Callan's, she thought with a hurting heart. She could definitely live with gazing into those eyes if she did nothing else. Although, Callan's eyes were warm and expressive. King Lucien's own were cold and blank.

Her heart hurt, but she was lucky. She could have done worse, she repeated in her mind. So, yes, she considered herself lucky after all.

Sally was grinning like a child as she skidded her way out of the palace. Danika watched her with a smile on her own face. Sally was right. She'd been so caught up with everything that had been happening lately, she had forgotten what it was like to leave the palace gates and go anywhere.

Sally was her usual cheerful person, stopping by every flower to pick a little part of it. She put it to her nose and inhaled deeply.

"Aah! It smells so good, my princess."

"It does, doesn't it?" Danika complied.

Sally stuck it to her hair and continued skidding away. Danika followed her in steady strikes. The people of Salem watched her as she walked in that aristocratic way that was like a second skin to her. She had her incredibly long hair in a bum at the back of her head, and her clothes, though simple, were ironed and fitted her body.

Eyes watched her curiously. The daughter of the monster, King Cone. They hadn't seen her in a while, only Remeta when her mother brought her out of the palace on their way to the market. It still left them speechless whenever the saw the 'ghosted one' looking so happy like a normal girl.

Danika was oblivious of the stares. She followed Sally and got to the point where the road was divided. One route led to the library and the other to the market.

"Which way first?" Sally asked, whirling around to look at her.

"Let's go to the library first. We can go to the market afterwards."

"Alright, my princess." Sally continued down the route to the library and Danika followed her.

At the library, Danika presented her card and they entered quietly. The library wasn't frequented by many, as lowborns had given up hopes of reading or learning how to write.

Danika took Sally to the inner room where the most interesting books were kept.

An hour passed while she read to Sally and helped her write. She also got a new book and had Sally read to her. Although, her words weren't all correct, Sally was making good progress and that made Danika happy.

Danika had Sally engaged in a book when she got up and started searching for another book to read. It excited her to gain new knowledge of things she never knew before.

She saw a book titled "Motherhood" and her interested piqued. She picked up the book and stared at the cover. A sketch of a pregnant woman was drawn on it. Would this book teach about how babies were made or the signs and symptoms of an expectant mother? Maybe how to be a mother?

She had never really been interested in such books before and she had no reason to be interested in it, but Danika found herself blowing out the dust that created a slight layer on the book and opened the cover.

Vetta stood in the small bedroom and watched through the peephole as Karandy talked with two women. They looked to be in their late forties and were so dirty. She couldn't make out the former slave trainer's words, but she knew that it was their plan he was trying to make a success.

Vetta kept herself hidden, watching both women nod their head in affirmation. She watched as he opened the door and let them out then came out of the bedroom after he locked the door. "Are you sure they can do the job right?"

Karandy nodded, chuckling. "They have a very bad grudge on the late King Cone. Zenia lost her only son because of him, while Coria lost her three children because of him. Trust me, Mistress, they can get the job done."

"That's good." She nodded. At least she was in a better mood now. Her meeting with the king—coupled with the fact that she had been unable to carry his child—had been grating on her nerves, but now...She was better, now.

"But what about that girl that follows her around?" Karandy asked.

Vetta waved him off. "I've made plans too to extract her. Don't worry about that one."

"What about the king's future bride? You said that she favor the former Princess Danika."

"Apart from the fact that she's on a walk with the king and will be spending most of the day with him, so she won't be able to hear what's happening outside the palace *when* it's happening?" She paused and added, "She won't be able to do a thing about it if she does find out about it. Even the king won't be able to do anything."

Vetta walked over to the window. People passed by to go to their various destinations. A mother was dragging a stubborn child who was crying. "I might not know much about royalty, but I know that they are taught well about leadership and the people. The only voice louder than a king's voice is the united voice of the crowd of his people," she mumbled.

Karandy nodded, seeing the sense of her words. He was getting the idea.

"A good king does not impose orders on his people when they are telling the truth. And a future queen knows that she cannot go around commanding the people. She knows that she will earn their trust, not force it."

"You're so smart, Mistress," Karandy praised, adjusting his hard organ. He longed to get his hands on Danika, but the mistress had been delaying the plans because she wanted to wait for the right time. In the meantime, he also wanted to fuck the mistress. She was a beautiful woman but with a dark heart. He wanted her.

But he didn't want to die yet.

Vetta smiled. "Of course, I'm smart. Trust me—today will be fun."

.

CHAPTER 16. THE DARK CLOUD.

Karandy watched the mistress's backside while she stared out of the window. Too bad she wasn't the one he was really craving to fuck.

"So, what about the other plan? Our main plan? When are we going to carry it out?" Karandy asked the mistress, licking his lips.

Vetta swiveled her head without turning around. "You mean when you'll get her within your clutches to do as you wish? The plan that involves you fucking her as much as you want?"

"Yes, Mistress. That's the plan," he said with real urgency. While he was happy that today that bitch, Danika, would be getting a little bit of what she deserved, he was not really all happy about this plan because it didn't involve him. He needed to get his hands on her. He wanted to have her. Damn, he was almost obsessed with the need to dirty her up.

The mistress turned her head back towards the window. "When it's the right time."

"It's been a month now, Mistress."

"You're impatient, Karandy. We need the prefect time because that plan is the ultimate plan that will ruin Danika completely in the eyes of the king and break her to pieces from the inside out. These ones are just for fun." She grinned.

He came up beside her to stand a few feet away, staring out of the same window and watching people passing. "This one will ruin her too."

"Only in the eyes of the people. Doesn't matter—the people already hate her. That's why it is for fun. Don't worry, our ultimate plan will come soon," she drawled.

Karandy gritted his teeth. He needed that plan to come sooner.

As Danika looked through the book, she felt the color drain from her face. Her hands became sweaty and her throat went dry like sandpaper.

Oh, Creator! No, please, it can't be. Most of the signs and symptoms that the book mentioned were ones Danika had been having. All the while, she'd thought she was sick because of the king's coldness towards her and his upcoming marriage to Princess Kamara.

But...

She swallowed tightly. No, no—she can't be pregnant. No, there's a mistake somewhere. Madam Baski had told her that she couldn't get pregnant because of the herbs she'd gave her on her second night with the king. So, there was just no way that she could be pregnant!

"Danika, you just can't be!" she consoled herself in a whisper. It was all a coincidence. It just couldn't be!

"My princess?"

Sally's soft voice startled Danika slightly. She took deep breaths and calmed herself for a few seconds before she plastered a smile on her face. She turned and faced her former personal maid. "Are you done reading?" she asked brightly.

Sally scrutinized her too-white face and eyes filled with fear. "Are you alright, my princess?" she asked worriedly.

"Yes. Yes, I'm fine. Of course, I'm fine. Can we go to the market now?" she asked breathlessly.

"Yes. I'm done." Slowly, Sally dismissed her worries and smiled brightly. "Let's go to the market now."

Danika dropped the book back to the shelve like it burned her. "Alright, let's go."

They left the library and began walking. Sally brightly began skidding ahead of her. "You walk as slow as a snail, my princess. I don't know why princesses are taught to walk such way. And they don't run better either," she called out from in front.

Danika pushed her terrifying prickling thoughts away from her mind and did her best to focus on Sally. "A princess has to walk gracefully. Well, not all of us were able to perfect that walk."

"I know, my princess. I remember that day we attended the princess's meeting. Princess Gretsha walked like a fat turkey," she giggled.

"Heavens! Sally!" Danika looked around to make sure that no one else heard then a smile crossed her cheeks. "The rebel princess would have you whipped for that, you know," she informed Sally.

Sally continued down her path. "I'm smart, my princess! I'd never call it to her to her face!"

Danika's lips stretched, but a sadness crossed her features. Sally would soon be married. Her only consoler, her best friend. How would she cope?

They walked until they entered the route that leads to the market. Sally stopped by the first shop and bought a bag for their goods. Danika followed her peacefully, missing the life that was once hers as she watched the children beggars, who were clothed in rags and sat lined up in a parallel line begging for money.

She missed having her own money—lots of coins—because she never hesitated to give to begging children when she was still a princess in Mombana.

Danika followed Sally dutifully and they began shopping for little things Sally would need after she got married. They were in the process of it when a maid walked up to them. "Sally, you're needed in the palace."

Sally turned towards the maid whose name she remembered to be Adelia. Those past few weeks, she had been serving the king's mistress exclusively as ordered of her.

"Me? But I took a permission from Madam Baski. She knows I'm going to the market and she permitted us," Sally explained.

"The mistress said to call you," the maid informed her.

"Me?" Sally repeated, pointing at her own chest in disbelief. The mistress had never summoned her alone in the past. She turned and looked at her princess, biting her lips.

Danika already looked worried and faced the maid. "Did she do anything wrong? Is there a problem?"

She shook her head. "It's nothing dire or anything. The mistress only needs her opinion on some new dresses she got. She said that Sally had a good taste in clothes and should help her pick the best clothes."

"Oh. Okay." Sally let out a breath of relief. For a moment there, she'd thought that the Wicked Witch of the West found out that she called her the Wicked Witch of the West behind her back. She turned to Danika, her face filled with indecision.

"It's alright." Danika took the bag from her. "I'll quickly finish up the shopping and meet you in the palace. You'll be fine."

"I'm not worried about me. What about you? Will you be fine, my princess?" Sally bit her lips.

Danika nodded. "I will be. Now run along so she won't punish you for being late."

Sally nodded and followed the maid out of the market.

Danika walked from one corner of the market to the other, buying the things she needed. Some people glared at her as she passed, but she bowed to them slightly and walked away with her shoulders high.

Pregnant?

No matter how she tried not to think about it, her traitorous mind kept going back to that awful possibility. Terror seized her system. *Heavens, no. It can't be,* she convinced herself stubbornly. There was no way---

A girl ran into her.

"Sorry! Sorry! Sorry!" the girl said as she pulled away from her.

Danika caught herself before falling and looked at the girl in front of her. The girl couldn't be more than eight years old, and she was dirty and dressed in rags. A lowborn.

"It's okay. No harm done," she said softly.

The girl nodded her head and took off in a run.

Danika continued walking. She hadn't walked for long when she began hearing commotions behind her.

"It's her! It's that daughter of a monster! She took the diamond necklace!" a woman's voice screamed behind her.

Danika turned back in sheer confusion. A small crowd of women were walking close to her and she wondered what was happening. Who was the woman they're talking about? Danika was most surprised when the crowd came in front of her and stopped. They didn't pass her.

"It's her! She's the thief!" a very angry looking woman shouted in front of her.

"Are you sure, Zenia?" one of the women asked even as she threw Danika an evil glare.

The woman, Zenia, nodded vigorously. Her eyes were blazing fire as she pointed at Danika. "She stole the diamond necklace from my store. I saw her steal it!"

The crowd gasped and faced Danika. They were all angry looking.

"Is this true!? Did you steal, you evil daughter of an evil man!?" one of the snapped angrily.

"I know, she stole it," another added.

"She wants to wear it later. Still thinks herself a princess, that bitch!"

"The apple does not fall far from the tree," another hissed.

There were murmurs and whispered from the small crowd, and those words were the only ones Danika was able to make out before she snapped out of the daze she'd entered.

This can't be happening! No, no, not her! The punishment for stealing! She swallowed and closed her mind from the horrible thought. Her heart squeezed in her chest.

"No! I didn't take anything! I'm not a thief!" she shouted, alarmed.

"She stole it, I saw her! Check her bag and you'll see it! I know she stole it, that bitch!" another woman shouted in the crowd.

Danika's body was trembling. She lifted the bag of goods she'd bought. "This is my bag. You can search it; I did not steal a thing!"

"If we find it, we'll crucify her!" a voice shouted in the crowd.

"We'll burn her!"

"We'll beat her up badly!"

"Hell, I've always wanted to get my hands on her!"

"We'll strip her naked too!"

The voices were too much; they were jarring in Danika's head. She was overwhelmed with the hatred that emitted from those words. Those people who hated her so much for a crime she didn't commit. Their eyes filled with rage. Hatred. They looked upon her with murder in their eyes.

One of them dragged the bag of goods from her and opened it and began ransacking it fanatically.

Danika just wanted it to be over. She was breathing erratically, her heart threatening to burst out of her chest. A thief? Thankfully, all her fears and feelings were well hidden on the inside. Her body quaked, but not visibly. She watched them coolly, waiting for them to vindicate her and for her to be on her way.

"It's really here! She stole the diamond necklace! It's here!" the woman gasped as she brought out a diamond necklace from the bag.

The whole crowd gasped.

Danika watched in horror. She had never seen that necklace before.

Those people would hurt her badly. It was right there in their eyes.

.

CHAPTER 17. GUT FEELING.

A thief. They all called her a thief. They found the diamond necklace in her bag—a necklace she had never seen before. Danika could only watch in a trance. She didn't know how to go about that; she didn't know how to start vindicating herself because she knew that all her attempt would be futile.

Those were people her father enslaved and tortured for the past ten years. They look upon her with hate, judgment and rage. Suddenly, she wished Sally was there with her. Sally. Anybody.

Those people would devour her. Her baby. *No—there's no baby, Danika.*

The words didn't convince her like they were meant to. She could only watch the angry mob in front of her. There was no pleading with them. Or begging them. It would change nothing. "I did not steal that. I have never seen that before," she tried anyway. Her voice was hoarse and calm, while her insides was trembling. Her blood ran cold and her heart was thudding in her chest.

One woman's hand snaked out from the crowd and slapped her cheek. Another grabbed hold of her hair. "You thief! You thief!"

"We will deal with you today!" another person shouted.

As they dragged her away, she thought:

Maybe, just maybe, this is how it was written in the stars.

Maybe, just maybe, this is the way it was meant to be.

Maybe, just maybe, this is the way I'll reunite with her mother again.

Baski was picking herbs with her daughter. Remeta was happy all day, and her expression was cheerful and bright. That was how it had been for a few weeks now. It gave Baski a special kind of joy. Today, they were picking newly fallen leaves.

Suddenly, Remeta let go of her bowl, and it fell to the ground. Her eyes went wide, and she began crying—a loud, distressed cry filled with so much pain.

"Remeta! Remeta!" Baski dropped her own bucket and ran to her.

Remeta's eyes remained wild, staring at the space in front of her unseeingly. "No, no, no!" She was crying. She was shaking her head.

Baski was filled with pain and panic at the sight. What was wrong with her daughter?

She grabbed hold of Remeta's arms and shook her roughly. "What is it, Remeta? Talk to me! Please, talk to me!"

"No! Please, let them go! Let them go! They did nothing, nothing! You're hurting Queen! And you're hurting Prince! Prince will leave! Queen will die! Stop, pleeeeeease!!" she screamed loudly.

"Stop! Remeta! What is it!? You're scaring me!" Baski shouted in panic. She couldn't understand her daughter. Was the former Remeta back?

The mad Remeta?

Tears filled Baski's eyes when Remeta continued screaming and crying. "They did nothing! Leave Queen alone! They're hurting Prince! Prince will leave!"

"It hurts! Mama, it hurts badly!" she screamed at her mother.

Baski tried to hug her, but she twisted out of her mother's arms. "No! Please! Let her go!" She took off in a dead run out of the woods. Tears streaming down her eyes, she was screaming at the top of her lungs as she ran.

Her hair was like wild fire—her battered heart hurting.

King Lucien did not like the gut feeling he was having. Inside, he did not feel comfortable, and it had nothing to do with the fact that he was out on a walk with his future queen. It was courting week, and he was determined to court her well. It was a duty required of him.

Lucien had long resigned himself to it, just like most of the kings out there who wanted the betterment of their kingdoms. His kingdom was most vulnerable because they just got out from ten years slavery and were still picking up the pieces of their lives.

Besides, he had no illusions in his life. He also had no decision about seeing his people ever suffer again. They needed a queen. They needed an heir. His chest tightened up—a different discomfort from the first. He watched Princess Kamara as she stood in front of the river. He was seated on the wooden bench—the same spot he sat the night before with Danika.

The king's mind was filled with her. He feared that if he breathed too much he would even take in that unique scent of hers. His head had been messed up all day. He came out to a walk with Princess Kamara, and he could only remember his walk the Danika. He did not want to be there with the princess. Instead, he wanted to be with his slave.

Strange. But it was a truth he had come to understand. He scowled at the awareness. His brows knitted in thought.

Before, when he thought of memories, his head only had his years in Mombana and the death of his family to offer him. Now, most of his memories comprised of the times he spent with Danika. It was weird and disturbing, but it was what it was.

"Your Highness?"

The voice of the princess had him coming out of his own mind. "Mm?"

Princess Kamara couldn't read it or figure out whatever was going through his mind. He had an unreadable look on his face, but she would have sworn that he wasn't enjoying her company. She didn't feel bad about it. Her mind was also occupied with her Callan.

"I said that this place is beautiful. Have you ever been here in the past, Your Highness?"

"Yes. I have been here." He looked around the place and could only see Danika standing there. The bad feeling in his gut returned tenfold.

Kamara did not know what it was that was in the mind of the king, but she knew that something was bothering him. She couldn't ask what it was for fear of overstepping her boundaries. His face was pulled in harsh lines, and he was scowling. His blue eyes met her again, and she was taken back to that very day Callan talked to her the first time. Callan was not a talker and he had always avoided her because of their difference in status. He was never so close to her, but she never minded.

Staring into the king's startling blue eyes, she wondered if Callan was ever thinking of her.

Her heart squeezed in her chest, and tears burned her eyes. Loving a man and getting married to another.

That was pure torture.

Sally did not like the feeling in her gut at all. It wasn't a good feeling. It wasn't sitting well with her. She sat uncomfortably in the bedroom of the mistress and waited for her to come back from wherever she went to. The maid had told her that the mistress would be with her shortly.

"Shortly" was turning out to be such a long time. Sally sighed and forced herself to keep waiting. But she was restless. So, so restless.

Sally stood and walked towards the window that overlooked the front lane in search of the mistress. The coast was clear; there was no sight of her. Her shoulders drew in and she waited. She left her princess alone in the market. The people hated her, but they wouldn't attack her unnecessarily, that much she knew.

The princess has been sick for a few weeks now, her mind whispered in remembrance. *What if she faints in the market and there's no one to help her?*

Sally swallowed and tried to dismiss the unfounded fears.

What if she faints and someone who hated her father takes her away and hurt her badly? Sally tried not to think of that, but no matter what, she couldn't just sit still. Her princess was alone unprotected in a market filled with people who hated her.

She turned towards the door then stopped. The Wicked Witch of the West would punish her severely if she returned and didn't find her. Could she risk her wrath? Sally didn't even wait for her mind to answer that. To discourage her. Her princess was above any other person.

She ran out of the room and looked around the hallway. It was empty, so she snuck her way out so that no one would see her. Then she took off in a dead run.

She ran to their bedroom but didn't find her princess. It confirmed that her princess wasn't back from the market.

A feeling of uneasy spread through her body. She took off in a run, straight out of palace.

Sally was most surprised when she ran through the roads that lead to the market and saw Remeta—or a girl that looked like Remeta? Sally ran faster to find out who the girl was, but the girl was running so fast and muttering things. She ran like there was fire on the mountain.

When she began catching up with the girl, Sally started hearing some shouts from crowds. Everywhere was deserted; she couldn't find anybody on the road or in any stores.

What was going on!?

She followed the sound of their voices to a gathering of a crowd.

"Let's burn her alive already! Thieves should not stay alive!" a woman screamed.

"Let's string her up the pole naked in the village square so that everybody will see! Thief!" another woman added.

Sally wondered what the angry mob was all about. And a thief? She didn't have time for that. She had to find her princess, knowing that her princess would never be found in gatherings like that. Princess Danika couldn't be in the middle of this crowd where they were beating up a thief, because her heart wouldn't be able to take the sight.

Sally turned to continue running her way when she heard a scream—Remeta's scream.

"Leave her *aloneeee!* Get away from *heeer!!*" She screamed so loud the crowd gasped and most people moved back.

Dread filled Sally's body. She ran into the crowd and began pushing through them to get to the front and see.

When she reached the front, Sally screamed at the sight before her.

CHAPTER 18. SILVER BOWLS.

D anika felt detached from her body. The beatings were too much. She can only breath pain as more kicks and hands hit her body.

She laid there sprawled down on the ground, curled into a ball.

She heard people scream but she couldn't make out who they were. She can't make out anything anymore.

Her body hurts badly.

Another kick landed on her back. Tears fell from her eyes. Her vision was too blurry, so she can't see anything. Or hear anyone.

They all sounded so far away. This must be what it feels like to die.

Another person kicked her and she only curled into a tighter ball. She has her hands wrapped to her middle, in a protective mode.

Why was she protecting her belly? There's no baby in there.

And yet, she couldn't move her hands. Not even when they rained blows on them.

Another kick landed on her lower back. She heard screams but she couldn't make out the people screaming.

Pitiful broken sobs filled her ears, and she found out that they were from her.

Her body hurts in a very bad way. Everywhere hurts.

Her lower belly was beginning to cramp too.

Sally screamed at the sight in front of her, horror filled her eyes as she stared at her princess curled into a ball on the ground, crying and trembling.

"Get away from her! Get away from her, all of you! What do you think you're doing!!!?" She screamed at the top of her voice, tears blurring her visions.

The crowd muttered and most of them moved away from Danika. The rest Sally pushed them away with all her might.

Remeta knelt in front of Danika, her whole attention on her as she still cried her head out. Sally, on the other hand, was glaring at the villagers with teary years.

"Get away from her, Sally, we don't want to hurt you. We have to teach this criminal daughter of a monster a lesson!" one of them shouted.

"Are you mad!? Are all of you insane!? How could you do this!? How!? Monsters! You all are the monsters! How can you do this!?" Sally screamed so loud they all heard it.

Shocked gasps filled the crowd. They didn't expect this reaction from the good-natured Sally, that always had a smile or two on her face for everyone.

"She stole a diamond necklace from Zenia's shop! It was found in her bag! She's a thief!" a voice came in the crowd.

"Yes! A thief!" they all echoed in rage.

If not for their love for Sally, they would have pushed her away and descended on Danika again.

"She is *not* a thief! She isn't! How can you all do this!?" Tears left Sally's eyes like a pool. Her heart was broken to pieces. "I'm so hurt beyond words! How could you all do this!?"

Guilt flashed in most of their eyes. The others just looked like they hated Sally's delay in their punishment.

"I fed you all in Mombana! All of you! Each and every one of you! How can you be so much of a hypocrite!? How can you treat her this way!? You call her a thief!? So, what if she's actually a thief!? *I was a thief too*!!!" she screamed loudly. "*I was a thief* when I was sneaked around every kitchen in the royal palace to *feed all of you*! We stole to keep you all alive! So, why don't you start beating me too!? How can you do this!? She will *never* steal anything from anybody! Ever!"

A few of them flushed red in guilt.

Sally swiped her hands through her face to wipe out most of her tears and see clearly. "You treat her this way because she's the daughter of the late king!? She is *nothing* like the late king! *nothing like him*! Why should a child be punished for a crime she didn't commit!? She never chose her father!! It is *not* her fault that she's his child!!!" She glared at all of them, her eyes red with fear and anger. "This woman you all are beating to death *fed you all* in Mombana! She fed *each and every one* of you!!"

Stunned silence came first. Surprised gasps echoed everywhere. Most of them who had some sticks raised before began lowering their sticks. There were murmurs in the crowd.

"No, that's not possible..." one voice said.

"She couldn't have..." another added.

"You're lying..."

"You're trying to save her with lies..."

Sally let out an empty laugh at their disbelief. Her heart was ripping out of her chest. "Did you stop to wonder why big foods were always possible to come to you most days!? Have you asked yourself why you ate from silver bowls!?" She whirled around to see all of them because they surrounded her. "When I *stole* food for you all, I was able to steal it from the servant's kitchen of the palace where food was made for the servants to eat. But you see the *main* royal kitchen!? I was never able to get in there, no matter how much I tried! It was always her! *always*!!" she screamed, pointing at Danika. "She went there and commanded the guards to let us in! She marched in there and started packing food in big silver bowls! She packed so much like a feast and gave it to me to give you all! If you have ever eaten from the big silver bowls of the palace, you should be ashamed of yourself because you are *biting the finger that fed you!!*" she screamed and sobbed.

All of them gasped. All of them.

Sally wasn't surprised because she knew that all of them had eaten from the silver bowls. Princess Danika had made sure of that.

"She was never in support of her father! Never! Her father punished her all the time whenever he found out what she's done! She is a good woman! She has never beaten a slave! She has never made a slave labour! She saved me when I was a child and still a slave! I was being tortured and she saved me and kept me with her!! And look at Remeta!!" They all turned and looked at a crying Remeta, who was crouched to the ground, crying and hugging Danika. "Do you think she would be like this if that woman was evil!? Remeta went through the worst! The worst!! And yet, she defends the daughter of the man of her nightmares. Haven't you all stopped to ask yourself why!? She is not *evil*!! She saved you all!! *SHE SAVED YOU ALL!!!*"

Most of those older women have started crying. A lot of them have dropped their sticks like it burned them. The young women were crying and looking regretful too.

Sally's red eyes found one woman in the crowd. "Coria, you! You hurt because you lost three children in the hands of King Cone, but you have two who survived and didn't die from hunger, right!? They ate from the silver bowls all the time, and it was because of her!!"

The woman named Coria looked pale like a ghost. Her eyes widened and she dropped to the ground and started bawling like a child.

"And you!? When your child was sick and dying, she ate from the silver bowls too!" She screamed at another woman. "And what about you!? And you!? And you!?" Sally asked every one of them but none could meet her eyes again. They were crying like she was.

One child ran from the crowd with a huge cup of water in her hands. She ran straight to Danika, knelt beside her, and began trying to help her drink the water. All the other children of the lowborns took it as their permission when Sally said nothing. They rushed to Danika and surrounded her. And they were crying and patting her body soothingly.

One particular girl that didn't look like she was more than eight years old was openly crying and glaring at her mother. The girl stepped forward bravely, but she was sobbing. "Please. Forgive me. I p-put the necklace in her bag."

The crowd gasped in sheer shock and outrage. Miserable cries of shocked and guilt-stricken women.

Sally lowered herself to that girl's height, still crying uncontrollably. "Why? Why would you do something like that?"

The girl turned and glared at her mother, who was looking guilty, and resigned. "Mama made me do it..."

Voices rose in the crowd.

"What!?"

"Zenia?"

"How could she?"

"Oh, heavens! What have we done!?"

"I'm so ashamed of myself..."

Sally glared at Zenia with a heart filled with rage and pain. Her job here was done. She turned to her princess and began bawling again at the bruises on her body. Her clothes barely covered her body because they'd been torn. Her eyes have closed, and blood is in every part of her body.

Why was there blood between her legs? Sally asked herself worriedly as she walked closer to her princess, but she didn't know how to start touching her bruised body.

The crowds were screaming and raging at Zenia, but it wasn't Sally's problem at the moment. Just then, the guards arrived.

The crowd parted, and Chad was the one leading them. His face looked so worried as he surveyed Sally for a few seconds to make sure she was alright before his eyes went to Danika. He bent down and scooped her gently into his arms. Her head rolled to one side, and her eyes closed. "She's unconscious."

"We have to g-get her...treated...please!" Sobs wouldn't let Sally talk anymore. It felt like a horse stomped hard on her chest and crushed it.

Chad took off in a dead run towards the palace. Sally and Remeta followed.

CHAPTER 19. IN THE WAKE OF THE DAWN.

When Remeta ran out on her mother, Baski had tried her best to chase her, but she was no match for a fifteen-year-old. Remeta had ran faster that lightening itself.

So, Baski went back to the palace building and waited for her daughter to return. She went to Danika's bedroom because she knew that it was the first place Remeta would come into when she returned.

The wait was killing her. She wasn't sure if her daughter *would* return, considering the way she ran out.

She tried to keep herself busy. The new herbal-leaves they picked, she emptied all on the table and began taking them one by one to grind.

She was in the middle of it when her door burst open and Chad entered the bedroom carrying—

"Oh, heavens! What happened to her!?" she shouted as Chad rushed to the bedroom and gently laid Danika on the bed.

Sally and Remeta entered behind him but they were crying their eyes out. Baski was happy to see her daughter safe and fine, but she begged to know what happened. "Why is Danika in this state!?" As she asked, she hurried around to dispose of a bowl of water to make use of the bowl.

Sally forced herself to push back her pain, and in halting tearful voice, she relayed everything that happened to Baski.

Baski was seated beside Danika and using the water to wipe the blood from all over her body by the time Sally was done talking. The blood between her legs caught and held her attention really well.

Did they rape her too!? she asked herself horrified. "Sally, rush to Argie's house and call him here immediately," she said.

Sally nodded vigorously, rushed out of the bedroom to get the royal medicine man. Baski dismissed Remeta too.

At first, Remeta just kept crying and refused to go. In the end, she turned and ran out of the bedroom.

Alone, Baski quickly got up and raised the torn pieces of Danika's clothes, but the blood was too much to be caused by rape. Her brows knitted.

Too much or too little, she wasn't sure anymore, but she had a strong feeling it wasn't rape.

Could it be?

No. No way; it couldn't be, she quickly dismissed. The king was sterile.

So, what could it be?

Baski rid her of the remaining torn piece of clothing, ignored all the other bruises, and focused on the blood that kept coming out from her privates. She began examining her.

Minutes passed. Her fears was confirmed. All the blood drained from Baski's face.

"By the gods..." she trailed off. Danika is pregnant. Danika is indeed pregnant.

Was pregnant, she quickly corrected herself, because the baby didn't seem to be there anymore. Baski stood shocked for one full minute. When the shock wore off, pain replaced it. How could she have done something like that?

How could she? She never expected it from Danika at all; why would she? "Oh, Danika. Why would you do something like this?" she groaned in an agonized voice. Tears filled her eyes.

So, just because she told Danika that she didn't need herbs that prevents babies, Danika thought that the herbs in her were still protecting her and she went to sleep with another man?

Baski closed her eyes doing her best to rein in the hurt. King's Slaves do that all the time in secret, cheating on their kings and hoping not to be found out. She just never expected that Danika would be like that too.

Was she raped by another but kept it a secret? No. If Danika was raped, she would have known about it.

Baski stood and disposed of the water then put in a new one. She hurried to her herb bag and quickly made herbs that would stop the bleeding first. For a moment—just for a moment—she contemplated making herbs that would flush the pregnancy out completely. Already, she thinks the baby is no longer there, but she could still give her herbs that would flush her system. Heaven knew that she'd be doing Danika and that child a favour.

The king would have her head if he found out about that development.

And poor Danika didn't know that the king could never father a child.

Should she flush the baby?

But then she shook her head. She couldn't make decision like that without the consent of Danika. She really had some explanations to make when she woke up. For now, she'd concentrate on saving her life.

Baski paused in the middle of pounding her herbs and looked at how bloody Danika's body was. Tears filled her eyes that the people would do something like this to someone. A pregnant woman.

For now, she would concentrate on saving her life, Baski resolved firmly.

Later, when she was awake, she could get really angry at her for cheating on the king and carrying another man's child.

Several hours passed. Night had fallen.

Chad stood beside his king in front of Danika's bedroom. King Lucien had been staring at Danika in that unreadable expression of his, and they'd been standing there for a very long time. More than an hour. His face might be unreadable, but Chad could have sworn that there was banked-up rage in his eyes.

The king had been coming back from his walk with the princess when he'd walked to him and told him everything that happened in the marketplace. King Lucien showed no visible reaction, but Chad

had seen his muscle tense. He'd looked like he wanted to punch someone. The violence and rage in his eyes when he heard what happened to Danika were unmistakable, and it had surprised Chad.

"Chad." King Lucien's deep voice pulled him away from the recent past.

"My king." He looked at the formidable man standing beside him. His eyes were still on the fragile woman who laid on the bed, bandaged in all part of her body.

"You ate from the silver bowls too, didn't you?" he asked calmly.

"Yes, Your highness. Many times." Chad groaned, still feeling bad. He had never felt any antagonism for King Cone's daughter—not even the first day she was collared. And today, he was relieved that he never hurt this innocent woman fighting for her life a few feet away from them.

The king's throat worked as he swallowed tightly. Chad wondered what was going through his mind. Whatever it was, he hadn't stopped staring at Danika for the past half an hour.

"The two women?" King Lucien asked.

"Zenia and Coria, the perpetrators? They are in the dungeon, my king."

He nodded. "The crowd?" he questioned, just as calmly.

Chad walked to the window of the bedroom and looked out of it. The crowd was still there at the gate. Almost all the people were sitting at the palace and refused to move away—those who participated in beating her up and those who did.

The information about Danika's goodness and innocence had gone round the town, and the people were feeling bad about what happened to her. They refused to leave until she was well again. It had been hours. No one had left the crowd to go and eat or do anything. The people of Salem were used to starving, so food wasn't their problem. Instead of reduction, the number if the crowd kept increasing. The children sat with their parents, and most of them were still crying.

Chad walked back to where the king stood and shook his head. "The crowd is still here, my king."

He remained silent. Time dragged by. So much time.

Chad didn't know how to ask, but he had to. "Isn't it time to leave, Your Highness?" He rushed on when the king said nothing. "It-It's courting week, and it wouldn't look good that you're here. The princess might find it disrespectful and offensive; she might take it the wrong way because your spare time is supposed to be hers alone during this period."

King Lucien said nothing. Did nothing. If he heard what he said, he didn't even blink an eye.

Chad was almost sure that the king had been standing here for more than two hours.

The king was still standing. The king hadn't stopped staring at Danika either.

"Chad?" he said at last.

"Yes, Your Highness."

"You can go back to your duties now. Tell anyone and everyone who looks for me that I am busy at the moment and shouldn't be disturbed."

"Yes, Your Highness."

"What about Vetta? Have you heard from her since morning?"

"No, Your Highness. But I heard that she went out of town to see a distance female friend of hers today. She should be back any time from now."

"She did not say a word about this to me," he reasoned in a cool blank voice. "Did she take the carriage?"

"I'm afraid not, Your Highness."

A pause. "You're dismissed."

Chad bowed his head and walked away.

Baski had developed a terrible headache. She watched Remeta, who laid on the bed of her bedroom, crying her eyes out. She had tried consoling her daughter, but Remeta was not consolable.

She kept sobbing and muttering, "He is leaving. He is leaving. So restless. He is so restless. He is hurting. He is leaving."

118

Baski was torn. She had tried to get Remeta to explain or elaborate, but she wouldn't say anything more, just kept repeating the same words over and over again.

Should she give her sleeping herbs like she gave to Sally? But she knew that Remeta wouldn't take them. She wondered what was happening to her daughter, and at the same time she was worrying about Danika.

The beating she got wasn't a minor one, and her bruises weren't minor either. She had to sedate Sally to sleep; she would have cried herself sick because of Danika's condition.

What she went through... Baski couldn't begin to imagine it.

For a pregnant woman, it was a miracle she was still alive after all those beatings. Though, she was barely hanging in there. And she wasn't sure if the baby was still there or not. Her bet was Danika had miscarried and the baby was no more in her.

She'd been able to stop the bleeding, but Danika had lost a lot of blood. Also, when the medicine man came, she'd been prepared to swear Angie to secrecy about Danika's pregnancy—at least until she had heard from Danika.

But Angie didn't detect a baby or any pregnancy in all the hours he stayed treating each and every cut and bruise.

It was safe to say that the baby was no longer in there.

Baski didn't know how she felt about the knowledge. As she began pulling out of her mind, she noticed that everywhere had gone silent. She swiveled her head towards the bed. Remeta had fallen asleep. She let out a breath of relief she hadn't known she was holding at the sight. She could now check on Danika again before she retired for the night.

Baski stood and headed out of her bedroom, closing the door as quietly as she could.

Today was the best day of Vetta's life.

On her way home, she'd asked one woman what happened in the market and the woman told her everything, how Danika was beaten brutally and mercilessly. Vetta hadn't waited for the woman to finish before she continued going back to the palace with a huge smile on her face.

Only for the smile to be wiped from her face when she got to the palace gate.

She saw a crowd seated just inside the gate. Most women were praying; some prayed to the gods they served, the others prayed to the one in the heavens. Other women held their sleeping children to their bodies and stayed quiet. Men were there too.

Vetta called out one of the women. "What is going on?" she asked in confusion.

"It's the slave princess. We won't leave here until we hear that she's alright!" the woman said passionately.

WHAT!? Vetta couldn't believe it. Surely, she hadn't heard the woman well at all.

The woman began crying. "What we did was so wrong! So wrong! Have to go back and keep praying for her!"

Before Vetta could ask if the woman was out of her mind, the woman was already hurrying away from her. She walked back to the crowd, sat down on her spot and began praying again.

What the hell was happening!? What was going on!? That wasn't part of the plan at all! What were all these people doing here!? They should be in their houses, happy and celebrating their revenge on King Cone's daughter. So, what were they doing there!?

And why were they crying!? Why the fuck were they praying!?

Vetta fumed in confusion as she made her way into the palace building. To calm herself down, she knew where her source of happiness would be coming from again.

She headed straight to Danika's bedroom.

She turned towards the hallway to see Baski standing outside the window, looking inside the bedroom with a passionate look on her face. A tear dropped from her eyes. She turned and saw Vetta walking closer and bowed her head slightly but didn't move away.

Vetta moved closer and noticed that the door was locked from the inside. Baski only stepped away from the window for her.

She stopped in front of the window, looked inside and froze at the sight in front of her.

120

Danika was bandaged in almost every part of her body. She looked terrible, a sight for sore eyes. She must be in so much pain, and her condition looks critical.

Indeed, her plan worked out more than perfectly. But Vetta wasn't looking happy at all.

Because beside Danika's bed, King Lucien was seated, staring at her. His guard was down because he didn't know anybody was watching. He looked so worried and concerned for her. In fact, there were so many emotions in his eyes, Vetta wasn't able to make out what they were.

But she knew for sure that none of them was hatred. Far from it.

Vetta was still watching when he lifted his hand, took Danika's smaller hand into his and squeezed slightly, his eyes closed intensely.

She watched when he placed her hand to his mouth and kissed it lingeringly.

Then he lowered his head to her belly and laid it there. For a man that hated touch, he hadn't let go of her hand.

In fact, he held her hand like he never wanted to let go again.

.

.

CHAPTER 20. THAT TIME WHEN THE HEAD IS ASLEEP AND THE HEART IS WIDE AWAKE

Vetta couldn't believe the sight in front of her. Her hand on the wall of the side of the window balled into a fist.

The king remained. He hadn't raised his head. It was as if a bond was holding his head to her belly, and he wasn't ready to pull away anytime soon.

The sight was hurting Vetta's eyes too much. She reached for the doorknob of the bedroom, but Baski held her hand. It forced her to look at Baski's face and the older woman was shaking her head. Baski wanted to talk but she couldn't do so there or they'd risk being seen by the king. So, she pulled Vetta away from the window and away from Danika's bedroom until they reached the hallway in the other side of the palace.

"No, you can't go in there, Vetta. Danika needs ultimate rest and she doesn't need to be disturbed at the moment," Baski informed her.

Vetta almost snorted. She had no intention of going in there because she was worried for Danika or anything. She wanted the king to see her and sever all physical contact with Danika.

"I heard all that happened, how is she?" she asked, feigning worry like she gave a damn.

"She is doing well. Hanging in there. She's been heavily induced; she doesn't need any disturbances."

"Oh. She must be in a very bad shape."

"She is," Baski admitted. "But at least it's a good thing that the two perpetrators were caught and they're in the dungeon."

Vetta's heart stopped beating. "What!?"

Baski nodded. "Yes. So some kind of justice will be found for what happened to her."

"Oh. I-I'm happy about that," she forced out.

"Yeah, me too. If there's a mastermind behind what happened, I wish nothing more than to see that person's head dangling on a pole, separated from his or her body." Baski's eyes flashed angrily.

Vetta shifted uncomfortably from one foot to another.

"Anyway, you can't disturb her tonight, Mistress—even if you're worried," Baski informed.

"I understand, Baski. I'll go back in the morning to check on her. It's too bad...what happened to her." Her hands were still curved into fists. She really wanted to go into that bedroom. But Baski had always been too smart for an old slave. No, she had to keep pretending like she was worried out of her mind like everyone else.

Vetta turned and began walking back to her bedroom. She couldn't stop thinking about how the king held Danika few minutes ago. She couldn't stop thinking about the crowd she met outside. She couldn't forget that the two women were in prison and they might just rat on Karandy, and Karandy would rat on her.

Everything was a disaster. Everything.

She stomped angrily into her bedroom and slammed the door closed. She took up the flower vase from her table and threw it to the wall with an angry scream. It shattered everywhere. The anger was still boiling in her. And fear.

For a moment, she contemplated going straight to the dungeon tonight, but she couldn't do that or everyone would get suspicious. No, she'd know how to handle that issue without being seen.

She squeezed her eyes closed and the image of the king holding onto Danika bled into her brain. It was courting week and he didn't even care! He wouldn't come to her but he would leave his chamber to the bedroom of a slave, sit beside her sickbed and hold her hand in the dark of the night!?

He wouldn't even let Vetta put her hands on him for long, for fuck's sake!

Her window caught her attention and she stormed towards it. There the crowd laid. They were all still there.

Most of them were praying in silence, while others had fallen asleep right there in the cold hard ground. Something a once-slave would never want to do again, they do it for the daughter of Cone!?

Vetta pulled off her clothes and laid down on her bed. Tears of anger, rage and bitterness filled her eyes.

She buried her face to her pillow and began sobbing her eyes out.

King Lucien had fallen asleep when he felt the body beneath his head stir. He woke and raised his head from her belly to look at Danika. His hand still clutched hers. King Lucien knew that it was way past midnight, but he did not think about that.

Danika's swollen eyes slowly slid open, and she looked at him. Her eyes looked so tired.

"My king," she whispered drowsily.

"I am not here," he groaned. He never expected to stay until she woke. She was never supposed to know that he was there.

Her eyes blinked slowly. "No. I know you're here."

He averted his eyes. "Doesn't matter. You're heavily induced with pills and potions; you won't remember a thing in the morning."

"I remembered... the last time."

"You did?"

"Yes. You said you have forgotten... what it's like to laugh."

Silence. His eyes were taking in the bandage on her thigh. "It doesn't matter. You're more induced this time."

Danika's eyes found her side where his hand was holding hers. "You're probably right." She dragged her eyes back to his face, and even in her drugged mind, she hadn't wanted to call his attention to her hand he was clutching so he wouldn't dislodge his.

"How are you feeling now?" he asked. His eyes weren't as cold. His face wasn't blank, and he wasn't scowling. In her drugged mind, Danika knew that it was the first time she was seeing him that way.

"You look... so handsome like this." Her voice was scratchy, she could barely say words.

124

He wasn't expecting that. He shook his head. "I am not handsome, Danika. You will not think that if you're in your right state of mind."

"But I think... about it all the... time... So handsome... beautiful... even with the scar... especially with the scar."

He said nothing. But his eyes was watching her carefully.

"How did you... get that scar?" Her eyes on his cheek indicated that she meant the scar that ran down his cheek.

"Cone decided that he'd learn to draw a straight line and needed a place to practice. He used an iron rod dipped in fire and carved my face up," he stated flatly, his eyes darkened in memory.

Danika's body hurt so much; she was afraid to move for the fear of shards of pain splintering through her body.

"How are you feeling, Danika?" he repeated, watching her carefully.

"My body hurts," she whimpered, her voice slurred. "My child. What about my child?"

The king didn't miss a beat when he answered; "She's fine. She's sleeping with Baski." He thought she was referring to Remeta.

It had gotten to his notice time and again that she talks of Remeta like her child, even though there were only a few years between them. Everyone in the palace knew how possessive she was of that girl.

"Oh," she breathed out in relief, her head rolling to a side. "My body hurts."

"The medicine man said that you will be fine. You have to be fine." His voice was a harsh command. His hand tightened on hers.

She kept quiet. Only breathed harshly, sweet pouring from her face. She was in a lot of pain. The king noticed. He let go of her hand and stood, then walked to the table and poured drinking water into the wooden cup. He took it back to her and raised her head slightly. "Here, drink this."

She followed his instructions and drank as much as she could. Afterwards, he dropped the cup beside him.

"You can't take another herb until morning. You have to endure the pain; it will pass." A look of remembered pain flashed in his eyes.

Their hands were close together, so Danika didn't need to stress herself for her hand to get to his. She twitched her hand, slipping it into his much deeper one. "Did it work... for you...? Did it... pass?" she asked, her mind too clouded, her head pounding.

He didn't say anything for a while. His eyes were pinned where her hand met his, and he wrapped his hand securely around hers. "Those on the outside eventually do." His throat worked. "If you're lucky, those on the inside eventually will too."

"Were you... lucky?" She could barely get the words out.

"No, I wasn't. I never am."

"I'm sorry."

"You should worry about yourself right now, Danika. Not about anyone else." He pulled his chair closer and placed his free hand to her head. He glowered at her. "You're burning up."

He might be glowering, but she saw the underlying concern in his eyes.

"I feel so sick," she admitted.

"That's because you are sick. You have to get well." He paused. "A lot of people are waiting for you to get well."

She blinked slowly to clear the sleepy fog in her eyes. "Are you... waiting too?"

"I am." He lowered his head and placed a kiss on her sweaty forehead. Then he pulled away and stood. "I have to go back to my chambers. Sleep well, Danika."

"Can't you... stay here... with me?" she forced out through a dry throat, her eyes filling up. "I don't... want to be... alone."

He turned and looked at her. For a moment, indecision flashed in his eyes before it was gone. "I cannot stay any longer. It is not appropriate."

"Stay with me... please... Just for tonight..."

Just for tonight. Her whispered words came with memories— memories of all the times when he'd make use of that same phrase. When he used those same words as an escape to feed so many unusual urge that slammed him where she was concerned.

The first night he took her on his bed, he let her sleep on it. That time he took pleasures from her body in a missionary position. That time he let her touch him, caress him. That day he was so sick, he let himself suckle from her lush breasts. That day he gave in to the urge to kiss her.

Memories of all their intimate times together only fed his strange hunger to stay longer by her side. Memories that fed another strange hunger to hold her stomach close to him for a little more time.

Lately, he found himself drawn to that particular part of her body and he didn't know why. But he did not know a lot of things Danika did to him, so he chalked it up to one of the numerous baffling things about her where he was concerned.

When he stood watching her with eyes that did not reveal much of whatever was going through his head, Danika felt the cramp in her lower belly begin again. In her foggy mind, she understood more than anybody the reason why he shouldn't be in her bedroom, but it did not stop a huge part of her from longing for the feeling of him beside her. It was as if something inside her wanted him to cuddle her up in his arms for the rest of the night.

The more he stayed away, the stronger her belly cramps became. A tear slipped from her eyes and she whimpered.

He began undressing himself, having been in his royal attire all along. He pulled off his well-embellished tunic, the gold work catching her tired eyes before it did a slow flip back to his face. He removed his surcoat, followed by his belt of gold.

Standing in his underthings, he walked closer to her. The cramps stopped and she felt a little bit better.

The bed dipped as he climbed in beside her, and she swiveled her head to stare at him with eyes that are barely awake. It was difficult keeping them open, but she did.

Then he laid beside her and pulled her into his arm. The movement hurt, but Danika endured it as he cushioned her to his chest and buried his face against her hair. She closed her eyes, breathing out in satisfaction as she snuggled up against him. His arm around her rubbed her shoulder soothingly. "I won't be here when you wake up in the morning, Danika."

"I know. I just want you... with me...when I fall asleep," she whispered.

It was well past midnight. The time for lovers. The time when a man's head went to sleep while his heart remained wide awake.

King Lucien pulled her head up and his lips found hers then kissed her passionately and intensely.

Like a man who was given awful news earlier in the day about his woman being beating up brutally.

Like a man who stood for hours watching his bandaged up woman fight for her life.

Like a man with so much burden on his shoulders and needed a solace, a refuge.

The kiss went from hungry and ravenous, to gently and reverent. In the end, his tongue tangled with hers slowly and thoroughly, his lips sucking hers persistently. When he drew back at last, Danika was breathing heavily. The pain in her body was momentarily forgotten, and the guards around his cold heart were momentarily down. There had been a huge crack in his heart and it reflected in his erratic breathing.

Seconds after the kiss, Danika fell asleep in his arms, her body going lax. The king held her head to his chest.

Another part of her called to him. He slipped his hand into her clothes and caressed her smooth belly soothingly without any thoughts.

Maybe because it was the only part of her that wasn't bruised and bandaged.

A great feeling of peace came over him and a lightness settled over his heavily-burdened shoulders. It hadn't taken long for him to fall asleep too.

.

EPISODE 21. KING CONE'S
CHILDREN NON-BIOLOGICALLY.

King Lucien walked into the dungeon. The two new prisoners got up and knelt before him in greeting.

"Your h-Highness," they said in unison, their voices showing their nervousness.

King Lucien stood at the entrance of it and looked at both women, Coria and Zenia. He had a fleeting memory of Coria back in Mombana. He had never known her to be wicked. Her actions were unexpected. He closed his eyes, and his mind was filled with the image of Danika lying down there, all bandaged and in pain.

The actions of his people. It was animalistic.

He just stood watching the two women, his expression as hard—as cold—as ever. It made both of them as nervous as ever. His silence wasn't making it any easier for them. They waited for him to talk, but he wouldn't say a word.

"We're so sorry! Oh, please! We're so sorry!" Zenia began crying in earnest.

Tears filled Coria's eyes, and she sniffled silently, looking as remorseful as Zenia. The two older women were still kneeling with their heads bowed.

"I am so disappointed in both of you." His voice was so calm, but they heard the intensity just the same as words that were shouted.

They cried the more, sobbing because the truth was that they were more disappointed in themselves. To think that they spent a great deal of time hating King Cone's daughter when she kept them alive in the only way she could have-when she did the things she could do to help them.

They should never have agreed with the former slave trainer. They should never have taken his money—or even taken the oath of secrecy. They never expected Cone's daughter to be innocent, and they never expected to be in this dungeon.

Coria and Zenia's hearts were broken. They were no better than King Cone. They should be punished accordingly.

"I'm r-ready to take any judgment you give out, Your Highness," Zenia whispered in resignation.

"Me too." Coria knew that even if the king gave them the death sentence they deserved, their children would be well taken care of.

With their heads lowered, the women waited for the king's judgment. It was a long wait.

The silence was deafening.

When he spoke again, it wasn't his judgment he was passing. "Did you two act alone?"

They stared at each other in fear, glanced at the king, and lowered their heads to the ground. They were scared of the former slave trainer. He made them take the oath of secrecy. Apart from that, it was rumored that he was a very dangerous man. They weren't terrified about themselves but about their children.

"We acted al-alone," they lied nervously. Coria squeezed her hands together against her plain dress.

People close to the king hadn't gotten used to his silence. They hadn't gotten used to the way he had to think his words through and say sentences one after another. Talk about two women in the wrong and awaiting a judgment that might mean their deaths.

The women almost peed their pants as they waited for him to say something. His silence was that unnerving.

Then he turned, giving them his back. "It is only fair that the woman you almost killed becomes the one to pass your judgment. Danika will decide your fate. If she demands your deaths, your heads will hang by the poles before sundown tomorrow."

He turned and walked out of the dungeon. He took three steps and stopped. "Before that happens, I will return and ask who the mastermind was. Again. You can also decide to tell me the truth then."

There was no sound of his footsteps as he walked away with his guards.

Coria and Zenia looked at each other. Silently, they began weeping again sorrowfully. Not only about their children's lives being in danger, but the late King Cone's daughter would definitely sentence both of them to death.

Danika drifted in and out of consciousness. Sally was right there by her side through it all.

When she needed to relieve her bladder, Sally helped her to the bathroom, and when she needed to take her bath, she was also the one to help her with it. Danika complained about her back aching and relieved her bladder a lot. Sally helped her patiently without any complaints at all. Instead, she just wanted her princess to be well again.

As the day progressed, Baski came in and gave her herbs. She changed Danika's bandages to new ones and gave her more sleeping pills. Baski wanted desperately to talk to Danika, but she hadn't been able to do so. She hadn't gotten the opportunity because Sally was right there with her, and the anesthetics Danika was given wouldn't let her stay awake long enough for that conversation.

Also, Baski hesitated because she knew more than anybody that it was not a good idea to put pressure on Danika, considering what she had been through. And her condition too.

That's if she was still pregnant. And it was looking like she was not any longer.

So, she waited. She came in every hour to give Danika medicinal potions, pills, and healing herbs. But when evening came, she returned to the bedroom and gave Sally an errand.

"But who will stay with my princess?" Sally asked, staring worriedly at Danika.

"I will," Baski assured the girl to soothe her worries.

Sally bit her lips. "She hasn't eaten lunch. She said she's not hungry."

"I'll make sure she eats something. Call Uyah on your way out and tell her to get some food from the kitchen."

"Thank you, Madam Baski," Sally whispered gratefully.

Baski only nodded, her sadness hidden well inside her. She'd seen the king in the wee hours of the morning going back to his chambers. No one knew that he stayed with Danika last night, and the way she saw the king the night before, holding Danika's hand and kissing it so tenderly.

Baski would have sworn that the king would not care less if Princess Kamara herself saw him in Danika's bedroom.

Then how on earth could Danika do that to him? Cheat on him with another man to the extent of carrying the man's child?

"Oh, Danika. What did you do?" she muttered miserably as she stared at the bruised figure sleeping on the bed.

She strode to the table and began grinding new herbs. A while later, Uyah brought in a tray of food.

Baski took the food from Uyah and walked towards Danika, and she sat down beside her bed.

"You have to eat, Danika." She woke her gently and carefully.

Vetta had a sleepless night the night before—a very restless night.

She couldn't leave the palace all morning because her quarters were being cleaned out, and it would make the maids suspicious if she went out by that time and out for long.

She waited impatiently; by afternoon, the worry was almost eating out her liver. When the maids finished thoroughly cleaning all the rooms in the mistress quarters, she sent them away. Then she dressed up in a yellow, well-embroiled corset and a very long veil to match so her face would be hidden when she left the palace.

As usual, it was a very long walk because she couldn't take the carriage. That would raise suspicion too.

Vetta knocked on Karandy's door when she finally arrived. It was so cold outside, and her insides were in chaos as she waited impatiently for him to open the door.

A few minutes passed before the door opened, and Karandy got out.

"You left me standing out here!" she hissed as she pushed past him into the house.

"I'm sorry, Mistress, but I had to discharge the woman that spent the night with me. We wouldn't want her seeing you here now, would we?"

That made her calm down. "You take whores to your house every day." Her disgust was apparent.

"A man has an appetite," Karandy answered as he locked the door.

"The two women we used were caught and held in the palace dungeon." Vetta moved straight to the point.

"I know. I heard all about it yesterday." Karandy walked past her and strode into his small kitchen to make something to drink.

"What are we going to do!?" Vetta burst out, unable to keep calm anymore. "Do you even have any idea what this means?"

He nodded, and that's when Vetta saw his worry too. "I'm more worried than you are, Mistress," he admitted. "I'm the person these women know. I'm the one that made a deal with them and gave them money."

"You said you swore them to secrecy!" She glared hard at him.

"I did. But you more than anybody should know how hard it is to be interrogated by the king. Hell, just standing in front of him is as unnerving as shit. Makes a man spill his guts." He downed the drink and slammed the wooden cup on the old table.

Vetta knew the truth of his words, and it did nothing to calm her nerves. She remembered vividly how Karandy himself implicated himself during his interrogation by the king. He was whipped and demoted as punishment.

What in hades did she get herself into?

She should have gone with her original plan. At least that one involved only Karandy, and it would have been a cleaner job.

"I know you think we should have gone for our original plan, right?" He didn't try to keep the smugness from his tone.

Admittedly, she nodded, then glared at him in superiority because she didn't like being in the wrong.

At that moment, Karandy didn't care. "It would have been a faster and cleaner job. I put on a blindfold, ambush the both of you, get her in a dark corner and fuck her brains out. You happen to watch it happen and tell the king all about it so that she can't hide it. So damn simple." He took a cigarette and a lighter from the wretched counter beside him then lit the cigarette up and took a long drag.

He was being disrespectful to her by smoking in her presence. In normal circumstances, Vetta could even order him to be whipped for such blatant disrespect. But this wasn't a normal circumstance.

"So, what do we do now?" she asked, ignoring his smoking.

He took another long drag. "I can take care of it. I can make sure those women never say a single word about me, no matter how they were interrogated."

Hope flared in her eyes. "You can?"

He nodded once. It was very easy to ensure that part happened.

"How will you do it?"

"I have...connections. You don't need to know, Mistress. I can get it done, but I'll need a huge reward." He planned to kidnap both women's children and send words to them in prison. He'd give them a choice.

Their silence or their children.

Mothers are too predictable. He smiled within himself and took another drag of his cigarette.

"Money is never the problem." Vetta reached into her corset, withdrew a small, wrapped cloth filled with coins, and dropped it on the table. "Just get the job done."

Karandy took the money greedily, as usual.

But this time around, he wanted something else too.

.

.

CHAPTER 22. SHE WILL NOT CRY. SHE WILL NOT CRY.

Karandy's eyes slid lustfully all over the mistress's body. She was clad in an expensive yellow corset designed with several spreads of lace all over it. Apart from the worried scowl on her face, the mistress was a beautiful woman—a beautiful woman with a black heart, he conceded as his eyes did a slow once-over on her.

But her black heart made her all the more attractive. He wanted her. Had wanted her for a long time. It was high time he made a demand he wanted.

Karandy dropped the unfinished cigarette on the table and looked at her. "I want something else too, Mistress."

She frowned at him. "What is it?"

He was nervous to ask, but he had no reason to be. They were in a dangerous situation, and it was not as if she could tell the king because it'd expose her too. He had always wanted to eat from the same plate the king ate from, and even though the woman he wanted more was the former Princess Danika, the mistress would have to do for now.

Karandy stood and walked closer to her, lust in his eyes.

Vetta saw it, and her eyes darkened in anger. "You'd better not say what I think it is you want to say," she hissed.

"I can give you pleasure, Mistress," he growled.

He raised his hand to caress her face but she slapped his hand away. "Don't ever put your hand on me! Ever again! I will not tumble the sheets with dirt! How dare you even have such intentions!? I am

135

the king's woman!" Her eyes filled with fire even as her traitorous body reacted, but she was determined never to lay with him. How dare he!?

Now that his intentions were clear, Karandy became bolder. "The king will never know. And it's just this once."

"You're not touching my body," she spoke through gritted teeth. "You take the money and get us out of this mess you put us in!"

Karandy almost reminded her that it was her idea to carry out that plan, but he didn't. Instead, he boldly ran his hand down her arm. "This mess is a big one, Mistress, and it will not look good if we're caught."

"Those women knows you only. They will rat on you only." She smiled superiorly.

"And I will rat on you," he informed her shamelessly.

The smile vanished from her face. Vetta's eyes narrowed angrily. "Are you threatening me!?"

He flushed guiltily but raised his chin all the same. "It doesn't have to be that, Mistress. It's just sex."

"If you're to fuck any of the king's women, it's supposed to be Danika. Not me."

"But I find you more attractive." He lied smoothly because the desire had really come to his body.

Vetta's eyes flashed. The woman in her that had always felt like Danika was better than her felt pleased immensely. She cleared her throat and averted her eyes. "Still, I'm not letting you put your filthy hands on me."

He shrugged and moved away then picked up the bag of coin from the table and gave it back to her. "Those women will just have to tell on me then. I can't guarantee that I will keep my mouth shut, Mistress."

"Don't be stupid and think with your head, you dirty slave. You will be killed!" she hissed at him. "Do you really want to gamble with your life!?"

He shrugged. "My life means nothing. And I'll be taking you with me."

Vetta's anger knew no bounds—mostly because she knew that she had been defeated. *This was NEVER supposed to happen!* She swore never to let a man without privilege touch her again in her life. She was no longer that slave!

But here it was again. This bastard wanted to pull her down to his level again! She would never forgive him for this!

Vetta hid her loathing well and crossed her arms. "Are you on herbs? Because I am *not* carrying your filthy seed inside me!" she snapped at him.

Karandy smiled triumphantly, not taking any offense from her insults at all. After all, he was about to fuck the king's woman. "Yes, Mistress. I cannot get you pregnant." He was a man that slept with cheap whores all the time, so he had to buy herbs from the medicine woman down the road every particular period of time.

Vetta nodded and began taking off her clothes. Outside, she looked cool and calm about it, but on the inside, she was sheathing in anger and rage.

Just the thought of what would happen was making her skill crawl.

But first things first: she would do this and come out of this particular mess.

Then he would regret this; she would make sure of it! She vowed inwardly as she undressed.

Baski shook Danika gently again. "You have to wake up, Danika. You need to eat."

"Not hungry," she moaned with her eyes closed.

"You need to eat anyway. You can't go on an empty stomach," Baski persisted, touching the part of her arm that wasn't bandaged.

But Danika had settled back into sleep again.

Baski glanced at the tray of food and noticed that Uyah didn't bring water. Uyah always forgot little things. Baski sighed and pulled away from Danika. She'd get the water before she came back again and wake her up.

Baski dropped the tray gently on the floor beside the bed before quietly walking out of the bedroom and closing the door. When she turned, she saw her daughter.

"Remeta. How---"

"The prince is in there." Remeta came closer and whispered to her mother as if in a conspiracy. "He's hanging in there but restless. He's hurt; barely in there...needs his father, but he's in there. Strong prince, like father!"

Baski watched her daughter, the pain blatant on her face. She couldn't understand what Remeta was saying, and no matter how much she wanted Remeta to explain, her child never did that.

Baski swallowed the lump in her throat and asked, "Please, explain to me, Remeta. Please, my daughter?"

Remeta only giggled like an excited child and skidded away.

Tears filled Baski's eyes, and a strong headache suddenly developed. She closed her eyes tight and allowed the pain to wash over her. It was as if her child became more insane as the days passed. But who was she to hurt about it? Remeta might be losing it, but she made a huge recovery. It hurt Baski to admit that she preferred this Remeta to 'the ghosted one' she used to be.

Her child would be fine; she consoled herself as she watched Remeta clap her hands in excitement down the hallway.

The water and the food were ready, and Baski woke Danika. She was persistent about it. At last, Danika opened her eyes reluctantly.

Baski got behind her head and pulled her up, helping her to lie in her arms. She supported Danika's head against her blossom. "You have to eat to keep strong. Your wounds will heal faster too."

"Alright, Baski," Danika whispered drowsily.

Baski spoon-fed her gently, and Danika ate obediently. In the silence that followed, Baski fed her the meal's first course from the tray. When the plate became empty, Baski dropped it beside the bed and picked up a plate of tomato bisque soup. She used the spoon to feed it to Danika. The more Danika ate, the more she began to feel better and less sleepy. She shifted uncomfortably on Baski's body, and the older woman knew she wanted up.

"Alright, here we go." Baski helped her to sit up. She got up behind her back and helped her lay her back on the headboard.

"Thank you, Madam Baski," Danika whispered hoarsely.

"You don't need to thank me this way, young lady. Thank me by getting better really quick and back on your two feet without any scars on your flawless body. That's the way to thank me," she said sternly but without vigor.

Danika felt her lips stretching into a little smile. "Alright, Madam Baski," she whispered again.

Baski pursed her lips and continued feeding her until the soup was gone. She reached into the tray and withdrew the third plate.

"I'm full," Danika protested.

Baski glared at her and shook her head. "You've not anything since morning. You're eating all of it."

Danika would have protested again, but she didn't bother to waste her breath when she saw the stubborn set of the old woman's cheeks. Her mind returned to the night before, but her memory was hazy. Danika could have sworn that the king had been there with her. She tried to remember, but her memory remained hazy. The last event she could remember clearly was being beaten up badly in the market. Sally screaming at the market women. Remeta crying all over her. The highly painful cramps that suddenly attacked her lower body----

"My baby!" Danika let out a high cry suddenly.

Baski paused in the middle of lifting the plate. All the blood drained from her face, and she stared at Danika.

Danika's face was paler. Her eyes implored Baski. "My baby. I lost my baby, didn't I?"

"You knew that you were pregnant?" Baski's voice was surprisingly neutral, but her eyes suddenly looked...cold.

Danika closed her eyes and nodded her head as pain washed over her. "I found out yesterday morning."

So, she'd been pregnant, and she'd lost the baby. Danika would not feel bad. She would not cry. It was for the best. The king would have Danka's head if he'd found out. A slave did not get pregnant by her master. And she wasn't just a slave, she was Cone's daughter.

She would not cry. She would not cry. It was for the best.

But tears slipped from Danika's closed eyes and rolled down her cheeks. "I thought I was protected. I never knew I'd get pregnant," she whispered.

"Of course, you never knew." Baski's voice was cold. "Here, open your mouth and finish this meal. I have some work to do." In her heart, that very part of her never believed that Danika would do something like that. But she never acknowledged that part of her because it would be ridiculous to do so.

But now, Baski pushed the pain away. She wanted to get away from here because she didn't think her poor heart could take Danika's betrayal. It hurt her so much because she cared for Danika like she was her own child too, just like she cared for the king

Danika's eyes remained closed in a world of her own. A painful world. "It's all for the best. This way, he'll never find out I carried his child. I won't have to die for that particular crime in such a humiliating way. The townspeople would just love to watch me die that way. For being stupid enough to let myself get pregnant for the king." She was crying softly as the words whispered out of her lips.

Baski sat frozen on the bed. The plate fell from her hand and shattered on the ground; the soup scattered everywhere. "W-What!?"

Baski's shout made Danika open her teary eyes, and she stared at Baski in sheer confusion. "Huh?"

"What did you just say?" Surely, she hadn't heard her clearly. Of course, she hadn't heard her clearly. Her ears must be failing her in her old age. There was no way she heard her clearly.

"I know it's stupid, too, to be crying," Danika continued cluelessly, raising her hand to wipe her wet cheeks. "I should be happy— carrying the king's child; it's stupid. It's a good thing the child is no longer in me." But even as she said that, the tears wouldn't stop falling from her eyes.

.

.

CHAPTER 23. A BASKET OF HOPE.

Baski's eyes went wide. She couldn't believe this! It was just too impossible! "Whose child was that, Danika?" she blurted out.

Danika looked confused and surprised at the same time. "Madam Baski?"

Baski's hand reached out and took Danika's hand into hers. She squeezed in agitation. "Tell m-me the truth. You know I'll never tell on you, right? The king will never find out! We'll bury it here and treat it like it never happened! As far as you promise me that it'll never happen again, the king will never find out! But you must tell me whose child you carried!" Danika's shocked mouth opened, but Baski rushed on, clearly fluttered and agitated. "Were you raped? Who did it!? Why did you try to cover it up!?" She shook Danika's hand again. "Just tell me everything, Danika. I need to know! Please!?"

Danika was speechless. She wiped the tears from her eyes to see Baski clearly and replayed every word Baski just said. Then it dawned on her that the older woman thought a man who was not the king had laid with her.

Baski thought she carried another man's child.

"No!" Danika snatched her hand from Baski's at the shocking realization. "No! Never! No other man has ever been with me that

141

way, Madam Baski! Never!" Her head began pounding, her heart racing, but she ignored those feelings and settled intense eyes on Baski. "It's always been the king! He's the only man that I've ever been intimate with, Baski! He's the man that took my virginity and it's been him ever since! Why would I degrade myself that way to be with another man?"

She raised her chin in reality, her eyes filled with fire. "I might be a slave now, Baski. I might be in plain clothes and do chores and mingle with all sorts of people. But I'd never degrade myself that way to let another man put his hands on me when I already belong to the king! I'd never do something that despicable and it hurts me that you think so low of me like that." She finished, swiping the tears from her eyes again and glared at Baski haughtily.

Baski raised trembling hands to cover her mouth. That intensity—that innocence and disgust—in Danika's eyes could not be faked. "Oh, Creator! No..." Baski shook her head in sheer disbelief. "No. It can't be."

Danika was the one who took one of Baski's hands that time around and placed it to her own chest. Their eyes held and she whispered, "I swear on my life. I swear on my mother's grave."

"No!" Baski snatched her hands away and tears began rolling out of her eyes in waves. "Heavens! No, oh Creator! His child? His child!? Oh, heavens! Gods! Creator!"

"Baski?" Danika called her name, shocked at her reaction. Why was she that way?

Baski wasn't looking at her. Instead, she kept exclaiming, her eyes wide. When she rose from the bed, Danika thought she wanted to leave the bedroom, but Baski began crying earnestly. "His child?" she cried, so much pain in her voice.

"Baski, what's wrong?" Danika was beginning to feel scared. She tried to move to go to Baski, but her body hurt, protesting the movement.

Baski sobbed like a woman who heard her child died. She clutched her chest and her legs gave out, falling to the ground and crying. "The king's child?"

"Please, you're scaring me. Please, stop crying, Madam Baski. I swear, I didn't do anything wrong. Please, stop," Danika pleaded, feeling awfully bad at hearing the broken sobs from the older woman.

Baski crawled closer to her and took hold of her hand. "You can't lose that baby, Danika! You just c-can't!"

"B-but—" Danika hadn't understood. It hurt her to see strong Baski fall apart that way. "Tell me what's wrong, please; tell me how to help you."

Baski shook her head sorrowfully. "You can only help me by that child, Danika. Oh, Creator, please! Why!? Why!? Danika, please help me," she cried.

"How!? How do I help you? Please, tell me what to do!" Danika shifted from the bed, ignoring the shards of pain that spread through her body. She reached for Baski, pushed the older woman's head beneath her chest and cradled her head there. She began rocking her softly. "It's alright. Please, stop crying."

Baski shifted her head to Danika's belly and only cried harder. "How c-could this happen? Oh, my Creator!?"

Danika couldn't comprehend much, but she did give Baski soothing words while rocking the woman as gently as she could. "It's okay, Baski. Please, stop crying."

It only made Baski cry harder.

Vetta dressed carefully and without words. Karandy was blabbing about how good it was, and how good he felt. She said nothing. As she walked out of his house, Vetta thanked the gods about her large corsets that covered every part of her lower body extravagantly. No one would see that she was almost limping and her legs were trembling.

That bastard, Karandy, almost killed her. He'd pounded her really hard, and for a moment, she'd thought the man planned to kill her. At first, she'd actually enjoyed it—she was no stranger to rough coupling. But then, the reminder came to her about who it was drawing pleasures from her body—a man who was lower than dirt—

and she'd dried up immediately. That was when he even began pounding her like she wasn't human, and it had hurt like hell.

"Animal!" she hissed as she stumbled upon a stone. Barely breaking her fall, she rose and glared behind her at his door. On the bright side, he was going to get her out of that mess first. Then she'd deal with him mercilessly for forcing her into that. Vetta wouldn't let him go! Never would she let him go for dragging her down to his level!

For now, Vetta forced herself to put him out of her mind. It was a long walk back to the palace.

When she entered the palace gates, she still saw crowds who came in occasionally to inquire about Danika's health. Apparently, the people had taken to the bitch. She hissed as she continued her way into the palace building. Thank heavens that she hadn't since that Princess Kamara for days. She'd heard from one of the maids that the princess preferred reading in her bedroom as her favourite pastime. For Vetta, that was a plus. Less time to run into that horror of a woman. She remembered the hot slaps the princess delivered to her cheek and did her best to tap down the anger.

Dealing with that princess was a small case. She just didn't have time at that moment.

Inside the palace building, Vetta was heading to the mistress's quarters when she saw the king coming out of the royal court. Her heart skipped several beats.

Oh, no! Oh, No! She could *not* run into the king at this moment. What if he demanded sexual pleasures? He'd definitely find her out, because that bastard's release smeared all over her thighs. And she had yet to clean up too! Vetta wanted nothing more than to reach her bedroom and wash his filthiness from her body.

The king was striding towards her, and she stopped at the sight of him, bowing in greeting, "My king."

"To my chambers, Vetta." He walked past her towards his chambers, his steps unhurried and his hands behind his back.

Vetta's heart skipped three beats. She followed him to his chambers, closing the door behind her when she walked in. "Is anything the matter, Your Highness?" Thankfully, her voice was calm.

He turned towards her, scowling. "You have been going out a lot lately, Vetta. And you do not take the carriage or any guards with you. Do you not value your safety? Or you do not want to obey my command?"

What!? She hadn't been expecting that.

"No, no, o-of course not, Your Highness. I just—I just needed those moments alone. It's not really some dangerous place; it's a friend of mine that lives just outside the boarder."

Silence. He seemed to be thinking about that. "And you go to see this friend without taking any escort like you are supposed to? Like your status is required of you?" he asked in that ridiculously calm voice of his. He might as well be talking about the weather.

Vetta didn't know what to say, so she said nothing.

The silence stretched between them. She wished she'd never seen him—at least until she'd taken her bath and washed away Karandy's filthy hands on her. Now, she stood in front of him, feeling very dirty. It was not a good feeling at all. She stared at him, and he had the usual blank face.

She had no idea what was going through his mind at all.

King Lucien began walking closer to her. He stood in front of her and palmed her jaw, lifting her chin. "I do not understand you these days, Vetta. It's as if something is going on with you right here under my nose and I do not know about it."

His sense of intuition had always creeped her out. "Nothing is going on with me, my king. I swear it," she rushed out.

"You just like to disobey my instructions." He let go of her and walked past her towards his desk. "I'm putting you under five days of house arrest for disobeying me so blatantly."

"My king!" The punishment was so unexpected, it had startled Vetta and horrified her.

"Guards," he called without raising his voice.

The door opened and two guards entered. They knelt and bowed their heads. "Your Highness."

"Escort the mistress to her quarters." His eyes found her horrified ones. "You do not regard your safety, but I do. You go out alone and come back so late after sundown. You do not take permissions from me. You do not inform me. A lot of things might have happened to

145

you, but clearly, you do not seem to be thinking about that." He walked to his desk and picked up his well-written scroll as he continued addressing her. "That is being rash. Stay in your bedroom for some days and clear your head, Vetta. Do not leave your bedroom."

His words brooked no argument. And, with the way he turned his back and took steady strides into his library, it was obvious he had dismissed her.

What the hell just happened? Vetta asked herself in shocked horror.

Danika did not know how long passed. It took a long time before Baski was able to get control of herself again.

"All hope isn't lost!" was Baski's exclamation as she pulled away from Danika. Danika watched her warily as the older woman began talking to herself, as if making plans.

"We aren't sure if the baby is gone or not, so we can't conclude anything yet. In the meantime, I'll go into the forest now in search of Albaress. Yes, Albaress! It's good for pregnancies, babies in the wombs. It soothes a mother and a fetus. Repairs the body. Stops bleeding. If the baby is hurting anywhere, Albaress can heal his wounds. Yes, I have to get that herbs. And so many other herbs! I need to make a list—"

"Baski! What are you doing?" Danika asked warily. Already, she was so tired and sleepy.

"Oh, Danika, we have to save that baby if there's any chance that you're still pregnant," she informed Danika.

"But..." Danika swallowed down the lump in her throat. "Isn't it for the best? That I lost the baby? The king will—"

"No! No, Danika, don't ever think that way! Ever! It's not for the best. We have to save your baby! If there's a chance, we MUST save that child!" Danika opened her mouth to say something, but Baski shook her head. "Heavens, I've stressed you much. I'm so sorry. It's not good for you at all, stress."

Baski walked to Danika and helped her lie down on the bed. "Here, get some sleep so that you'll feel better and stronger later.

Princess Kamara has come here countless times today to see you, but you've been sleeping and aren't strong enough for visitors yet. For now, just focus on getting better, and I'll take great care of you."

Danika was feeling so very tired so she didn't bother arguing. Baski had behaved really strange with her today, but she didn't let herself think about it.

Baski rushed to the table and brought her potions and helped Danika swallow them. "It'll help you sleep well for a long time. A good sleep is best for your health."

Danika stared through dazed eyes as the older woman fused over her. Finally, Baski drew her blanket over her and kissed her on the cheeks.

"Thank you so, so, so much, Danika," she whispered.

Danika's mind was already halfway asleep, but she still murmured, "For what?"

"For. Everything." *For being a ray of sunshine and a basket of hope to our people.* But Baski didn't say it out loud.

As Danika fell into soft slumber, her thoughts were with King Lucien: How much she missed the king. How much she wanted to be with him. Lie against him.

Her conscious self might not remember the events of the night before, but her fuzzy drugged-up mind remembered.

As she fell asleep, she wondered if the king would come to her again tonight.

.

.

CHAPTER 24. THE UNKNOWN MAN.

Princess Kamara hadn't been able to go to sleep. She stood by her window and stared out of the dark night. Her mind was filled with the image of a man who wasn't her future husband. Callan occupied her mind.

Every night, she dreaded the thought that the king would summon her for her duties on his bed. While she wasn't untouched, she wasn't a loose woman either.

And now, she has fallen in love, which made just the thought of another man putting her hands on her that way fill her with dread.

In an ordinary way, she should have gone to the king and demanded her right to be on his bed during that season. But she only felt relief when time passed, and the king did not summon her.

She worried about Princess Danika too. The beatings she got were brutal. Danika had always been brave for a princess, which was why she could withstand such pain. Kamara couldn't even think about that. It sends shivers down her spine.

She had tried to visit Danika countless times but always found her sleeping. The potions she was on must be too much.

A bird flew across the window, forcing Kamara's attention to it. Memories of the day she'd written some words and sent them to Callan on a messenger bird filled her mind. She closed her eyes tight and reveled in the memories. He'd written back, which had surprised her. Callan was a peasant, and peasants did not know how to read and write. But apparently, Callan was way different because he wrote back to her in short, concise words and very masculine handwriting.

She smiled at the memories. He'd thanked her politely for taking care of him and his injuries. Thanked her for sending Henna to care for a peasant like him.

He had always been very polite with her, and he did not know the feelings she harbored for him.

Following the memories came a sting at the back of her eyes. The world difference between them was too painful. Even if she didn't marry King Lucien, ending up with her Callan was the most impossible thing in the world.

She stood there for a long time.

Finally, she wiped the tears from her eyes and walked away from the window. As she strode towards the bed, she wondered…

Does Callan think of me too?

Madam Baski was still very shocked about what happened in the afternoon. The new things she learnt earlier in the day. Danika had been pregnant for the king. That child was the king's baby.

Nighttime, she sat down on the chair in her bedroom and revived the events of the day. Danika was a different kind of light shining on their people. She'd gotten pregnant for the king, something that no other woman had been able to do.

Baski's biggest pain came from the fact that she wasn't so sure if the baby was still there. That was what hurt her the most.

Heavens, let that baby be in there. Let that be alright.

She wouldn't know for a few weeks for sure. She couldn't check the natural way again without harming the mother and the baby. They are both so vulnerable now; she couldn't afford to do that.

Baski had been so overjoyed that she'd practically run to the king and given him the shocking news, but she knew that it was out of the question until they knew that Danika was still pregnant.

It would hurt the king without measure if he found out that he'd been able to impregnate a woman but the child died. It would be an incomprehensible pain.

So, yes, she'd have to keep it to herself for now. Creator, let that baby be alright!

Baski was about to get up and prepare for bed when the bed ruffled, and Remeta shifted sleepily beside Sally. She'd made Sally come to sleep with Remeta because she'd planned to sleep in Danika's bedroom and keep watch over her.

Remeta shifted again on the bed and rose slowly. She rubbed her sleepy eyes. "Mama?"

At the murmured words, Baski got up from the chair and strode towards the view of her daughter, where Remeta would be able to see her clearly. "Remeta? Sweetie, I'm right here. Go back to sleep."

Remeta rubbed her eyes sleepily, "I'm worried, Mama."

"Why, my dear?"

Silence descended as Remeta kept rubbing her eyes. "I'm really worried, Mama."

"About what?"

"My Queen. The Prince. I—" she paused as if trying to sort through herself. "I really feel so much pity for King Lucien."

Baski kept quiet as she tried to understand what Remeta was saying. Her Queen… Prince… King Lucien…

The Prince… The Prince?

The Prince!?

"Oh, my heavens!" Baski exclaimed when it all suddenly made sense to her. "Oh…creeps!" Her eyes were wide like saucers as she stared at her daughter like she was just seeing her for the first time.

"This was what you meant all along! That was exactly what you meant all along! And I thought you were losing your mind! Oh, Creator! I should have seen this all along!"

Remeta watched her mother without saying a word. Baski was trying to put two and two together. She remembered yesterday they were picking herbs in the bush. Her daughter had been able to feel Danika's pain even from afar. She could still remember how Remeta dropped everything she was doing and ran out to where Danika was.

Did that mean that her daughter had some special ability or something? Baski filed it away as it dawned on her that Remeta said she was worried.

Baski held Remeta's hand in reassurance. "Tell me, dear. Tell me why you're so worried."

"It's the prince. The future---" she cut off suddenly. "I still don't know if he will stay," she whispered.

King Lucien tried to lay down his pounding head and go to sleep, but sleep remained so far from him. He wasn't surprised, but still he tried. When he finally slept, his dreams were the usual nightmares. The memories of Declan played themselves one after another in his head.

He woke up sweating profusely and breathing hard. It was the middle of the night and silence already descended everywhere. Memories of Declan did not hesitate to break him down. Would a day every come when he would remember his beloved cousin without such intense pain gripping his chest? Declan never deserved that kind of horrible death. He did not deserve it at all.

A pounding headache nagged him. He got up from the bed and walked out of the bedroom. He had no destination in mind, but his legs carried him towards Danika's bedroom. He took the key from the guard standing and sent the guard away.

The king opened the door but made no move to enter deeper into the bedroom. With his arms crossed together and his face inscrutable, he watched her sleep.

She looked so small on the big bed, her blonde hair spread out everywhere. Even while bandaged up like a sacrificial lamb at the altar, she looked as beautiful as an angel and as forbidden as sin.

He did not plan to be found out. He didn't want her to know that he had ever come here.

It had been three nights since his future bride came to the palace, and he hadn't summoned her to his bed. That was not the way things should be. The courtship was for the king to get to know his queen—to spend all his spare time with her—and for the queen to warm his bed and satisfy his sexual urges.

He had no desire of all of that. In his mind—so very deep in his mind—he acknowledged that he had the desire to spend more time with Danika than his future queen.

But then again, when a man performed his duties, he did not have to like them. It was called a duty because it was an obligation—whether you fancied it or not.

His eyes took in her bandaged arms. Was she doing better?

He watched her sleep for a little while. The rise and fall of her belly in breathing fascinated him. He walked into the bedroom, getting close to her, then bowed a little and placed a hand on her belly.

Just a feather-like touch of assurance. Is that what it was?

He frowned a bit and straightened himself to his full height. He did not know how long passed as he stood there and watched the rise and fall of her chest, of her belly.

Finally, he tore his eyes away from her.

Danika's bladder woke her up all of a sudden. She'd kept her eyes closed, trying to put off the feeling of having to get up from the bed and use the bathroom, but the pressure was suddenly unbearable for her. She stirred, stretching herself a little bit. The moment she took that first step into consciousness, she felt his presence.

King Lucien is here. He really did come tonight.

Her eyed opened and found his, standing beside her on the bed.

IN THE KINGDOM OF NAVIA

So late at night, no one was awake anymore. Just the guards on duty.

A small house was located in the secluded part of the town. Darkness surrounded the house; it was way past midnight.

Time for lovers. Time for nightmares.

Inside that house, it's owner laid on the bed and he was having nightmares. He breathed heavily and thrashed on the bed, lost in the tight grip of his nightmares.

He lost his memories a long time ago, and so, his nightmares did not make sense to him. All he knew was that it was hard for him to have a peaceful sleep, and his nightmares did not reveal much. They were only filled with images that weren't complete. Horrible suffering he did not understand.

But that particular night, he heard words in his nightmares for the first time.

Someone shouting a name. The person's voice was filled with so much pain and desperation.

"Declan! *Nooo,* leave him alone! *declaaaan!!*" The voice roared so loudly.

Callan shot up from the bed, sweating profusely. His breathing erratic as he tried to catch his breath.

The voice would not stop calling to him and pleading on his behalf.

Declan, the voice called him, instead of Callan.

CHAPTER 25. ANOTHER TOGETHER.

Danika's bladder woke her up all of a sudden. She'd kept her eyes closed, trying to put off the feeling of having to get up from the bed and use the bathroom, but the pressure was suddenly unbearable.

She stirred, stretching herself a little bit. She felt his presence when she took that first step into consciousness.

King Lucien is here. He really did come tonight.

Danika's eyes opened and found him standing beside her on the bed.

"My king..." Danika whispered sleepily.

"Get some sleep, Danika. I was not here." His deep voice blended with the night and sent shivers down her bruised body.

"Yes. You were not here." She easily agreed with him to make everything easy. Her mind was all slurred up by dozens of potions and pills. But no matter how hazy her mind was, she knew the king was standing there. And she didn't want him to go.

"How are you feeling?" His arms were crossed around his chest, and he was dressed for bed in his casual attire.

He didn't look like a man who had gotten any sleep. He must have been busy all day.

"I feel...better than I did yesterday," Danika told him truthfully. Whatever Baski had been giving her, it was making her feel better.

He nodded once and turned to leave.

Her bladder only pressured her all the more. She made a move to get up from the bed, wincing when her body protested.

He turned to her and scowled when he realized she was trying to get up from the bed. "What are you doing?"

The deep command of the calm question halted her, and she glanced at him warily. "I w-want to use the bathroom..."

His scowl went blacker. "No one is here with you? Baski should be here. Or your former personal maid."

"They were here w-with me all day. Madam Baski might h-have left for a little...while to put...Remeta to sleep..." Danika rushed defensively so that he wouldn't get angry at them.

He made no move, but she noticed some of the tension left his body. He was still frowning as he watched her struggle to get up from bed.

Finally, he walked away from the door, and she expected he would go out. But instead, he walked towards her and took hold of her arm gently. His help startled her. If he noticed her startled look, he said nothing about it. "Lean into me."

She followed his soft command, leaning heavily into his body, letting him take most of her weight.

He smelled so good, she breathed him in deeply and held it for a moment, before she let it out.

In steady steps, they made their way to the bathroom. He pulled up her nightwear and began untying her underthings.

Danika flushed red, staring down at him as he worked the robes of her linen shorts till he untied them. He pulled them down and looked at her meaningfully.

"Thank you, my king." Danika's face was crimson as she did her business. He waited patiently for her, holding most of her weight.

Afterwards, he buttoned her up and dressed her clothes before leading her out of the bathroom. He helped her get on the bed before he took a step back.

Danika lay under the coverlet, drinking in heavily the very sight of him. She'd carried his child and lost it too. The reminder sprang tears to her eyes.

"Are you alright?" he asked at the sight of the tears.

She nodded rapidly. "Yes. My wounds hurt." Her internal wounds hurt more than the external ones now.

A muscle ticked in his jaw. "You'll be fine."

"Thank you, my king," she whispered. Danika did not want him to go. Although it was inevitable, she wanted to keep him close for as long as she could...no matter how little.

"Can I ask something...?"

He untangled his hands, walked towards her, and sat beside her on the bed. "You can."

"How was your day?"

King Lucien spared her a glance because the question was unexpected. Unbiddenly, he searched his memory and realized she was the first person to ever ask him that. Baski would, if she was ever allowed to, and Chad would too. His mistress wouldn't. His brows knitted at the thought.

She saw it and shook her head. "I'm so sorry for asking..."

"I spent most of the day in court. A lot of things to do. A lot of decisions to make. It was quite a strenuous day," he answered at last.

"I'm so sorry--"

"Stop apologizing for things you have no control over," he chided, but his voice was unusually soft.

It must have been the softness in his voice that gave her courage. Or was it the way he had been with her lately? Or the fact that he won't punish her now because her body was a massive bruise?

She wasn't really sure where her courage came from when she whispered, "Come and hold me..."

Silence met her request—a silence that stretched while he looked at her with blue eyes that wouldn't reveal anything.

"Do not think you can ever order me around," he stated, at last, a muscle ticking in his jaw.

"I'd never think...of something like that," she whispered hoarsely.

"Do not think you can ever tell me what to do."

"God forbid that I'd ever do something...like that," she countered softly.

Silence. Then, he looked away. "If I hold you, I will want to stay here with you. It is not proper."

"Oh..." Her face fell. She wished that, just like yesterday, he would forget what was proper and what was not.

Danika's mind wasn't the only mind troubled. The king was also battling his innermost self.

It was not proper to be there with her, but when he returned to his bedroom, he would not sleep either. And when he managed to, nightmares plagued his subconscious—memories of his dear little brother.

Would it be so wrong to lie down with her and escape...just for a little while? His body wanted hers so much. His dick had thickened since he helped her use the bathroom, and it only made him scowl at himself. Wanting to bury himself deep into a woman who was badly beaten up and trying to recover did not make sense. It was unlike him.

Danika wondered what ran through his mind that was bringing such a deep frown to his face. She bit her lips. She should never have asked him to come and hold her. It was ridiculous and so unlike her. She opened her mouth to apologize, but then his words about apologizing stopped her. He would not accept it. She looked away, staring at the empty space ahead of her.

When the bed dipped, her breath caught. She swiveled her head to see the king climbing onto the bed beside her.

"I will not be here when you wake in the morning, Danika." His deep voice resonated in the silent room.

Happiness spread through her bruised body inwardly. On the outside, she nodded her head. "I will never request that of you, my king."

For the first time, Danika was forced to wonder if the king really did hate her—if he still hated her as much as he did all those months ago. In her hazy mind, she could only think of a few things he had done that she had never expected. She slid her eyes close and tried to remember the last time he'd ever punished her like a master would punish his slave...

It's been such a long time, her mind whispered as he pulled in beside her. She turned herself into his arms, ignoring her protesting body. His large hand wrapped around her body, drawing her closer to him. She bit back a wince. Instead, she melted into him completely.

She felt him on her lower body. He was hard for her.

Raising her head, she stared up at him.

"Get some sleep, Danika. I will not make any demands on you. Not in your condition," he stated flatly.

Her heart raced, and her mind whirled. He would be with her until she fell asleep, and then he'd return to his chambers. What if he summons his mistress to satisfy him? Or Princess Kamara...?

Danika's heart tightened in her chest, the thought leaving a bad taste in her mouth. She wanted to be the one who satisfied him. He's this way because of her. The thought of him drawing pleasures from the body of another woman—or another woman bringing him to sexual release—did not settle well with her at all.

As Danika nuzzled her head to his wide comforting shoulder, she acknowledged that she had no right to feel this way. She was merely his slave, while the other women were his mistress and his future queen. She should not be feeling possessive of him in this way, but she couldn't help herself.

Acting on impulse, she lifted her face and pressed her mouth to his. Wherever her courage came from, she had no idea. But she didn't cower or falter, not even when he stiffened against her.

She slipped her eyes closed and did the things his lips taught hers, whirling her tongue softly to the contours of his lips. She kissed him wholeheartedly.

Time passed, and he wasn't kissing her back. That was when she self-consciously began pulling back. Then, he muttered some explicit but inaudible curses before snaking his hand at the back of her head, pulling her closer to meet his descending lips. He began kissing her thoroughly, holding her closely. His tongue tangled with hers, and their breaths became one. He suckled on her lower lip, and she moaned breathily.

She felt the fierce crush of his mouth with awed pleasure. He tasted of masculinity and male, and his lips were devastatingly expert.

Her arms went under his and around him; her hands savored the taut muscles of his broad shoulders.

Danika clung to him, her body trembling with a kind of pleasure that terrified her while his hard mouth took everything it wanted from hers.

Then her hand reached out and she pulled up his robe and began untying his underthings.

Princess Kamara gave up on sleeping when it kept eluding her. She put on her robes and headed out of her bedroom on a night walk. She needed company.

She'd check on the king to know if he was awake too. Maybe they'd go on a walk together.

Baski mentally blamed herself to death for getting so carried away while making herbs she forgot to check on Danika for such a long time.

She was on her way to Danika's bedroom when she heard soft cries and a male grunt. The king was in there with Danika.

The king's chambers were lightly soundproofed—only a scream or a roar could be heard from his bedroom. But other quarters weren't—including Danika's bedroom.

Her ears flushed, and Baski suddenly felt like she was in a place she wasn't supposed to be. Worry filled her. What if the king was making demands on Danika? She wasn't physically capable of being intimate with a man like him. Apart from her bruises, there was still her uncertain but vulnerable condition.

Just then, Baski heard footsteps coming towards the king's chambers. She turned and saw Princess Kamara approaching the king's chambers, and her eyes widened. If she comes any further, she'll hear the King and Danika, and if she goes to his bedroom, she'll find out he isn't there!

Baski hurried towards her immediately. Her steps were quick and fast to cover more ground. "My Princess?"

Princess Kamara stopped and confided, "I couldn't sleep. I'm going to try and take a walk---"

"I'll give you something to help you sleep, Princess. Do not worry, you're in the right hands. Come on, come on," she urged as she led the princess away from her destination. "I make the best of herbs; you can ask anyone in this kingdom. I'll give you something to help you sleep like a baby."

"Oh. Okay." Princess Kamara allowed the older woman to lead her away.

.

.

CHAPTER 26. PEACE OFFERING AND GIFTS.

"Danika," he breathed into her mouth.

"Please, let me." She reached inside and wrapped her hand around his warm flesh. His breath hitched as she caressed the length of him.

When his breathing hitched, she half-expected him to pull away from her—to stop her from touching him. But his kisses only became more ardent and intense.

She let out a breath she didn't know she was holding and withdrew her hand. His kisses were like a drug to her system; nothing else existed than his hands on her body and his mouth on hers.

Danika reached her hand behind her towards the table and withdrew the gel Baski used on her body. Without breaking the kiss, she opened the lid and dipped her hand into it. Her hand came out wet and dripping. She wrapped it around his thick hardness and began working him determinedly with her hands. Their unsteady breathing filled the air as the two lovers lost themselves in the arms of each other.

King Lucien broke the kiss, and his hand working a little unsteady on her cotton nightie. He freed her breast from the confinement of her gown, dipping his head lower, and his searching mouth found her pert nipple and he began sucking ardently. Danika cried out. Shards of pleasure overrode the pain that sizzled through her body as she arched her back towards him. Her breasts were so sensitive that the rough urgency of his mouth was hurting and pleasuring her at the same time. She circled the wide head of his massive thickness, and he grunted unsteadily, his hands holding her back to him contracted softly.

"Danika!" His voice broke, but her touch had an inevitable effect on his reserve. She felt him tremble against her, heard his tortured breathing as he tutored her with his mouth.

With each tug of his lips, she felt it in between her legs. She was so wet; she was all liquid fluid down there. What he was doing to her had her tethering on the edge of climax without falling over. The movements of her soft hands increased jerkily, and she melted into him completely giving herself up to him without holding back.

When he convulsed, crying out in ecstasy, she forced her flushed, aroused, eyes to lift, to look at him. It was incredible, watching him come apart in her arms like that.

King Lucien pulsed in her grasp, helpless, blind, deaf, to anything but the fierce pleasure that was coursing through him. He pulled his mouth from her red nipple and lifted his head, then devoured her mouth. He kissed her with fervor, his lips hard and fast against hers; he took her breath away. When the last jet of his release spilled, Danika reached for one of the towels Baski had been using to press hot water to her body without breaking their feverish kisses. She used the towel to wipe him clean before he broke the kiss at last.

His eyes scrutinized her, taking in the unspent desire in her dazed innocent eyes and the slight trembling of her body. He freed her other breast from its confinement and lowered his head to it to give it the same treatment he gave to the other. She cried out at the sensitivity and intensity of it all; it was almost too painful. Her hand held on to the back of his head, trying to push him away, but it was like trying to move an unmovable wall.

Then she felt his hand trail behind her back. He intentionally didn't touch any of her bruises so he wouldn't hurt her. His large hand snaked into her underthings from behind and he caressed the small, sensitized nub of her womanhood. Danika clung to him and made soft music for him with the things he was doing to her. He played her body like a keynote and she responded with soft music. It was the first time he had done something like that to her, it dawned on her hazy mind. The first time he touched her with his hand in such an extensive blatant way.

162

He pushed two fingers into her, and her body tensed and she came in shuddering breaths. He patted her soothingly without being persistent, so that she didn't hurt herself.

Finally, he pulled back and wrapped her in his arms.

They fell asleep that way. He held her all night.

He didn't leave until dawn.

As days passed, Danika started getting better. It was a gradual and steady step, but she did it. Sally and Baski was right there with her to help her as much as they could.

She was determined to be well and strong for Sally's upcoming wedding, which was the greatest reason she pushed hard. She took all her herbs; never left a pill she was supposed to take.

Remeta was also right there with her, but she was back to her usual playful, child-like behaviors of being happy all the time and chasing crickets. If you had no knowledge about her, you'd never believe she had any gift of foresight.

A week passed, and Danika was able to walk around without help anymore. Most of her bruises had faded to red marks, and the wounds are almost gone.

Sally worried herself to death as her wedding approached and she hadn't been able to buy her sandals. She hadn't been able to go to the village since what had happened to her princess. Now, her princess was getting better, and she still didn't want to leave her for a single minute.

Danika found out what was happening and was horrified. "Your wedding is fast approaching, and as a bride, you don't have your sandals!? What are you going to wear!?"

"I'll still go out one of these days and buy one," Sally admitted, flushed. "I have the money to buy very nice shoes."

"You do?" Danika asked, feeling happy for her best friend.

Sally nodded and confided excitedly. "The king gave Chad big money for us to make good preparations. I'm so grateful to him!"

Danika was also happy and grateful; she'd informed Sally that they'd be going to the market to buy her footwear. She'd informed her that a new bride shouldn't wait to buy anything.

Sally was horrified. She hadn't forgotten what had happened the last time they went into the village. How could she forget when her princess was barely getting out of the ordeal? She'd tried to protest, but Danika only shook her head and refused.

"I can't be inside the palace for the rest of my life without any freedom to walk around as I please just because I'm scared of being implicated and beaten up. That is not living, Sally," she stated vehemently.

Sally kept quiet because she knew that her princess was right. That very day, two weeks ago, her princess had passed out before she could hear the things she'd screamed to the people.

Her princess wasn't aware of how she had been saved, and when she'd heard about the crowd that stayed awake in the palace gates because they wanted her to be alright, she never believed it either.

"They must have been there for another reason. Those people hate me too much. It can't be that," she'd told Sally.

So, when they walked out of the palace together, Sally was right there beside her to help her when she got tired and needed to lean on her.

As Danika walked and staggered, Sally caught her and steadied her before leaving her alone so that she'd keep walking on her own and getting stronger. It reminded Danika of three months ago when Sally was raped and brutalized by the kings. They'd also walked this way during her healing process.

How time flies. It felt like ages ago.

Immediately after they stepped out of the palace, all eyes were on Danika. Passersby stopped to look at her, and others just stood and watched warily. Danika noticed the blatant stares---how couldn't she when it was way too obvious?---and it made her uncomfortable. But she was determined to keep her shoulders high and walk with Sally. These people almost killed her two weeks ago, and now they look at her like they're seeing a complete stranger. The few glances she got of their faces, she couldn't see the usual malice, the pure hate they'd always emitted.

164

They got to a point where a little girl, who didn't look older than six years old, walked up to them. The girl hesitantly offered her a gift. Danika stopped and stared at the chocolate in the little girl's outstretched hand. It touched her immensely that this little girl would offer her such gift. Being a lowborn, or less privileged, they barely had enough to eat and sustain themselves. Now, this little girl offers her the little she had.

Danika lowered herself to eye level with the child. "Thank you so much," she whispered as she accepted the gift.

The child beamed at her and ran away. Before Danika could take another step, other children began walking up to her and offering her chocolates. There were so many children, their smiles sincere as they crowded her and made peace offerings. Tears sprang from her eyes as she accepted and thanked them all.

Then the women, men, and older people walked to her and apologized vocally about what they did to her. It was so unexpected; Danika couldn't control the tears. Sally was there, patting her back occasionally as Danika forgave them all for ganging up on her and beating her up.

The people of Salem hadn't expected her easy forgiveness, and when it came, it only made them feel more guilty and their consciences so heavy. Indeed, they'd preyed on an innocent. Indeed, they'd bit the finger that fed them.

The former Princess Danika was nothing like her father.

As Danika and Sally continued to buy what they came for, people were very good to her, and most women even gave her a gift from their shops. They bought Sally's sandals at a discounted price.

When Danika entered the palace, everyone took one look at the gifts she carried and knew it for what it was. Peace offering and gifts. Danika had found favour with the people.

The maids had stopped being mean to her after they found out about the things she did when they were still slaves in Mombana. They looked at their hands and saw the gifts from the people and smiled at her in acknowledgement.

"You deserve it." Was practically written on their faces.

The mistress was the only person that glared hard at her as she passed with her sets of maid and saw the gifts. Vetta didn't say any words to her, but she didn't need to. Her eyes and stiff posture showed her anger and rage. Thankfully, she just walked passed Danika, marching straight to her quarters.

But other people—each and every one of them—looked at Danika with kindness and appreciation. Danika felt so emotional, and for the first time in two weeks, she decided that her pain was worth it. The beatings were worth it too. If that was what it took for the people to accept her and stop seeing her in the same light they saw his father, then it was definitely worth it.

And yet, a part of her prayed to the creator for the baby inside her to be alright. She shouldn't have had a prayer like that because that child would only cause more problems for her. For one, the king might order her execution if he found out about it. For another, his mistress or his 'queen' might order her to be whipped or force her to take a body flusher—just like most queens and mistresses did in other kingdoms.

She wasn't particularly afraid of Princess Kamara because she was a good person. But the king's mistress was more wicked than the others; she might do that to her and more.

Body flushers did kill the woman on some occasions, too, under overdose. Most people used very dangerous herb combinations for it.

A slave did *not* carry the king's child; it was simply not done. And yet, no matter how much she crossed her heart on wishing her baby had left her, Danika still found herself wishing otherwise.

"Oh, Danika, what did you do?" she whispered to herself alone in her bedroom in the evening.

Well, she shouldn't worry about it now. Although, she still had all her symptoms of pregnancy. Baski said they wouldn't be sure until she did her first checkup tonight.

In the meantime, she forced her mind away from it and focused on the beautiful gifts in her hands.

Several minutes later, the king summoned her.

CHAPTER 27. FORGIVENESS.

Vetta was in her bedroom with her heart in her throat. She'd heard that today that the fate of those women she'd hired to mess Danika up would be decided. She couldn't sit still, so she paced around the bedroom. Karandy had told her that he would make sure those women did not spill the beans, and she had paid dearly to make sure he got that side of his job done.

She just hoped that nothing went wrong. She needed to get out of this without really being inside of it. And then she would deal with that bastard for having the effrontery to threaten her and use her body that way without respect. It had taken more than a few days for her body to heal, and because she had been given house arrest, she hadn't been able to get pills to stop the ache.

Vetta had put her fertility pills aside just to be sure that the idiot's seed did not take root first before she could continue her pursuit of carrying the king's seed.

It was the courting week delaying her from being intimate with the king. The king hadn't summoned her to give him pleasure because of the stupid courting week.

It had been two weeks; she wished that it would end already. Once it did, she'd take her pills, go back to the king and get pregnant. She needed to carry his child before he was married to that wild woman, Princess Kamara!

Danika entered the king chambers and bowed her head. "You summoned me, my king."

King Lucien was dressed in his royal attire. He came out of the library with a book in his hand and walked straight to his desk. "It's time I take you to the dungeon," he stated matter-of-factly.

Danika's heart flew right out of her chest. Had she done something wrong? The dungeon? She snapped her mouth shut and only nodded. "You wish is my command."

He walked past her, leading the way. She followed him dutifully, and all the while, she couldn't stop wondering what going to the dungeon was all about.

They walked out of the royal quarters towards the servant's quarters where they entered the hidden wing that led to the underground palace. At the gate of the dungeon, the guards rushed towards it and opened the chains. The king walked in and turned towards Danika. She walked right in behind him and saw two women she recognized from two weeks ago in the market square. They had beaten her up very badly.

"It is only fitting that the woman who they almost killed becomes the one to pass judgment on them," was all the king said.

"Your Highness?" Her voice mirrored her confusion.

"These women were the mastermind behind your beating in the market. They stole the necklace and put it in your bag for you to be beaten for it," he declared, his cold eyes on the women.

Danika looked at both women, who were looking sad and resigned at the same time. They had dried tears in their eyes, and from their expressions, they already sentenced themselves to death. They were just waiting for her to say the words.

Four pair of eyes stared up at her, and then lowered their heads in shame.

Danika walked deeper into the cell, walking past the king. She stood directly in front of them. "Rise."

At her soft but firm whispered, both women wearily rose to their feet. Coria looked at Zenia with the resignation and the knowledge that this would be the last time she'd be seeing the woman ever again. The daughter of Cone had not deserved what they did to her, and it was very unlikely that she wouldn't sentence them to death.

Just as they expected and predicted, the former slave trainer took their children captive in exchange for their silence. They'd gotten the word right there in the dungeon. Their fates had been decided a long time ago, so there was no need to kill their own children too just because they wanted to live. And so, they had snapped their mouths shut and waited for the inevitable.

"I forgive you both." Danika said the words so softly, it took the women a while to assimilate the words. When they did, their eyes widened and looked towards her in shock. Even the king's eyes flashed with surprise, but only for a second. He did a better job at hiding it. Her eyes held theirs and she continued. "I forgive you both, but I hope you won't treat another person the way you treated me. In the future. You must learn to give people a chance."

Each softly spoken word touched the deepest part of the women, and Danika wasn't done yet. "My only crime is being my father's daughter, but I had no choice. I wasn't given the choice as to who my father would be. I only came of age one day and realized who my parents were. So, please, do not hate and punish people for sins they did not commit so you don't shed the blood of an innocent because of it."

"Yes, princess! So, so sorry!" Zenia was crying. Danika's forgiveness was so unexpected it was like the strike of an arrow to her chest. She knelt and kept thanking her and also asking for her forgiveness at the same time. The way she spoke made them forget the rags she was wearing and hear the authority of the words of a princess.

When both women fell to the ground, crying and thanking her and saying sorry at the same time, Danika lowered herself to the ground and hugged them both. "It's alright. I forgive you," she whispered.

Danika and the king walked back into his chambers. The silence was uncomfortable. She picked the hem of her dress nervously, while waiting for the king to dismiss her. He hadn't said a word since the dungeon, and it had her worried. Was he angry that she released the women? He had given her rights to their judgment. She shifted uncomfortably from one foot to another.

"Danika." He had his back to her when he called her name. That tone. The very tone of his voice had shivers going down her spine. It was the same voices he used whenever they were in bed together. The same tone when he calls her name while taking his pleasure from her body.

"Y-yes, Your Highness." She fidgeted with her dress; her voice wasn't past a whisper.

"What am I going to do with you?" The question, so unexpected, rubbed her of speech. So she snapped her mouth shut and prayed to the heavens for him not to be so angry at her. "You make forgiveness so simple. People ganged up on you and beat you up so badly you nearly died, and there you are, forgiving them as if they committed a crime as simple as lying," he said.

Danika wished she could see his face to discern if he was angry or not. She swallowed tightly. "I felt like letting it go, Your Highness."

"Why?"

"The whole world is driving by a will, blind and ruthless. In order to transcend the limitations of that will, we have to learn to let go. That is the only way to move on."

Silence met her words, as if he was contemplating them. She let him have all the time he needed. Finally, he turned towards her and she got a good look at his face. There was no hate or anger. Just...warmth. "You can go now, Danika," he stated.

She bowed her head to him and turned to leave, but his hand snapped out and caught hers. He jerked her towards him and kissed her.

A gasp of surprise slid past her lips as he kissed her hard, fast and hungry. His hand held the back of her head while he ravished her mouth. She closed her eyes and kissed him right back. She had been starved for him for the past two weeks, she grabbed onto crumbs, needing anything he could give her at all.

The kiss lasted forever before he pulled back. His eyes blazed fire as he stepped back. He didn't look like a man who had practically led devoured her just some seconds ago.

Danika's feet were unsteady as she bowed to him again and walked out of his bedroom.

The rest of the evening passed methodically, and Danika found herself smiling more times than she could count.

The smile lasted until she was examined by Baski in her bedroom at night.

Vetta was more than happy when the maids gave her the news about the release of those women. She was standing in the shadows of the hallways that led to the dungeon, and that's where she stood when Danika and the king passed. She was also there when both crying women were released. Now, that chapter was closed and done. Vetta took a deep breath and stared at the route Danika and the king followed.

It had been a plan that would have gone so perfectly but Danika and her useless maid, Sally, had to ruin everything. Now the people are on Danika's side!

So, what if she ate from the silver bowls? And so? It was all in the past and this was the present!

Vetta admitted to herself that she ate more than most people from the silver bowl in Mombana. She had always been competitive and so damn hungry; she never hesitated to grab onto a silver bowl whenever food was brought in. But that was all in the past! And it didn't matter if Danika gave them food! It did nothing to erase the pain and punishments her father gave to them! Food had nothing on the whippings! The forced-sex!

Vetta turned and began striding away. It didn't matter of her plan hadn't gone the way it was expected. Vetta would find another way to deal with Danika. This time around, she'd find the best way because she wanted to deal with Karandy, too, while she was at it. They would regret messing with her—

A hand suddenly grabbed hold of hers from behind. Vetta startled and turned around. Remeta was holding onto her hand, staring ahead, and began speaking in a robotic way.

"You get away with it this time around, but what about next time? Don't. When it comes to your head, ignore it. Don't." She finally looked Vetta in the eyes. "Don't do it. You'll hurt queen. You'll hurt Prince. You'll hurt his father. And you will get hurt. You get away this time around, and you get hurt the next. Your nemesis is coming in form of a person."

Then she let go of Vetta's hand suddenly and walked away.

.

.

CHAPTER 28. INDECISION AND UNCERTAINTY.

Princess Kamara just got words from her father's kingdom that she should stay put here in Mombana for some time because there was a problem in Navia. Her father detected a spy in his cabinets, and until the spy was found and flushed out, it wasn't safe for her to come back.

It made Kamara angry and sad at the same time. She missed home. Most importantly, she missed seeing Callan. Once she gets returned, she would try to find a way to make seeing Callan possible. It had been so many months; it was like an ache in her flesh.

She had been very lucky for the past two weeks; the king hadn't summoned her to perform her duties to him. He hadn't summoned her to warm his bed. But she wasn't sure how long her luck would last. The thought made her restless and wary.

Kamara and Henna were coming back from an evening walk when Kamara collided with someone.

"Don't you look!?" Vetta sputtered angrily when someone collided with her. She looked up to see it was Princess Kamara.

Henna had her hand to her mouth because she hadn't seen the accident in time to stop her princess and the mistress from colliding into each other. Vetta, herself, had been deep in thought of the things Remeta had said to her. She hadn't understood anything, and frankly, it wasn't bothering her that much. It was unfortunate that Remeta's madness only continued to worsen. It was really a pity. But Vetta had wondered what the insane girl meant by 'the prince' and 'the queen' and not hurting them. It had Vetta confused because she knew that

Remeta referred to Danika as a queen, and also Princess Kamara was the king's future queen. So what had she meant?

Those had been the thoughts running through Vetta's head when she collided into the princess.

Princess Kamara stepped back from Vetta and looked at her like she was seeing a bug. Her hand itched to slap the mistress again, but the only thing keeping her was the polite warning the king gave her about beating his mistress.

"*You* ran into *me*." Kamara glared at her, emphasizing through gritted teeth.

Vetta really hated the princess, but she knew her place too. Her cheeks hadn't forgotten the slaps. "I'm sorry, Princess. I didn't mean to run into you." The apology left a sore taste in her mouth, but she had no choice.

Princess Kamara remembered the way the mistress had beaten Princess Danika weeks ago for colliding with her. A very wicked mistress, that one was. Just like Mistress Donna, her father's main mistress.

Princess Kamara stepped closer to Vetta, suddenly feeling that anger she always felt for her father's mistress—the same bitch that advised her father to marry her off just because she fell in love with a peasant.

Kamara's hand snatched out and she grabbed hold of Vetta's hair.

"Ouch! Let me go!" Vetta shrieked at the unexpected reaction.

Princess Kamara's hand only tightened in her black mane. "You beat up a former princess because *you* collided with her few weeks ago, and now, here you are—a *mere* mistress—colliding with *me*, a princess! Your future queen!"

"I already apologized, didn't I?" Vetta snapped, not used to answering to anyone but the king for such a long time.

Kamara yanked hard on her hair, pulling a few strands with her. She hissed, "You watch that tone with me, *Mistress,* or I will have you whipped for such insolence."

"I am sorry, Princess." Vetta gritted out again.

Kamara held on for a few more seconds before she let go of her hair and stepped back. She squared her shoulders and walked past the mistress. "Make sure to keep out of my way!"

Vetta kept glaring at her back until she disappeared from the hallway. Her scalp burned from such treatment, and anger was boiling in her blood.

That wicked bitch!

"Oh, heavens! You're still pregnant, Danika!" Baski declared with renewed joy on her face as she stared up at Danika from between her legs.

Danika's face was pinched with pain from the tiny thing Baski inserted in her body. "Please, get it out. It hurts my lower belly," she whispered.

Baski's face was radiant as she held her thighs in reassurance and began extracting the small test tube. When she pulled it out, she was still smiling and happy. She gazed at Danika like the sun rose and sets on her head. "Your child is healthy and strong and still hanging perfectly in there after everything!"

Excitement and dread filled Danika at the same time. "Creator, what do I do!?"

"You're going to tell the king! That's what---"

"Never!" Danika stated heatedly, "He can't find out!"

"What!? But he has to know. Danika, he fathered a child! He should know---"

"No." Danika shook her head adamantly. "No, please. He'll have me killed! You know this! He'll punish me! Why are you so excited about telling him, Madam Baski? Do you want him to order my execution!?"

Baski paused, deep in thought. She understood where Danika was coming from, but Danika didn't know the condition of the king. She didn't know that the king was thought sterile, and she couldn't tell her about it. The king was a very private person, and that was not a secret a person just revealed. Even Vetta didn't know about it.

"Danika, my dear, he might be very happy about it. You'll never know unless you try," she informed uncertainly.

"Might?" Danika whispered. "I should walk up to him and risk my life for 'might'? I can't do that, Baski. I'm not strong enough."

"But pregnancy is not something a woman hides, Danika! Sooner or later, he'll find out about it. Your pregnancy, especially, shouldn't be hidden, because a lot of care should be taken. A whole lot of care!" Baski reasoned.

"I can't. No, he can't find out!" Danika was remembering when she was a child and had heard her father sentence two slaves to death for getting pregnant with his child. No matter how much those slaves pleaded and said they had taken body flushers, he had been adamant in sentencing them to death by beheading.

"No way, I'll never!" she reinstated more firmly, her hands going around her belly protectively.

"But---"

"If you tell him, I'll run straight to the nearest bush and chew on Alka," she vowed heatedly.

Baski's mouth hung open in shock. "That's the most poisonous herb ever!"

"My thoughts exactly."

Baski bit her lips helplessly. The firm set of Danika's jaw showed that she was very stubborn about it—that infamous stubbornness most brave princesses inherited. She didn't have what it took to tell the king about something like that because even she didn't know what his reaction would be.

But still, keeping him in the dark was very dangerous. "If he doesn't find out, how does he know that he shouldn't be intimate with you?"

"Huh?" Danika didn't understand that part.

"Your pregnancy is in a very vulnerable stage, Danika. Coupled with what you've already been through, the king shouldn't be intimate with you for more weeks to come. And even after those weeks, he would have to be extremely gentle with you when you both are intimate." She paused for her to digest that part.

Danika's cheeks heated but it didn't stop her from pointing something out. "The king is not g-gentle when it...um...when he..."

Baski nodded. "The king is not a gentle man; you know this much more than I do. That's the sole reason he should have this knowledge, or else you'll be killing that baby and endangering your own life whenever you go to bed with him."

176

"Oh." A headache began pounding at her head. Danika palmed her head in indecision, shaking her head miserably. "You know I can't deny him."

"I know. That's why I worry for the future when he will summon you to his bed."

Minutes passed before she called. "Baski?"

Baski came closer and patted her head in a motherly way. "My dear?"

"Do you have hundred percent certainty that he won't kill me if he finds out?" she mumbled.

Baski opened her mouth. Closed it. Opened it again. At last, she snapped it closed because she truly didn't know the answer to that. The king was the most unpredictable man she'd ever known, and great chances were he might not believe that the child was his. He might never believe.

Danika put Baski's thoughts into words. "You, Baski, found it hard to believe that I was pregnant by the king, for reasons I don't know. And what about the king? Will he just sit down and take the news that I'm pregnant for him at mouth-value? Without disbelieving it or questioning it?" She glanced up at Baski. "You gave me a chance to explain and swear, but the king wouldn't give me that chance if he doesn't believe me. I'll pay a dire price."

Baski knew that she was right too. There were just too many things at stake there. She wanted nothing more than to let the king know that he was not as sterile as everyone thought, but at the same time, she didn't want to risk Danika and her baby's life for it either.

"I'm so worried, Mama, because I'm still not sure if the prince will stay." Remeta's word filled her ears.

The reminder made Baski shiver. "You know what? We'll take it one step at a time. We'll keep it a secret for now while still looking for a way to break it to him without putting your life in danger. Pregnancy is not something that can be hidden for long, Danika. Very soon, you'll be running out of time."

Danika drew her knees up and hugged them tight to her chest. She began to rock herself, unable to stop worrying.

It was very late at night when King Lucien finished the last petition he had been writing and rolled the parchment closed. He held it closed with a band and kept it beside him where the other scrolls were.

He knew he could no longer put it off. His duty.

It was long overdue.

"Who is there?" he called as calmly as ever when a knock came to the door. He got up from his chair and lifted the scrolls from the desk.

The door opened and Zariel entered his chambers. "Your Highness!?"

He took the scrolls to the inner bedroom and arranged them on the library where it would be easier for him to extract them in the morning then came back to his bedroom and walked back to his desk in those steady regal strides of his, that practically screams power and authority.

His eyes found Zariel and he stated, "Tell Princess Kamara I summon her."

.

.

CHAPTER 29. HIS FUTURE BRIDE.

In the kingdom of Navia, Callan rose from the bed when he couldn't sleep anymore. He was sweating profusely from the nightmare he just had. Bits and pieces of images hadn't made sense, filled with screams and human torture. He knew it was slavery at its peak, and that was one thing he knew for sure about himself: He was a slave and he was left for death.

A young woman saved him somehow by bringing him to this kingdom. A privileged woman in this kingdom had been so dedicated to taking care of him. He knew her as 'Lady'. He address her as 'My lady' because he didn't know her name. She came here often with her personal maid, bringing him foods and herbs and helping him.

He would forever be grateful to her, even though he hadn't seen her in a long while. She stopped coming around one day, and only recently, he found out that she was the princess of this kingdom. She went to another kingdom to court with her suitor.

He strode towards the window and looked out into the dark. His house was isolated from most houses because he didn't like noises and disturbances. He built this small house here five years ago and liked it.

Crossing his arms, he watched the night and allowed his mind to wander where he never allowed it to do so before. *My lady*. He wondered how she was. Did she have a good suitor who would take good care of her? She was a good woman—the best he had seen among privileged women—and he was so surprised when he found out that she was a princess.

She wasn't spoilt, mean and wicked like other princesses he had heard about. Instead, she was cool, reserved and an elegant lady. He'd never seen a more beautiful woman. It had been a long time, but he still couldn't forget what she looked like and what her smile was like.

He'd wondered time and again why a woman like her would mingle with the likes of him, and always, he got no answer. She'd seen a peasant like him almost dying at the side of the road five years ago with no memories of his past and no name or identity. And yet, she'd gotten people to carry him to shelter where she had been nursing him since.

Three women aided him and saved his life: a young woman from his own kingdom who gave him water to drink after he was left for death; the old woman whose chariot he'd hidden inside and drove all the way from his kingdom to this place; and his lady, Princess Kamara—the only princess of the kingdom of Navia, soon to be married to the king of Salem.

As Callan stood before the window, wondering how she was doing and her wellbeing, he heard that name again in his mind.

Declan.

He had been hearing that name since the night a man roared out that name in his nightmares. Was *he* Declan?

Who was that man? Why hadn't he tried to look for him? Had he tried and hasn't found him?

Who was that man?

Princess Kamara had gone to sleep when she was awakened and given the message about the king's summon. Her heart flew right out of her chest. She knew that she had exhausted her luck and it was time to perform her duties.

Tears prickled the back of her eyes as she got up and put on her robes. She made her way out of her chambers and started towards the king's chambers.

It was well past midnight. She bypassed sleeping guards and a few guards on duty. Getting to his door, she paused and took a shaky breath. Then she knocked hesitantly.

Silence met her soft knock. She waited patiently, trying to still her racing heart and calm herself down. Nerves racked her, and her eyes wouldn't stop prickling.

"Come in," came the deep voice of the king.

Kamara opened the door and entered his room. Inside, the king was seated behind his desk, scribbling on the scroll in front of him. It made her remember her father, who was always writing when he wasn't dealing with matters of the court and his people—when he wasn't with her mother or listening to the advice of Mistress Donna.

"You summoned me, Your Highness." Thankfully, her voice was calmer than she felt—the shivers working inside her had not reflected on it.

King Lucien looked up from the scroll towards her. "Give me a minute." Those short-clipped words more than anything confirmed her fears: The king would take her to bed tonight.

"Take all the t-time you need, my king," she whispered. Princess Kamara tried to pull herself together. It was just coupling—nothing she hadn't done before. She could survive the night. All she had to do was just to close her eyes and take it.

She walked on shaky legs to the bed and lowered herself on it. He continued writing while she sat down, her body racked with nerves. If she hadn't known better, she'd say that he was also trying to delay their coupling.

The silence between them stretched. Only the cool breeze of the night was heard occasionally.

Finally, the king placed the inked feather gently back into the lid and closed it, picked up the scroll, and began rolling it methodically then set it on the desk.

Then the sound of a chair pulling back interrupted the silence of the night as the king got up and walk around his desk. He crossed his arms and leaned against his desk. "Take off your clothes, Kamara."

Kamara got up from the bed and began pulling off her clothes. Her hands were trembling, but she tried her best not to let her anxiety show. Taking off her robes, she stood in her flimsy nightwear and stared up at him.

The king wanted nothing more than to order her to the table and have her give her back to him. He wanted it swift and fast, to get it over with. He did not want to have to touch her or for her to touch him. He did not want anybody's hands on him.

But she was a princess and would be his future queen. She didn't deserve such treatment from him. So, he forced himself to pull away from his desk. He strode towards her, coming up to her from behind. He placed a hand on her shoulder and she jumped slightly.

"It's okay. Relax," he said softly.

She jerked her head into a hesitant nod and waited, her hand clutched to her undergarments. He placed a kiss on her shoulder and it left a sore taste in his mouth. King Lucien turned her around to face him. She was doing her best to hide it, but the fear in her eyes couldn't be hidden.

His eyes fluttered to her face and he saw Danika. He blinked hard and looked again. But it was Kamara. Why would he think about Danika at such time like this? Putting the thoughts away, he dreaded what would come next, but it did not stop him from trying to get it done. The sooner, the better.

He lowered his head and took her lips with his. Swallowing her whimper, he coaxed her lips with his, while his hand hung loosely on her shoulder. Kamara squeezed her eyes shut and tried not to let her uncertainty show. Her hands felt useless by her side, so she placed them on his clothed shoulder. He stiffened instantly. Every large part of him froze like stone in front of her, and he pulled back, breaking the kiss.

Her chaotic mind refused to process and reminded her at the moment that this man did not like to be touch, because her nerves were shot all over the place.

"Kamara," he breathed her name.

"Yes, Your Highness." Her voice shook.

"You aren't ready for this, are you?"

She was surprised that he asked. She knew that they did not ever ask or care. During the princess's meetings, they talk and confide in each other, and the married ones tell them some secrets of the marriage bed. The kings don't care if you want it or not, and it was never pleasant. You just lie there and take it so you can make a baby.

"No. I'm not ready." She almost added that he should get on with it because she might never be ready, but she didn't want to push her luck. She wasn't brave enough.

He stepped back, causing her hand to fall away from his shoulder. Kamara could have sworn that it was relief she saw in his eyes before he blinked it away and gave her that blank stare that had become perfectly his. "Get on the bed and lie down," he ordered her all of a sudden.

Her eyes widened at the command; her own relief shot to dust to be replaced by dread. She nodded jerkily and walked to the bed. She laid down on it and curled into a ball, a protective move she couldn't help, and peeked at him beneath her long eyelashes. But he didn't follow her. Instead, he turned away from her and walked back to his desk. He sat down there and unrolled one unused scroll.

Kamara watched him warily. That must be his way of getting her relaxed and ready for him. The bed was very soft and comfortable, but her rankled nerves wouldn't allow her to feel it. She watched him like a trapped mouse would watch a predator cat.

He began writing. Time dragged by.

So much time passed, Kamara began feeling sleepy, but she did her best to jerk her eyes open. If he saw that she was sleepy, he might abandon his scroll and come over to get it over with. She forced her eyes to remain open, even as all the nerves drained out of her gradually. She laid there pliant and sleepy.

King Lucien knew the exact moment she fell asleep. He paused and stared at her.

She'd put her hands on him, and the touch had felt so strange and uncomfortable, it made his skin crawl. It was not a new feeling, because everyone's touch made him feel that way.

Except Danika.

Danika, whose touch he almost...anticipated. Craved. Who made his dick harden and thicken with just her presence. Whose lips he could spend a good amount of time kissing. Danika was who he wanted in his bed—who he wanted to lose himself in.

He picked up the scroll and folded it. In the privacy of his mind, he could admit this to himself.

He knew that if he tried hard enough, he could get hard for his skittish future bride and perform his duties. But.

He did not want to try hard enough. At least, not for tonight.

Tonight he did not want her hands on him, and he did not want to touch her.

They could try again another time.

.

.

CHAPTER 30. SALLY'S HAPPINESS.

The king summoned Sally two days later.

Sally's heart was in her throat when she got word that the king was summoning her. It was the first time she'd be standing before him that way, and as she stood in front of his door, her legs were practically shaking.

She knocked, and his deep voice ordered her in. Sally entered the empty room, but the sound coming from the inner bedroom indicated that he must be in there. She squeezed her hands together nervously as she waited for him.

The door opened, and the king came out of the inner room. She bowed her head to him. "You summoned me, Your Highness."

He walked towards her and stood in front of her. He said nothing, but his eyes scrutinized her thoroughly. Those eyes that revealed nothing almost made her squirm. She kept her head lowered and waited agitatedly.

"You have been Danika's personal maid for a long time, right?" he asked finally.

"Y-yes, My king."

"And you're getting married to the chief of my security guards in a few days, right?"

"Yes, Your Highness."

"Why?"

"Um?" The question, so unexpected, took Sally by surprise.

He crossed his arm to his chest and picked her with blue eyes that revealed nothing. "Why are you getting married to him?"

Sally thought about that and swallowed tightly. "I love him."

He turned away from her and strode towards his desk. Without turning towards her, he continued. "Do you know that Chad means more to me than his status as my chief security, personal bodyguard and assistant?"

"Yes, Your Highness." She had heard much about the king from her betrothed to know that the king favors him very much.

"Even before we were enslaved, Chad had always meant more to me. And then, once we were enslaved, he made so many sacrifices for me." He paused and turned around. "Will you treat him right, Sally?"

"I will do my best, Your Highness." She loved Sire Chad, and she knew that he loved her too.

In their world, in their time, two people did not marry for love. Marriages were arranged. Also, brides were betrothed to their husbands at a very young age. Love rarely came in, and when it did, it was mostly after marriage. Marriage for love was as rare as rain in their world.

That was why their relationship fascinated King Lucien as much as it gladdened his heart. If any man deserved such luck and fortune, it was Chad.

He turned towards the girl that would be marrying his good friend and scrutinized her again. They were both damaged people. Could she handle him? "Chad, he..." The king paused. "He has some problems. After we were enslaved, he went through some horrible things that damaged him. Do you know about this?"

Sally nodded because Chad had told her all about it. She knew about his sleepwalking problems and the rapes the kings subjected him to. Chad also told her that it affected him because his body became used to the horrors he had endured. She did not understand what he meant, but she knew she would stand by him. She loved him too much.

The thought of their wedding night filled her with nerves, but she didn't have to think about it beforehand. She did her best to put it out of her mind.

"He told you?" The king was surprised. Chad was tight-lipped and very private; he did not confide in people much, just like the king.

"Yes, he did, Your h-Highness." The reminder made tears burn through Sally's eyes. Whatever she had been through was nothing compared to what her Chad had been through.

The king saw her fighting tears and most of the coldness left his face. A muscle ticked in his jaw. "Lately, he has looked...better. Happier. I see a different man, and it gladdens my heart. If any man deserves to be happy, that man is Chad."

And you. But Sally knew better to voice out her thoughts. If only the king would give her princess a chance.

Then he pulled away from his desk and walked around it. He opened the cabinet and withdrew a small, wrapped bag.

The king walked up to Sally. "You make him happy. That is enough for me. Take this."

At the soft but firm command, Sally reached out with both hands and took the wrapped package. Her eyes widened to unbearable degrees. It was a small bag of coins.

"You can pay dowry with that on your wedding day," he said.

"Thank you so much, Your Highness! Thank you so much!" Sally gasped; her heart filled with gratitude. Her hands trembled as she held the unexpected gift with both hands like the cherished feat it was. She had been worried sick about how to get this money, and even though she had saved up, it was never enough. She had hidden it from Danika so that her princess wouldn't worry herself sick. And here the king is, offering her this large amount of money. Her knees hit the ground; her head lowered. Tears of gratitude spilled from her eyes as she thanked the king over and over again.

"You are welcome, Sally. I want you to get married and live well. Also, from today, you seize being a palace slave. Chad is getting married to a young beautiful common girl, not a slave. I already gifted him with a small but comfortable house just outside the palace. It is a wedding gift," he stated.

Sally's eyes widened in fear. She couldn't stop being a slave because it would tear her away from her princess. She'd have no reason to be in the palace anymore.

When he saw her face, the king added, "Do not worry. You can work as a palace maid afterwards. If you want to."

A heady wave a relief filled Sally. She thanked him so much, never expecting such kindness from him. She had always known—and heard—that the king was a good man, but the things he went through hardened him. Today, she witnessed firsthand how thoughtful and kind he was. Her mind went to Danika. Her poor princess. She wished one day the king's heart would heal completely and he would forgive. She wished one day her princess could witness his kindness and mercy too. She wished that one day he would remove the collar from Danika's neck and free her too.

Sally thanked him again and he nodded curtly before he ordered her to go. She was on her way out when his deep voice stopped her.

"Sally."

She turned. "Yes, Your Highness?"

He kept silent for long. And then, "You are a good girl, a loyal companion. I appreciate your selfless sacrifice. Chad is exactly like you. I know you both will have a good life."

"Thank you, Your Majesty." Her head riled as she walked away. Her selfless sacrifice? Could he be talking about that day she took her princess's place in the courtroom? That day the kings brutalized her? But why would he appreciate her for that day? Could it be that he'd felt relieved—even happy—that she took Danika's place?

Sally stopped outside the door and looked back at the door in puzzlement.

Could there be any chance—any chance at all—that the king had feelings for her princess?

It had been five days since Baski confirmed that Danika was still carrying the king's child inside her, and four days since the king had summoned Sally, but the time that passed did nothing to solve Danika's problem—to alleviate her worries.

Danika woke up in the morning of the sixth day feeling sick. One good thing about it was that she already knew her symptoms for what they were as she ran to the bathroom and disposed of her breakfast.

How would she tell the king about this child? What did she do? What if the mistress finds out? Five days hadn't given her an answer to those questions. She pushed it all to the back of her mind, wiping her mouth clean.

She had been avoiding the king, and every night, she went to bed with her heart in her throat, praying that the king would not summon her for the night. She missed him so much, and she craved to be in his arms so much it was almost physical pain. But a lot is at stake now and coupling with him was dangerous for her—for her baby.

"No, Danika," she muttered, shaking her head. "This isn't a day to think about this. It's a special day today."

"My princess! How do I look!?" Sally shouted happily as the door of the bathroom burst open and she waltzed inside.

Danika took one good look at her and a smile spread across her lips. "You look beautiful, Sally."

Sally whirled around, a big smile on her face. She was getting married to Chad today and Danika wanted this day to be so beautiful for her. She had been happiest when Sally narrated her confrontation with the king: the gift he gave her, setting her free, and also giving her a chance to work in the palace. Emotion had welled up in Danika and tears had filled her eyes. She was most happy. Sally deserved every happiness in the world, and she was determined to make sure that today remained so good for her.

Sally had always been so protective of her; it was Danika's turn to protect Sally and make sure her morning sickness did not ruin her day.

"Are you alright, my princess?" Sally asked worriedly, glancing at the breakfast Danika just disposed of.

Danika had tried to keep the knowledge of her pregnancy all to herself but was forced to tell her when Sally woke up in the middle of the night and caught her crying. She'd told Sally, who had been as horrified and as helpless as she was. She couldn't have done it these past few days without Sally's encouragements.

"Everything will be alright, my princess. You will be fine, my princess. Carrying a child is a blessing and not as evil as slave masters makes it look like. You will be fine, my princess."

"Yes, I'm fine. This dress really matches you and you look so good in it." She grinned at Sally, shoving her problem down.

The worry dissolve from Sally's face was replaced by a smile. "I know, right? Are you feeling queasy?"

189

"A little," she admitted. "But I'll be fine. Come on, let's get you ready for your wedding. You wouldn't want to be late."

She prayed that the creator would help her today. She had been feeling faint and dizzy a lot lately because of her condition, and she would be giving Sally away in front of a lot of people—even the king, if he would attend.

What if she felt dizzy during the ceremony? Or worse, what if she fainted?

Heavens, please, help me, Danika thought as she led Sally out of the bathroom.

.

CHAPTER 31. WOUNDS HEAL. SCARS DON'T.

Sally and Chad married in the local church, and many people attended. Danika was shocked that almost all of Salem came to witness their legal union. Mombana came, too, and for the first time in a long time, she saw the familiar face of most of her people.

Tears sprang to Danika's eyes when her people walked past her and bowed to her. Even when dressed in rags, they still recognize her as their princess.

And the king was there too. He was seated at the front with his guards behind him, and Chad's joy about his presence was clearly written on his face. He knew how busy the king's schedule was, so he knew the sacrifice the king made to be present on his special day.

Princess Kamara sat on the king's left side with a kind smile, and Vetta was seated by his right side, glaring at the church's door. That was where the bride and her handler stood.

Apparently, the mistress did not like weddings. But the way she was glaring at the door, you'd give it a second thought. Was it truly the wedding she didn't like or the bride's handler?

Danika stood beside Sally at the door of the church. Sally had no other family, so Danika acted as her handler who would give Sally away.

Sally wore a beautiful white extravagant ball gown and Danika in a red, less-extravagant gown. Both looked beautiful.

Sally had a bright smile that made her face radiant and glowing, but she was so nervous. Danika took her hand and smiled at her in

191

reassurance. She walked her down the aisle, and the wedding rituals began.

A lot of time passed before the old priest finally pronounced Sally and Chad man and wife. The couple's joy was so apparent it brought tears to Danika's eyes. So many things were urging tears to her eyes. Her Sally was getting married, and after today, Sally would no longer be here for her all the time because she was a married woman and her husband would come first. She would miss Sally so much.

And then, the love in their eyes. It was obvious that Chad loved Sally so much; the always-brooding guard wore a warm smile. If only the king would love her this way.

Her eyes darted towards the king at the opposite side of the church and widened when their gazes collided. He'd been watching her. His eyes pinned hers, and she didn't know why he had looked at her that way. She quickly averted her eyes, her heart racing. If only wishes were horses, she sighed dreamily.

But wishes weren't. The only man she loved so much was one man she could not have.

"We call on the bride's handler to give a little speech about the bride." The priest's voice jerked her back to the present.

All eyes turned to her.

Danika got up from her seat and took a step forward. Suddenly, her eyes blurred.

Oh, no! Creator, please not here! Not now! She took another step, and another wave of dizziness slammed her so much the world blurred around her.

Baski was sitting beside her and noticed when Danika almost lost her balance. The older woman stood immediately and went to Danika to hold and steady her. "You can't, Danika. Not here!" she whispered heatedly into Danika's ear.

"I feel so dizzy, Baski. I don't think I can make it to that altar," Danika replied, her fear apparent in her trembling voice.

"Holy Creator," Baski whispered under her breath.

Danika blinked hard and looked up. Everyone was watching her. They looked worried and confused about how she staggered to a stop in the middle of the aisle, and Baski held her. Danika's eyes darted towards the king. He was still watching her, but this time, his brows furrowed.

Baski raised her voice. "I apologize on behalf of the handler. As you all know, a week ago, she was beaten up badly in the market and has yet to recover fully."

The confusion cleared from most faces but guilt and sadness remained. Sally looked relieved by Baski's intervention and watched as Baski led her back to her seat.

The king's expression didn't change.

Danika sat down again and tried to level her breathing. The old priest continued other activities, jumping the parts that involved the handler. The wedding progressed from there until it was finally done. Danika felt guilty that she almost ruined things for Sally. Her face reflected her guilt when they came out of the church afterwards. She was hugging Sally and apologizing for almost ruining her day.

"No! Don't ever say a thing like that. My day is not ruined. I'm very happy that Madam Baski was able to cover it all up. I can't begin to imagine how disastrous it would have been if your condition had been found out so publicly. It would mean hell for you, my princess."

Danika sighed as she pulled back. "Those were my thoughts exactly, Sally."

"I'm so nervous about tonight, my princess," Sally confided nervously, her beautiful face with light makeup filled with uncertainty.

Danika took her hand in reassurance. "You don't have to be, Sally. You're going to be with a man you love. That basically means that everything will be fine."

"You're right; you're right." She took a deep breath and smiled anxiously.

"Oh, Sally, I'm going to miss you so much!" Danika hugged her again, emotion clouding her throat.

Sally closed her eyes, holding her tight. "I'll miss you too, my princess. I'm glad that you have Madam Baski and Remeta. If not, I don't know how I would have coped with leaving you all alone here! I'll still be working here, so I'll see you almost every day!"

They stayed that way for a while before they had to pull away.

Danika watched the king as he strode to his carriage. She picked up his stiff shoulders and the tension that radiated from his body even from afar. What changed? He had been so relaxed during the wedding. What happened to make him look that way?

Sally followed her eyes to see the king entering his carriage, ready to go back to the palace. Sally bit her lips at the hunger and longing on Danika's face. Her princess wore her deep love for the king on her face whenever she was looking at him. Sally wondered how no one else had been unable to notice. She was glad they hadn't. It would only mean more problem for her princess.

Sally bit her lips. "When will you tell him?"

Danika knew she meant the pregnancy. "I don't know, Sally," she answered truthfully. Just the thought of the king finding out had her belly tied in a knot.

"You can't hide it forever, my princess."

"I know, Sally, I know. But..." she waved her hands uncertainly, trying to explain her thoughts. In the end, she let her hands fall to her sides. "I'm too scared. I don't know how to go about it."

"Sir Declan had once talk about marriage to me, my king. I know he would be happy for me on this day if he were here."

King Lucien blinked hard and shook his head to get Chad's heartfelt words away from his mind, but the words kept whispering to him over and over again until he drew taut with tension like a drawn bow.

If only Declan were alive. Chad had made the innocent comment after his wedding while he was greeting and thanking the king for attending his special day. He'd clamped his mouth shut immediately after saying those words and apologized regretfully.

"Declan is not some forbidden topic just because he's dead. It's okay, Chad." Those were the words the king replied with. But the harm had been done. If only Declan were still alive. If any of his family were still alive.

He was all alone in the world. His mother, his father, his sister and then, his cousin. All killed by one monster.

But as the day progressed, those words tormented the king. Declan and his horrible death tormented him until he developed a pounding headache. His shoulders weighed heavily. Restlessness filled him. He had spent the rest of the day in court, and by evening, he was back in his chambers with a cold heart and a hard face.

He got behind his desk and unrolled a new scroll. He had to send a petition to the kingdom of Ijipt on the morning of the morrow.

Just then, the door opened and Baski entered. She took one look at him and her steps faltered. A huge frown marred his face, and tension came off him in waves. The frown wasn't unfamiliar, but there was something slightly different about it.

Cold. The raw coldness she hadn't seen on his face for a while was right there.

He spared her a glance and took in the wooden cup she carried. He said nothing, but his eyes asked the questions.

"I m-made you a tea for headache and relaxation, Your Highness." Baski forced herself to answer with a braveness she didn't feel.

He focused back on the scroll in front of him. "You know that those herbs do not work so well on me, Baski."

"I know, my king, but this one will definitely work." She began walking closer to him. "It's a new recipe I decide to try today." She offered it to him so expectantly.

The king paused and took the wooden cup from her then downed the contents in one swing of his arm.

Only the king would drink something so awfully bitter with such a cold straight face, Baski thought as she watched him sadly. She took the empty cup from him and stood, racked with indecision. She knew that something troubled him; something very terrible that must have caused such coldness and tension in him.

As Baski watched him uncertainly, she didn't know how to go about the reason she came. She'd wanted to find a way to tell him about Remeta's gift and foresightedness. Baski knew that if she could tell him all about her daughter and he believed her, that would be the first step of warming him up for the news of Danika's pregnancy— for the news that a woman is carrying his child. All that would be remaining for her would be to find a way to coax Remeta to come and talk to him about the child. This part she knew would not be easy because Remeta didn't talk until she was 'pushed' to by her gift.

She'd cross that bridge later. First things first.

Baski glanced at him again and tried to find a way to start, but he allowed his inked feather to drop suddenly. He looked up at her with cold blue eyes. "You can go, Baski. I want to be alone."

"Of course, Your Highness." She would try another day when his mood wasn't so black and scary. *Oh, whatever was going through that head of his?* Baski bowed to him and turned towards the door. She took two steps when he called her back.

"Baski." His voice was cold and hard.

"Yes, my king?" She turned expectantly.

"Tell Danika I summon her."

Fear and worry slid down her old spine. Summoning Danika in a mood like the one he could not be a good thing.

Baski thought fast. "Danika isn't around, my king. She---"

He only glanced up at her. He didn't say a word. He didn't have to. His chilling blue eyes said it all.

"I will find her, Your Highness," Baski whispered.

.

.

CHAPTER 32. MY MASTER. MY KING.

Sally and her husband arrived at their new house, and a feeling of excitement and peace was apparent in their expressions and how they looked at each other.

They held hands all the while since they were seated in the carriage, and now in the confinement of their new home, they were reluctant to let each other go.

They changed out of their wedding clothes and headed outside. Most of the day they spent lying at the beach, all cuddled up. They weren't strangers to being in each other's arms because that was how they had spent the last few months: always pressed together, always touching each other innocently. And now, they were married.

Sally had been nervous all day because of what tonight meant for them. But now, in his arms, she let nothing worry her. They talked about little things already used to talking with each other. They enjoyed the peace and quietness of the beach. The sound of water flowing before them and the warm touch of the evening air. It was beautiful.

Sally began noticing that her husband had grown silent with time. "Is anything the matter?" she whispered, her head on his chest, her finger trailing his parch of hair.

Chad looked down at his wife. He still could not believe that she was finally his. He did not deserve this woman, but he would look his blessings in the eyes. He could only make sure that this beautiful woman, who was a box of sunshine, wouldn't regret marrying him for the rest of their lives. Chad would make sure that she was always happy.

"I was too excited about our union. I'm afraid I must have said something to the king I shouldn't have," he admitted, stroking her soft auburn mass.

"Really?" She bit her lips in concern. "Is it something so bad? Is he mad at us?"

Chad shook his head, hating the sad concern on her face. "No, dear. He isn't mad at us, but it did put him in a sore mood. I just hope he'll be alright. The king had no one, and I have always been by his side for many years. I hope he'll be alright."

Sally had the same thought. Her princess had no one, and she had been with her for such a long time. She wished that Danika would be alright. "He is a strong man. He will be fine," Sally said, rubbing his chest in slight reassurance.

Chad nodded distractedly. He knew the kind of man the king was and it worried him. A damaged man in every aspect of that word, the king would rather push people away than let them get too close to him. Already, the former Princess Danika was working her way into the king's heart, and he was completely unaware of it. Chad wished it would not remain that way for long because it would be a rocky road when it dawned on the very stubborn broken man who had lost every single one in his life in a very brutal way that he was falling in love with the daughter of his nightmare creator.

Chad hoped that he wouldn't be hurting Danika and himself too much when that time came because if any man ever deserved to be happy, it was the king.

If any man deserved to laugh again, it was king Lucien.

Baski walked out of the king's bedroom with her heart in her throat. This summon filled her with dread.

She walked to Danika's bedroom and saw her lying down on the bed, her breathing evened out. She knew that she was sleeping even before she walked towards and saw her closed eyes. Even in sleep, lines of worry marred Danika's face. Baski knew that the poor girl was more stressed lately with everything she was going through. And now this…

She touched Danika gently. "Danika, dear you have to wake up."

Danika mumbled incoherently and settled back to sleep.

"The king summons you, Danika."

Her eyes snapped open and she sprang up from the bed with so much force, her head spun.

Baski held her. "Easy, easy…"

Danika fixed her with a worried gaze. "For what? Do you know why, Madam Baski?"

The older woman shook her head. "I don't know, Danika. But he's not in a good mood at all."

All the blood drained from Danika's face. "Do you think it has something to do with what happened in the church today? Or…" she swallowed tightly. "Or he's going to want to…"

"I don't know, Danika, but there's every possibility that he's going to want to draw sexual pleasures from your body." She shook her head miserably. "That is not a good idea, Danika. And with the way he is now, I fear for you."

Danika's heart flew away from her chest. "Is his mood that bad?"

Baski nodded calmly.

She swallowed tightly and stared down at her hands. Danika had dreaded this constantly for the past few days; she had worried herself sick. She missed being in his arms, but not like that. It was downright terrifying.

"What do I do, Baski? I think I'm about to die from panic." Her voice trembled as she looked at the older woman helplessly.

"Here…" Baski pulled her to sit towards the edge of the bed. "Wait right here for me. I'll be right back."

Danika nodded and watched Baski as she hurried out of the room. She wrapped her arms around herself, suddenly feeling cold. The king summoned her and he wasn't in a good mood.

Oh, whatever was it that blackened his mood? she asked herself worriedly. If it had anything to do with the things her father did, then she really had something to worry about.

The door opened again, and Baski entered with a small, wrapped ball like a small stone and some gel. "I read about this herbal seed so many years ago when I was young and still learning herbs from my grandma. One of her herbal old books had words about this seed in its pages," she began. "They say it keeps a baby in the womb firm and healthy even during hard times...like the mama had an accident or something. I don't really know because I don't read so well, but we don't have much of an option. I harvested the seeds after I found out that you were pregnant. Just in case."

Danika bit her lips, staring at the weird-looking seed. "Do you think it will work?"

Baski looked unsure. "I don't really know, Danika, but I can't just send you to the lion's den unprepared."

"I'm scared, Madam Baski."

Baski took her hand into hers and squeezed lightly. "You'll be fine, my dear. You're Danika and you've always been strong and brave. All my life, I've seen the worst kind of slavery, and yet most of us are able to give birth during the worst kind of it all. Back in Mombana, I knew a few women who the guards molested every single day, even when they got pregnant. Some were subjected to very hard labour. A few of them were able to give birth to that strong child, too, and come out healthy." Baski smiled at her in reassurance.

"A few?" Danika could only mumble, her throat dry like sandpaper.

"We go through a lot, Danika. Slaves. Most of them couldn't survive." Her voice took on a sad note.

"How is that supposed to be an encouragement, Madam Baski?" Danika cried out.

"Oh!" The older woman flushed guiltily. "Um, well, let's see..." She seemed to be in thought for a few seconds. Then her eyes brightened. "The king is...quite partial to you, and you love him so much. Surely, that will help a lot. You'll be fine, Danika."

Danika took a deep breath; she didn't even need to ask how Baski knew that she loved the king because she had a bigger problem to worry about. However, surprisingly, Baski's encouragement worked. Not really much of the words, but because she was really trying to encourage her. Danika knew that if anything went wrong, Baski would be there for her.

Another deep breath. Danika took the seed from Baski and threw it down her throat. The older woman gave her water and she washed it down. Then Baski gave her a small bottle of gel. Danika took it from her, murmuring her gratitude, and opened it. Her confusion was apparent as she glanced up at Baski for explanation.

Baski's wrinkled cheeks flushed a little. "Vetta once referred to the king as a no-preamble man. Just in case...um, you have to be prepared."

Danika would have refuted the mistress's notion, but she was too worked up to try. Indeed, the king was not big on foreplay, and he didn't like to be touched, but he was different with her. That gave her a pause. He was different with her. Surely, everything would be alright. That, more than anything, calmed her.

She took the gel from Baski, entered the bathroom and used it then came out a minute later and walked towards the door.

"Danika?"

She turned at the sound of Baski's voice. "Hm?"

Baski hesitated. "The king is a very damaged man. He might look well on the outside, but he is broken on the inside. He needs help, but he is not a man that will allow it."

Danika knew all that, but hearing Baski say it squeezed her heart in her chest.

The older woman smiled sadly, wet her lips and continued. "Do you know that sometimes, when he takes so much time to reply words or give commands, I think it's because he's trying to hear the words above the ones in his head? His head is a war zone."

"Madam Baski---" Danika began.

But she walked closer and took Danika's hands again into her older ones. "So, please, be patient with him, okay? Don't struggle. Don't fight him. If any woman can reach him and draw him out of the abyss, it's you. You have done it before. I have complete faith in you."

Danika smiled nervously. The thought of the king hurting did not settle well with her. She nodded. "Alright, Baski."

Stepping back, Baski severed contact. "Go, now. And hurry. Keeping him waiting will only put him in a worse mood. Getting all worked up in that calm way of his. Not good for you."

Danika nodded again and walked away towards the king's quarters. With each step she took, the hammer in her chest beat louder and harder.

She reached his door and knocked on it so hesitantly, her heart pounding.

She waited for his command. The wait was killing her.

"Enter," his deep voice came.

She shivered. She could feel the hardness and coldness of it even with a closed door between them.

Calm down, Danika. Calm down. At this rate you'll panic yourself to death right here before you even stand before him. She opened the door and entered, locking the door behind her. She took a step inside and stopped.

Baski was right. He was in a very black mood. The worst kind.

The man who was seated behind the desk without sparing her a glance—whose whole attention was focused on the scroll in front of him—wasn't the King Lucien that took her out for an evening walk and gave her memories she'd never forget. The large, formidable figure that began folding his well-written scrolls into a neat roll in front of her, wasn't the man that visited her sick bed and stood for hours watching her sleep. He wasn't the man that held her in his arms and kissed her senseless and held her all night.

No. The man in front of her was her master. The man that hated her and drips with his loath for her father. The man that took her virginity.

He is my master, not my king.

He raised cold chilling eyes to her and uttered only one word.

"Strip."

.

202

CHAPTER 33. TROUBLED MIND. BROKEN SOUL. ESCAPE.

The word sent a chill down Danika's spine, shredding her heart right out of her chest. This was truly not the man she had been with recently, and she didn't know what happened. She didn't know how to reach him—how to reach her king and not her master. Fear gripped her, but she was determined to try.

"My k--" she began, only to cut off suddenly when his cold eyes glared at her. *Do not dare.* Those eyes said the words his mouth didn't.

"Strip," he repeated, putting the scroll away.

Danika's heart beat wildly as she raised her shaky hands and began undressing. What happened to him? What went wrong? During the wedding, he was cool and refined—his usual self lately. Something must have happened after the wedding to tick him off. Or was it about the past?

Untying the ropes of her chemise, Danika let it drop to the ground and stepped out of it. The sound of the king's chair pulling back was unusually loud in the room as he stood.

He looked wild. Fierce. Animalistic. Angry.

Chilling blue eyes—eyes she had not seen in a long time—pinned her as he began striding towards her. She'd pulled off her garter and stepped out of it, too, left in her cotton underthings. He didn't give her the time to pull them off. Instead, he grabbed hold of her arm and pulled her back, twisting her almost immediately until Danika suddenly saw herself pressing face-front to the wall. She shot out her arms immediately to either side of her to steady herself and prevent from colliding with the wall. He came up behind her almost immediately. She felt his breath to her ear.

"Please," she gasped, trying to tap down her terror. "Please, calm down, Your Highness."

A large hand circled her neck, and she froze up, expecting him to choke her. Relief coursed through her when his hand lowered. But her relief was short-lived because he wasn't dropping his hand. Instead, he circled the button of her collar.

She had never forgotten the cold metal around her neck that branded her as his slave. A collar-shock in her condition would kill her. Terror closed up Danika's throat, and she began shaking her head vigorously. "Please, please, not the collar. Please, don't press it!"

"I'm your master. I am not your king." His voice was positively animalistic—so deep it was a growl.

The king Lucien Danika had come to know lately was not in there anymore. Tears filled her eyes. "Yes. Master." The whispered words left a bitter taste in her mouth.

He caressed her collar button for a few more seconds then dropped his hand to her waist. The relief made her tremble, but the fear remained. His body drawn taut felt like stone behind her back as he pressed close to her. Danika gasped when she felt his massive erection on her lower back, thick and hard poking her. But only for a second.

The next second, he pulled back a bit, and with one firm yank of his hand, he tore her chemise from her body. Her breasts spilled out. Another yank of his hand tore the cotton trousers that covered her lower body, leaving her completely naked before him. The swift and rough way he handled her had her almost hyperventilating with panic. And, for the first time since she became a slave, she found herself struggling to be free from him.

His muscular strength and powerful exertion scared her. If he touched her that way, he'd hurt her very badly. Her mind registered and it only made her struggle all the more.

Oh, Creator! Whatever is wrong with him!?

But the more she struggled, the rougher he became. Caging her with his arms, a groan emitted from his throat when he had her easily confined.

"Please. Oh, please. I'm pregnant," she whimpered, tears welling in her eyes. The words tore from her throat before she could hold them in. Her head no longer worked; she had not known the words she uttered. But whatever her words were, it didn't seem to get to him. To stop him. Whatever it was she was saying wasn't working at all.

The ruffle of clothes registered distantly through the roaring on her ears. She tried to think through her fear. She needed to think. She feels like she was missing something important, but her mind was too clouded to think clearly—

His bare hardness pressed against her back, and it dawned on her that he wouldn't be touching her intimately or preparing her body. She struggled more frantically.

"Please stop, you'll hurt me! You'll hurt our child! Please, I'm pregnant!" her whimpers were louder as she tried all her might to be free of him, but her strength was nothing compared to his.

He wasn't hearing her. The more she tried, the rougher he became. It was as if he became more of an animal the more she tried to break free. As if he didn't want to let her go.

He gripped her tight like he life depended on holding her close to him. His leg kicked hers apart, his large hand gripped her thigh and lifted one of her legs baring her open for him.

******

King Lucien's demons had completely taken over him. He was dragged down deep into the abyss; he couldn't see or hear anything. Demons of his past. His memories. His parent's death. His cousin's death. His pregnant sister's death right here behind him in his library. Her screams as she called to him and he couldn't answer. Her lifeless tear-filled eyes as she gazed into space, dead.

Screams. So many screams.

Children being raped. Men being whipped. Declan's roars. Vetta's screams. Baski's cries. Remeta's pain-filled shrieks. Chad's howls as he was brutally raped. Cone's devilish laughter. The smell of death. The lifeless eyes.

So many voices. Calling out to him for help.

So many voices in his head. He couldn't help!

They called to him as they died. As they took their last breath, they begged their king to save them.

He couldn't. They all died. Declan died. And it was all his fault.

Screams in his heart.

Screams in his head.

So many screams.

Escape! *Escape!! ESCAPE!!!*

He needed to escape from them. To get away. To make them stop.

They overpowered him. Overwhelmed him. His head was filled with screams and shouts.

But he put his hand on her and it got better. Whoever she was, she made the screams louder and restless. Uncomfortable. He had to keep her close. He had to keep her close. *Not letting go!* He could not think past the roaring in his ears. He couldn't think past burying himself inside the soft flesh caged before him.

She kept saying something to him but he couldn't hear her. He could not hear past the roaring in his ears.

She smelled so good and he wanted her so much. To devour her. Bury himself so deep inside her until nothing separated them. To dominate her body completely. To own her. Until he could not think of anything else but her. Until he could forget everything else but her.

She. Is. Mine.

Baski was as restless as a husband whose wife was in the hands of the midwives. She couldn't sit still, so she got up and began pacing around.

She didn't know how long had passed, but she couldn't bear staying in Danika's bedroom anymore. She walked out and went in search of her daughter. Who knew? Her daughter might already be 'pushed' into foresight, and she might be able to tell her a thing or two about the big situation at hand.

Baski walked towards the backyard but couldn't find Remeta. She went to the river to see if her child had chased her crickets to that part of the kingdom, but she still couldn't find Remeta.

In the end, she went back to the palace building. Entering inside, Baski walked to her bedroom and opened the door. Remeta's back was to her as she stood before the bed, her dyed-red hair asleep and beautiful behind her back, resting just before her waist.

"Remeta! There you are. I've been looking all over for you!" Baski said as she entered and closed the door.

Remeta turned towards her mother at the sound of her voice. There were tears in her eyes and all over her cheeks.

Panic and relief filled Baski's bones. Panic because of her tears and relief because she was foreseeing something. She grabbed hold of Remeta's arms and shook her slightly. "What is it, Remeta!? Tell me what it is!" The answer Baski got was more tears rolling down her eyes. Eyes that stared right at her but weren't really seeing her. "Remeta!" She shook her desperately, "This is not a time to keep quiet!"

Remeta sniffled and remained silent.

"Alright, that's it." Baski got up with a new purpose. She was going to the king's chambers to get Danika out. She had no idea how she'd achieve that, but that wasn't what her mind was thinking about at the moment. She had to save that pregnant girl who had already had so many complications at such early stage of her condition!

Getting up, Baski pulled away from Remeta and hurried to the door. A hand grabbed her. She turned to see Remeta clutching her tightly.

"It's too late. Don't," Remeta whispered hoarsely.

"No, I have to---"

Remeta began rambling in a low voice. "You can't take them from him. You can't take them from him. Don't take them from him. He won't let you. He won't let anyone. You can't take them from him. If you take them from him, what will happen to him? He needs her. He needs them. He's hurt. Gone. Mad. *Hurt. Hurt. Hurt.*"

Baski turned towards her daughter completely, trying to make sense of the things she was saying. Remeta was saying she shouldn't take them away from the king? Danika and her unborn child? She knelt before her daughter, who was already trembling and crying softly. She tried to know if Remeta could say more for her to understand. "Remeta? My baby? I don't understand."

A full minute passed in tense silence that was only interrupted by the sound of her sniffles and soft cries. And Baski's loud heartbeats. Then Remeta looked her mother dead in the eyes with the saddest eyes Baski had ever seen. "It's not his fault. He is hurting badly, Mama. We're losing him. He had been fighting for five years, but every man has a breaking point. She is the only one that can help him."

"Danika?" Baski's breath caught in her throat. Fear sizzled down her spine.

She nodded once. "We can only hope that she reaches him on time. Or he will hurt her badly. And we will lose him completely."

.
.

CHAPTER 34. ANIMALISTIC INSTINCTS.

Escape! Escape!! Escape!!!

He had to keep her close. He had to keep her close! Not letting go!

King Lucien could not think past those animalistic urges that beat down on his head. Could not hear past them.

She struggled against him. It angered him that she was trying to get away from him. She was not leaving like his sister did! Not like Declan did! He'd do everything to keep her close!

Never! She was not getting away! He was not letting her go!

He palmed her thigh and lifted her leg, baring her to him. Pure animalistic instincts rode him so hard he was shaking with the urge to bury himself deep inside the soft flesh he caged before him. Positioning himself blindly, he bumped against her, but her body restricted his invasion. An animalistic growl tore from his throat and he tightened his hand on her waist and on her thigh.

"Take. Me. In!" The deep guttural growl tore from him as he nudged her opening with his dick again more roughly and urgently. He breached her a bit, shoving the head of his erection into her.

Danika cried out, the pain rolling off her in waves. It had been so long since he'd taking intimate pleasures from her body, and she'd tried to prepare herself like Baski instructed her, but she wasn't able to achieve that because the finger she'd gently put inside herself had hurt. She had given up after a few attempts.

Her lean dainty finger was nothing compared to the king's hardness. Absolutely nothing.

209

"Oh, Creator! P-please! Please!" She struggled blindly to pull free from him, unable to think of anything else at that moment.

Another savage growl emitted from his throat and his hand on her waist tightened to iron grip. He withdrew jerkily, spread her wider for him and slammed into her again with so much force he breeched her body and buried himself to the hilt.

A scream tore through the air that sounded very distant to his roaring ears and her spine arched under his onslaught of savage greed. He pulled back almost immediately and thrust harder again. And again and again.

Danika felt *pierced*. She burned from the inside—a very intense painful burn. She screamed again and cried out against the very uncomfortable feeling as he plummeted her body over and over again. With each thrust, he tried to go deeper like he wanted to brand them together. Like he wanted to glue her to him so that nothing separated them ever again.

"Not...letting... go!" He thrusted with each word, harder and harder, his body coming over hers completely.

She laid her head on the wall in front of her, yelping with each stroke he took inside her. She felt like she was sandwiched between two hard walls. The tension that emitted from the king's taut body was too much, and as he took her body so roughly, she felt as if he was owning her soul too. Animalistic growls of pleasure left his throat with each thrust, his head pressed to her neck, his breathing erratic. Tears licked from her eyes, her forehead pressed to the wall. Her leg—the one that met the floor—was trembling, unable to hold her. Whimpers after whimpers tore from her throat.

His hand shot to her hair, and he grabbed hold of it and gripped it tightly. Danika stopped breathing. Her body tensed up and her eyes snapped close as she tried to prepare herself for the searing pain she knew would come when yanked on her hair.

She waited, but he didn't yank on it. Instead, he only held on as he kept plunging in and out of her. Relief crashed through her that he wasn't pulling on her hair. Her king might not be in there, but whoever was behind her wasn't intent on inflicting blatant physical pain. No, he was only intent on possessing her with his body like he wanted to brand himself in her. Like he owned her.

He was gripping her so tightly and so close like he was afraid of letting her go—like he was afraid of her leaving him.

The way his family left him. The voice ghosted inside her, startling her.

Suddenly, Danika remembered Baski's words. *"Please, be patient with him, okay? Don't struggle. Don't fight him. If any woman can reach him and draw him out of the abyss, it's you."*

Could this be what Baski was talking about? Was he truly holding her that way because he was afraid that she'd leave him like his family did? Could she truly reach him?

Danika squeezed her eyes shut, and the fight suddenly went out of her. She stopped struggling and melted into his hard body. Her eyes closed, her head tilted in surrender, and she gave herself to him and waited, her heart pounding.

He kept plummeting her body roughly. His hand let go of her hair and grabbed hold of her breast, which he squeezed roughly. Her fear skyrocketed, and the need to struggle threatened to overwhelm her. She forcefully shoved it down and shut her mind to it. Instead, she only arched back into him.

It went on and on. A low growl—more like a vibration—emitted from his chest behind her, like a hungry panther. Suddenly, she felt some of the hard tension leave him. He didn't loosen her hand, but his strokes lessened somewhat. It gave her hope and courage to take the next step. She reached behind her and touched him for the first time. She caressed his bare hips tentatively—like a person soothing an angry lion—half expecting him to snatch away her hand or did anything physical to hurt her.

He stiffened. A shudder worked through his body.

She didn't stop.

A soft hand touching him hesitatingly penetrated his drunk haze. So soft, and oh so soothing.

It reminded him of when he was a young lad on his mother's knees. His mother would read to him and teach him how to do math. She would praise him and pat the soft curls of his head when he did things right.

211

The small hand that caressed his thigh, and now his hair, was like a soothing balm to his wounded soul. To his head raving mad.

One by one, his demons began receding. One by one, the dark memories began fading. They loosened their fierce hold on him. Only a bit.

For the first time, he became aware of his surroundings. Of the soft trembling body he pinned to the wall, thrusting savagely and hungrily into her.

Danika.

He loosened his hold on her breast, but his control was still shot to dust. He only slowed his strokes, but he didn't stop. He couldn't. He pressed his sweaty head to the side of her face. "Danika?" he breathed for the first time.

Relief was like a river flowing inside Danika. She didn't stop touching him or caressing his hair. Running her hand up and down his hipbone, she whispered, "My king."

"I... can't... stop..." His deep groan vibrated her ear. "I need you."

Danika closed her eyes and those three words washed over her. It was the first time he had ever said words like that to her. He didn't tell her he wanted her. He *needed* her.

Suddenly, a rush of power and love filled her and made her swell with it. This man who she loved so deeply; this man who was so powerful, who had never needed anybody, needed her.

Her head rolled back to his chest, and her fingers held on to his hip and the back of his head. Her love for him was so pure and deep, she gave herself completely to him.

"Then take me. Take anything you want. Take everything you need," she whispered hoarsely.

A deep shudder worked through his body. He buried his face to her neck and inhaled deeply, causing her to shiver.

"Danika?" He sounded unsure. His deep voice was barely a hot breath to her neck.

His hand left her breast and held her belly, pressing her closer to him. He run his hand up and down her smooth flat abdomen, his breath puffing out hotly on her shoulder. Even without his awareness, he held their child in his grasp.

"It's okay. It's alright. I'm right here. With you. For you. It's okay. I'm not going away. I'm right here. I'm not leaving. It's okay." Those whispered words spilled from her lips unrestrained. She had no idea where her consent—her words—would take them, but none of that mattered to her anymore.

Not minding how tightly he held her, how savage his thrusts were, she knew that she'd wear his bruises for days to come, but she kept her body molded to him and held on tightly to him.

He pulled out of her then and turned her around. She faced him, and he closed in on her. She wrapped her arms trustingly around his neck. He lifted her and wrapped her legs around him. He plunged back in, his thick dick pressed deeper and his body smothered hers.

He thrust once, gritting his teeth. "I can't be slow. Don't ask me to be slow."

Danika nodded, stroking his back, thrilling with fear and want. And a deep need to soothe. "Take me however you need." As she uttered those words, she closed her eyes and prayed to the creator to protect her child—their child that nestled inside her.

In that moment, all her fierce protectiveness rounded and centered on the father of her baby. She left the rest to the creator— or whoever up there that was listening to her prayer. Whoever up there saw the impossibility of her situation. That saw how much she loved this man who held her body plastered to his.

This man—who seemed to be battling what another man would never have survived—became her main priority.

.

.

.

CHAPTER 35. THE KING'S HEART.

Is body slammed into her once, twice. He switched from barely-human back to animal. He let go of everything. His hips pulled back before colliding with hers with a ferocity that echoed in her heart. Everything about him switched to possessive greed.

His face shut down. Lips pursed. Sweat beaded.

"Danika," he growled, driving into her. He repeated her name like it was a lifeline and he was hanging on to it. Like he needed the reminder that it was her to hold onto sanity.

Every stroke of his phallus claimed ownership, and she closed her eyes and let him steal her away. Nothing else existed but him inside her and his hard heat surrounding her. She locked her legs tighter, pulling him achingly deep. He bumped her cervix and she yelped.

Her eyes watered. The pain was out of the world. She pulled back immediately and dislodged him a bit. His mouth latched onto her neck, sucking, biting. Sparks of gold and silver whizzed in her blood, intoxicating her—making her body come alive in his arms.

"Yes. Take me," she panted as King Lucien drove violently into her. Every thrust he lost himself until she didn't know which man she held in her arms—her master or her king.

Her buttocks rammed on the wall as he took everything he had to offer. He was right. It wasn't gentle. It wasn't sweet. It was dirty and cruel and broken. But she took it all.

His hands landed on her hips, holding her in place as he increased his rhythm. His face twisted until he looked furiously angry. Her heart no longer beat—it hummed like a hummingbird as every thrust unlocked a power deep inside her. A power over that man. Over her fate. Over her sadness and happiness and future.

"Danika," he kept repeating.

Love swelled like a typhoon in her chest, evolving, growing until it filled every space and cavity. She visualized love protecting the new life inside her—spreading to King Lucien and healing him. It kept growing until her body had no more space and it exploded out of her, showering them both in emotion.

"I—I can't stop." He reared back, his face shiny with sweat. "I'm hurting you." His eyes were wild, skin ashen. "Make me stop. Make me to stop." His teeth gritted as he drove particularly hard into her.

As if she ever could. Her feelings for him were stark in her eyes. Their child nestled right between them.

She was so close to falling over the precipice of a release she felt was profound.

This was between her and him.

Life and death.

Possession and ownership.

She threw her head back. "You're not hurting me. I..."*I love you; I love you, I'm pregnant for you, I'm carrying your child, I love you, I love you so much!*"I trust you."

He groaned, increasing his rhythm until she felt sure she'd snap in two. His guttural moan vibrated through his chest as the first ripple of need travelled down his dick, massaging her with the fierceness of his impending orgasm. Her body clenched, tightened, and wound, taking her out of that stratosphere and placing her on a shooting star—a comet where everything was happy and perfect and there was no tragedy or sadness. No memories. No slavery. No pain.

Grief tried to steal her from his embrace and she clamped her eyes shut, focusing only on his heat and vitality.

Danika wrapped her arms around his shoulders, dragging him close against her. He moaned as his entire body went bow-string tight. He pulled her away from the wall, lowered them to the floor and landed on top of her. His hands went to either side of her head, his hips positioned as she held on, never letting him go. Their breathing mingled, panting out of control.

Every stroke was delicious; every motion sent her higher up the mountain of claiming the most incredible orgasm of her life. She relished in the fierceness of him, the absolute ownership of his body on top of her.

Full body contact. Something completely new.

She loved hugging him.

She loved being blanketed by him.

The first spindle and body-shivering band of her release teetered just out of reach. Danika's dug nails into his ass, curving into him, meeting his every thrust. He cried out with all the torture in the world—lost in whatever mind-warp he suffered.

"I—I need you so much," he snapped, violence tinging every part of him.

That was all she needed. The knowledge he needed her gave her the strength to brave the unknown future. Gave her the courage to keep loving this broken man.

Danika came with a loud wail. She unraveled and combusted all in one go. The orgasm wasn't just in her wet sheath; it existed in every blood cell, in every breath she took, in every part of her. On and on the waves rolled, mimicking the crashing surf of the river down the palace. She cried his name repeatedly, bulking under him.

His mouth found hers then in a battle of lips. His mouth devoured hers, stealing her breath completely.

Danika felt complete. She hadn't even known a lot was missing until he gave her everything he was. Until he lost himself completely and had to find himself again in her arms. She'd never be free of him, just like he'd never be free of her. She knew this with every fiber of her being.

She cried out as the contractions of her release squeezed around his dick. He shivered and thrust harder. And again.

King Lucien came apart.

His thrusts lost uniformity, driving relentlessly, seeking pleasure, seeking a release.

His orgasm tore down his back, rippling like a powerful wave over his muscles. He spurted deep inside, splash after splash.

Her release kept going, intensifying as their life mingled. She found, for one brief second, eternal happiness.

Gradually, he slowed before coming to a gentle rock. Then he collapsed on her, going completely still.

But Danika's breath wouldn't slow. No matter how much she tried to catch her breath, it wouldn't slow down. She gulped in air in large quantity, her gasp filling the air. She panted heavily, her chest rising and falling rapidly. She panted and panted. Her head was spinning, and the world blurred around her. *And tilted.*

Yet, she still held him.

The world closed in on her. She came dangerously close to passing out. And she still gulped in air.

She gripped her neck as if she was trying to loosen whatever was clenching her neck and cutting off her breath. Her other hand, she placed on his soft curls, unconsciously patting him soothingly.

King Lucien opened his eyes and took in his environment. He was in his chambers. He felt disoriented and very tired.

More importantly, he noticed the soft body beneath him and the quick rise and fall of her chest, the panting sounds as she tried to drag in breath.

Danika watched the king through blurry eyes as he looked down on her, his sweaty brows knitted and creased with concern.

"Are you alright, Danika?" he asked, his hand touching her forehead.

"Can't...catch...my...breath!" she gasped.

"I will send for the medicine man---"

"No!" She grabbed hold of his arm, still panting. The medicine man would find out that she was pregnant even before she was able to find a way to tell the king.

His eyes touched her body, examining it. Pain and regret flashed in his eyes, but he blinked and it was gone. The warm glow and tiredness from what he had been through—and what they just did—remained in their wake. He lowered his head to hers and kissed her forehead. "You're alright, Danika. It's okay. Try to take a deep breath. Not short breaths. Try to take in a lot of breath, hold it for a second and breath out."

Danika closed her eyes and blindly followed his soft commands. She did as he instructed her.

"That's it. That's it," he added, then he dipped his head and took her lips into his. He wasn't kissing her. Instead, he gave her air.

Breathing in deeply, he released it gently into her mouth. He did it repeatedly until she felt so much better.

Danika's eyes watered at the intimacy. Somehow, this—what he did right then—felt more intimate than his kisses. And his kisses had always been intimate.

"I'm better now," she whispered, at the same time wishing he wouldn't stop, but she already had too much air.

He pulled back and looked at her again to confirm. Danika began dreading that he'd get up and go back to doing one of his kingly activities. She wanted him lying down right here on the floor of his chambers. She wanted him to be with her, even for a few note minutes.

He pulled away from her body completely, but he didn't leave. Instead, he laid down on the floor beside her and placed his head in between her breasts. Her arms felt like water, but she was able to raise them and wrap them around his head. They cuddled that way. They listened to the sound of their breathings. Allowing the silence between them to stretch, it was a comfortable silence where the king tried to remember the details of what just happened, and Danika tried to suppress the feeling of worry for her child.

What was done, was done. At least if she lost the baby, it would save her from all the stress and worry about the king finding out, she tried to console herself.

She concentrated on the feeling of the king's head in between her breasts. His hand was caressing her skin the same way hers did to his head. They almost seem like real couples, Danika thought with an inner sad smile. She closed her eyes to enjoy the moment.

"Thank you, Danika." His deep voice broke the silence at last.

Her eyes opened and she looked down at him. He turned towards her, his eyes on her face. He looked like a better version of her king because he looked more relaxed than she had ever seen him.

"I scared you. Then I took you so savagely. Already some parts of your body where I gripped you are turning red," he said to her.

If only her body was her biggest problem. Her external comfortlessness, bruises and body was the least of her problems. The thoughts that she'd be saying goodbye to the life inside her was the main source of her problem.

"I'm fine," she whispered, giving a small smile to emphasize that notion.

He laid his head back on her body, listening to sound of her breathing. What happened a few minutes ago still shook him. How he had lost it. He'd needed her badly. Never wanted to let her go. He could still remember how overwhelming it had all been. He never needed anybody the way he'd needed her few minutes ago.

And she'd been there. She was right there. And she never left.

He'd scared her. He'd hurt her severally and the thought did not sit well with him. She was choked to her throat with terror and the need to escape him. And yet, she didn't. She gave herself completely to him. Touching him. Urging him on. Caring for him. He closed his eyes and the feeling washed over him. For the first time since his father died, he felt connected to another person. She never let him go. And, for the first time in his life, he was willing to keep that connection. To fully give out his trust to her. She would never betray him. Or leave him.

A cherished memory prickled his head. He found himself opening his mouth to talk about it. "When I was a lad, my father was very strict when teaching me everything about being a good prince."

Danika released her breath softly and listened attentively. She couldn't resist touching him, and she didn't. She whirled her fingers around his earlobes, slid it down to the stubble parch of his cheek and rested it there.

"He would teach me how to shoot an arrow. How to hunt and to fish. How to make decisions in court. My father said that the strongest king is the king of his people, not the king for his people." His eyed her plump breast with interest as he spoke. "After every learnings from him, I always felt bombarded and overwhelmed. I would run to my mother's chambers and fight with Melia about who would get the favourite spot to sit and listen stories. In the end, we would sit anywhere, and she always read to us. Told us lots of stories. As a child, she was my escape. After every tough day, I would go to her and she would make it all go away." He swallowed tightly. "And then, one day, she was no longer there."

Danika didn't stop touching him. He pulled closer to the crook of her arm so that her breasts became a breath away from his face.

"I'm sorry," she breathed, not knowing what else to say.

He peaked out his tongue and licked her nipple twice. "It was difficult because I had to suddenly resume responsibility of so many people because my parents died, and still I failed them all. We ended up in slavery and experienced hell for ten years. Ten horrible years that lives at the back of my head, tormenting me all the time."

The way he paused in between few words told Danika how difficult it was for him to talk about, and yet he was telling her all about it so effortlessly.

He wrapped his mouth around her nipple and suckled in soft tugs, and a shiver worked down her spine. He was fixated on her breasts to distract himself from his revelations.

One arm around his neck, and the other obsessed with his face, Danika held him like a woman would hold a child who nurses on his mother's breasts.

He let go of her nub with an inaudible pop and his eyes found hers. "I made Declan a promise that I would get him out of that hellhole. I failed to keep that promise and it haunts me. I held on to Declan like a lifeline because he was the last of my relatives. The only person I had left." Blue eyes fluttered closed and he pulled her back into his mouth, sucking with more urgency this time around, causing her to grimace. Her breasts were bigger and more sensitive.

He released her puckered nub reluctantly and began playing with them. "His death was not an easy one. I don't think I can ever get over it."

Emotion welled inside Danika that he'd open up to her like this. She swallowed down the lump on her throat. "Death of a loved one is never easy to get over, but we have to keep trying. That is because we're alive, and we have to survive and keep our head above the waters." She paused and debated if she should say the next thing on her mind. Would it upset him? She took a blind leap at it. "When my father died, I mourned him. He was never really a father to me, but he was all I had. That was before I found out how animalistic he was. That was before I found out that he was a monster who never loved anyone but himself. I don't have anyone but Sally. And she keeps me going. Now she's married." Her throat closed up and she blinked hard to keep the tears. Her friend was married and she was happy.

He swiveled his head, pulling his attention away from her breast, and looked at her beautiful face laced with languid exhaustion. King Lucien liked being this close to her. Maybe, just maybe, he could take a chance. Maybe, just maybe, he could try to let one more person in—someone who would not ever betray him. Someone who he could give more of his trusts. Someone who would never leave him.

"Promise me, Danika," he whispered hoarsely.

"What, my king?"

"Promise me that you will never betray me. Promise me that you will never break my trust." His voice took on a hard edge.

Danika swallowed. This was the second time he had said those words to her. They sent a shiver down her spine. "I promise," she vowed in a low voice.

"Promise me." He buried his face in her neck. "Promise me you'll never leave my side."

The vulnerability he showed her shocked her so much. She could not imagine how difficult those last words must have been to come from a hard and powerful man like him.

Her throat cloaked up, but she whispered hoarsely, "I promise."

He looked up at her. Warmth filled his eyes for the first time in years. He lowered his head again and kissed a small bruise on her neck. "I will never forgive you if you break any of those promises, Danika," he stated softly but vehemently.

"I will never forgive myself either." She would never betray this man. Why would she ever betray him?

A man who had known more heartbreaks and emotional suffering than all the slaves in the whole twelve kingdoms, why would she ever betray him?

He took a deep breath, licking her neck. Silence descended.

Can I tell him about my pregnant now? Danika thought.

Just the thought had her heart in her throat. She opened her mouth, "I... I... I'm..."

He raised his head and looked at her. "What is it?"

She swallowed tightly, "I'm... I'm... I'm pr...." But the words caught on her throat.

"What if I get pregnant?" she blurted out.

He stiffened all over. One moment he felt like a man, and next, he felt like stone beside her.

The silence that followed was nerve-wracking.

Then, "You should never worry about that. I have never given you to another man. I have never shared you before, and I do not have plans to share you with anybody." He looked her dead in the eyes. "So, that is not possible, Danika. That, I can assure you."

.

.

CHAPTER 36. BARING HIS HEART.

Baski couldn't sleep; she worried herself sick. How was Danika doing? What was going on in that bedroom? Would the child be alright? She was standing at the window, almost sick with worry. She'd heard Danika's screams, and since then, her heart refused to leave her throat.

Baski made the decision already. On the morn of the morrow, she would do everything within her power to get a good duration of time with the king—to explain about Remeta's gift. If he knew and believes in Remeta's gift, all that would remain would be to get Remeta to go to him and break the news to him. It was their best chance of telling the king about Danika's pregnancy without endangering Danika and her child. On the morrow, she must find the courage to talk to him.

But for tonight. What was happening in that room? She worried herself.

"Stop worrying, Mama. Come to bed. I feel scared," Remeta's sleepy voice came to her.

She turned to see Remeta sleepily rubbing her eyes. "I'm coming, my child."

"You need not worry about the prince. He's fine in his father's arms now. Worry about the near future that scares Remeta, Mama. Worry about the three W's," she whispered sleepily.

A shivered worked down Baski's arm. "What scares you, my child? What is the three W's?"

Remeta only laid back on the bed and fell right back asleep.

Baski watched her laboured breathing as she slept peacefully. In the end, she took her advice and joined her on the bed.

Tomorrow was another day to worry about.

Sally stood in front of the mirror, looking worried and so nervous, and her hands were sweaty. It was her wedding night and she didn't know how to go about it. She had tried not to think about it all day, but night had fallen and she was more nervous than a cat.

Madam Baski had called her to the privacy of her bedroom yesterday. She'd talked to her like a mother would do and told her the things to expect on the marriage bed. Madam Baski had told her that it was completely different than what the kings did to her and what the guards did to her, too, when she hustled to feed the slaves back in Mombana.

"I don't know how it'll be different, Madam Baski," she'd whispered confidingly.

"You'll see," the older woman had replied.

Standing in front of the mirror, Sally stared at herself. She'd bathed in scent water Madam Baski told the maids to arrange for her. She was dressed in her flimsy nightwear, her red hair pulled down well past her waist, and her eyes emphasizing her nervousness. But she had kept her husband waiting for long.

She came out of the bathroom and walked back into one of the bedrooms that had become theirs.

Chad just finished putting on his shorts when his new wife entered. She looked so small and nervous, and oh, so beautiful. He had never wanted another woman so much. He walked close to her and took her hand into his. "I will never hurt you, Sally. I never ever want to hurt you. You look so scared. Maybe we will not lay together until you are ready. I can wait. I don't want to hurt you."

His sincere words ceased some of her nervousness. The way his concerned eyes looked at her like she was the most beautiful woman—the most desirable woman. She found herself shaking her head. "No, I want to be with you."

His hand cupped her cheek tenderly, "Are you sure? I can wait---"

"Yes. I'm very sure, my husband." The word sounded strange but very sweet to her. She loved him so much.

That was all Chad wanted to hear. He pulled her closer and took her lips into a soft kiss.

Danika's heart flew right out of her. The king lowered his head again and closed his mouth around her nipple, sucking and playing with the other one.

The courage deserted her at his reply, and the fear of what he'd do when he found out doubled. She must be a coward because she couldn't tell him about it anymore.

At least, not for today.

She'd talk to Baski and they'd think of another way to telling him...another day. Today, she just wanted to enjoy the peace and solitude and happiness of lying right here on the floor with him and seeing a completely different side of him. She didn't have the guts to ruin this moment for them. She earned this beautiful moment. A moan slipped from her throat as he nibbled her softly.

"Is it my imagination or did your breast get bigger?" He pulled back and asked observingly. His finger plucked the rigid peak of her other breast. "And your nipples got darker too."

The question shocked her. It shouldn't have. She had always known that the king was very observant; she just didn't know that his observance would extend to where her body was.

"Um. It must be your imagination, my king." She prayed he wouldn't be suspicious.

"Mm." He dipped his head and licked around her nub.

What if I get pregnant?

The question shook him and made his heart ache. He couldn't blame her; it was not her fault for asking. She didn't know about his medical issues, and he had been drawing sexual pleasures from her body a lot. She was bound to ask. It didn't make it hurt any less.

Apart from the death of Declan, the next reason he knew affected him so much was the pain of knowing that his father's bloodline would die on his reign. It was an unbearable pain. His generation had been on the throne and kept their bloodline going for more than a thousand years. And, suddenly, it had to come to an abrupt halt on his own reign.

If any of his male relatives were alive, he would have given him his queen for them to make an heir that would continue their bloodline, as many royal families have done over the years.

But he had no one. No relatives. No family. No child.

"Please, stop thinking about it." Danika's soft melodic voice filled the air. "Whatever you're thinking now, please stop."

His eyes found hers. He saw the worry in hers and the deep pain in his. He blinked once and put the thought away—for her. "I want to keep you close to me, Danika," he breathed to her.

Her eyes watered at the heartfelt words. The king really liked her, she reasoned delightfully. He might not love her, but he had taken to her. She swiped the tears from her eyes. That was big progress compared to the way he was with her when he made her his slave. "I want to be close to you too, my king."

He kissed her lips; his tongue mated and danced with her in a song as old as time. She wrapped her arms around his neck, clinging to him. Making the moment last.

Finally, he pulled back. "There's a spy activity suspected in the kingdom of Navia, so Princess Kamara will still be here. The courting week will still go on, so I will not be able to be with you constantly. It is an act of disrespect to her and her family, and I would not want to do that."

Once a princess, Danika understood perfectly what he was saying. She nodded sadly, but at the same time, relief filled her. The courting week would stop the king from taking sexual pleasures from her whenever he wanted to, and it was a good thing for her.

He laid his head back to her chest, enjoying the feel of her plump breast beneath his ear. "But once the courting week is over, you are mine, Danika."

Her heart skittered away. "I've always been yours, my king." She had always been the king's slave.

"Yes, you have always been mine. And you will keep being mine. I will stop restraining myself with you, Danika. You're the only woman that has seen all of me. You saw all and you are still here with me. You held me when I needed contact the most. You keep me sane," he groaned hoarsely.

She felt each words vibrate her heart, her soul. Her throat closed up with feelings.

"My upcoming marriage has weighted heavily on me for a long time. A woman who will have to touch me, try to talk to me, try to be in my personal space. It does not please me, but a king must do what he must, for his people."

"Yes, a king must." It hurt her so much to agree with him. She wanted to be the only woman in his life. But she also knew how demanding the weight of duty is. If only she were still a princess.

She closed her eyes against the pain. She no longer regretted how her fate turned out. She no longer had pains about it. If she was never a slave, she would never have known King Lucien. She would never have had a chance to be with a man like him.

"But I will keep you close to me, Danika. You know me, and I can trust you. You have proven trustworthy. I had no one, but now I have you." He looked her in the eyes. "I am not letting you go."

Vetta stood frozen behind the door. Her eyes were wide and her heart cold as ice. She'd heard those words clearly. Shock was her first reaction.

She couldn't sleep, so she had gone to seek him out. To hell with courting week, she'd stated with all the intentions of coming to his chambers and seducing him to lay with her.

.

CHAPTER 37. A NIGHT IN THE MOON. A NEW MEMORY.

The kiss Chad gave Sally was very tender and sweet. Her thoughts turned off as his touch inundated her. An insidious weakness invaded her system. Her eyes closed and her body trembled as she felt light sips taken from her mouth. His lips moved to her cheek, up to her forehead, and then to her ear. He kissed all parts of her face reverently.

Her breathing fractured. Her hands slowly released their grip on her nightie and moved to curl around his head. They kissed for very long minutes. His hand cupped her soft breast, moving so that he could feel the nipple hard in his moist palm. "So beautiful."

Sally tried to breathe normally, but she couldn't. Her hand went to his broad chest and moved involuntarily over the hair-roughened muscles. Her head tilted back, inviting his mouth.

He lifted her petite body. She weighed almost nothing, and he carried her to the bed. He felt fear that he might break his promise and hurt her. He didn't want to, but he was a big man, and she was a small woman. He laid her down very carefully on the bed like she was porcelain then he began kissing her again because he couldn't help himself. He shifted her back onto the bed, sweeping the pillow out of the way.

He undressed her with slightly unsteady hands. She watched as he rid himself of his clothing too. Naked, he laid out on top of her and fused their lips so he wouldn't look down at his body and get more scared. He had scars, and Sally had seen them before when she unexpectedly came in on him when he was undressing. His scars made no difference to him, just like hers made no difference.

Slowly, deliberately, he knelt between her soft thighs and pushed them wide apart. His black eyes stabbed down into hers. His breath was audible as he looked down at her with possession. He began touching her intimately, caressing her sensitive bubble, and she shivered in his arms. Her soft arms were wrapped around him, and she pulled him closer, their lips dancing to the music as old as time.

She moaned into his mouth as he rubbed her with slow, tender movements. Breaking their kiss, he pulled back and watched her reactions.

"You're so tight. You feel like a maiden," he bit off with a grimace. "I don't want to hurt you, but I'm afraid I'll do that. You're going to feel it when I go into you."

"I love you so much, my husband. I really want to be with you," she whispered feverishly and bravely, laying her head on his shoulder.

He wanted to be with her just as much, but he was also determined to take it easy and as gently as possible. He kissed her hair down to her forehead, her neck. Then he lowered his head and took her rosy nipple into his mouth. She cried out, her head thrown back. He suckled her rhythmically, loving her body so gently.

"Oh," she sobbed in his arms as he treated her two gloves to the same treatment while he touched and fingered her gently.

He was able to get a finger inside her wet sheath, and he worked her with it until she soaked his fingers, writhing all over him.

"Please, please, I need you," she cried mindlessly when she couldn't take more, and she wanted more body contact from him.

He moved down over her, catching his weight on one elbow while his hand continued its maddening sweep against the moistness of her body. "I'm going to make you climax. When you do, I'm going inside you. Don't want to hurt you."

The blunt statement made her flush, even though the desire overwhelmed her. Her lips parted with a shocked breath.

"I need you so much," he whispered, bending to her breasts to kiss them again. "You make me complete."

"You complete me, too," she confided shyly. She wondered if she could faint lying down. What he was doing to her body was like slow torture. She opened her legs even more, coaxing him, as the pleasure began to build into something frightening.

Her helpless little cries of pleasure were arousing him intensely. His mouth opened on her breast, and his tongue worked at the hard nipple while his hand became insistent on her body. She was shivering rhythmically, lifting her hips to encourage him, incite him, to give her pleasure. Her head thrashed on the pillow.

"Chad?" she gasped in fear, her eyes wide. What was he doing to her?

That must be what Madam Baski meant when she told her that it was different, she realized with mindless pleasure. She had never felt anything so good. She never knew women could feel like this in the arms of men because she had never felt that way. She only knew pain and torture from men, so this was really new and frightening.

He pulled back from her breast and kissed her forehead. "Trust me, sweet wife. My beloved. Just let go."

Her hands gripped either side of her head. She moaned harshly, her teeth clenching, as she started up a spiral of incredible tension.

He lifted his head and looked straight into her eyes, feeling the tension build. "Open your eyes and look at me," he bit off.

She could barely focus. Her body was lifting and falling with every throb of pleasure. She ached for something just out of reach. Her mind was focused on the distant goal that was so very close. She gasped with every touch, her dazed eyes staring into his almost fearfully.

"It's over to let go, my sweetness. I'll be right here to catch you," he whispered roughly, unblinking. His own heart was shaking him.

He felt his body throbbing with insistence. The words didn't make sense, and then they did. She was reaching, reaching, almost there, almost...there...!

"Oh!" she cried hoarsely as her whole body suddenly convulsed on a wave of pleasure so intense she thought she might die of it.

"Yes," he moaned. He withdrew his hand from her dripping wetness and moved suddenly over her, almost shaking with the urgency of how he needed her.

He got in between her and pushed down, impaling her. Sally's eyes glazed over, she felt the sharp intrusion, but the burn became part of the pleasure, part of the throbbing heat that shook her body. His lean hands gripped her wrists and his weight crushed her into the mattress as his hips moved roughly, his body penetrating in a fever of anguished need. She stared into his eyes as she convulsed, seeing his face harden, tighten, his eyes like glittering black diamonds. He was groaning, his body shivering as the rhythm became insistent, urgent, fiercely demanding.

He bent to kiss her bruisingly, his breath mingling with hers in the anguished rush for fulfillment. His body was throbbing in time with hers, his powerful legs trembling as he drove into her. He wanted her too much. It hadn't been easy, having her so close for months but unable to touch her. And now, she was his forever. Tonight, he'd fought really hard for control and he won.

He lifted his head and looked into her eyes at point-blank range as the rhythm built to utter madness and the sound of the springs was as loud as their rough, frantic breathing. Suddenly, he arched down into her and stilled, his eyes wide and black as his lean body began to convulse.

"Sally," he ground out hoarsely. "I love you so much," he whispered unsteadily, holding her eyes while the world went blazing into oblivion.

The words made the fever burn even higher. She watched him as satisfaction shook him above her, his face clenched hard, his eyes closing finally in the maelstrom of passion that rocked his own body. It was beyond imagining. She felt him burst inside her, felt the heat of their passion explode. He cried out and she watched until he blurred in her wide, shocked eyes. She relaxed suddenly, feeling him impale her even farther as he drained the climax of its final weak throbs.

He collapsed into her arms, damp with sweat, shivering in the aftermath as she was. She held him weakly, tears rolling down her cheeks as she moved involuntarily against his still-aroused body to hold on to the echoes of fulfillment that stabbed into her with exquisite little thrills of pleasure.

Oh yes, this is exactly what Madam Baski meant. She sighed, her chest rising and falling.

He lay over her, feeling her body move. He was awed. No sexual experience of his entire life compared with it. He'd known so much horror and terror, this was an ultimate taste of Heaven. He never expected it to be half this way.

He pulled her tired body into his arms. "Thank you so much, Sally."

"No, I should be the one thanking you, Chad," she whispered tearfully.

"We will just thank each other," he groaned, watching her sleepy eyes.

"My husband?" she whispered.

"Yes, my wife?"

"When you sleepwalk tonight or any other night, you can go around and come back here to my body. I will welcome you so much," she breathed shyly, burying her face to his chest.

Chad felt his heart tighten in his chest. He could never deserve this girl, but he is never letting her go.

"I would want that too," he groaned hoarsely.

Vetta was sheathing as she walked out of the bedroom. Suddenly, she wished she had never gone there. She wished she never heard the incoherent mumbles, and never pressed her ear so glued to the door to decipher the things they said. She wished she never got curious.

"Good night, Mistress." A maid greeted her with a bow as she passed.

Vetta only glared daggers at the maid and marched right past her. What was so good about the night!?

There was nothing—*absolutely nothing!*—good about this night!

Danika was right there inside that bedroom.

The king drew sexual pleasures from her body and sated himself on her. During courting season. Not only that, but he was also saying such ridiculous words to Danika she never expected him to say.

Words she kept hoping the king would say to her!

Vetta whirled around and glared at the hallway that led to the king's chambers. She was raging. A new urgency filled her. Over her dead body would he be able to keep that witch close to him. She would break whatever was between them; she would scatter it to pieces beyond repair.

And she knew where to start.

She whirled around and marched right out of the hallway. She would deal with this issue really well.

And she knew the right place to start. She headed for Princess Kamara's bedroom.

King Lucien and Danika laid down there, doing nothing and thinking of absolutely nothing. Just taking a break from the world.

A lot of time passed as they touched each other and enjoyed being in each other's arms. They talked and talked about their past lives—the parts that weren't filled with so much pain.

"I am very tired, and my head is pounding. I feel dizzy too," the king finally said.

Danika had her hand running lazily at his broad back and chest. She was tired too, and oh, so sleepy. She wished the night would never end because she didn't know what tomorrow would bring. She wanted this moment with the king to last forever. But as midnight drew closer, it became a struggle to keep her eyes open.

"I am sleepy too," she admitted. Then she asked hesitantly, "Do you want to get on the bed?"

He shook his head, kissing the top of her breast. He spent years lying down in a cold cell. This was nothing. "No. I don't want to move an inch from here."

"Me either," she whispered.

He stretched his hand, reaching for his discarded robe. He picked up the big fur cloth and wrapped it around them. "There are no guards at the door or I would have called them. You need to shout for them. Can you do that?"

He'd hidden their nakedness, so she nodded. He gave a nod of approval.

"Guards!" she shouted, burying her red flushed face to his chest.

A minute passed before they heard the sound of a key going into the lock from behind the door. It opened and a guard entered. Shock blanketed his face when he saw the king lying on the ground with his slave. He was quick to mask his shock and bowed his head. "My king, you sent for me."

"Reach the bed and get me the big bedsheet, Zariel."

"At your command, Your Majesty." In quick strides, he reached the bed and withdrew the huge bedsheet that decorated the bed.

He didn't need to wait for the command, instead, he covered the king and the former princess's body with the big blanket.

"You can go now," the king said.

Zariel bowed again and walked out, closing the door behind him.

The king pulled his furcloth from under the bedsheet and dropped it aside. He pulled her closer, raised her leg and threw it over his hip, opening her up to him. He began surging into her.

She cried out, her eyes going wide. She was sore down there.

"I won't hurt you more. I will take it easy." He breathed into her neck. "I want to sleep inside you."

Her heart fluttered. The things he said to her always had this effect on her. She also wanted to be that close to him. So close, the closest she could get.

"I want that too. I want to fall asleep with y-you inside me," she whispered shyly, thankful that he wasn't looking at her. Instead, he was nibbling on her neck.

His hips pulled back and slowly. With a gentleness she never knew he possessed, he pushed himself into her. Inch by delicious inch. Sore tight muscles gave slowly, they stretched to accommodate him. Her breath hitched; she bit her lips. She was sore, but the feel of him was heavenly.

Finally, he was so deep inside her, she almost panicked that he'd hit her cervix again. But he stopped pushing and took a deep breath against her.

She breathed out and relaxed in his arms.

Wrapped in each other's arms, spread out on the floor of his chambers, the king's head to her bosom and a part of him buried so deep inside her, they fell asleep.

They fell into a peaceful sleep, because their hearts were at peace.

CHAPTER 38. THE KING'S WOMEN.

Vetta knocked on the door of Princess Kamara's bedroom. She waited impatiently for the door to open. She knocked again and again and again. Finally, she heard footsteps and the door opened. The princess stood behind the door, and from the look of it, she'd been sleeping.

"What are you doing in my bedroom?" Kamara asked, surprised to see the mistress standing behind her door.

"I need you to come and see something," Vetta stated to her. The mistress looked a little smug too.

Kamara crossed her arms. "Why would I want to go anywhere with you in the middle of the night? For all I know you might be a woman of bad mind and you would want to harm me."

"Why would I want to do that!?" Vetta hissed. She didn't like the insult—being addressed as a woman with a bad mind.

"I do not know. You tell me."

"Listen, I only want to show you something. I wanna be of help. You can either agree to go with me or you don't. Either way, I won't stand around wasting my time and getting insulted." Vetta turned and marched out of her the door. She walked slowly, watching behind her through the corner of her eyes. She really hoped that the princess would get curious and follow her. She walked a few more steps before she heard faint elegant footsteps behind her. She turned smugly; her eyebrows raised as she looked at the princess.

Princess Kamara already had her robes on to cover her nightie. "This better be worth my time, Mistress Vetta. I do not have time I waste a lot."

Vetta smiled wickedly. "Oh, it's so going to be worth your time. Tell me, Princess, do you like to be disrespected?"

"You must be dumb to ask, Mistress. No princess likes to be disrespected."

"My thoughts exactly." Vetta smiled wickedly, still leading the way.

Kamara cocked her head in thought, wondering what the woman is up to. They walked in silence through the hallways until they arrived at the king's Chamber.

"What are we doing here?" Kamara asked, confused.

"Follow me." Vetta said simply. She really wished that the king hadn't sent Danika away. Kamara really needed to see that.

She walked towards the window and quietly drew the curtain open. She looked inside and her heart tightened with rage and satisfaction. It was even worse this time around. The king still laid on the floor— *on the floor*—with Danika wrapped tightly in his arms and the blanket spread over them.

They were sleeping like two lovers that found each other and never wanted to let go ever again. Stupidly pathetic!

"What are you doing, Mistress Vetta!?" Kamara kept her voice very down as she hissed. It was a very punishable crime to be spying on the king.

Vetta masked her rage and plastered a smile on her face. "Come and see, Princess."

"I am not moving an inch," Kamara declared.

"Trust me, you don't want to miss this."

Kamara took a deep breath and walked closer towards her. Vetta stepped aside and crosses her arms. The princess looked through the window. Vetta waited smugly with her arms crossed as she waited for the princess to come to terms with the sight before her. She watched Kamara's face closely.

Blatant shock that slackened her jaw and left her mouth wide open was her first reaction. And then her face closed up.

Kamara remained by the window, just staring inside as time passed. She couldn't stop staring at King Lucien and Danika curled up on the floor, their bodies tightly pressed together. The king did not like to be touched, that observation was the main reason why it shocked the devil out of her to find him in that position with Danika.

"Oh," was all she said.

Vetta know they couldn't stay for long. "We have to be out of here before we get into trouble."

Kamara nodded and pulled back from the window. She followed the mistress and they walked well away from the king's chambers.

"So, tell me, Princess, was it worth your time or not?" Vetta drawled smugly.

Finally, it started making sense to Kamara. The reason why the king was so hesitant in taking her to his bed. The reason why he couldn't summon her, not once in all the two weeks she had been here. Finally, she understood what that look on Danika's face all the time whenever she was staring at the king. Of course, it was love. How could she have missed that?

Danika was very much in love with the king. So in love, she wore it on her face. And the king? He must love her too, to be in that position with her. It all made sense finally.

"Are you not going to say anything?" Vetta huffed in frustration when the princess remained silent on their way back.

"What do you want me to say?" she asked calmly.

What!? That was *not* what Vetta expected. She expected the princess to be raving mad and angry right now. To barge into the king's chambers and demand for an explanation and an apology from the king for disrespecting her like that. To have Danika whipped for such insolence.

Her, taking it so coolly, wasn't what Vetta wanted at all.

Vetta turned to her when they walked far away. "It's courting week. You're in your bedroom while the king summons his slave sate his hunger every night. He prefers his slave to you, and this is your week. Tell me, you do not feel disrespected?"

"I feel very disrespected," she conceded softly.

That's something. Vetta nodded in satisfaction. "It's very bad for him to treat you this way. And Danika pretends to be your friend, but she goes right behind you and sleep with the king during *your* courting week." Kamara said nothing to that. Instead, she resumed walking.

Vetta followed closely behind her. "So, what are you going to do about this?" Vetta urged her.

"I do not know. What am I going to do about that?" She kept walking.

"There are so many things you can do about that. The king disrespected you in such a bald way, you can go to him, stand your ground and demand from him. He will do your wish because he did wrong."

"And what do I demand from him?"

"To make Danika a Mine Slave instead of the king's slave. You can also have her whipped for such insolence."

Kamara turned to her. "And why would I want to do that?"

"*What?*"

"The king is the only one with the right to summon his slaves, and his command cannot be disobeyed. He summoned her and she responded. I do not see how this is her fault," she stated matter-of-factly.

"How can you think that!?" Vetta couldn't believe that. She was almost breathing fire in sheer frustration.

Kamara crossed her arms. "Tell me, Mistress. Have you ever been in love?"

Vetta opened her mouth to shout to her that she loved the king! And that is why she was trying to have him to herself! But telling the king's future queen that you love the king was *not* a good idea. She kept her mouth shut.

"My guess is that you have never been in love," Kamara continued. "You do not know what it's like to be in love, Mistress. Maybe that is why you are so bitter."

Vetta was taken aback. "Why are you insulting *me*!? How is this *my* fault!?"

Kamara cocked her head to the side in thought, her well-brushed hair falling in front of her. "Why do you hate the king's slave so much? Shouldn't you be happy that the king has only one slave? Only one mistress? Other kings have more than twenty."

Yes, but I bet they cannot have the king feeling so attracted to them. It's almost like Danika has a powerful man like King Lucien in her control! And

238

she is even King Cone's daughter! Vetta swallowed those words. Instead, she replied, "I don't hate her."

"Liar," Kamara whispered.

Vetta resumed walking. "Anyway, I saw something I know isn't fair to you, that was why I came to call you. Obviously, I have done something so wrong for trying to bring such disrespectful act to your notice."

Kamara said nothing and resumed walking too.

Vetta felt a small amount of victory. No matter how much the princess looked indifferent and what her reasons were for her not to want to take immediate actions, Vetta could swear that the princess *did* feel disrespected. That in itself was a victory on its own. The woman was a vixen. If she placed Danika on her bad side, that would be a very bad thing for the bitch. Vetta smiled.

At least she wouldn't be the only one Princess Kamara hated. This woman really hated her for reasons she didn't even know. And the worst part of it was that the king was planning to get married to her. What in old bones would happen to her when this woman became the queen? She might even find a reason to order her death one day.

Maybe she should try making friends with her. If she was going to be the queen—IF—maybe she could try to be friends with the bitchy princess. It would also work in her favour if the princess is on her side. Danika would suffer more, and together, they would push Danika away. Then she would push the princess away and the king would be hers alone. Again.

That thought intact in her head, Vetta slowed her steps so that the princess would catch up with her. "So, how is it back home?" she asked in an effort to make a conversation.

"I do not understand," Princess Kamara replied without sparing her a glance.

"I mean, how is it like back in your kingdom? I've never really known a lot of places, you see. The only place I know is Salem, and then, Mombana, when we were taken into slavery. We really suffered, you know," she confided.

Just as Vetta predicted, the princess lost some hard lines on her face. Pity always got more to people than conversations. Vetta smiled inwardly and continued as they rounded another hallway that led back to Kamara's chambers. "It wasn't easy being under the reign of Cone. He was—"

"King Cone."

"What?"

Kamara spared her a glance. "He was King Cone. Just because he was wicked and brutal—and is dead—doesn't make him any less of a king. He was a king. He was royalty. Address him as one."

Vetta gritted her teeth. This princess was almost more annoying than Danika. Almost.

"It wasn't easy being under the reign of...King Cone. He was a brutal and heartless man. He treated us like dirt because we were slaves." They reached Kamara's chambers as she continued. "I remember that time it became a routine for me to get whipped and beaten and raped and brutalized all in one day. It was so horrible—"

"And yet, you treat slaves that way now."

"What?"

Kamara stopped and turned to her. "You treat slaves like there are not worth the leather shoes on your feet when you've been through being a slave. Shouldn't you be kinder to them? I see the way you beat the maids and slap slaves. I saw the day you mistreated the former princess Danika, too, just because her status is reduced. Shouldn't you be better? Kinder?" Princess Kamara paused, shaking her head. "When you treat people like that, you become a monster. Tell me...are you any different from King Cone?"

With that, Princess Kamara walked right past her to her bedroom and closed the door.

.

.

CHAPTER 39. DANIKA'S DELIMMA.

Danika's bladder woke her several times in the night. She had to untangle from the king and use the bathroom each and every time, and when she returned, he took her right back into his arms—even with his eyes closed.

They overslept. When they woke the next morning, the brightness of the day was harsh inside the king's chambers. As she stirred, his eyes opened too. They looked at each other in the light of the day. It is probably one of those times in life when time stands still. Danika's mind was filled with uncertainties.

What would happen now in the light of the day? Would he go back to being so cold to her? Try to forget the events of the night before?

"Good morning, my king," she whispered.

"Good morning, Danika." His voice was anything but cold—just the voice of a man who woke up after a good night's sleep.

Then he leaned closer and took her lips into a searing kiss that was sweet, ravishing, and breathtaking at the same time. Her worries disappeared like the wind and were replaced by her heart filled with so much love for this man.

She'd almost lost him last time. To the past. To the demons that hovered in his sleep and haunted his waking moment. Her hand tightened on his shoulder, and she kissed him back as thoroughly as he kissed her.

A long time passed before he pulled back. King Lucien wanted nothing more than to spread her out on the floor again, bury himself to the hilt and sate his hunger to the maximum satisfaction in a way he knew only her body could give him. But in the light of the day, he saw the faint bruises, red skin and grab marks he'd inflicted on her the night before, so he let her go because he knew she would be sore from it all.

"I have so much to do today. A case to settle in court, according to my royal advertiser, Lord Dumbleton, and shooting with the new recruitments of the department of security," he said as he got up from the floor.

Danika nodded, pleased that he was confiding in her about his activities of the day. She bit her lips. "Then you must get ready, my lord. I'm so sorry. I think I made you oversleep."

"And I feel most grateful to you for it." He walked to his wardrobe and took out a rope he tied around his waist.

Danika watched him with lazy eyes appreciatively. He was large and powerful. Not fat—never fat. His presence commands so much respect, even from a stranger who had never met him. She watched as he wrapped the rope efficiently and without hurry. He never did anything in a hurry. His steps steady and regal, he walked into the inner bedroom.

Alone, she got up from the floor, wincing as her body protested massively. Every part of her—especially her inner body—felt the intensity of his passion the night before. She stood up and began putting on her robes. She didn't bother asking permission to use his bathroom because she knew he had greater needs for it as he had to get ready for the day.

As she finished putting on her robes, she was surprised to see him leaning against the door of the library and just watching her.

A blush spread all over her face. He slept inside her the night before. The blush only intensified.

The king would have laughed at her struggle if he had been a laughing man. But he was not. So, he simply kept watching her like a man would watch his favourite meal.

She turned towards him and bowed to him. "I have to go now, my king."

A pause. He pulled away from the door and walked closer to her. "Do not forget anything we talked about last night. Do not forget the promises you made me."

242

Her heart fluttered. "How can I ever forget?"

"Never forget. I will mostly restrain myself because of the courting week, but once it is over, I will keep you close. I will not let go." Blue eyes slid over her face as he repeated what he had said to her the night before.

She wished that before that time came, she'd be able to tell him that she was in a family way. "I am yours, my king."

His hand palmed her cheek and tilted her chin, making her eyes meet his chiseled face. What would it feel like to see this man smile? The thought, so unexpected, made her heart constrict. What would it take for him to smile? A heartfelt full-blown smile?

"Meet Baski the instant you go away from here. Let her take a look at you and use her medicinal herbals on you. I..." he paused. "I apologize for being so rough with you."

Knowing that apology was not easy for a man like him melted her inside. She searched his face, but it was hard to read. Was he feeling guilty for the way he handled her?

"Do not feel guilty, Your Highness. I will meet Madam Baski, but I feel perfectly fine," she reassured him. And it was no lie.

She had never felt any better in such a long time.

Later in the day, cleaned up, and after another round of sleep, Danika went in search of Baski. She found her in the woods with Remeta, picking a basket full of herbs.

They all walked together to the palace and back into Baski's bedroom. The older woman was livid and worried, but Danika went right ahead to explain what had happened in the king's chamber. She gave her the general reason, skipping the intimate memories she had made with the king. Those were private and hers alone to cherish.

She told Baski about how he was so deeply buried in the past that he almost lost his sanity with her and how she came close to telling him that she was pregnant and his response.

"Oh, dear." The older woman palmed her wrinkled forehead, "I'm glad you withdrew when you did. I can't begin to imagine what would have happened to you if you had told him and he took the news badly. He really believes he can't father a child, and no one can blame him."

"You're right. I just couldn't go on with it. I didn't have to courage," Danika said sadly.

"I'm watching closely for his schedule to loosen up, then I will find the time to go to him and explain Remeta's gift to him. His schedule is packed to the teeth. He is a very busy man."

"He is."

"Oh, thank you so much, Danika, for pulling him out of that abyss. I know you could do it. I never lost hope that if any woman would be Abel to reach him when he's losing the fight with himself, it will be you." Baski teared up as she put herbs on her body.

Danika looked around and noticed that Remeta had disappeared again. She hadn't said a word to her all morning, just a lot of smiles and happiness.

In the time that passed, Baski rubbed herbs and liquid concoctions she had never seen before on her but knew better than to question the older woman's extensive knowledge of herbs.

Already, her body started feeling better. Soothed. The pains lessened.

Finally, Baski's face took up a concerned note. "Do you feel any discomfort in your stomach? Have you had any blood droppings from your body, even if it's just a little, since last night?"

"No, I feel perfectly fine. Not even a drop," she answered truthfully.

Baski let out a breath she didn't know she was holding, her face a light of relief. "Thank heavens. If you feel any sharp pain or see any blood, no matter how little, you have to inform me, do you hear me?"

Danika nodded her head.

Seven weeks later, Danika was watching Remeta play around in the palace garden. Remeta giggled as she ran around, her new friend—a fox—following her everywhere. She still couldn't believe that this was the same girl who, five months ago, was so afraid of her shadow and almost mad with the horrors of a past that a girl her age should never have.

She was just like a different person. Actually, Remeta was like three different people.

The sad haunted girl she promised that there would be 'no more bed' for.

The child who ran around the woods chasing crickets, carrying a fox around and being happy.

And, the seer that kept warning her of a big danger coming.

"Beware of the three W's." That had become a new mantra for the seer, Remeta, whenever she talked to her. Danika had tried so much to find out what was the three W's, and even Baski had tried, but there was no way for them to know that. Remeta wouldn't say anything.

Once the seer, Remeta, decided to keep quiet, she did not say anything. And that was the problem they had been having for more than a month.

"See the sky, my queen!" Remeta shouted, pointing at the sky.

Pulled out of her thoughts, Danika glanced up at the yellow sun that rose in the sky, giving the evening and the garden a beautiful, serene glow.

"It is so beautiful," she whispered truthfully, drawn away from her problems to the beautiful sky.

"Yes. It looks almost as beautiful as you, my queen." The girl turned and grinned at her. "Almost. You are the most beautiful sun. The most glowing moon. And the most alluring star on earth and in the sky."

Danika's heart swelled with love for the fifteen-year-old girl that had stolen her heart a long time ago. A smile touched her lips. "Thank you so much, Remeta. You're just as beautiful."

The girl only grinned wider before she began plucking beautiful flowers and inhaling them excitedly.

"Remeta?" she called, just to try her luck again for the countless time.

"Yes, my queen?"

"What are the three W's?" she asked softly.

As always, Remeta frowned a bit. Then she looked at her with a smile and continued doing what she was doing. This time, she continued plucking the rose flower before her.

Danika sighed in defeat. So much to worry about. So much to think about. Her biggest problem was that she was more than three months pregnant, and the king didn't know she was carrying his child. She was thirteen weeks gone.

Baski was finally able to get a moment with the king, and she explained Remeta's gift and ancestry to him. She'd told the king the truth about her great grandfather, a big fearsome shaman there in Salem. There were healers and shamans in her ancestry.

The king believed perfectly. He had heard stories of the great Gunther and knew through his father that the great Gunther was Baski's great-grandfather.

So, the king didn't find it hard to believe that Remeta had the gift of foresight.

Danika could still remember that day. They were so happy. So very happy that the king believed them. All that remained was for Remeta to go to the king and tell him about her condition.

That was where all the problems lay. Till today.

No matter how they begged Remeta and told the girl about how dire their situation was, Remeta wouldn't say a word about going to the king. At one time, Baski had told her to wait when Remeta would 'see' another future, so they would plead with her then.

They'd waited long until the day Remeta came to her bedroom, tugged on her clothes and warned her of the three W's for the first time. She'd begged the girl then to go to the king and give him the news herself so that the king would believe, but Remeta only shook her head.

"It is not yet time," she'd said in a robotic monotone.

Danika had tried to find out what she meant by that, but the girl only blinked hard and came back to her normal self. She'd grinned at her and skidded out of her bedroom.

Now, she was at a crossroads. She was so worried she wasn't sleeping properly anymore. Her hand touched her stomach caressingly. Her belly was no longer as flat as it used to be. There was a slight bump to it.

And while she could easily pass it up for something she ate, how would she explain the hard surface of her belly?

Karama's stay in Salem had protected her for long. She had spent time with the king outdoors, taking walks, riding with him, and strolling the lanes with him.

She smiled at the memory. After that night in the king's chambers, he had become freer with her. Closer to her. She had come to crave and enjoy every single minute they spent together. He hadn't taken sexual intimacies from her again since that night in respect of the courting week. They kissed a lot and she had even taken him into her mouth and sucked him occasionally, but they hadn't had sex since then.

He must be sating himself with his future queen. Her chest constricted at the thought like it always did. She tried not to think about it. It became easier to deal with if she wasn't thinking about it. Kamara was going to be his queen. One day, Kamara would be married to him and become his legally.

Every princess was raised with the concrete thought of how important it is to be joined with a prince or a king in holy matrimony. His wife would always come first before his mistresses. And then his slaves. Kamara would always come first to him. And then Vetta.

Danika blinked hard, pushing the pain away. There were so many other problems to think about right now. Like the fact that the courting week would be ending the following day, and Princess Kamara was going back to her kingdom.

The king had already told her something in the morning when she served him the tea Madam Baski gave her to take to him. He'd drawn her closer, his eyes sliding all over her hungrily. He'd placed his head on her swollen bosom and groaned. "You will spend tomorrow night with me, Danika. Here, in my bed. All night."

A shiver of anticipation and dread went down her body at the reminder.

She got up from the grass and walked towards Remeta. She pulled the girl's arm, causing her to stop plucking the flowers and look at her.

"Remeta?"

"My beloved queen," she replied with a pure smile.

Danika knelt to become at eye level with her. She began in a gentle, coaxing tone. "Please, Remeta, you have to save me. Save my child. 'The prince' like you call him. The courting week had ended, and I need the king to know that I'm carrying his child before he finds out by himself and thinks I've betrayed him by keeping it from him. Not to mention when he gets the idea in his head that he isn't the father of our child. I shudder to think of what will happen to me then." She shook Remeta's arms slightly to see the intensity of her pleas. "Please, Remeta, you have to go to him and tell him. I'm tired of carrying this secret, but it's too heavy. It's weighing me down, stressing me badly. I don't know what else to do. Please, Remeta?"

Silence met her pleas. Her knees on the grass began hurting as time passed; it seemed like forever.

Then Remeta placed her hand on her cheek. "My beautiful queen."

"Yes, Remeta?" she answered readily and hopefully.

"Beware of the three W's," was all she whispered before she turned and ran away.

CHAPTER 40. DANGEROUS GROUNDS.

D anika walked hand in hand with Remeta after their time in the garden. She hadn't been able to get a meaningful response or anything at all from Remeta. It worried her and made her feel on the verge of tears. Her time had run out. The near future wasn't looking good for her.

They were almost at the front of the palace when she saw Kamara and her personal maid, Henna. They were coming out of the royal quarters.

Kamara saw her and her steps faltered. Danika watched the princess warily. Kamara had been really scarce in the past few weeks; she was exactly the typical princess like she had been, always holed up in her room, reading, reading, eating, more reading. Was that what it was, or was there another reason?

Danika took another look at Kamara's oval face and noticed the few almost invisible details she missed the first time. Kamara's eyes were dull and she looked tired. Not physically. Emotionally tired and sad.

"Give me a minute, Henna," Kamara said with a look over her shoulder.

"Yes, my princess," Henna agreed with a bow of her head. She turned and walked back through the hallway they came out from.

Danika turned to tell Remeta to excuse them, too, but Remeta already ran towards the other side of the palace, probably in search of her mother.

Kamara started walking close, and Danika met her at the center. Danika inclined her head slightly. "Princess Kamara."

"I already told you to call me by my name, Danika." She continued walking, leaving Danika to walk with her.

Danika matched her steps with hers. Silence descended between them as they walked. The silence was supposed to be comfortable, but for some reason, Danika felt tense.

"Are you angry at me for something?" she blurted out suddenly as soon as the thought popped into her head. That would explain a lot of things, like the reason why Kamara hadn't sought her out for the past few weeks. And, when they ran into each other in the hallway, she only inclined her head and kept going without stopping.

Her chest constricted at the appalling thought. "You ARE angry at me." It wasn't a question this time.

Kamara said nothing, just kept on walking.

Danika worried on the inside, but she remained cool on the outside. Her elegance and sophisticated demure mirrored Kamara's with each step, and they looked like sisters.

"I saw you and the king that night. In his chambers. On the floor. In each other's arms, asleep," came the calm reply at last.

Danika didn't have to think hard for the mental image to come. When it did, her blood ran cold. She saw her intimate night with the king. "Oh," Danika muttered guiltily. She didn't know what to say about that. Once a princess herself, she could understand the disrespect Kamara felt. Not to mention the anger and even hurt.

Kamara let out a deep breath. "I'm not angry at you. I'm not even hurt, or I would have done something about it these past few weeks."

"You aren't?" Danika asked, uncertain and bewildered.

"No, I'm not. Sadly, what I saw made it easier for me to understand a lot of things. I made peace with it."

"I don't understand."

Kamara turned towards Danika. Her lips curved a bit, her eyes watching her. All too knowingly. Her seeing gaze unsettled Danika, but she didn't let it show. The only person who could see her weak and unsettled was the king.

Kamara turned forward and continued walking. "I will tell you a story. In Navia, there is this man that suddenly appeared in our kingdom. I took one look at him and knew immediately that he wasn't from Navia." Danika listened attentively; they rounded another corner. "Women in the village told stories of how the man washed up our shores, almost drowned and drained and injured severely. I was making rounds in the village to take note of the crop growth and market activities when I saw him first. His blue eyes were the first features of him I noticed."

"Blue eyes?" Danika's asked curiously.

Kamara nodded, her eyes dazed in memory. "Very blue. Deep blue, like the sea. A lot of people have blue eyes, but only few have ones so deep they can easily captivate."

"Like the king's."

"Huh?"

Danika shrugged. "The king's eyes are that same deep blue."

"Yeah. I noticed immediately when I stood in his presence. But unlike the king, that man stole my heart."

"What?" Danika started. That was completely unexpected.

Kamara's lips curved sadly. "I fell in love with him, Danika. He wasn't a man of status; he lives in a small hut in a secluded part of town, and he was mostly so sick. Henna and I took care of him most of the time, and we nursed him back to health."

"Your father allowed it?" she asked, surprised. Her own father would punish her severely for something like that.

Kamara shook her blonde hair. "No, he didn't. I visited him in secret."

It all started making sense to Danika. "Let me guess, your father found out and matched you with the king."

Kamara nodded. "Yes."

"I'm so sorry." *No wonder she kept herself holed up in her bedroom,* Danika thought sadly. She understood Kamara's plight on a very personal level.

"So, that was it. I understand what it's like to be in love. You're in love with the king."

Danika's mouth opened and closed. Her jaw dropped. She never thought Kamara would find her out. She bit her lips worriedly. This was not a good idea.

"Do not worry. I have no intention of being a 'bitch' about it. That is why I told you my story." She paused. "Falling in love with a peasant is as dangerous as falling for the king. My father found me out and I'm paying for it. You keep hoping that the mistress never finds out about it. She might use it as the perfect opportunity to have your head in a spike."

"I know. Thank you, Kamara. I avoid the mistress like the plague. She doesn't like me very much," Danika confided softly.

"No, she doesn't. Loving the king is dangerous; a lot of things can go wrong." She shook her head. "Besides, you already have so many problems on your hand without me adding to them."

Danika's steps faltered. She turned her head and glanced at Kamara.

Concern marred her face. "The second most dangerous thing a slave can do is to fall for her master. The first and foremost is getting pregnant by her master."

Danika felt a huge wave of dizziness. Kamara's hand was around her immediately, steadying her.

"Oh, heavens." She felt cold on the inside. She had always known that, but hearing Kamara say it out loud reminded her of how dangerous a land she was threading.

Kamara let her go gently when she found her footing. She turned to face her completely. "Maybe that is why I feel a little bad about going home. That mistress will eat you raw and spit you out if she finds out about your condition. That is if she hasn't found out yet. If you escape being murdered by the king, that mistress will definitely do the job. You thread a dangerous ground, sister."

"Y-you know?" Danika couldn't believe it. *Kamara knew she was pregnant. She knew.*

Kamara nodded her head solemnly. "I would be a fool not to realise. I watched you from afar. The symptoms are written all over you. The fatigue. The sleeping. The day you had to vomit your lungs out in the backyard." She paused. "I know, Danika."

Danika was speechless; she didn't know what to say about that. It shocked and scared her. "You're not...mad? About it?" she forced herself to ask at last.

Kamara shook her head. "No. I love Callan so much, and I would like to carry his child anytime," she informed her proudly. "You love the king. It is only fitting that you do not have the heart to rid yourself of his child, even when your life is practically hanging on a thread because of it. I feel so happy that I will see my Callan again after so many months, you do not know how happy I feel." Kamara continued. "But I worry for you, Danika. That mistress will do anything in her power to make your life hell if she finds out. Beware of her."

"Danika is carrying the king's child. She is pregnant," Vetta announced in a voice that was deceptively calm.

Karandy watched the woman who was seated in the wooden chair at the other side of the room looking at him with a cool expression that revealed nothing. It had been two months since he saw the king's mistress, and it particularly surprised him to hear her impatient knock on his door that morning. Another surprise were the words pouring from her mouth.

"It is not possible for her to be with child for him. Why would she risk herself so dangerously? The former princess is smart," he contributed.

"Oh, she is very smart. And that is why she got pregnant for the king. It is a dangerous game. Either the king kills her for it, or he accepts her. If the latter happens, her status might change for the better and she will be a very important person in his life. She is smart," Vetta conceded, before she added, "But very foolish."

"How did you know she's pregnant?"

"I have my maid keep an eye on her; she reports everything to me. She is with child," she repeated with certainty.

Karandy watched the king's Mistress. He was surprised she wasn't raging and mad as hell. Calmness was an oddity to the woman he had come to know both physically and intimately.

"You are calm about it. Does that mean you are okay with it?" Karandy asked carefully.

253

Vetta laughed then. It sent a chill down Karandy's arms. The sound was hollow and empty.

"I wouldn't be here if I was okay with it, would I?" she growled at last.

No, she wouldn't. Karandy watched the beautiful woman with deceptive calmness in her demure. No, she wouldn't be here if she was truly okay with it. After that day he drew sexual pleasures from her body, she disappeared. That was two months ago. He missed her; he missed her body. Eating from the same plate the king eats from is a definite turn-on. The feeling only intensified because the mistress didn't like him at all, and she despised his status to the teeth. Yet, she spread her legs for him.

His dick jerked in his pants, and he adjusted himself and walked to the other side of his small hut in an effort to mask his reaction to her. He had no plans whatsoever to do something about it. Not today. Not when the mistress was behaving so out-of-sorts with her calmness over a finding that was supposed to make her blow with rage and shout to the moon.

They become deadly when they keep quiet, his father always said to him.

Vetta got up then. "I have to go. I have an appointment with a healer."

Why would she have an appointment with a healer? Was she sick? Why did she come at all when she wasn't going to give him a plan?

He watched her warily and realized that there was something different about her. She looked...colder, meaner.

"The courting week is ending tomorrow morning. I plan to be on the king's bed tomorrow night," Vetta informed him.

"Wouldn't he want to spend that time with Danika?" She'd told him once before how the king favors Danika's bed to hers. He wouldn't blame the king. Princess Danika was the most beautiful woman he had ever seen in his life, and not to mention that air of royalty around her wherever she went.

It had been almost a year in slavery for her, but that had never changed. Her elegance and royal sophistication remained as blatant as if she still had the expensive big clothes on.

"Wouldn't the king want to spend tomorrow night with Danika?" he repeated to her.

"I wouldn't be giving him a choice," she replied simply as she began rolling her hair to get the black mass into the hood she hid herself in when she showed up.

Her hand found the hood behind her back and she covered herself up with it. He watched her as she walked out of the door.

They become deadlier when they keep quiet.

.

.

.

.

CHAPTER 41. WHO YOU ARE, WILL NEVER CHANGE.

D anika was carrying the king's child. She was pregnant by him. As Vetta took steps to the healer's house, those words wouldn't stop ringing in her ears. Her hands fisted to her side, and her eyes blazed in anger and banked-up rage.

How could something like this happen?

She had been trying for months now to carry the king's child, and she had been trying. She hadn't been able to achieve that.

Instead, she carried Karandy's seed inside her.

It was a thought she didn't like remembering. The past few weeks hadn't been good for her, only for Danika to come and ruin it completely.

As a slave—being treated like anything less than an animal—she swore to herself that she would never go back there again. And she would have no connection to such stinky life again.

When she found out from the new healer uptown that she was carrying a child, a few thoughts came to her head, like pinning the child to the king and getting everything she wanted in life.

But it made her very uncomfortable. Not being found out but carrying something so dirty inside her.

Any child that wasn't from the king was one she did not want to carry. Over her dead body would the dirty child of that dirty bastard remain in her.

So, she'd gone to another healer named Monah, that heals best in the twelve kingdoms, and collected an herb to rid herself of the baby.

Her plan was simple. Once the child was gone, she would return to the healer and take new fertility pills.

The next time around, she had confidence that it would work. According to Talia, her maid, many women from the village testify to that healer's herbs.

The healer had given her the herbs and assured her that it would work. She was supposed to bleed for just one day, according to Monah. However, she bled for more than five days non-stop. That was two weeks ago. On the sixth day, she'd been ready to return to the healer, but the bleeding stopped. So, she'd pushed it all away.

Now she needed to collect fertility herbs from Monah. She needed them for the night of the morrow to be intimate with the king. Already, Danika had gotten pregnant before her, and if she gave birth, that child would be recognized as the firstborn of the king.

Not that she would ever give birth to that child.

Vetta smiled at the thought as she rounded the corner that led to the healer's house. Danika was foolish this time around.

Kamara reached her door, Danika standing beside her. She turned and faced Danika.

"I will be going back to my father's kingdom on the morning of the morrow. I will miss seeing you, Danika."

"I will miss seeing you too, Kamara." Danika shifted on her feet, already tired from standing for too long. "I wish you the best with your Callan."

"I wish myself luck too. I still have a few weeks with him before the next step to my marriage when King Lucien will come to ask for my hand." Kamara's lips curved sadly. "I wish a miracle would happen, and I'd be with Callan instead of King Lucien. But then again, wishes have never been horses."

"Yes, they have never been," Danika echoed, remembering her current situation. She shook her head. "I remember when I was a princess too."

"You should never forget something like that, Danika. You are royalty. Never forget that you are royalty. The mistress would do everything within her power to get rid of you and your baby. She hates you that much, and you will not blame her because she wants the king too." Kamara took a step forward and placed her hand on Danika's cheek. Looking her in the eyes, she continued intensely. "But you should not forget that once upon a time you were authority. Once upon a time, you commanded an army of princesses. You were brave! Very bold and courageous! Do not forget that woman, Danika. That princess *nobody* could ever step on."

Danika remembered that woman vividly. It hurt just thinking about the princess she once was. But she was a slave now. She began shaking her head miserably.

But Kamara only nodded. "I know you are a slave now, and you have limited choices. I know you have to survive, my sister. You have survived this long, and I am so proud of you. I respect you for it. Any princess will be very proud of you and respect you for it because not all of us would be able to survive one week in slavery. But I don't want you to forget Princess Danika. Do not forget that brave, elegant, and sophisticated princess that always raised her voice when she needed to be heard!" Kamara held her shoulders and shook her firmly. "A princess that commanded other princesses! This time, it's no longer about you alone trying to survive in every possible way you can, but you have to protect your child too. In every possible way you can.

"I keep praying that my marriage with the king will never work out. I don't know what I will do if it works out, Danika. Because according to law, you and your child will either be killed or banished away from the palace...because the queen's child will always be the heir to the throne. There should be no elder child. It was the law in all twelve kingdoms. A law I hate but will have to come to pass if I become queen."

Danika knew that, too, and she wished a time would never come when such a law would force Kamara to be against her. She only wanted to be by the king's side. That was all she wanted. The throne and its heir had never been a thought to her.

Kamara let her go and turned towards her door. "I don't even want to be queen, Danika. All my life, I've had that responsibility. It is not something I want anymore." Kamara shook her head sadly. "I want to live a normal life with Callan. A simpler life without big responsibilities. Without the weight of the world resting on my shoulders. I want to be with him. I do not want the burden of the crown."

Danika understood her words perfectly on a more personal level. Being a princess could be very tiring at times. "I hope everything works out for you in the end, Kamara. If anybody deserves to be happy, it is you." She inclined her head in a respective bow. "You are a good woman, and I'm glad I got to know you on a more personal level, Princess Kamara."

Kamara smiled then—a beautiful, sincere, heartfelt smile as she pulled Danika closer to her for a hug. "Do not forget to fight for your child, and fight for yourself, any way you can."

"I will not forget." Kamara gave her strength to brave the future. Whatever that future may be.

"It was nice knowing you on a more personal level, Princess Danika," Kamara whispered as she pulled back.

"I am no longer a prin---"

"Clothes change. Status changes. But what you are will never change, Princess Danika." That said, Kamara turned and entered her bedroom.

Vetta knocked on Monah's door, waiting impatiently. The cold outside wasn't favourable for her.

It took a long time before the door opened, and the older woman came out of her door. She took one look at her visitor and bowed her head in greeting. "Is everything alright, Mistress?"

"I have reasons to be here, or I wouldn't be here," Vetta hissed angrily and stormed into the small old house. She turned and glared at the woman. Monah couldn't be more than fifty-years-old. She looked small and frail, but rumors has it that her status was deceiving.

Monah followed her inside. "That's my mistake for asking such a stupid question, Mistress. Forgive me."

Vetta nodded, taking a seat at the other side of the room.

"How were the herbs I gave you three weeks ago?"

"You said I was going to bleed for one day, Monah." She crossed her arms and leveled the woman with a stare. "I bled for five days. Five extremely painful days."

"Oh, that is strange." The woman's brows knitted with thoughts. "Are you sure?"

"What sort of question is this? Do you think I would be lying about something so important!?" Vetta fumed through gritted teeth.

Monah nodded. "Kindly get on the table. I need to examine you."

"I don't need to be examined. I need you to give me the best fertility pills you possess. That is the reason I came here today."

"I don't think that is a good idea, Mistress. You just came out of a very bad condition, and you should not think about getting pregnant again so soon. Your body has been stressed a lot---"

"My body," Vetta cut her off with deceptive calmness, "...is mine. Now, you will do exactly what I tell you to do."

Monah hesitated. But she was a smart woman who knew that the king's mistress would punish her if she kept disobeying her—even when it was for her own good. "I will get the very best of them pills, Mistress," Monah said at last, turning towards her inner bedroom where she stores herbs.

"Do not keep me waiting," Vetta ordered. She had a lot to do. So many things to do.

When Monah disappeared to her inner bedroom, Vetta waited impatiently, tapping her foot on the ground. Danika was pregnant for the king. Danika carried the king's child. The words would not stop ringing in her ears. She laughed hollowly.

Over Vetta's dead body would Danika have that child. She never wanted to go to Karandy's place again, but after discovering something huge, she knew that, eventually, she had to go. She needed his help.

Well, now she had a plan. A very good plan that would kill three birds with one stone.

Monah came out later and gave her the pills. "Here it is. It is called Door-ga. They are very strong and very effective. Twenty women have used it. Twenty women have had children because of it."

"Good. That is what I want." Vetta took the pills and paid her.

"But can I at least examine you? I need to know your body's status and capacity, Mistress, because you will take a pill as strong as Door-ga."

"My body is strong and capable, Monah. It's been two weeks since the miscarriage. Now I'm healthy and capable of trying again—from the right source this time." Vetta turned towards the door. "I have to go."

Monah watched her leave. She felt concerned. Door-ga was a very powerful pill, and the mistress just had a bad miscarriage that might have caused complications. Bleeding for five days might be normal, or it might not be a good sign. Then Monah shrugged and closed her door. Her patient would be fine since it was her first miscarriage.

CHAPTER 42. AT THE FRONT OF THE DARK TUNNEL.

In the evening, Danika was in her bedroom brushing her hair when Baski walked in.

"The king requests that you be the one to bring his dinner to him in his chambers," she informed her with a concerned smile.

Danika's heart skipped three beats. "Baski?"

The older woman walked closer and took the comb from her. She watched her through the mirror as she combed her long blonde hair. "My dear?"

"I've run out of time," she whispered, her hand caressing her slight bump.

"I know." Baski let out a shuddering breath. "I know, Danika. But the heavens are with you. They will guide you."

"Courting week ends tomorrow. He wants to spend the night with me."

"I know that too. I thought maybe we should go together to tell him about your condition. If I go with you, I might be able to reach him before disaster happens." Danika swiveled her head and looked up at the older woman. "Maybe," Baski amended.

Danika took a deep breath and turned towards the mirror again. "I don't know what to do anymore. Remeta was our best shot."

"Seers cannot be told what to do. They hardly do what is expected of them. My mother told me so much about my great grandfather, Gunther, to know that much."

Danika looked down at her hands. Her fingers picked at each other nervously at her midriff.

"We will find a time together, and we will go to him, alright?" Baski assured her in a low voice.

Danika wished Sally was there. She missed Sally so much.

"Okay," she answered softly. "I have to go to him."

Baski packed her hair and clipped it behind her back.

Karandy was preparing to go out in the evening when he got a knock at the door. He put on his coat, his socks, and his shoes, then headed for the door and threw it open. The mistress stood behind the door as usual, looking impatient and angry.

"Mistress." He inclined his head in greeting.

"It took you ages to get the door. I was freezing outside." She walked inside towards the small fireplace.

"I am sorry I kept you waiting, Mistress." He was observing her carefully, watching the features of her face.

She strode towards the old chair and lowered herself into it. She crossed her arms, her gaze sliding over him slowly. "Are you going somewhere?"

"I am. I want to go to the brothel downtown." He didn't try to mask his meaning.

She snorted in disgust. "Going to pick a prostitute for the night?"

"That's the idea."

"Well, this isn't the time to tumble the sheets with dirty whores. I have a plan. You can be in on it or not," she announced rather reluctantly.

Karandy's brows knitted in thought. This plan of hers, she was giving him a choice to either want in or not, would most definitely favour him. "Let me guess, our main plan? The first plan?" He tried to tap down the anticipation already coursing through him.

She nodded once. "With a little change."

A change? "What do you have in mind?"

"I will get Danika out to the back of the palace and you'll grab her. There's a small hut back there. Take her inside and do everything you want with her. A maid will happen to come across you two lying in an intimate position. She will go and report to the king."

Karandy found the nearest chair and sat down on it. He didn't want to miss this for the world.

Vetta smiled inwardly at the sight of his eagerness. "It is something you have wanted for such a long time, starting from when you were still a slave trainer in the mines."

"You have no idea. I have wanted her for a long time. The bitch only got me demoted and caused me pain." His eyes narrowed to slits. "She will finally pay."

"She will. On the day after tomorrow, you will be getting Danika. Drugged and at your mercy. You can do everything you want; no need to control yourself. I don't care what you do, but don't kill her, and don't bruise her where it'll be visible. A lover's bite is okay."

Karandy glanced at her suspiciously. "You have it all planned out."

"I do," she stated calmly. "So, you are taking the opportunity, or should I find someone else?"

"Of course, I'm taking it. It's the main reason I tangled with you, Mistress, from the beginning. You promised me you could give me Danika."

Her lips split into a smile. "I'm about to fulfill that promise."

Danika went to the royal kitchen. The cook already had the king's food on his tray and everything set for her on the table.

"Here it is," The cook pointed.

"Thank you." Danika carried the tray of food out of the kitchen towards the king's chambers. She rounded the servant's quarters only to see Remeta sitting down on the pavement of the stairs, staring into pace.

"Remeta? Are you alright?" Danika asked, slowing her steps and watching the girl with concern.

She had her fox in her hand, stroking its auburn body. The fox was watching Danika with eyes that creeped her out. Danika wouldn't be surprised if that fox wasn't an ordinary animal. It creeped her out that much.

"Remeta is worried, my queen." Her eyes found Danika's. "Remeta is scared."

"Why?" Danika forgot about the food she carried, her concern for the girl sitting beside her. "Did anything happen?"

Remeta hesitated. Then she shook her head.

"Alright, go to your mother's bedroom. I need to give the king his meal. I will be back."

Remeta gave her a small smile and nodded her head in affirmation. Danika returned her smile and walked past her.

"My queen?"

Danika turned, "Mm?"

"I am sorry, my queen, but it is written. But the gods favor you. The heavens favour you. Darkness all around you, but a bright light so blinding is ahead of you. Just a little out of reach. Hang in there, my queen." She smiled at her sadly. Then she turned and walked away.

Danika stood there for a full minute, trying to comprehend what the girl had just said.

In the end, she gave up and continued her journey towards the royal quarters.

Danika reached the king's quarters and knocked on the door. She waited patiently.

"Come in," came the deep voice of the king.

She hadn't heard his voice since the day before, and it coursed a shiver down her spine. It made her heart flutter too. She had it bad for him. It wasn't something she didn't already know, but the knowledge never ceased to hurt her. Love was not supposed to soothe and hurt at the same time, but hers did.

She opened the door quietly and let herself into his chambers. He was rolling a well-written scroll up and dropping his inked pen on the desk. He raised his head and looked at her.

"I brought your food, my king." She inclined her head.

He gestured his head towards the table without saying a word. She nodded and walked to the small eating table situated on the other side of his chambers. She cleared the scrolls and parchments on it and began arranging his food methodically. It had been that way in the past few days. He always requested that she be the one to bring in his food. Or help him with his clothes. Or to help him write and translate.

She felt more intimate with him, even though he hadn't been taking sexual pleasures from her body. "Your food is ready, Your Highness," she announced softly, turning towards him when she was done.

His eyes were on her. It unsettled her, and a flush spread through her cheeks.

King Lucien could not stop staring at her. The past few weeks had not been easy, having her so close, but he was forced to curb his hunger for her. When his control slipped, he'd call her and have her take him deep into her sexy little mouth. It was mostly enough for him and satisfied him because his innocent Danika was very good with her mouth. The best part of being with her was her selflessly wholehearted eagerness to please. He did not regret letting her in. He did not regret trusting her.

Maybe, just maybe, he would be able to believe in another person again. *Maybe, he would be able to finally heal.*

"Your H-Highness?" her soft voice stuttered out as she shifted nervously on her feet.

The weird urge came again, just like it had for the past few weeks. The weird urge to let his cheeks stretch into a smile. His brows knitted in confusion. "I am coming," he responded to her, shutting his mind to the thought.

He got up and walked around his desk and started for the table.

Danika inclined her head again and turned towards the door.

"Do not go." The words were firm but gentle at the same time.

She turned and looked at him seated in the classy chair made for a king, his eyes on the food in front of him. "Your Highness?"

He did not raise his head as he stated, "Come and sit with me. I do not want to eat alone. I do not want you to go."

Karandy was still thinking about that plan. "The maid that will report us to the king, won't she call my name? That will get me killed," he reasoned.

"She doesn't know you. All she knows is that she caught the king's slave fooling around with a man at the storeroom of the palace."

"Wouldn't Danika tell on me during interrogation?"

Vetta couldn't help herself, and she chuckled at his naivety. "If you think the king would give her a chance to be interrogated after such a crime, then you don't know the king at all. My best bet is that he will order her execution immediately. Betrayal is a crime worse than murder to the king."

Karandy wasn't surprised. King Lucien was not to be messed with.

Vetta continued. "Why do you think she hasn't told him about her pregnancy? She is very scared about how he'll take it. If I were still a slave, I'd rather die than get pregnant for a master like the king," she stated vehemently. "As a slave, Danika threads the most dangerous ground."

"So, why don't you just go to the king and tell him his slave is pregnant? That will be a win for you, too, and a loss for her."

She leaned back in her chair. "It wouldn't kill three birds with one stone."

"I don't understand." His confusion was apparent.

She waved him away. "You won't. There's no greater win than the one which will come from the king's conceptual belief that Danika had a lover all along. It is the worst kind of betrayal. He'll find out about her pregnancy then, and it will be disastrous for her. I look forward to seeing the king kill his own child by his own hands."

Karandy winced. That plan was perfect and very harsh. It reminded him of how wicked the mistress was. Dread filled him for the first time since he forced her to sleep with him. Was he safe?

"Is there more to the plan?" he asked her, trying to tap down his doubts.

She shook her head with a purse of her lips. "No. That is all. Do not worry, it is a perfect plan. You and I will get what we want."

His excitement was apparent on his face, and she had to resist the urge to laugh out loud. The useless bastard.

He had no idea.

CHAPTER 43. THE HEALING KING.

"Come and sit with me. I do not want to eat alone. I do not want you to go."

Danika turned towards him at the deep baritone of his voice, her heart doing a somersault. He didn't want her to go. He wanted her to stay with him. "As you wish, Your Highness," she replied hoarsely.

She walked back to the dining table and sat down beside him. He dug into the broth in front of him, scooping it up and into his mouth. She watched him eat, keeping quiet because she knew how much he loved his silence. There was no food in front of her, but she wasn't really hungry. Just having that moment to watch him eat was enough to feed whatever hunger was in her. She loved him that much.

Folding her hands on her lap, she resisted the urge to caress her baby. It was a bad habit she had developed over the past few weeks, touching and caressing her belly in private whenever she was thinking of the king. A bad habit considering her situation, but one she couldn't stop.

The king raised his head, catching her watching him. Her cheeks heated at being caught, and she quickly lowered her eyes.

"Guards," he spoke in that calm voice of his.

A few seconds passed. The door opened, and Zariel entered. "You summoned me, My Lord?"

"Go to the kitchen and get an extra plate of food. Do not forget to get a basin of water and linen towels, too," he ordered, chewing softly on the meat in his mouth.

"Your wish is my command, Your Highness," Zariel answered immediately and hurried out of the room.

"I am not hungry, my king," Danika protested softly. Those days, her appetite had taken a vacation away from her. Not that Baski cared. The older woman always forced her to eat everything, saying it was good for her child. She tried her best to eat them but had very little appetite.

The king glanced at her. "You look a little skinnier. You will eat."

She swallowed a gasp at his innate observation. It was almost creepy how he would notice the very slight difference in her weight. She was suddenly thankful that she had been wearing big double corsets lately to hide her condition. He would have noticed otherwise.

You will spend the night naked in his arms tomorrow, Danika. He will definitely find out.

She shut her mind against the frightening thought and focused on watching the king eat in silence. She watched how he scooped up some little potatoes and directed them to his mouth.

The door opened, and Zariel entered with an identical tray to the one the king had. If the king noticed that he brought food for her on a plate meant for a queen to eat from, he said nothing. Instead, he picked up the wine and drank from it.

Zariel walked around the table towards her and dropped the tray of food in front of her. In the minute that followed, he set the food as it should be in front of her before he bowed to the king and walked out of his chambers.

She thanked him for the food and dug into her plates. They ate in comfortable silence.

Vetta was coming back from Karandy's house. She had been having a very beautiful day as she rounded the corner that led to the gate of the palace. Then, a small body bumped into her, dragging her out of her thoughts. She looked down to see a small boy who couldn't be past seven staring up at her.

"How dare you throw such a dirty body at me!? Do you want me to have you whipped!?" she hissed angrily, shoving the boy hard.

The child fell and began crying. A heavily pregnant woman ran towards them, and her eyes widened when she saw who her child had run into. "I-I'm so sorry, Mistress. Please, forgive my son! I'm sorry!" the woman cried, fear gripping her because she knew the rumors about the king's mistress being short-tempered and intolerable.

"He should have looked where he was going, the hellion!" Vetta hissed.

The woman's eyes widened at the anger in the mistress's voice. The woman knelt and began crying and begging. She feared her son would be taken into the palace and whipped.

Vetta dusted her dress clean, hating the dirtiness she was feeling. She turned to the boy and narrowed her eyes at him. "Make sure you look where you're going next time!"

The boy only cried harder, running to his mother to hug her tight.

Vetta noticed she was beginning to draw the attention of other people, so she turned and stormed away. "Ugly dirty lowlifes!" she fumed as she walked.

When she arrived at the palace, her thoughts returned to Karandy, and a smile touched her cheeks, wiping out the ugly event from outside the palace a few moments ago. The useless bastard really had no idea. There was so much more to her plan than he knew. She would be killing three birds with one stone. That included Danika, her child, and the idiot, Karandy.

Vetta had something to smile about for the first time in a few weeks. Something really cool. She headed for the king's quarters.

She reached the door, but Zariel stopped her. "The king is having dinner. He does not like to be disturbed."

Of course, she knew he didn't like to be disturbed when eating. She had no plans to invoke his anger by doing so. "I will come back later." She turned to leave and stopped when her eyes caught at the closed window.

Two shadows sitting down and eating. The king and Danika.

Vetta pushed down the anger she felt. It didn't matter; they had limited time to spend together in the future, anyway.

Let Danika have that moment.

She turned and walked away. Reaching into petticoat, she withdrew the fertility pills she got from Monah. He would be hers tomorrow night; she would make sure of that.

Danika noticed that the king was troubled. It showed on his face as their meal progressed.

"What troubles you, my king?" Danika asked, her eyebrows creased with worry.

King Lucien wasn't used to sharing his problems. He said nothing.

She noticed his defensive hesitation and didn't press. He had let her in long enough for her to know him for who he was—a man who was more used to keeping to himself than talking to people. But she already had his trust. He had already let her in. He would tell her when he was ready and not before.

After the meal, she got up and began clearing the plates. She got to his side and packed up his plates. She was about to carry it up when his arm suddenly wrapped around her midriff.

"Don't. Don't turn around," he ordered, stopping her impulsive movement.

Danika froze. Her heart was in her throat because the king's arm was crossed over her belly. Could he feel their child?

His head came down on her lower back. "Let us be like this just for a moment. Just for a moment."

He didn't notice. She let out a shuddering breath of relief.

They stayed that way for long. She dropped the plates she had in her hand back to the table. Then she began patting his hands rhythmically. His deep breaths fanned her butt. She imagined his eyes sliding close. Finally, he unwrapped his arms from her and raised his head. She took it as her cue to turn towards him. His hand rubbed his forehead as if trying to soothe a headache. She allowed herself to sit back on the chair behind her.

Finally, he moaned in a low voice. "Downtown, the crops are dying. Their lower market hasn't been selling well lately. It has been this way since the beginning of this year, but I thought things would change. It hasn't."

Danika had heard about this before from the maids. They talk about a small part of town downtown having trouble feeding because crops are no longer growing.

"Crops are dying. There has been no rain in this kingdom for two years. It is unsettling, but it happens in other kingdoms too. Salem is vulnerable because of what we've been through at the hands of King Cone. We are still trying to stand back on our feet. That's why it's harder for my kingdom. The farmers are trying, but there is only so much they can do."

Danika listened quietly as he poured out his mind to her. She could tell that this had weighed heavily on him from the way he talked about it. No wonder he looked so worn out.

"It gets worse as time goes by," King Lucien continued. "This past few weeks, they've been getting food from the palace, from the servant's kitchen. I have the cooks send food downtown, but it can't go on like this for long."

Danika felt compelled to assure him. "The people of Salem are very strong, my king. They have survived on their own for a long time. The people downtown might be lowborns, but they are survivors. Do not worry so much."

"I cannot help but worry," he groaned.

She bit her lips. "Can I make a suggestion, Your Highness?"

He rubbed his hand over his face. "You can."

"There is a lot of water from the ground here in the palace. Why don't we connect a pipe from the palace to downtown? It would supply water there, at least enough for them to keep the crops growing and be able to feed and sell. It can sustain the people until rain comes," she presented softly.

King Lucien hadn't thought of that before. He raised his head and looked at the woman before him. He felt like a heavy load had lifted from his shoulders. "This is a very good idea, Danika," he said truthfully.

Danika nodded, inwardly feeling pleased with herself. She was glad that she was able to help.

"I will tell Zariel to do that first thing tomorrow morning." He paused. "I want you to go over there when you can to oversee the project."

Danika's eyes widened. That was usually the work of a queen or a person from a privileged position. Definitely not for a slave.

"But---" she began.

He got up and walked towards his wardrobe and began undressing his royal wears. "You can ensure that every house will be able to fetch the water they need."

She snapped her mouth shut, but her heart filled with happiness that he would put her in charge of such a big important project when he had a future queen and a mistress. It made her eyes water. "I will make sure not to disappoint you, my king," she breathed.

Silence descended. Left in his underthings, he walked to the bed and laid down on it. His eyes closed, and he continued rubbing small circles on his forehead.

"I feel so tired." He paused. "Come and hold me, Danika." The request made her heart jump. She hesitated. "Do not worry about the courting week. I will not try to take your body. That will be on the night of the morrow. Now, I need to sleep. That works best in your arms," he murmured without opening his eyes.

She realized that he hadn't just openly confessed something so important to her, but he also gave her a weakness of his. He slept best in her arms. He trusted her enough to tell her that much.

Her legs carried her to him, and she got into bed beside him. The king needed her. For the first time in a long time, she felt genuinely happy. He might not love her, but he did feel something for her. Something beautiful. He must, for him to be able to let her in...and keep letting her in.

Her eyes found the door of the library behind him—the place where his sister, Princess Melia, was killed by her father. She could still remember that day he warned her never to go into that library. He was so angry he'd told her that he would kill her the day he found her in that library. And since then, she had never been inside there. It was also a part of him he had kept away from her.

Would the day come when he would let her inside that library? With the way he had been with her lately, she had hope. With time, he would trust her enough to let her in completely.

Automatically, he pulled her closer and wrapped his arms around her. "This is better."

"Yes." She closed her eyes and burrowed into him, and a sigh of pleasure left her lips. She loved being in his arms. Had craved it in the past few weeks.

"I know something much better." He pulled back and began untying the ropes of her corset. Finally, the ropes came free. He pulled it down and freed a plump, creamy breast. A groan of satisfaction left his lips before he took the perk nipple into his eager mouth.

Danika couldn't hold back the moan that escaped her lips. That part of her had always been sensitive. More so now that she was pregnant. With each tug of his lips, she felt something that secret place of her womanhood. She pushed down the feeling and closed her eyes again and began patting his short black curls.

Time passed.

That seem to be all he needed. It didn't take long before his breath evened out and he fell asleep.

.

CHAPTER 44. THE QUEEN OF MANIPULATION.

The next day, Danika and Baski didn't get to see the king because the day had been filled with activities.

Just as the king said, the next morning, he told Zariel about the plan for irrigation and water distribution to the people. He also told Zariel that Danika was in charge.

So, she left the palace and went into town with them, where she supervised and directed the sharing of water. Coming outside town reminded her of Sally, her former maid, who had been at her side for years. She missed Sally so much even though she wrote to her from time to time. It paid off that she taught Sally how to write.

Sally might not be perfect and might get most of the words wrong, but what mattered to Danika was that she was able to return her messages, and she was also able to comprehend Sally's messages after a few careful reads. She hoped that one of these days, she would have the time and permission to leave the palace and visit her best friend.

Down the town, she was dedicated to her duty, making sure that the sharing of water worked well and properly.

The people were so happy about the water; it showed on their faces and their attitudes, on the smile they gave her each time they passed with their big buckets. They thanked her and the king as they fetched their rounds. She made sure every family got their share.

Danika was still making her rounds when a little boy fell into her. She grabbed the child to steady him so the boy would not fall. He did not look older than six years to her. "Are you all right?" she asked, concerned, staring at the boy's clothes and not-so-clean hair.

The boy had fear written all over his face. "I'm sorry! I'm so sorry! Please, don't hurt me!"

"I have no plans to hurt you, dear. Please, don't cry. What is your name?" she asked softly.

He took two steps away from her, still crying. The boy hesitated.

Danika patted his hair in reassurance giving him a beautiful smile. "It's okay. It's okay."

"I'm Corna," he mumbled at last.

"Stop crying, Corna, okay? I won't hurt you."

A heavily pregnant woman came running out immediately with her own bucket in her hand, and her eyes widened at the sight in front of her. She dropped her bucket immediately as if it bit her. She rushed to Danika and knelt in front of her. "Oh, please! Please, have mercy on him, please! Corna is very clumsy and reckless and always running without watching his way. Please, have mercy, please!" the young woman cried bitterly.

Danika was already shaking her head. She helped the pregnant woman stand up. "Stop panicking. He only runs into people; he isn't hurting anybody. Don't let it bother you so much."

"Corna has no control at all. Yesterday, he ran into the mistress, and he almost got whipped for it. Please have mercy, please! I'll try to hold him as often as I can."

"You can only try your best, but it's okay. He's just a boy, and he's already scared out of his mind." She spared the little boy a glance and saw how he shivered in fear. The sight broke her heart. Not minding the boy's dirty state, she lifted the boy into her arms. He was quite heavy, but she held him. Danika consoled him with soothing words while the poor mother stood beside them, gawking at her. The woman never expected such treatment from a woman who was once of privileged status—a woman who was fathered by a monster.

Time passed, and the boy stopped crying, but he refused to get down from Danika's arms. Instead, he burrowed his head into her shoulder and stuck his hand into his mouth and sucked on it.

No matter how his mother tried to get him to come away from Danika and allow her to work, the boy turned deaf ears. In the end, Danika just smiled and walked away, carrying the boy.

She held the boy as she continued doing her job. She made sure the older people in the village got enough water, too, while Zariel and the guards stayed several miles away from her, getting the pumps working well.

It was evening by the time King Lucien finished in court. He was feeling so tired, as always, after a long day in court. That day, he had to deal with a married couple who wished to separate and the little kids in the orphanage of Salem. Those children lost their parents at the hands of King Cone during slavery. The reminder made his head hurt.

The king was almost at his chambers when a maid ran to him, breathing heavily and seemed to have come in a hurry. He turned towards her and waited for her to talk.

The maid fell to the ground and bowed her head. "My name is Kaya. I'm the personal maid of the mistress. She is so sick, Your Highness! So, so, sick, and she requests you."

That had the king's brows creased in worry. "How is she? What is the matter? Is she doing alright? "

"No, my king. She is not doing so fine. She scares me."

"Take me to her."

The maid nodded vigorously and got up from the floor. She led the king to the mistress quarters.

When the king entered, he saw Vetta lying down on the bed. It had been so long since he saw his mistress he felt guilt. He and Vetta had been through so much together; it was unfair that he had been so unconcerned about her for the past few weeks.

The king turned to Kaya. "Leave us."

"As you wish, Your Majesty." The maid responded with a bow of her head before she turned and hurried out of the room.

Vetta's eyes opened a little. "My king," she whispered in a hoarse voice.

He walked towards the edge of her bed and sat down. "How do you feel?"

Vetta tried to read him, but it was as impossible as trying to force rain to fall. His face was as hard as it was carved out of granite, but his eyes weren't so cold.

"I feel very bad." She had him exactly where she wanted him. Buying the body-weakening and swollen-face pills from the black market was definitely worth it. It gave her inner joy. Outside, her eyes watered as she watched him. The seller did tell her that the illegal pill did make a person an emotional mess. She was glad about that part too. She needed all the game she could get.

"What is wrong with you?" he asked in a calming voice.

"I started having lots of pain in my belly and so much weakness. I couldn't control the pain; it was too much." It wasn't exactly a lie.

"I should have Baski take a look at you. She might be able to help."

"No. Not Baski." She shook her head. "Wouldn't want to be a burden to her. Kaya already called Angie, the medicine man, and he has examined me. He made me some herbs to take too."

Her eyes went to the table beside her, leaving the king's eyes to follow. Indeed, there were drugs on the table but they were her fertility pills and body-energizing potions.

The king nodded. "You will be fine, Vetta."

"Thank you, my king. I'm just so s-scared." She swallowed, looking frightened. "I hate being sick. It reminds me so much about that horrible place. I don't ever want to live with the thoughts of that hideous past in my head."

He raised his hand. Hesitated. Then he placed it on her arm, a muscle at his jaw ticked in that telltale indication that he didn't like touches. He didn't pull his hand, though. "Try not to think about it. We are free, Vetta. The drugs might make you delirious but try not to get buried in that awful memories." His eyes clouded. "I know what it feels like to drown in them. It is not a good feeling."

She knew that he knew how awful and tormenting their past had been for him, which was exactly why she was using it. Tears filled her eyes and overflowed. Being delirious was her best strategy.

"I feel so alone," she cried.

"You are not alone."

"Lucien?" she whispered, knowing he wouldn't punish her for it.

278

He stiffened. She'd called him that a few things in slavery after a massive torture session. "Mm?"

More tears. "Can you please stay this night with me? I'm so scared. I don't want to be alone. I'm so scared to be alone."

Danika was tired and worn out by the time the project finished.

She took Corna back to his mother's house and dropped him at the front porch. Lowering herself to become eye level with the boy, she ruffled his hair again. "You'll be fine, Corna. Be a good boy, okay?"

Corna nodded obediently. "You are a good queen. Very beautiful queen."

Danika smiled at him, even as she wondered what was with the little boy addressing her the same way Remeta addressed her. "I'm not a queen. I was a princess, Corna. But not anymore."

The boy reluctantly released his finger from his mouth with a pop. He moved closer and placed his little hand on her belly. He touched every corner of it like a doctor would do during an examination. He looked up at her confused face and smiled. "Pwince of Rwain. Ewerything will be fine."

Danika returned his smile even though she hadn't understood most of his halting words. The door opened, and his mother came out with a warm smile. She thanked Danika for everything.

"Because of you and the king, we will have so much to eat again. We have water again. Thank you so much. You are so different from your father. I am so sorry that you have been hated because of him. You are a good woman, Princess Danika." The woman smiled at her before she took Corna into the small house.

Danika's heart was filled with happiness as she walked away from the premises. It was a good day today.

Her happy mood only lasted until she entered her bedroom, and Baski informed her that the king would be spending the night with his mistress in her bedroom.

She should feel relief---it would buy them more time to tell the king about her pregnancy, which she and Baski had already decided they would do on the morning of the morrow. If the king didn't spend the night with her, he wouldn't have to find out by himself and accuse her of betrayal.

She should be giddy with relief. But all she felt was sadness. Her chest tightened, and her eyes watered. She turned away from Baski so that she wouldn't see her tears. "It's a good thing for me anyway. I can just use this opportunity to get some much-needed sleep. I've been so stressed; I need the rest and---"

Baski came to her front and hugged her close. "It's okay to feel bad, Danika. No one ever gets used to the bitter fact that a man who was supposed to be hers is in the company of another woman."

Danika swiped the tears away. "The king is not mine."

"You're right, he isn't. You are not the only woman the king has. Several mistresses and slaves belong to the king, but a king belongs to his queen."

The answer only made her hurt the more. It reminded her of the things she could never have—of her former status she lost.

"Our king already has his future queen, but guess who he has feelings for?" Baski added.

Danika stiffened, pulling back to see the older woman's face clearly.

Baski nodded. "I don't know what those feelings are, and I can bet that he has no idea either. But he has feelings for you, Danika. Feelings that are not hate. Feelings that he does not have for any other woman that belongs to him."

Baski smiled as she began walking to the door. "Why don't you keep that in mind as you try to get that much-needed sleep? And you're going to need that sleep very well. It's a big day tomorrow. And we don't know what it will bring."

After she left, Danika walked to the bed and sat down on it. Her heart was light and filled with hope.

Did the king really have feelings for her?

Well, Baski was right about one thing. It was a big day tomorrow. They would go together and break the news of her pregnancy to the king. No more going back.

What will tomorrow bring?

Will it change her life for the better?

Will it change her life for the worse?

Will tomorrow end her life?

Danika took her bath and came back to her bedroom. Lying on the bed in a simple night cloth, she couldn't shake the bad feeling that settled in her gut.

Why did it feel like tomorrow would change her life forever?

.

CHAPTER 45. THE DARK SUN UPON A BRIGHT STAR.

Vetta spent half of the night reminiscing their days in captivity. It made the king on edge, and as hours passed, he was tense like a coiled snake waiting to snap.

It was exactly what Vetta wanted. Why would he want to forget what they'd been through? Why would he try to forget what shaped him into the man he is now?

Vetta took her fertility pills around midnight, the bone-weakening pills already wearing off like the woman told her. An hour after taking her pills, she was horny as hell and ready to have the king to herself.

He was lying behind her, tense and ready to sleep. But he had always been a man who sleep did not favor, so she knew he was awake even when he was as quiet as the blazes.

She turned towards him and reached boldly for him. She did not think it was possible for him to get tenser, but that happened when she placed a hand on his chest.

"Not tonight, Vetta." she felt the vibration of his deep groan.

"I need you, my king. I need you so much," she whispered, untying his rope.

His hand stopped hers. Blue eyes like bottomless pits of hell met her face. "You are sick. You do not need this."

"Yes, I do. Please. It's been so long. Danika came along, and you no longer want me. You treat me like I'm dirty like you no longer want me. It pains me," her voice sad, she articulated.

"Vetta---"

She rose from the bed and pulled off her clothes. She'd prepared for this night, so she wasn't really wearing much. Sitting up naked beside him, she shook her head miserably. "I am your mistress, my king. I feel like I'm no longer good enough for you, maybe because I wasn't born with royal blood inside me. Maybe because you have forgotten everything we've been through. Maybe you glance at me and remember dirt." Tears filled her eyes and she sniffled. "The same dirt King Cone created when he raped my mind and my body right in front of you."

King Lucien slid his eyes closed; the memory made his heart—which was warm earlier in the day—go cold.

"He dropped a burger. Wanted me to crawl on my hands and knees and eat it out straight from the ground with my mouth. Like a dog." He remembered one of the events.

"Something so utterly degrading and demeaning for you," she whispered.

His head moved in a nod. "I would not do it, so he starved me for three days. Came back afterward to force such humiliation again in front of twelve slaves. He raped you brutally right in front of me because I would not do it."

She closed her eyes at the shameful remembrance. She didn't have to fake the tears; they came all on their own.

"I can still remember that like yesterday. Your screams. The blood. I never forgot, Vetta. There are some things that can never be forgotten," he said quietly.

"These memories stayed with me," she admitted, her hand on his chest again. "When you keep me so far away like you have done these past few weeks, I cannot help but feel dirty. You do not want me anymore."

He rose and palmed her cheek. "That is untrue. I do want you. And about your past, they do not define you, Vetta. What defines you is your present and your future."

She lowered her head then and kissed his lips. His hand on her waist tightened, a small reaction, but with the king, it did not get any bigger. She pulled back and sniffled. "See. I repulse you. You can't even bear to kiss me, but you do so with Danika all the time. She was the princess. The Untouched. The Unraped. The Pure. The innocent. And I am just dirt."

"I do not kiss Danika for those reasons, Vetta," he indicated at her miserable cry. "And you are not dirt. I do not like such an assessment. If being battered makes dirt, then I would be mud."

"Then kiss me. Take me to bed, just like old times. I crave it: the pain, the pleasure, the pressure, everything. I crave you." At that whisper, she kissed him again.

He remained unresponsive for a few seconds. Then he took over. Kissing her, he undressed. Naked like she was, she wet her hand with the lube on the table before touching his phallus. She took hold of his length and stroked him to arousal.

They laid on their sides, with her back to him. Raising her leg, she moaned when he pushed into her to the hilt. His thrusts were restrained and controlled,as if his body was with her but his mind wasn't.

She reached behind him and circled his neck, aching her back to push him deeper into her. "Let go," she moaned. "Let me have the man that has fucked me for more than five years. The pain, pleasure, the animalism, I want it all."

It reminded him of that day he was overwhelmed, and he lost *all* control with Danika. He has taken sexual pleasures so unrestrained from his mistress before—but he has not lost the real control with her.

"Be careful what you wish for," he grated out.

"I know you want it too," she persisted, rotating her hips on his, in a way she knew he enjoyed. He emitted a low groan. She continued. "That man will always be in you. The one who loves to inflict pain and pleasure at the same time. I don't cave in the face of pain and you know it. It is one of the things Danika can never give you."

"Do not pretend you know her. You do not."

"I know her likes." Swiveling her head to watch him over her shoulders, she panted. "Would she want you to yank on her hair as you fuck her hard enough to hurt? Would she want you to bite hard on her neck enough to leave a mark? Pinch hard on her nipple, not to pleasure but to hurt?" Her voice lowered more to an octave. "Would she let you take her in the ass?"

"Vetta—"

"She would not want to. She can't. You know it and I do." Her pants increased, and so did his thrusts. "She c-can never sate that broken man in you. The monster her father created." Her eyes glazed over as she pushed down on him over and over again. "I want that monster. I can feed him. You know I can..."

His erratic breathing was all that met her words, and his thrusts increased as he neared climax.

Vetta watched him lazily the next morning as he put on his clothes in that unhurried way that had always been a thing with him. Her eyes followed him greedily, a smile plastered on her face. He had been with her all night, even though he held some part of him back. It didn't matter much to her because she knew she got to him, and there was a part of him that would always be hers.

"You are going to the training ground and will be training new guards today, right?" she asked, lying naked and sated on the bed. She had no desire to put on her clothes.

He reached for his gold-colored robe and pulled it over his head. "You have that right."

"There have been some silent rumors between the maids..." she trailed off.

He spared her a glance as he tied his royal belt, which he had worn when he'd come to her yesterday. "What is that?"

She bit her lips. "They said that Danika is seeing another man. According to the rumors, she has another lover."

Eyes so cold they would freeze the toughest of men snapped up and held hers. He spoke no words, but he didn't need to.

She'd pushed him too hard.

Vetta backpaddled immediately. "W-well, I wasn't the one that s-said it. It was a rumor I overheard—"

"I do not ever want to hear such a thing from you again," he cut in.

"My king, I didn't mean—"

He turned away from her. "Danika is not that kind of woman. She was trained better than that. She has more morals and principles than most princesses. She would not do it—not when she finds it degrading and beneath her status."

She sputtered in indignation, taken aback. "She is a slave."

"She was a princess. For twenty-two years."

Why would he defend her like that!? It annoyed Vetta greatly, but she tapped it down. It would make it all the more entertaining and interesting when her plan proved him wrong. In fact, it only solidified her belief that the king would execute Danika when he found her in the arms of another man.

Poor Danika. Vetta smiled greatly. It was a promising day.

"I have to be in court." He strode to the door.

"I enjoyed last night, my king," she produced in a surd tone. "I am yours to summon whenever you want. Even when your forced to indulge your broken self and have...special needs. I am yours."

King Lucien reached for the doorknob and stopped. He turned and walked back to her until he stood in front of her. There was a slight ting of pity in his eyes as he watched her.

"I am trying to heal, Vetta. Maybe it is time you try to do the same." With that, he turned and walked out of her bedroom.

Danika woke up feeling unwell. It was not unusual for her ever since she got pregnant, but this day was worse than the others. She vomited her lungs in the toilet, lowered herself to the floor beside the seat, and laid her head on it to try to get some sleep. She was feeling that sleepy.

A knock came, followed by the creek of the door. "Danika?" Baski's voice came through.

"In here." She tried to shout, but it came out like a croon.

A few seconds later, Baski appeared at her door and looked at her with concern. "Your food is down the drains."

"I couldn't keep it in. I feel very queasy this morning. More than the other days."

Baski walked closer and helped her get up from the floor. She led her out of the bathroom. "That's what being pregnant is like. Some days are better—or worse—than the others." She led her to the chair and sat her down on it. She began rubbing Danika's back in an attempt to calm her queasiness. "You have to come back during early afternoon to put something in your stomach again. If you eat again now, you won't be able to keep it down."

"Okay. Zariel said we have to go and distribute water to another part of town that was having the same water and crop issues. Theirs aren't as severe as those downtown, but they still have problems with cultivation because of water," she explained softly.

"That is good. I still can't believe the king entrusted you with something so huge. I never expected it. He is so unpredictable."

"I never expected it either. I plan to go and see Sally when I'm in town too. I've missed her so much."

"I know she misses you too. That's how it is when you recently get married. You miss your family and friends, but you can't do anything about it for a while. You have new responsibilities, and that is taking care of your new husband, trying to make a family and trying to adjust to your new life," Baski enunciated to her in an educative way.

"I understand. Thank you so much, Baski. For everything." Danika raised her head and smiled at her in gratitude. "You're the mother I lost when I was young. Thank you for being here for me."

Baski shook her head, still rubbing her back. "You are a good woman, Danika. I knew almost immediately when I came to see you in the dungeon two days after the king collared you." The older woman smiled at the reminder. "You were looking so elegant. So very beautiful and proud like the princess you are. But behind that bravado, I saw a vulnerable woman in terror of the new strange world she found herself in. I didn't let myself feel for you because of your father."

"What changed?" Danika asked, curious.

"Your strength. Your braveness. Your heart. The goodness in you. The light in you shines too bright; it cannot be ignored," she answered without missing a beat.

Danika's eyes watered, and she averted her eyes. "You give me so much credit."

Baski only smiled and gave her back the last pat before she pulled away from her and stood up, "The king is in court this morning. He has a lot to do. We will go to him when you come back this evening."

Danika nodded. "Alright. I will go to the backyard to pick up the clothes I hung out there to dry."

Danika rounded the corner that led to the backyard when all of a sudden, a strong hand grabbed her from behind. She opened her lips to scream, but the hand slapped over her mouth while still holding her tight against his hard body. A knife poked at her side from behind. "Make a single noise and cut you apart like a cloth."

The deep dreaded voice of the former slave trainer reverberated Danika's ears. She froze automatically in fear as he dragged her to the store room and slammed the door shut.

.

CHAPTER 46. THE DUSK BEFORE THE DAWN.

Sally woke up that morning with a sick feeling in her gut. A very sick feeling of impending doom. Staring at the wall clock, she wasn't surprised that she woke up late, considering how late she had fallen asleep last night. A small smile split her lips, followed by a red that spread across her cheeks.

Chad had been very demanding—more demanding than he'd always been with her. It was beautiful. And speaking of her husband. She looked around the empty bedroom for him, but he wasn't in the room. Then she heard the faint sound of an axe hitting some wood repeatedly.

She got up and entered the small bathhouse, her face glowing as she felt the aches in her body that were a perfect memory of everything he had done to her the night before. She loved being married to the love of her life. She never thought her life would ever turn out like this.

A few moments later, she was dressed in a plain yellow petticoat and a beautiful small-rounded hat on her head. She strode to the kitchen to try and fix something to eat for them.

That bad feeling came again in her gut—this time around, stronger, deadlier. Her princess, Danika.

She paused in the middle of cutting vegetables and savored the feeling of longing for her princess. She had missed seeing her princess so much. So much it was almost a physical ache.

Sally had always planned for a while now to go and see her princess, but she had never found the time to do that because she and her husband were still trying to settle in. They were working around the house and renovating in their spare time.

Standing on her toes, Sally looked out of the kitchen window, watching Chad as he broke the woods. He'd told her that he wanted to build a storeroom for them.

Oh, Princess Danika, I miss you so much, Sally thought sadly. She resolved to make time today—no matter how little—to go and see her princess in the palace.

"Why do you look so worried? Are you alright, my dear?"

Sally sighed when she heard the voice of her husband close behind her. His hand wrapped around her waist. She must have been too wrapped up in her thoughts she didn't hear him walk in.

"I'm worried about my princess. I woke up having a very bad feeling in my gut," she explained softly. "I miss her badly."

"I think about the king, too, from time to time. We should make out time to make a visit to the palace." Chad played with her soft hair, washing her cook.

Sally nodded. His words should have alleviated her worry and calmed her heart, but they didn't.

The sickening feeling in her gut only worsened.

Callan was working at the back of his house. Peace and serenity was his only companion with him, exactly how he liked it. The chirpings of birds in the morning. The sound of giving flowed down the hill a few miles away. The soft sweeping of wind every moment. He was deep in thought as he caught the linens he wanted to use as new cotton for his house.

He was quickly jerked out of his thoughts when he heard a soft but firm knock on his front door. He dropped the scissors and the linen cloth and got up from the wooden chair. He walked back to his house through the backyard and entered the sitting room, going straight to the door where he pulled it open.

It was a visitor he never expected after months of absence—after he heard of her impending marriage to a king.

"Good day, My Lady." He extended with a bow of his head, opening the door wider for her to enter.

"Hello," Princess Kamara greeted. She was almost nervous, and he had never known her to be anything but sparkling.

Kamara removed the hood she used to cover herself while making this forbidden journey. Her father would be very mad at her if he found out about this, but she just couldn't stay away any longer. She needed to see him. Not seeing him the past few months hadn't been easy, coupled with her one month in Salem, and he was all she thought about since she returned yesterday.

Her eyes took him in the same way he watched her. He was one of the most handsome she had ever met, with those devastating blue eyes that were very expressive, unlike King Lucien's.

Kamara admitted that she was a nervous mess. Her insides tingled just at the sight of him. Her heart raced, and her cheeks were faint red.

Callan was the only man that always reduced her to this state. She would have been ashamed of herself if she hadn't found out about her deep feelings for him.

"I'm so sorry for dropping in so unannounced. I ---" she paused, not knowing the way to say it. "I just needed to see you."

"It's no problem or hardship, my lady. I-I was not expecting to see you at all," he stuttered out, obviously flustered by her presence.

"Oh, should I go?" She must have caught him at a bad time. She shouldn't have—

"No, no, that's not it, my lady." He was quick to clear her doubts. He looked behind her in search of something.

He must be looking for Henna, Kamara deducted. She had never visited him before without her personal maid. In fact, she rarely went anywhere without her.

She pushed the strands of her hair to her face, and an almost-shy smile appeared. "It's just me today. I came alone."

"Oh." He balanced his weight on the other foot. His eyes were everywhere but at her. He pointed behind him. "I am working out back."

"Can I stay with you while you work? I wouldn't disturb or yell or distract you. I will—"

"Yes, please," he replied, cutting her off.

Her eyes brightened and she looked at his face more. It calmed most of her nerves to see that he was as flustered as she was. Maybe, just maybe, he felt her absence when she stopped coming around.

"I can stay?" she asked in clarification.

He held the door wider for her, and his eyes finally met hers. "Yes. You can stay for as long as you want. I don't mind."

The last of Kamara's worries about invading his privacy disappeared like the wind, and her lips stretched into a wild smile as she walked into the house.

Karandy slammed the door shut before he released Danika from his arms. A wicked victorious smile stretched his lips as he looked at the former princess. "At last," he groaned to himself in satisfaction. "At—fucking—last."

Danika glanced at the man that suddenly grabbed her away and locked her in the store room with him. Terror filled her because he had a knife with him. "Let me go!" she demanded, meaning to keep most of the intoxicating fear from her voice.

"You are in no circumstances to give commands, Princess," he mocked, chuckling at her.

Danika took deep breaths and tried again, walking right past him to the door. "Please, let me go. Why would you bring me here!?"

He dragged her by the hair and yanked her right back to him, pressing the knife to her lower back again. "Don't ever do that."

Danika froze. "The king will murder you for this. You better let me go, or I will report this to the king!"

That devilish laughter came again. Then Danika felt his hand wrapped around one of her breasts and he squeezed hard. A scream erupted in her throat at the excruciating pain, and his hand shot to her mouth, smothering the pained sound. He didn't stop squeezing until Danika thought he'd crush her breast and her nipple would fall off.

"Stop! Please!" Her pleas were muffled through his hand, and she writhed against him, thrashing so hard in an effort to pull free.

"Let me make something clear, Princess. You do not get to threaten me. Not today. You can only ask the gods to keep me in a better mood on this day so I won't strangle you after I take what I want from you over and over again." Finally, his hand released her abused plumpness and he stepped back.

Her eyes watered, and she looked around fanatically for an escape. *This can't be happening! This can't be!!* She had a sickening feeling in her gut about what 'he wants from her' and bile rose in her throat. Over her dead body would she allow that!

"Money! I will give you money if you will just let me go!" she screamed at him. Her fear and will to escape that hellish fate overrode her sense of reasoning, and she made a run for the door again.

Before Karandy could reach for her, a huge wave of dizziness found her first. She cried out as the room tilted. She lost her balance, but his repulsive hand caught her and lifted her off her feet.

"Let me go! Let me go now! *Help*!!!!" she screamed again.

Karandy forced her down on the hay he made in the storeroom and came down on top of her aggressively. He wrapped his hand around her collared neck and squeezed tightly, cutting off her scream...and her breath.

She made choking sounds, trying to drag in breaths to her system. Karandy was already raving mad about her stubbornness. He was truly tempted to beat her brutally and strangle her to death, not minding the mistress's instructions. But he tried to get himself under control by taking deep breaths to calm his anger. Taking sexual pleasures from her body as much as he wanted and anyhow he wanted when she was too drugged, he could do. But sleeping with her dead body was not something he wanted.

"Will you keep your mouth shut and do everything I want, or do you want me to strangle you to death!?" he snarled angrily, his hands tightening on her throat.

Danika's lungs burned from lack of air; she couldn't breathe at all. Helpless tears wouldn't stop flowing from her eyes down her ears to the white piece of cloth he spread beneath her. She nodded her head vigorously, thrashing under him in her effort to throw his hand off and take oxygen into her lungs.

Finally, he loosened his hand and pulled back from her. She gasped in air in large quantity, and all the fight knocked out of her. Suddenly, she was feeling so tired of everything. Her throat hurt. Her inside burns. Her breast were aching badly.

"Useless cunt. You think yourself all high and mighty?" He leaned closer, grabbing her jaw and forcing her to look at him. "The only thing I have ever wanted from you was your body. If you had allowed me to take you whenever I wanted then—if you had agreed to my offer, then in the mines—none of this would be happening!"

"Please, let me go. I'm feeling so unwell, and you're hurting me," she cried miserably, wanting to be everywhere but where she was at the moment. "I'm p-pregnant. You're h-hurting me."

"I know you're carrying the king's child. Good luck with that one. You have a death wish, keeping an abomination like that thing in your belly." He reached for her clothes.

She crawled back until her back hit the wall, scurrying out of his reach. "No! Please, don't hurt my baby. Don't hurt me. I'm s-sorry for everything I did, but please, don't do this!"

He had wasted enough time. This woman had featured in every one of his erotic fantasies, and now he had a chance to live them. Having her well away from people behind closed doors and at his mercy had given him a hard, painful boner. Blazes, he couldn't wait to explore her. He wanted to take her body while she screamed and fought him—the thought turned him on so much—but he knew he couldn't risk it. The plan was to drug her senseless; they were so close to the palace.

He reached for the table behind his head and withdrew the pill that would make her very high for his cock, and then he would be able to fuck her as long as he wanted before the maid whom the mistress would send came.

"Take this." He extended it to her casually.

Danika watched the small brown pill with terror. What was that pill? Would it kill her? Hurt her severely? Whatever it was must not be a good thing. She shook her head vigorously, pressing herself to the wall.

Karandy hissed impatiently and glared at her. "Listen to me. It's either you take this all by yourself, or I force it down your throat after

I've beaten you within an inch of your life and strangled the breath out of you. You will have no choice but to take the pills."

Her cheeks were wet from crying, and she felt very dizzy and tired. "P-please stop. I feel f-faint," she cried truthfully.

"These pills will help you. Keep you energized and happy. I will make you very happy, and you will only want so much more," he enunciated smugly.

Her eyes skittered to his pants which were distended by his engorged dick. Just the thought of his hands on her body repulsed her greatly, not to mention that part of him. She would never be able to survive it if he raped her body. She would fall apart. She would break beyond repair.

"No!" she began screaming at the top of her lungs. "Somebody help me! Some---"

He grabbed hold of her hair and yanked her towards him, cutting off her breath. He covered her mouth with his and kissed her brutally, shutting her up. Danika fought him and nausea with everything she could. She struggled against him, but her strength was no match for him.

He pulled back.

She opened her mouth to scream again.

He forced the pills down her throat and grabbed hold of her neck in that instance so she wouldn't throw it up.

It was either she swallowed or it choked her to death.

Danika closed her eyes in defeat and helplessness and swallowed.

CHAPTER 47. THE SETUP.

Vetta couldn't stop smiling. She was having a very beautiful day, and it showed on her face. She might be carrying the king's child. She might be pregnant for him already. The thought couldn't stop making her smile. Not to mention that her plan was already in motion. She'd been watching when Danika walked to the backyard to get her clothes and didn't return. Vetta didn't need to be a seer to know that Karandy must have grabbed his quarry.

Poor pregnant woman. And poor Karandy too.

Men will always be men, Vetta thought as she turned and began walking outside in search of the king. The useless asshole might have noticed that there was a loophole in her plan, but lust blindsided him. His obsession with Danika's body had blocked him from seeing every other thing—including his own doom.

"Did you see the king?" Vetta asked the first maid she saw outside the palace building.

"I saw him at the training field. He just finished teaching sword fights to the trainees. I think he is about to leave," the maid answered with a bow.

She nodded curtly and continued her journey. Once she entered the vicinity of the big training field, she saw him at first glance and stood for a moment, admiring him. Vetta had always loved having that man as hers. A man so powerful and so different from other men who belonged to her, who listened to her and needed her so much before. And then Danika had to come along and take him from her. Danika ruined everything Vetta had spent more than six years working so hard for, and she didn't even deserve him. She was the daughter of the monster who created the monster the king was today—who created the monster she, Vetta, was today. Danika was the very spawn of the devil himself.

And today, she would pay in unspeakable ways. Even if it meant the king would kill his own child by his hands—if Karandy hadn't done the job.

"My king!" she called from the entrance of the field.

King Lucien turned and acknowledged her with an inclination of his head before he faced away from her and began walking out of the field through the other end. She hurried her steps to get to him. When she reached him, she fell into steps with him. "I saw the trainees, my king. You must have done a pretty good job leading the training today."

"Most of them are still far away when it comes to swordsmanship, but they will get there," he replied as calmly as possible.

"I believe so too. You have always been the best swordsman. A warrior to the core. It was one of the things King Cone feared so much and the reason he locked you away all the time."

King Lucien continued walking, his arms together behind his back. The palace workers bowed and greeted him at every turn, and he inclined his head slightly in acknowledgment of their greetings.

"What are you doing out here, Vetta? Shouldn't you be picking a new dress to give your seamstress at the market?" he asked after a little silence.

Vetta smiled beside him, feeling all fluttered up. He remembered the ball she told him about last night, that she'd been invited to by Lady Mirabeth. Wiping the smile from her face, she took on a sad look. "I lost a sample of the new dress I had in mind for the ball, my king."

He spared her a glance. "How did that happen?"

"I have no idea, My Lord. I think I must have misplaced it, and it hurts me a lot."

"I apologize for that. Maybe you should tell the maids to help you search?"

Vetta nodded. "I will keep that in mind for later, my king. For now, I just want to accompany you on a walk."

They got out from the vicinity of the field, and the king stopped suddenly. Vetta raised her head to see why and saw Baski ahead of them.

The older woman seemed to be searching for something, but when she saw the king, she strode towards them and bowed her head. "Good day, my king."

"You look worried. Are you alright, Baski?" His voice was neutral, but there was a thread of underlying concern.

Baski's face mirrored her own worry and concern. She was out of breath like she'd been running. "I've been looking for Remeta all morning. She woke up crying this morning, and then she ran out of the palace. I've not seen her until now."

"You should not let it bother you, Baski. Remeta will be back. You know how she loves roaming the wild," the king speculated.

Baski calmed a bit, but she was still agitated. "I know, my king. But she ran out of the palace. She looked scared and in pain. I don't know what to do for her."

The king continued walking slowly, and Baski fell into steps with them. "Maybe you should just give her a little space. It might be all she needs since she ran out of the palace."

"I thought so too. I thought maybe she'd gone to town to stay with Danika during water supply," Baski injected.

"I do not think Zariel's group has left the palace yet. Zariel is still getting the supplies they will need ready."

Baski's steps faltered. "You mean they are still in the palace, Your Highness?"

The king nodded. "That is the message I got this morning."

Baski's brows creased in worry. If Zariel's crew hadn't left then, where was Danika? When she went to her bedroom in search of Remeta and didn't see any sign of her, she'd thought that Zariel's crew had already left. That was strange.

"I do think that they might have already left for town, my king," Baski repeated, staring up at the king.

He shook his head to indicate that she was wrong. Then he turned to his three guards, who followed a few feet behind them. "Has Zariel left?"

"No, Your Majesty. They are still making preparations," one of them answered after they all shook their heads. Another guard was carrying the king's sword and its patch.

The king swiveled his head and continued walking. Baski felt worried. Where was Danika?

Vetta did not like how the king carried on a conversation with old Baski without her. So she looked to the sky and inserted her voice. "Isn't it a beautiful morning?"

"I guess it is," was all the king said.

As Baski walked with them, she tried to calm herself with many possibilities—many reasons why Danika had disappeared. She must have fallen asleep in one corner. That might just be it because poor Danika tended to fall asleep every time and everywhere. Or maybe she had gone to see Sally like she indicated she would in the morning.

They got to a curve—two routes: one led to the woods while the other led to the backyard of the palace.

"Can we go through this route?" Vetta asked, pointing at the one that leads to the backyard. "I want to stop by the storeroom. There are some clothes I gave my maid to take out yesterday and keep in the store until it's time to take them to the village and distribute to woman of poor backgrounds. I think I must have mistakenly packed in those samples I was talking about."

"Alright," the king responded.

Satisfaction sizzled through Vetta like a bird in the wind. They started down the part leading to the storeroom, and she couldn't help but smile again. Karandy better have used his short time to take as much pleasure as he needed from Danika's supple because the real show was about to hit the road—a show that included his death, Danika's death, and her child's death too.

All of a sudden, Remeta's words came back to her. Her steps faltered. "*You get away this time around, but what about next time? Don't. When the plan comes to your head, ignore it. Do not do it. You will hurt queen. You will hurt Prince. You will hurt his father. And you will get hurt. You get away this time around, and you get hurt the next. And your nemesis is coming in the form of a person.*"

Goosebumps worked their way down Vetta's spine at the vivid reminder of those creepy words from a very creepy young adult.

Remeta had always been crazy, Vetta. It solidified her resolve, and she pushed the words away from her mind.

Remeta was just crazy.

He had wasted so much time because of the fight she had put up. So much time. Karandy counted on kidnapping her, drugging her and fucking her mindless. He never counted on her putting up so much fight due to her present condition.

Watching Danika victoriously after the swallowed the pills, he let go of her neck and watched her with the joy of a cat that caught a mouse in its trap.

Danika began sobbing. She pulled herself from his grasp to get away from him, and he let her. He knew that she would come crawling back.

"What did y-you give me?" she croaked, her voice hoarse from being choked twice.

"You will find out soon enough," was his smug response.

Danika did not want to be there at all. She wanted to be away from there! She staggered to her feet and started towards the door, and her head tilted. The bedroom spun around her. The pills in her system battled her body, causing her stomach to hurt. She cried out and grabbed hold of her belly, trying to steady herself as she took another step towards the door.

Karandy frowned slightly. She was supposed to feel the effects of the drugs now, not feeling sleepy still. It should be energizing her. The seller said it would make a woman want sex and keep her energized for it. The seller didn't know that the woman in question was pregnant.

Karandy's arms folded, and he arched his brow while he observed her stagger unsteadily at her feet. Would her pregnancy alter the effect of the drug?

It did.

He watched her eyes slide close and she fell. His arms shot out, and he grabbed her, lifting her off her feet in his arms. She was sound asleep.

Karandy wanted her energized, not asleep. His eyes caressed her incredibly beautiful face, the soft rise and fall of her chest. The wetness of her cheeks. He had never seen a more beautiful woman in sleep. He had to have her. He wanted her too much.

Turning, he walked back to the hay he had prepared for this and laid her down on it. Swiping his fingers across her cheeks, he dried her tears and kissed her lips. "At last. I have you to myself," he groaned triumphantly. Her sleep did not alter their plan. The maid didn't have to see them having sex; she would just have to catch them asleep in each other's arms—like lovers.

Quickly, he got up and undressed himself completely, leaving only his white undershirt on. Then he began undressing Danika. He took off all her clothes from her corset and petticoat down to her drawers and inner drawers. He pulled back and looked at her. She was left in her flimsy white cotton gown, which was the last of her inner-wear. He raised the gown, revealing her white cotton panties. His mouth watered at the flawless sight of her inner thighs.

Even the mistress's hidden parts did not look as good as Danika's.

Anticipation and impatience beat down on him, and he reached for her panties and pulled them down her legs, leaving her womanhood bare. Her creamy breasts tempted him from the cotton of her underthings. With unsteady hands, he unbuttoned her and freed one breast, which he fumbled eagerly, closing his eyes to savor the moment. He lowered his head and sucked her into his mouth at the same time he massaged his cock. He groaned and moaned, his other hand caressing her face and flawless white skin.

He couldn't wait any longer. He rolled, taking her with him so that he lay on the hay and her weight fell on top of him. He worked a finger into her and groaned as her muscles squeezed him. Hades! She would feel heavenly on his cock. And the pills did do something right. They made her very wet for him. He quickly extracted his finger and grabbed her waist with both hands. He raised her, positioning his cock to her opening and—

Sounds of footsteps made him pause. He heard the voice of an older woman.

Was she the maid that would catch them? Shit!

He thought fast. He could just lay her on him, close his eyes and pretend to be asleep with her. They were already in a compromised position. Before the maid would be able to reach the king, he would be able to have Danika and disappear. Holding that thought, Karandy laid her on his pelvis without penetrating her, and pushed Danika's head from his left shoulder to his right so that her head and hair in disarray would hide his face.

A second after he achieved his aim, the door opened.

But it was nothing that Karandy expected.

Baski was the first to enter the storeroom, followed by Vetta and the King.

The image in front of them spoke volumes—words that looked self-explanatory. Danika lay on top of her lover in an intimate position, and they were obviously sleeping after having a hot interlude together.

Baski gasped. "Oh, heavens!" She covered her mouth with trembling hands, her mouth wide in shock. She threw a glance at the king.

King Lucien stared at the scene in front of him blankly for a few seconds, as if his head hadn't been able to process what he was seeing. When it did, his face closed up like a book.

"By the Gods! What is going on here!?" Vetta gasped, looking as shocked as ever. She turned too and watched the king.

King Lucien said nothing. Absolutely nothing as he kept watching the scene in front of him so intensely—like he expected the illusion to disappear if he watched it too much.

Baski felt her heart break to pieces for the king. He had been healing. He did not need this. He did not need this at all.

At the voice of the mistress and the pregnant silence that followed, Karandy realized that something was wrong.

Something had gone extremely wrong.

He opened his eyes and peered at his environment through Danika's hair. The king?

THE KING!!!

He pushed Danika away from him and sprang up from the bed. That was *not* what he expected! This should *not* be happening!!!

This was *not* the plan!!!!

302

"My K-King!" he stuttered as he tried to get up from the bed.

The way he shoved Danika so hard woke her up from her slumber. She stirred, feeling so disoriented.

Karandy's legs tangled on Danika's clothes on the bed, making him fumble and struggle clumsily to get up from the bed.

"Dargak," the king spoke for the first time. That deadly monotone sent a chill down a confused Baski's spine.

"Y-Your Highness!" The guard with the sword answered at the door and hurried forward.

Then Karandy was able to untangle his legs from the clothes and he hurried out of bed. His legs touched the floor as he opened his mouth, "Your H-Highness, I can explain—"

The king moved so fast; it took only a few seconds. He reached for his sword, pulled it out from its sling and waved it once towards Karandy's neck. Baski screamed as Karandy's head separated from his body and rolled to the floor. His body followed suit. Blood filled everywhere.

The scream jolted Danika more awake. She opened her eyes, feeling very disoriented. Getting up from the bed, she rubbed her knuckles into her eyes, trying to clear her blurry eyes and understand where she was and what was happening around her.

The king turned towards her, a savage expression on his old hard face.

Baski began crying her eyes out, still unable to believe what was happening. Under that cold blue eyes, she watched the king shatter before her very eyes. The king took two steady steps towards Danika, and before Baski could comprehend his next actions, the king raised his hand.

Baski didn't think. She had no time to think.

"No, please! Not the collar! She is pregnant! Not her neck; she is pregnant!" Baski screamed instinctively.

But it was too late.

It was too late the minute they opened the door of this storeroom and stepped into this place.

It was too late, for he did it before she was able to get the words out.

.
.
.

WATCH OUT FOR THE LAST PART.

MY WOMAN
MY POSSESSION

WHAT MY BODY WANTS (Her Sex Addiction)
By Kiss Leilani

ROSIANNA

I'd done something stupid. I'd done something really stupid.

Why did I have to enter the room? I should have stayed outside. I knew he was having sex in here, I knew he was fucking two women in this bedroom, so why the hell did I come in here?

What gave me the impression that I could pull it off like I did when I was eighteen? I was no longer eighteen. I was not that sweet little virgin anymore. No, I was quite the opposite. So, why the hell did I enter the room, and worse, allow myself to sit through it?

My whole body was on fire. Every little part of me. I needed relief and I needed it quick, or I'd break down right in front of Santos. It was the one shame I'd rather die than go through in front of him.

"Rosy? Are you alright?" he drawled, not really concerned but amused.

"You're a first-class bastard, Santos," I whispered, my voice almost shaky and hoarse with the strength of my anger and desire for that man.

He chuckled softly and walked away from me to the bed and started folding the sheets. "We've already established that long before I went abroad."

My pussy clenched. I felt shaky on the inside. I *needed* to leave. Now.

I stood up quietly, a movement that belied the urgency and desire coursing through me. Suddenly, I regretted putting on high heels because I was shaky on my feet.

"Don't tell me you're leaving, Rosy, when you just arrived?" he asked with an arch of his brow.

"Oh, I didn't just arrive. I've been here for almost the hour it took you to fuck two women right in front of me," I spat.

"Is that jealousy I smell in your voice?" He seemed amused at the prospect.

305

"Just conviction," I shot at him, lying through my teeth.

I turned and started for the door, almost having the urge to run before I did something really stupid. Like beg Santos to fuck me.

I was almost at the door when a hand curled around my shoulder. I suddenly found myself against the wall and trapped between Santos and it.

"Oh, Rosy," he whispered, his voice sending shivers down my heated body. "Do you remember?"

"What?" I asked even though I feared I already knew what he was asking.

He leaned closer to my ear. "That night six years ago? Right here, in this house, in this room...you begged me to fuck you"

I closed my eyes again at the pain of the memory. "You wanted me," I whispered.

"Oh, I did," he admitted. "So damn bad. Desperately. You were a craving then, almost like very expensive alcohol. I was sure I'd get addicted to you if I touched you."

Silence.

"Is that why you didn't?" I finally asked, trying to keep it simple, but that was a pain that had been with me forever. How could I not know it?

Santos shook his head, his eyes staring pointedly at my lips. "I stopped because you were a virgin who deserved more. You deserved better than a man like me. I would have spoiled you."

I would have laughed if my chest wasn't hurting so bad. If my body wasn't on fire, *burning* for this man.

"Let me go, Santos."

He ignored me. Instead, he leaned in. "I was stupid that night, you know. Quite stupid of not taking what you innocently offered, even though I wanted to, so damn much."

I loved you! I loved you, you bastard! I wanted to throw these words to his face, but I refrained. He didn't need to know.

I felt his hand move from my waist down to the edge of my dress before snaking inside. My dress rode up as his hand moved in a caress and rested on my panties.

"What do you think you're doing, Santos?" I protested, doing my best to ignore the shards of pleasure that shot through me.

"Fuck, you're soaked," he muttered, caressing my pussy through my silk panties.

"Leave me alone, Santos. I don't want you. Not anymore." Trying to keep the pain from my voice, I pushed him, but it was like trying to move a wall.

"That's not what your body says, darling." He pushed the panties aside and stroked my bare clit. I couldn't stop the moan from escaping.

"What my body wants and what I want are two different things," I said truthfully, even though in this case, my body and I wanted the same thing.

Anger darkened his eyes as he dipped his head and kissed my neck, his arousal pressed against my thigh. "But what did you do, Rosy? After that night we made out—after that night I tasted you—what did you do?"

My brain was still trying to process that information when he suddenly pushed away from me, severing all contact. "The next day, you offered my best friend the same thing you offered me!" he spat venomously.

I stopped breathing. Something curled up inside me and died. "What?"

He laughed mirthlessly. "You thought I wouldn't find out!? You thought Jason would keep it silent!? You went right ahead to slept with my best friend, you ungrateful slut!"

Santos didn't shout the words, but his deep, angry voice still cut like a whip. *Oh, God. Oh, my God.*

"The same day I left was the day you gave yourself and your virginity to my best friend. Why, Rosianna? You couldn't keep it in your pants, right? The same mouth you used to profess your love for me that night was the same mouth you used to scream for my damn best friend!" He was really angry, his hands fisted. His eyes held hatred as he glared daggers at me. "I'll never forgive you for that, Rosianna. Ever. You might have given your virginity to Jason, but I own your body and I'll take what's mine. One of these days, I'll have you on my bed and I'll take everything you have to give and more. Not out of love for you—no, not anymore. But because you owe me, Rosianna. Your body is mine."

That said, he turned and walked to the bathroom without a backward glance, leaving a disoriented, close-to-tears me behind.

Available on Kindle stores. Free on Kindle Unlimited.

OTHER BOOKS BY THIS AUTHOR.

THE ALPHA KING OF NATURIAH SERIES.

- Mate To The Alpha Predator
- Mate To The Alpha Called God
- Mate To The Alpha Of All Alphas

THE BREATHING DEAD (Spirit Of Christmas) A short novella.

WHAT MY BODY WANTS (Her Sex Addiction)

THE HOMELESS BILLIONAIRE —Coming out March 2023

For updates, follow my new page on facebook: KissLeilani
Library and kissleilaniauthorpage
My Facebook Account: Kiss Leilani
On TikTok: kissleilaniauthor
Instagram: kiss_leilani